ABSENCE OF LIGHT
a Charlie Fox novella

incorporating

FOX FIVE
a Charlie Fox short story collection

plus

Across The Broken Line
a Charlie Fox short story

ABSENCE OF LIGHT
a Charlie Fox novella

incorporating

FOX FIVE
a Charlie Fox short story collection

plus

Across The Broken Line
a Charlie Fox short story

Zoë Sharp

Murderati Ink [ZACE Ltd]

Murderati Ink [ZACE Ltd]
Registered UK Office:
Kent Cottage, Bridge Lane, Kendal, Cumbria LA9 7DD

This edition published 2013
Murderati Ink [ZACE Ltd]

ISBN-13: 978-1-909344-35-8

ISBN-10: 1-909344-35-4

Typeset in 11/14pt Century Schoolbook

For Andy, Derek and Jane
The people who made this happen ...

And for the victims, survivors and rescue and recovery teams of
the major earthquakes of the twenty-first century

CONTENTS

A Bridge Too Far
intro

This was the very first short story I ever wrote featuring Charlie Fox.

The story is set at roughly the same point in her life as the opening book in the series, KILLER INSTINCT, when Charlie is living in Lancashire in the UK and making a living teaching self-defence to local women.

She has been out of the Army for several years by this time, but has not yet plunged into a new career in close protection. Such a possibility is a long way from her mind, even though she already demonstrates the cool-headedness in a crisis that makes her so well suited for the job.

A Bridge Too Far came about because I was invited to submit a story for the UK Crime Writers' Association short story anthology, GREEN FOR DANGER: CRIMES IN THE COUNTRY, by the editor, Martin Edwards. (I did not tell him that I had never attempted a short story before until after he had accepted it for publication.) But as soon as Martin mentioned the requirement of a rural setting, a true story sprang to mind.

Some years ago a friend told me about being a member of a local Dangerous Sports Club. Bicycle abseiling was one of their pursuits, if I remember right—and yes, that is just as crazy as it sounds.

Bridge swinging was another speciality, which did take place from an old disused railway viaduct that stretched across a farmer's field. And the farmer did indeed object to their activities for exactly the reason stated.

But after that, all bets were off and I let my imagination take hold!

As well as the original CWA anthology, A Bridge Too Far also appeared in *Ellery Queen Mystery Magazine*.

A Bridge Too Far

I watched with a kind of horrified fascination as the boy climbed onto the narrow parapet. Below his feet the elongated brick arches of the old viaduct stretched, so I'd been told, exactly one hundred and twenty-three feet to the ground. He balanced on the crumbling brickwork at the edge, casual and unconcerned.

My God, I thought, *He's going to do it. He's actually going to jump.*

"Don't prat around, Adam," one of the others said. I was still sorting out their names. Paul, that was it. He was a medical student, tall and bony with a long almost roman nose. "If you're going to do it, do it, or let someone else have their turn."

"Now now," Adam said, wagging a finger. "Don't be bitchy."

Paul glared at him, took a step forwards, but the cool blonde-haired girl, Diana, put a hand on his arm.

"Leave him alone, Paul," Diana said, and there was a faint snap to her voice. She'd been introduced as Adam's girlfriend, so I suppose she had the right to be protective. "He'll jump when he's ready. You'll have your chance to impress the newbies."

She flicked unfriendly eyes in my direction as she spoke but I didn't rise to it. Heights didn't draw or repel me the way I knew they did with most people but that didn't mean I was inclined to throw myself off a bridge to prove my courage. I'd already done that at enough other times, in enough other places.

Beside me, my friend Sam muttered under his breath, "OK, I'm impressed. No way are you getting me up there."

I grinned at him. It was Sam who'd told me about the local Dangerous Sports Club who trekked out to this disused viaduct in the middle of nowhere. There they tied one end of a rope to the far parapet and brought the other end up underneath between the supports before tying it round their ankles.

2

And then they jumped.

The idea, as Sam explained it, was to propel yourself outwards as though diving off a cliff and trying to avoid the rocks below. I suspected this wasn't an analogy with resonance for either of us, but the technique ensured that when you reached the end of your tether, so to speak, the slack was taken up progressively and you swung backwards and forwards under the bridge in a graceful arc.

Jump straight down, however, and you would be jerked to a stop hard enough to break your spine. They used modern climbing rope with a fair amount of give in it but it was far from the elastic gear required by the bungee jumper. That was for wimps.

Sam knew the group's leader, Adam Lane, from the nearby university, where Sam was something incomprehensible to do with computers and Adam was the star of the track and field teams. He was one of these magnetic golden boys who breezed effortlessly through life, always looking for a greater challenge, something to set their heartbeat racing. And for Adam the unlikely pastime of bridge swinging, it seemed, was it.

I hadn't believed Sam's description of the activity and had made the mistake of expressing my scepticism out loud. So, here I was on a bright but surprisingly nippy Sunday morning in May, waiting for the first of these lunatics to launch himself into the abyss.

Now, though, Adam put his hands on his hips and breathed in deep, looking around with a certain intensity at the landscape. His stance, up there on the edge of the precipice, was almost a pose.

We were halfway across the valley floor, in splendid isolation. The tracks to this Brunel masterpiece had been long since ripped up and carted away. The only clue to their existence was the footpath that led across the fields from the lay-by on the road where Sam and I had left our motorbikes. The other cars there, I guessed, belonged to Adam and his friends.

The view from the viaduct was stunning, the sides of the valley curving away at either side as though seen through a fish-eye lens. It was still early, so that the last of the dawn mist clung to the dips and hollows, and it was quiet enough to hear the world turning.

"Hello there! Not starting without us, are you?" called a girl's cheery voice, putting a scatter of crows to flight, breaking the spell. A flash of annoyance passed across Adam's handsome features.

A young couple was approaching. Like the other three DSC members, they were wearing high-tech outdoor clothing— lightweight trousers you can wash and dry in thirty seconds, and lairy-coloured fleeces.

The boy was short and muscular, a look emphasised by the fact he'd turned his coat collar up against the chill, giving him no neck to speak of. He tramped onto the bridge and almost threw his rucksack down with the others.

"What's the matter, Michael?" Adam said, his voice a lazy taunt. "Get out of bed on the wrong side?"

The newcomer gave him a single, vicious look and said nothing.

The girl was shorter and plumper than Diana. Her gaze flicked nervously from one to the other, latching onto the rope already secured round Adam's legs as if glad of the distraction. "Oh *Adam*, you're never jumping today are you?" she cried. "I didn't think you were supposed to—"

"I'm perfectly OK, Izzy darling," Adam drawled. His eyes shifted meaningfully towards Sam and me, then back again.

Izzy opened her mouth to speak, closing it again with a snap as she caught on. Her pale complexion bloomed into sudden pink across her cheekbones and she bent to fuss with her own rucksack. She drew out a stainless steel flask and held it up like an offering. "I brought coffee."

"How very thoughtful of you, Izzy dear," Diana said, speaking down her well-bred nose at the other girl. "You always were so very accommodating."

Izzy's colour deepened. "I'm not sure there's enough for everybody," she went on, dogged. She nodded apologetically to us. "No-one told me there'd be new people coming. I'm Izzy, by the way."

"Sam Pickering," Sam put in, "and this is Charlie Fox."

Izzy smiled a little shyly, then a sudden thought struck her. "You're not thinking of joining are you?" she said in an anxious tone. "Only, it's not certain we're going to carry on with the club for much longer."

4

"Course we are," Michael said brusquely, raising his dark stubbled chin out of his collar for the first time. "Just because Adam has to give up, no reason for the rest of us to pack it in. We'll manage without him."

The others seemed to hold their breath while they checked Adam's response to this dismissive declaration, but he seemed to have lost interest in the squabbles of lesser mortals. He continued to stand on the parapet, untroubled by the yawning drop below him, staring into the middle distance like an ocean sailor.

"That's not the only reason we might have to stop," the tall bony boy, Paul said. "In fact, here comes another right now."

He nodded across the far side of the field. We all turned and I noticed for the first time that a man on a red Honda quad bike was making a beeline for us across the dewy grass.

"Oh shit," Michael muttered. "Wacko Jacko. That's all we need."

"Who is he?" Sam asked, watching the purposeful way the quad was bearing down on us.

"He's the local farmer," Paul explained. "He owns all the land round here and he's dead against us using the viaduct, but it's a public right of way and legally he can't stop us. That doesn't stop the old bugger coming and giving us a hard time every Sunday."

"Mr Jackson's a strict Methodist you see," Izzy said quietly as the quad drew nearer. "It's not trespassing that's the problem— it's the fact that when the boys jump, well, they do tend to swear a bit. I think he objects to the blasphemy."

I eyed the farmer warily as he finally braked to a halt at the edge of the bridge and cut the quad's engine. The main reason for my caution was the elderly double-barrelled Baikal shotgun he lifted out of the rack on one side and brought with him.

Jackson came stumping along the bridge towards us with the kind of rolling, twitching gait that denotes a pair of totally worn-out knees. He wore a flat cap with tar on the peak and a tatty raincoat tied together with orange bailer twine. As he closed on us he snapped the Baikal shut, and I instinctively edged myself slightly in front of Sam.

"Morning Mr Jackson," Izzy called, the tension sending her voice into a high waver.

5

The farmer ignored the greeting, his eyes fixed on Adam. It was only when Michael and Paul physically blocked his path that he seemed to notice the rest of us.

"I've told you lot before. You've no right to do this on my land," he said gruffly, clutching the shotgun almost nervously, as though suddenly aware he was outnumbered. "You been warned."

"And you've been told that *you* have no right to stop us, you daft old bugger," Adam said, the derision clear in his voice.

Jackson's ruddy face congested. He tried to push closer to Adam, but Paul caught the lapel of his raincoat and shoved him backwards. With a fraction less aggression the whole thing could have passed off with a few harsh words but after this there was only one way it was going to go.

The scuffle was brief. Jackson was hard and fit from years of manual labour but the boys both had thirty years on him. It was the shotgun that worried me the most. Michael had grabbed hold of the barrel and was trying to wrench it from the farmer's grasp, while *he* was determined to keep hold of it. The business end of the Baikal swung wildly across the rest of us.

Izzy was shrieking, ducked down with her hands over her ears. I piled Sam backwards, starting to head for the end of the bridge.

The blast of the shotgun discharging stopped my breath. I flinched at the pellets twanging off the brickwork as the shot spread. The echo rolled away up and down the valley like a call to battle.

The silence that followed was quickly broken by Izzy's whimpering cries. She was still on the ground, staring in horrified disbelief at the blood seeping through a couple of small holes in the leg of her trousers.

Paul crouched near to her, hands fluttering over the wounds without actually wanting to touch them. Sam had turned vaguely green at the first sign of blood, but he unwound the cotton scarf from under the neck of his leathers and handed it over to me without a word. I moved Paul aside quietly and padded the makeshift dressing onto Izzy's leg.

"It's only a couple of pellets," I told her. "It's not serious. Hold this against it as hard as you can. You'll be fine."

Michael had managed to wrestle the Baikal away from Jackson. He turned and took in Izzy's state, then pointed the shotgun meaningfully back at the shaken farmer, settling his finger onto the second trigger.

"You bastard," he ground out.

"Michael, stop it," Diana said.

Michael ignored her, his dark eyes fixed menacingly on Jackson. "You've just shot my girlfriend."

"*Michael!*" Diana tried again, shouting this time. She had quite a voice for one so slender. "Stop it! Don't you understand? *Where's Adam?*"

We all turned then, looked back to the section of parapet where he'd been standing. The lichen-covered wall was peppered with tiny fresh chips but the parapet itself was empty.

Adam was gone.

I ran to the edge and leaned out over it as far as I dared. A hundred and twenty-three feet below me, a crumpled form lay utterly still on the grassy slope. The blood was a bright halo around his head.

"Adam!" Diana yelled, her voice cracking. "Oh God. Can you hear me?"

I stepped back, caught Sam's enquiring glance and shook my head.

Paul was already hurrying towards the end of the bridge to pick his way down beneath the arches. I went after him, snagged his arm as he started his descent.

"I'll go," I said. When he looked at me dubiously, I added, "I know First-Aid if there's anything to be done and if not, well—" I shrugged, "—I've seen dead bodies before."

His face was grave for a moment, then he nodded. "What can we do?"

"Get an ambulance—Izzy probably needs one even if Adam doesn't—and call the police." He nodded again and had already started back up the slope when I added, "Oh, and try not to let Michael shoot that bloody farmer."

"Why not?" Paul demanded bitterly. "He deserves it." And then he was gone.

It was a relatively easy path down to where Adam's body lay. Close to, it wasn't particularly pretty. I hardly needed to search for a pulse at his out flung wrist to know the boy was dead. Still, the relatively soft surface had kept him largely intact, enough for me to tell that it wasn't any shotgun blast that had killed him. Gravity had done that all by itself.

7

I took off my jacket and gently laid it over the top half of the body, covering his head. It was the only thing I could do for him, and even that was more to protect the sensibilities of the living.

When I looked up I could see half of the rope dangling from the opposite side of the bridge high above my head, its loose end swaying gently. The other end was still tied around Adam's ankles. It had snapped during his fall, but why?

Had Jackson's shot severed the rope at the moment when Adam had either lost his balance and fallen, or as he'd chosen to jump?

I got to my feet and followed the rope along the ground to where the severed end lay coiled in the grass. I used a twig to carefully lift it up enough to examine it.

And then I knew.

The embankment seemed a hell of a lot steeper on the way up than it had on the way down. I ran all the way and was totally out of breath by the time I regained the bridge. But I was just in time.

Diana was crouched next to Izzy, holding her hand. Paul and Sam were standing a few feet behind Michael, eyeing him with varying amounts of fear and mistrust. The thickset youth had the shotgun wedged up under Jackson's chin, using it to force his upper body backwards over the top of the parapet. Michael's face was blenched with anger, teetering on the edge of control.

"He's dead, isn't he?" He didn't take his eyes off the farmer as I approached.

"Yes," I said carefully, "but Jackson didn't kill him, Michael."

"But he must have done." It was Paul who spoke. "We all saw—"

"You saw nothing," I cut in. "The gun went off and Adam either jumped or fell, but he wasn't shot. The rope gave out. That's why he's dead."

"That's ridiculous," Diana said, haughty rather than anguished. "The breaking strain on the ropes we use is enormous. No way could it have simply broken. The shot must have hit it."

"It didn't," I said. "It was cut halfway through. With a knife."

Even Michael reacted to that one, taking the shotgun away from Jackson's neck as he swivelled round to face me. I could see the indentations the barrels had left in the scrawny skin of the old man's throat.

8

Chances like that don't come very often. I took a quick step closer, looped my arm over the one of Michael's that held the gun and brought my elbow back sharply into the fleshy vee between his ribs.

He doubled over, gasping, letting go of the weapon. I picked it out of his hands and stepped back again. It was all over in a moment.

The others watched in silence as I broke the Baikal and picked out the remaining live cartridge. Once it was unloaded I put the gun down propped against the brickwork and dropped the cartridge into my pocket. Michael had caught his breath enough to think about coming at me, but it was Sam who intervened.

"I wouldn't if you know what's good for you," he said, his voice kindly. "Charlie's a bit of an expert at this type of thing. She'd eat you for breakfast."

Michael favoured me with a hard stare. I returned it flat and level. I don't know what he thought he saw but he backed off, sullen, rubbing his stomach.

"So," I said, "the question is, who cut Adam's rope?"

For a moment there was total silence. "Look, we either have this out now, or you get the third degree when the police arrive," I said, shrugging. "I assume you *did* call them?" I added in Paul's direction.

"No, but I did," Sam said, brandishing his mobile phone. "They're on their way. I've said I'll wait for them up on the road. Show them the way. Will you be OK down here?"

I nodded. "I'll cope," I said. "Oh and Sam—when they arrive, tell them it looks like murder."

Nobody spoke as Sam started out across the field. He eyed the quad bike with some envy as he passed, but went on foot.

"I still say the old bastard deserves shooting," Michael muttered.

"I didn't do nothing," Jackson blurted out suddenly. Relieved of the immediate threat to his life he simply stood looking dazed with his shoulders slumped. "I never would have fired. It was him who grabbed my hand! He's the one who forced my finger down on the trigger!"

He waved towards Michael, who flushed angrily at the charge. I replayed the scene again and recalled the way the stocky boy had been struggling with Jackson for control of the gun. It had looked for all the world like a genuine skirmish but it could just as easily have been a convenient set-up.

When no one immediately spoke up in his defence, Michael rounded on us.

"How can you believe anything so *stupid?*" he bit out. "Adam was a good mate. I would have given him my last cent."

"Didn't like sharing your girlfriend with him, though, did you?" Paul said quietly.

Izzy, still lying on the ground, gave an audible gasp. I checked to see how Diana was taking the news of her dead boyfriend's apparent infidelity but there was little to be gleaned from her cool and colourless expression.

A brief spasm of what might have been fear passed across Michael's face. "You can't believe I'd want to kill him for that?" he said and gave a harsh laugh. "Defending Izzy's honour? Come on! I knew right from the start that she's not exactly choosy."

Izzy had begun to cry. "He loved me," she managed between sobs, and it wasn't immediately clear if she was referring to Michael or Adam. "He told me he loved me."

Diana sat back, still looking at Izzy, but without really seeing her. "That's what he tells—told—all of them," she said, almost to herself. "Wanted to hear them say it back to him, I suppose." She smiled then, a little sadly. "Adam always did need to be adored. The centre of attention."

"You're just saying that, but it wasn't true," Izzy cried. "He loved me. He was going to give you up but he wanted to let you down gently, not to hurt your feelings. He was just waiting for the right time."

"Oh Izzy, of course he wasn't going to give me up," Diana said, her tone one of great patience, as though talking to the very young, or the very slow. "He used to come straight from your bed back to mine and tell me all about it." She laughed, a high brittle peal. "How desperately keen you were. How eager to please."

"And you didn't *mind?*" I asked, fighting to keep the disbelief and the distaste buried.

"Of course not," Diana said, sounding vaguely surprised that I should feel the need to ask. She sighed. "Adam had some … interesting tastes. There were some things that I simply drew the line at, but Izzy—" her eyes slipped away from mine to skim dispassionately over the girl lying cringing in front of her, "—

well, she would do just about anything he asked. Pathetic, really."

"Are you really trying to tell me that you *knew* your boyfriend was sleeping around and you didn't care at all?"

Diana stood, looked down her nose again in that way she had. The way that indicated I was being too bourgeois for words. "Naturally," she said. "I understood Adam perfectly and I understood that this was his last fling at life while he still had the chance."

"What do you mean, while he still had the chance?" I said. I recalled Michael's jibe about Adam having to pack in the dangerous sports. "What was the matter with him?"

There was a long pause. Even Jackson, I noticed, seemed to be waiting intently for the answer. Eventually, Izzy was the one who broke the silence.

"He only told us a month ago that he'd been diagnosed with MND," she said. Her leg had just about stopped bleeding but her face had started to sweat now as the pain and the shock crept in. When I looked blank it was Paul who continued.

"Motor Neurone Disease," he said, sounding authoritative. "It's a progressive degeneration of the motor neurones in the brain and spinal cord. In most cases the mind is unaffected but you gradually lose control of various muscle groups—the arms and legs are usually the first to go. You can never quite tell how far or how fast it will develop because it affects everyone in a different way. Sometimes you lose the ability to speak and swallow. It was such rotten luck! The chances of it happening in someone under forty are so remote, but for it to hit Adam of all people—" he broke off, shook his head and seemed to remember how none of that mattered any more. "Poor sod."

"It was a tragedy," Izzy said, defiant. "And if I gave him pleasure while he could still take it, what was wrong with that?"

"So," I murmured, "was this a murder, or a mercy killing?"

Diana made a sort of snuffling noise then, bringing one hand up to her face. For a moment I thought she was fighting back tears but then she looked up and I saw that it was laughter. And she'd lost the battle.

"Oh for God's sake, Adam didn't have Motor Neurone Disease!" she cried, jumping to her feet, hysteria bubbling up through the words. "That was all a lie! He *wanted* you to think of him as the tragic hero, struck down at the pinnacle of his youth. And you all fell for it. All of you!"

Paul's face was blank. "So there was nothing wrong with him?" he said faintly. "But he said—"

"Adam was diagnosed HIV positive six months ago," Diana said flatly. "He had AIDS."

The dismay rippled through the group like the bore of a changing tide. AIDS. The bogeyman of the modern age. I almost saw them edge away from each other, as though afraid of cross-contamination. No wonder Adam had preferred the pretence of a more user-friendly affliction.

And then it dawned on them, one by one.

Izzy realised it first. "Oh my God," she whispered. "He never used ..." She broke off, lifting her tear-stained face to Michael. "Oh God," she said again. "I am *so* sorry."

Michael caught on then, reeling away to clutch at the bridge parapet as though his legs suddenly wouldn't support him any longer.

Paul was just standing there, staring at nothing. "Bastard," he muttered, over and over.

Michael rounded on him in a burst of fury. "It's all right for you," he yelled. "You're probably the only one of us who hasn't got it!"

"Ah, that's not quite the case, is it, Paul?" Diana said, her voice like chiselled ice. "Always had a bit of a thing for Adam, didn't you? But he wasn't having any of that. Oh, he kept you dangling for years," she went on, scanning Paul's stunned face without compassion. "Did you really not wonder *at all* why he suddenly changed his mind recently?"

She laughed again. A sound like glass breaking, sharp and bitter. "No, I can see you didn't. You poor fools," she said, taking in all of their devastated faces, her voice mocking. "There you all were debasing yourselves to please him, hoping to bathe in a last little piece of Adam's reflected glory, when all the time he was spitting on your graves."

Michael lunged for her, reaching for her throat. I swept his legs out from under him before he'd taken a stride, then twisted an arm behind his back to hold him down once he was on the floor. *Come on Sam! Where the hell were the police when you needed them?*

12

I looked up at Diana, who'd stood unconcerned during the abortive attack. "Why on earth did you stay with him?" I asked.

She shrugged. "By the time he confessed, it was too late," she said simply. "There's no doubt—I've had all the tests. Besides, you didn't know Adam. He was one of those people who was a bright star, for all his faults. I wanted to be with him, and you can't be infected twice."

"And what about us?" Paul demanded, sounding close to tears himself. "We were your friends. Why didn't you tell us the truth?"

"Friends!" Diana scoffed. "What kind of friends would screw my boyfriend—or let their girlfriends screw him—behind my back? Answer me that!"

"You never got anything you didn't ask for," Jackson said quietly then, his voice rich with disgust. "The whole lot of you."

Privately, part of me couldn't help but agree with the farmer. "The question is," I said, "which one of you went for revenge?"

And then, across the field, a new-looking Toyota Land Cruiser turned off the road and came bowling across the grass, snaking wildly as it came.

"Oh shit," Paul muttered, "it's Adam's parents. How the hell did they get to hear about it so fast?"

The Land Cruiser didn't stop by the quad bike, but came thundering straight onto the bridge itself, heedless of the weight-bearing capabilities of the old structure. It braked jerkily to a halt and the middle-aged couple inside flung open the doors and jumped out.

"Where's Adam?" the man said urgently. He looked as though he'd thrown his clothes on in a great hurry. His shirt was unbuttoned and his hair awry. "Are we in time?"

None of the group spoke. I let go of Michael's wriggling body and got to my feet. "Mr Lane?" I said. "I'm terribly sorry to tell you this, but there seems to have been an accident—"

"*Accident?*" Adam's mother almost shrieked the word as she came forwards. "Accident? What about this?" and she thrust a crumpled sheet of paper into my hands.

Uncertain what else to do, I unfolded the letter just as the first of the police Land Rover Discoveries began its approach, rather more sedately, across the field.

Adam's suicide note was brief and to the point. He couldn't face the prospect of the future, it said. He couldn't face the dreadful responsibility of what he'd knowingly inflicted on his friends. He was sorry. Goodbye.

He did not, I noticed, express the hope that they would forgive him for what he'd done.

I folded the note up again as the lead Discovery reached us and a uniformed sergeant got out, adjusting his cap. Sam was in the passenger seat.

The sergeant advanced, his experienced gaze taking in the shotgun still leaning against the brickwork, Izzy's blood-soaked trousers, and the array of staggered faces.

"I understand there's been a murder committed," he said, businesslike, glancing round. "Where's the victim?"

I waved my hand towards the surviving members of the Dangerous Sports Club. "Take your pick," I said. "And if you want the murderer, well—" I nodded at the parapet where Adam had taken his final dive, "—you'll find him down there."

Postcards From Another Country
intro

This was the second short story I wrote featuring Charlie Fox. This story follows my ex-Special Forces turned bodyguard heroine fairly early in her close-protection career, working as part of a security detail for the affluent Dempsey family. Tension is high among Charlie's team after an attempt is made on the life of one of the family, but sometimes the threat comes from an unexpected source, with equally unexpected consequences.

I wrote this story specially to go into the back of the US paperback edition of the fourth Charlie Fox novel, FIRST DROP, as an added extra. This is the only place it has been available previously.

It always bothered me slightly that Postcards From Another Country stood apart from the novel, rather than linking into it in some way. However, when I wrote the ninth book in the series, FIFTH VICTIM, I was finally able to do something about this by using the character of the Dempseys' wayward daughter, Amanda, as one of the integral players in that story. In fact, Charlie's previous history with her made their subsequent relationship far more complex and interesting.

Postcards From Another Country

Somebody once said that the rich are another country—they do things differently there. It didn't take me very long working in close protection to realise that was true. Hell, some of them were a different planet.

The Dempsey family were old money and that put them at the outer reaches of the solar system as far as real-world living was concerned. Personal danger came a distant second to social disgrace, which was always going to make life tough for those of us tasked to keep them from harm.

The family didn't seem bothered so much by the attempted assassination—and that was how they referred to the botched hit that sparked my involvement—so much as the fact it was carried out with no regard to the correct etiquette.

So, they put up with the movement sensors in the grounds and the increased numbers of staff who regularly patrolled the boundaries, but they baulked at having the infrared cameras I'd recommended to blanket the exterior of the house, and absolutely dug their heels in about close-circuit TV coverage inside. It was my job, I was told firmly, to stop anyone from getting that far. *No pressure, then.*

The radio call came in at just after 3:00 AM, when I was in the east wing guest suite I'd commandeered as a temporary central control.

"Hey, Charlie, we just apprehended someone in the summer house," came the crackling voice of one of the new guys. "I think you'd, um, better come take a look."

"Stay where you are, Pierce," I said, alerted by the hesitation when he'd been well-briefed on how to handle a situation of this type. "I'm on my way."

The summer house was an architectural flight of fancy writ large. Just goes to show what happens when the wealthy get bored and start doodling.

As I made my way across the lawn and skirted the swimming pool the summer house was lit up like a beacon, lights blazing from every window. I jogged up the steps that led to the ornate entrance and pushed open the door.

As soon as I saw who Pierce had cornered, I understood his reaction. The girl was eighteen but could have passed for twenty-one, and she was utterly beautiful, wearing a mask of blasé bravado and a top that was barely legal. She sat sprawled on one of the cane sofas, one long leg dangling with apparent negligence over the arm. Only the nervous swing of her foot gave lie to her insouciance.

She'd been practising her best sultry pout on Pierce and did not look pleased when I arrived to spoil her fun. Another few minutes and she'd probably have wheedled her way loose. If the scowl she shot in my direction was anything to go by, she realised it, too.

"OK," I said grimly. "I'll deal with this." As he hurried past me, looking flustered, I added quietly, "Stick to procedure, Pierce. And wake the boss."

"Oh … really?" His eyes flicked longingly over the girl before he caught my eye and mumbled, "Yeah, OK, no problem."

As the door closed behind him I turned back and found the girl watching his departure with glittering eyes.

"You've obviously made quite a hit there," I said dryly.

"Hmm," she agreed, letting a secret little smile briefly curve her lips that died when she switched her gaze back to me. "I get the feeling you're not quite so easily impressed, though."

"No, I'm not," I said, and for nearly half a minute we stared each other out. Then I sighed. "It was foolish to think you could get past us, Amanda," I said, voice mild. "Your father hired us because we know what we're doing."

"Damn watchdogs," Amanda Dempsey said with a sneer. "I've been evading people like you, sneaking out, sneaking in, since I was thirteen years old."

"Well, we caught you this time, didn't we?"

"Yes, you did," she drawled and something flashed through the back of her eyes, quick and bright. Then it was gone. She shrugged. "Well, you can't win them all."

17

She sat up, suddenly restless, and reached for the inlaid ivory antique cigarette box on the glass table in front of her. "Mind if I smoke?"

"Yes," I said, slamming the lid shut before she had a chance to reach inside, and leaving my hand there. Open-mouthed, she thought about making an issue of it, but took one look at my face and decided not to, shrugging like it was of no importance.

"You know that someone tried to kill your father less than a week ago," I went on, allowing some of the exasperation I was feeling to leak through into my voice. "Is this all just a game to you?"

"What if it is?" she said. "Just because someone's decided to take a pot-shot at the old man—and the number of likely suspects must be *legion*—and he's chosen to shut himself off like some old hermit, it doesn't mean *I* have to be a virtual prisoner in this mouldy old place, too, does it?"

The house had every modern convenience. As well as the outdoor swimming pool and the indoor swimming pool, there were tennis courts, stables, a home gym that made the pro place I used seem positively under-equipped, and a dozen full-time staff to pander to the family's every whim. I knew ordinary people who paid a fortune for weekends away at a place like this. I shook my head. What was that about familiarity and contempt?

"You want to go out, you're free to go by the main gate," I said mildly then. You don't have to scale the back wall."

"Yeah, right." She gave a cynical snort of laughter and threw me a challenging stare. "So I can go out, huh? Alone?"

I smiled and shook my head. "Not a chance."

"OK, so who'll come out with me and spend the night clubbing? You?" She let her eyes flick me up and down, deliberately insulting. "What if I get lucky? Are you going to wait outside the bedroom door like a good little watchdog while I—"

"Only if you let me strip-search the guy at gunpoint first," I said easily. "Mind you, some of the guys you've been hanging around with lately are used to that kind of thing, aren't they?"

"How dare you check up on me," she gritted out, her cheeks flushing, a dull red that did nothing for her porcelain skin.

"We checked up on everyone," I said.

She jumped up. For a moment she just stood there, trembling with anger that had her on the verge of tears.

18

"I should have known you wouldn't take my side," she said, sounding much younger, almost petulant. "My father says 'jump' and the only thing you spineless wimps give a damn about is how high."

"You have to admit that your old man's money has come in very useful for getting you out of a few scrapes over the years," I said cheerfully. "Drug possession and drunk driving, to name but two."

"How much trouble do you reckon I would have got into," she said bitterly, "if I hadn't spent half my life trying to live up to Daddy's impossible ideals?"

"You could have got out from under," I pointed out. "He doesn't exactly keep you locked up in the basement."

She laughed, as though I'd suggested something ridiculous. "And done what? Gone where?"

I refrained from rolling my eyes. "You're young and moderately bright. You didn't have to be a lapdog all your life," I said, unable to resist getting my own back for her earlier jibe. "You could have gone anywhere and done anything you set your mind to. Most people," I added, "have to work for what they want in life. They don't get it handed to them on a hallmarked silver platter by a flunky wearing white gloves and a tailcoat."

Amanda paced to one of the windows even though the lights made it impossible to see anything outside except her own reflection in the glass. Maybe that was all she was after. Eventually, she turned back.

"You don't come from money, do you, Charlie?"

I thought of my parents' affluent country home in the stockbroker belt of Cheshire and laughed. "My folks aren't quite down to their last farthing, thank you very much."

I shifted slightly so I was between her and the open doorway, just in case, glancing through it as I did so. Lights had come on in the main wing of the house and I could see figures moving across the lawn. Pierce might be new and green, but it seemed he had remembered what he had to do, at least. "I certainly don't go running to *my* father," I went on, "to bail me out every time I hit a problem."

"If that's what I've done," she said, lip twisting, "it's because I'm just doing what Daddy taught me from the cradle."

"Which is?"

"That money is the answer to everything."

19

Into the silence that followed, my walkie-talkie crackled into life.

"Hey, Charlie," came Pierce's voice, loud and clear, "you were right. We got him. Some punk kid with a sawn-off. Southwest corner. The situation's contained and the police are on their way."

"Good. Thank you." I put the walkie-talkie back in my pocket and glanced across at the girl. "Sorry, Amanda," I said with no regret in my voice. "Your diversionary tactic didn't work. Who was he, by the way—your latest bit of rough? Did you really think he'd get to your father before we could stop him?"

I put my head on one side and watched her as she turned away from the window and staggered back to the sofa, dropping onto the cushions like her legs would no longer support her. But when she looked up, her eyes were wild, defiant.

"You'll never prove anything," she said. Fine words, spoilt only by the shaky tone.

"She doesn't have to."

Behind me, the door pushed open and her father stepped into the summer house. He'd put on a silk robe over his pyjamas, but he was still a commanding figure.

Amanda stiffened at the sight of him, then dived for the cigarette box on the table in front of her, scrabbling inside it.

"If you're looking for that nice little semiautomatic you hid in there," I said, regretful. "I found it this afternoon."

Her colour fled. She gave a shriek of rage and flew out of her seat. I was never quite sure if it was me or her father she intended to attack, but I didn't give her the chance anyway. Before she'd taken more than two strides I'd grabbed her arms, spun her round, and dumped her back onto the sofa again. I was tempted to get a punch in, but she *was* my principal's daughter, after all.

I settled for a verbal blow instead. "Not so much watchdog, Amanda," I said. "More guard dog."

She snatched up the cigarette box and hurled it instead. It never came close to target, hitting the wall next to the door and cracking in two, scattering filtertips across the Italian tiled floor. Then she began to cry.

Her father regarded this display of temper without expression, while I received another message from Pierce to say the police were at the main gate.

20

"Let them in," I said. I looked across at Dempsey. "Do you want them to take her, too?"

Dempsey pursed his lips briefly before shaking his head. "That won't be necessary. He motioned with a vague hand. "We'll get her ... help of some kind."

"Your decision, sir, of course."

He hadn't taken his eyes off his daughter. "Why, Amanda?" he asked softly. "What do you possibly gain from my death?"

Her lip curled. "My freedom."

He frowned at that. "But you've had everything you could possibly wish for."

"No. I've had everything money could buy," she said in a brittle voice, throwing her head back. "And if you don't know the difference there's no earthly point in my trying to explain it."

There was a long pause. Dempsey finally broke his brooding survey and flicked his eyes at me.

"I'm not dealing with this tonight," he said, like it was some minor irritation. "Just get her out of my sight, would you." And with that he turned on his heel and stumbled from the summer house. It doesn't matter how much money you've got, if your children hate you enough to try and kill you. Either for or because of it.

I moved over to his daughter. She rose from the sofa. "Not quite such a game now, is it, Amanda?" I said.

"On the contrary," she said, eyes glittering, head high. "Now it gets interesting."

Like I said: the rich are a whole nother country—they do things differently there.

Served Cold
intro

In this collection of short stories featuring Charlie Fox, this story is unusual as it is not written in first person—in Charlie's voice. Instead, the story is that of a waitress and stripper called Layla, who has reached a rock-bottom turning point in her life and has made a momentous decision.

This story came about when Megan Abbott invited me to contribute to the anthology of female noir, A HELL OF A WOMAN, which she was editing. The theme of the anthology was to celebrate the girlfriends, secretaries, sisters and other female characters who normally play sidekicks and walk-ons in noir fiction. This was their chance to shine.

While I was thinking about what to write for A HELL OF A WOMAN, we had a trip planned by ferry from Scotland across to Northern Ireland. It was a long drive to the ferry port at Stranraer, and traffic was slow and heavy. In brief, we just failed to make the boat, arriving at the port just as the security gates were closing. We had no choice but to hang around in Stranraer for several hours until the next boat.

This was how I ended up sitting in a little café, drinking a pot of tea and idly watching the waitresses moving mostly ignored between the crowded tables. And that's when the character of Layla first began to form.

She's seen life from the seamy underside, found and lost love, been discarded, betrayed and abandoned. But now she has a plan ...

Served Cold was nominated for the Crime Writers' Association Short Story Dagger in 2009, and was chosen to appear in THE MAMMOTH BOOK OF BEST BRITISH CRIME, edited by Maxim Jakubowski.

Served Cold

Layla's curse, as she saw it, was that she had an utterly fabulous body attached to an instantly forgettable face. It wasn't that she was ugly. Ugliness in itself stuck in the mind. It was simply that, from the neck upwards, she was plain. A bland plainness that encouraged male and female eyes alike to slide on past without pausing. Most failed to recall her easily at a second meeting.

From the neck down, though, that was a different story, and had been right from when she'd begun to blossom in eighth grade. Things had started burgeoning over the winter, when nobody noticed the unexpected explosion of curves. But when summer came, with its bathing suits and skinny tops and tight skirts, Layla suddenly became the most whispered-about girl in her class.

A pack of the kind of boys her mother was usually too drunk to warn her about took to following her when she walked home from school. At first, Layla was flattered. But one simmering afternoon, under the banyan and the Spanish moss, she learned a brutal lesson about the kind of attention her new body attracted.

And when her mother's latest boyfriend started looking at her with those same hot lustful eyes, Layla cut and run. One way or another, she'd been running ever since.

At least the work came easy. Depending on how much she covered up, she could get anything from selling lingerie or perfume in a high-class department store, to exotic dancing. She soon learned to slip on different personae the same way she slipped on a low-cut top or a demure blouse.

Tonight she was wearing a tailored white dress shirt with frills down the front and a dinky little clip-on bow tie. Classy joint. The last time she'd worn a bow-tie to wait tables, she'd worn no top at all.

The fat guy in charge of the wait staff was called Steve and had hands to match his roving eye. That he'd seen beyond Layla's homely face was mainly because he rarely looked his female employees above the neck. Layla had noted the way his eyes glazed and his mouth went slack and the sweat beaded at his receding hairline, and she wondered if this was another gig she was going to have to try out for on her back.

She didn't, in the end, but only because Steve thought of himself as sophisticated, she realised. The proposition would no doubt come after. Still, Steve only let his pants rule his head so far. Enough to let Layla—and the rest of the girls—know that he'd be taking half their tips tonight. Anyone who tried to hold anything back would be out on her ass.

Layla didn't care about the tips. That wasn't why she was here, anyhow.

Now, she stood meekly with the others while Steve walked the line, checking everybody over.

"Got to look sharp out there tonight, girls," he said. "Mr Dyer, he's a big man around here. Can't afford to let him down."

He seemed to have a thing for the name badges each girl wore pinned above her left breast. Hated it if they were crooked, and liked to straighten them out personally and take his time getting it just so. The girl next to Layla, whose name was Tammy, rolled her eyes while Steve pawed at her. Layla rolled her eyes right back.

Steve paused in front of her, frowning. "Where's your badge, honey? This one here says your name is Cindy and I *know* that ain't right." And he made sure to nudge the offending item with clammy fingers.

Layla shrugged, surprised he picked up on the deliberate swap. Her face might not stick in the mind, but she couldn't take the chance that her name might ring a bell.

"Oh, I guess it musta' gotten lost," she said, all breathless and innocent. "I figured seeing as Cindy called in sick and ain't here—and none of the fancy folk out there is gonna remember my name anyhow—it don't matter."

Steve continued to frown and finger the badge for a moment, then met Layla's brazen stare and realised he'd lingered too long, even for him. With a shifty little sideways glance, he let go and stepped back. "No, it don't matter," he muttered, moving on. Alongside her, Tammy rolled her eyes again.

Layla had the contents of her canapé tray hurriedly explained to her by one of the harassed chefs and then ducked out of the service door, along the short drab corridor, and into the main ballroom.

The glitter and the glamour set her heart racing, as it always did. For a few years, she'd dreamed of moving in these circles without a white cloth over her arm and an open bottle in her hand. And, for a time, she'd almost believed that it might be so.

Not any more.

Not since Bobby.

She reached the first cluster of dinner jackets and long dresses that probably cost more than she made in a year—just for the fabric, never mind the stitching—and waited to catch their attention. It took a while.

"Sir? Ma'am? Would you care for a canapé? Those darlin' little round ones are smoked salmon and caviar, and the square ones are Kobe beef and ginger."

She smiled, but their eyes were on the food, or they didn't think it was worth it to smile back. Just stuffed their mouths and continued braying to each other like the stuck-up donkeys they were.

Layla had done this kind of gig many times before. She knew the right pace and frequency to circulate, how often to approach the same guests before attentive turned to irritating, how to slip through the crowd without getting jostled. How to keep her mouth shut and her ears open. Steve might hint that she had to put out to get signed on again, but Layla knew she was good and he was lucky to have her.

Well, after tonight, Stevie-boy, you might just change your mind about that.

She smiled and offered the caviar and the beef, reciting the same words over and over like someone kept pulling a string at the back of her neck. She didn't need to think about it, so she thought about Bobby instead.

Bobby had been the bouncer in a roadhouse near Tallahassee. A huge guy with a lot of old scar tissue across his knuckles and around his eyes. Tale was he'd been a boxer, had a shot until he'd taken one punch too many in the ring. Then everything had gone into slow motion for Bobby and never speeded up again.

He wore a permanent scowl like he'd rip your head off and spit down your neck, as soon as look at you, but Layla quickly realised that was merely puzzlement. Bobby was slightly overmatched by the pace of life and couldn't quite work out why. Still plenty fast enough to throw out drunks in a cheap joint, though. And once Bobby had laid his fists on you, you didn't rush to get up again.

One night in the parking lot, Layla was jumped by a couple of guys who'd fallen foul of the 'no touching' rule earlier in the evening and caught the rough side of Bobby's iron-hard hands. They waited, tanking up on cheap whiskey, until closing time. Waited for the lights to go out and the girls to straggle, yawning, from the back door. They grabbed Layla before she had a chance to scream, and were touching all they wanted when Bobby waded in out of nowhere. Layla had never been happier to hear the crack of skulls.

She'd been angry more than shocked and frightened—angry enough to stamp them a few times with those lethal heels once they were on the ground. Angry enough to take their overflowing billfolds, too. But it didn't last. When Bobby got her back to her rented double-wide, she shook and cried as she clung to him and begged him to help her forget. That night she discovered that Bobby was big and slow in other ways, too. And sometimes that was a real good thing.

For a while, at least.

"Ma'am? Would you care for a canapé? Smoked salmon and caviar on that side, and this right here's Kobe beef. No, thank *you*, ma'am."

Layla worked the room in a pattern she'd laid out inside her head, weaving through the crowd with the nearest thing a person could get to invisibility. It was a big fancy do, that was for sure. Some charity she'd never heard of and would never benefit from. The crowd was circulating like hot dense air through a fan, edging their way up towards the host and hostess at the far end.

The Dyers were old money and gracious with it, but firmly distant towards the staff. They knew their place made sure the little people, like Layla, were aware of theirs. Layla didn't mind. She was used to being a nobody.

Mr Dyer was indeed, a big man, as Steve had said. A mover and shaker. He didn't need to mingle, he could just stand there, like royalty, with a glass in one hand and the other around the waist of his tall, elegant wife, looking relaxed and casual.

Well, maybe not so relaxed. Every now and again Layla noticed Dyer throw a little sideways look at their guest of honour and frown, as though he still wasn't quite sure what the guy was doing there.

Guy called Venable. Another big guy. Another mover and shaker. The difference was that Venable had clawed his way up out of the gutter and had never forgotten it. He stood close to the Dyers in his perfectly tailored tux with a kind of secret smile on his face, like he knew they didn't want him there but also knew they couldn't afford to get rid of him. But, just in case anyone thought about trying, he'd surrounded himself with four bodyguards.

Layla eyed them surreptitiously, with some concern. They were huge—bigger than Bobby, even when he'd been still standing—each wearing a bulky suit and one of those little curly wires leading up from their collar to their ear, like they was guarding the president himself. But Venable was no statesman, Layla knew for a fact.

She hadn't expected him to be invited to the Dyers' annual charity ball, and had worked hard to get herself on the staff list when she'd found out he was. A lot of planning had gone into this, one way or another.

By contrast, the Dyers had no protection. Well, unless you counted that bossy secretary of Mrs Dyer's. Mrs Dyer was society through and through. The type who wouldn't remember to get out of bed in the morning without a social secretary to remind her. The type whose only job is looking good and saying the right thing and being seen in the right places. There must be some kind of a college for women like that.

Mrs Dyer had made a big show of inspecting the arrangements, though. She'd walked through the kitchen earlier that day, nodding serenely, just so her husband could toast her publicly tonight for her part in overseeing the organisation of the event, and she could look all modest about it and it not quite be a lie.

She'd had the secretary with her then, a slim woman with cool eyes who'd frozen Steve off the first time he'd tried laying a proprietary hand on her shoulder. Layla and the rest of the girls hid their smiles behind bland faces when she'd done that. Even so, Steve took it out on Tammy—had her on her back in the storeroom almost before they were out the door.

The secretary was here tonight, Layla saw. Fussing around her employer, but it was Mr Dyer whose shoulder she stayed close to. Too close, Layla decided, for their relationship to be merely professional. An affair perhaps? She wouldn't put it past any man to lose his sense and his pants when it came to an attractive woman. Still, she didn't think the secretary looked the type. Maybe he liked 'em cool. Maybe she was hoping he'd leave his wife.

At the moment, the secretary's eyes were on their guest. Venable had been free with his hosts' champagne all evening and his appetites were not concerned only with the food. Layla watched the way his body language grew predatory when he was introduced to the gauche teenage daughter of one of the guests, and she stepped in with her tray, ignoring the ominous looming of the bodyguards.

"Sir, can I interest you in a canapé? Smoked salmon and caviar or Kobe beef and ginger?"

Venable's greed got the better of him and he let go of the girl's hand, which he'd been grasping far too long. She snatched it back, red-faced, and fled. The secretary gave Layla a knowing, grateful smile.

Layla moved away quickly afterwards, a frown on her face, cursing inwardly and knowing he was watching her. She was here for a purpose. One that was too important to allow stupid mistakes like that to risk bringing her unwanted attention. And after she'd tried so hard to blend in.

To calm herself, to negate those shivers of doubt, she thought of Bobby again. They'd moved in together, found a little apartment. Not much, but the first place Layla had lived in years that didn't need the wheels taken off before you could call it home.

He'd been always gentle with Layla, but then one night he'd hit a guy who was hassling the girls too hard, hurt him real bad, and the management had to let Bobby go. Word got out and he couldn't get another job. Layla had walked out, too, but she went through a dry spell as far as work was concerned, and now there were two of them to feed and care for.

Eventually, she was forced to go lower than she'd had to go before, taking her clothes off to bad music in a cheap dive that didn't even bother to have a guy like Bobby to protect the girls. As long as the customers put their money down before they left, the management didn't care.

Layla soon discovered that some of the girls took to supplementing their income by inviting the occasional guy out into the alley at the back of the club. When the landlord came by twice in the same week threatening to evict her and Bobby, she'd swallowed her pride. By the end of that first night, that wasn't all she'd had to swallow.

Even Bobby, slow though he might be, soon realised what she was doing. How could he not question where the extra money was coming from when he'd been in the business long enough to know how much the girls made in tips—and what they had to do to earn them? At first, when she'd explained it to him, Layla thought he was cool with it. Until the next night when she was out in the alley between sets, her back hard up against the rough stucco wall with some guy from out of town huffing sweat and beer into her unremarkable face.

One minute she was standing with her eyes tight shut, wondering how much longer the guy was going to last, and the next he was yanked away and she heard that dreadful crack of skulls.

Bobby hadn't meant to kill him, she was sure of that. He just didn't know his own strength, was all. Then it was his turn to panic and tremble, but Layla stayed ice cool. They wrapped the body in plastic and put it into the trunk of a borrowed car before driving it down to the Everglades. Bobby carried it out to a pool where the 'gators gathered, and left it there for them to hide. Layla even went back a week later, just to check, but there was nothing left to find.

They stripped the guy before they dumped him, and struck lucky. He had a decent watch and a bulging wallet. It was a month before Layla had to put out against the stucco in the alley again.

How were they supposed to know he was connected to Venable? That the watch Bobby had pawned would lead Venable's bone-breakers straight to them?

A month after the killing, Venable's boys picked Bobby and Layla up from the bar and drove them out to some place by the docks. Bobby swore that Layla wasn't in on it, that they should leave her alone, let her go. Swore blind that it was so. And eventually, they blinded him, just to make sure.

Layla thought she'd never get the sound of Bobby's screaming out of her head as they'd tortured him into a confession of sorts. But even when they'd snapped his spine, left him broken and bleeding on that filthy concrete floor, Bobby had not said a word against Layla. And she, to her eternal shame, had been too terrified to confess her part in it all, as though that would make mockery of everything he'd gone through.

So, they'd left her. She was a waitress, a dancer, a hooker. A no-account nobody. Not worth the effort of a beating. Not worth the cost of a bullet.

Helpless as a baby, damaged beyond repair, Bobby went into some institution just north of Tampa and Layla took the bus up to see him every week for the first couple of months. But, gradually, getting on that bus got harder to do. It broke her heart to do see him like that, to force the cheerful note into her voice.

Eventually, the bus left the terminal one morning and Layla wasn't on it.

She'd cried for days. When she'd gotten word that Bobby had snuck a knife out of the dining hall, waited until it was quiet then slit his wrists under the blankets and bled out softly into his mattress during the night, there had been no more tears left to fall.

Layla's heart hardened to a shell. She'd let Bobby down while he was alive, but she could seek justice for him after he was dead. She heard things. That was one of the beauties of being invisible. People talked while she served them drinks, like she wasn't there. Once Layla had longed to be noticeable, to be accepted. Now she made it her business simply to listen.

Of course, she knew she couldn't go after Venable alone, so Layla had found another bruiser with no qualms about burying the bodies. And, once he'd had a taste of that spectacular body, he was hers.

Thad was younger than Bobby, sharper, neater, and when it came to killing he had the strike and the morals of a rattlesnake. Layla knew he'd do anything for her, right up until the time she tried to move on, and then he was likely to do anything *to* her instead.

Well, after tonight, she wouldn't care.

She slipped out of the ballroom but instead of turning into the kitchen, this time she took the extra few strides to the French windows at the end of the corridor, furtively opened them a crack, then closed them again carefully so they didn't latch.

By the time Layla returned to the ballroom, the canapés were not all she was holding. She'd detoured via the little cloakroom the girls had been given to change and store their bags. What she'd collected from hers she was holding flat in her right hand, hidden by the tray. A Beretta 9mm, hot most likely. As long as it worked, Layla didn't care.

A few moments later someone stopped by her elbow and leaned close to examine the contents of the tray.

"Well hello, *Cindy*." A man's voice, a smile curving the sound of it. "And just what you got there, little lady?"

Thad, looking pretty nifty in the tux she'd made him rent. He bent over her tray while she explained the contents, making a big play over choosing between the caviar or the beef. And underneath, his other hand touched hers, and she slipped the Beretta into it.

"Well, thank you, sugar," he said, taking a canapé with a flourish and slipping the gun inside his jacket with his other hand, like a magician. When the hand came out again, it was holding a snowy handkerchief, which he used to wipe his fingers and dab his mouth.

Layla had made him practice the move until it seemed so natural. Shame this was a one-time show. He would have made such a partner, someone she might just have been able to live her dreams with. If only he hadn't had that cruel streak. If only he'd touched her heart the way Bobby had.

Poor crippled, blinded Bobby. Poor *dead* Bobby ...

Ah well. Too late for regrets. Too late for much of anything, now.

Layla caught Thad's eye as she made another round and he nodded, almost imperceptibly. She nodded back, the slightest inclination of her head, and turned away. As she did so she bumped deliberately into the arm of a man who'd been recounting some fishing tale and spread his hands broadly to lie about the size of his catch. He caught Layla's tray and send it flipping upwards. Layla caught it with the fast reflexes that came from years of waiting crowded tables amid careless diners.

She managed to stop the contents crashing to the floor, but most of it ended up down the front of her blouse instead.

"Oh, I am *so* sorry, sir," she said immediately, clutching the tray to her chest to prevent further spillage.

"No problem," the man said, annoyed at having his story interrupted and oblivious to the fact it had been entirely his fault. He checked his own clothing. "No harm done."

Layla managed to raise a smile and hurried out. Steve caught her halfway.

"What happened, honey?" he demanded. "Not like you to be so clumsy."

Layla shrugged as best she could, still trying not to shed debris.

"Sorry, boss," she said. "I've got a spare blouse in my bag. I'll go change."

"OK, sweetheart, but make it snappy." He let her move away a few strides, then called after her, "And if that's caviar you're wearing, it'll come out of your pay, y'hear?"

Layla threw him a chastised glance over her shoulder that didn't go deep enough to change her eyes, and hurried back to the little cloakroom.

She scraped the gunge off the front of her chest into the nearest trash, took off the blouse and threw that away, too, then rummaged through her bag for a clean one. This one was calculatedly lower cut and more revealing, but she didn't think Steve would object too hard, even if he caught her wearing it.

She pulled out another skirt, too, even though there was nothing wrong with her old one. This was shorter than the last, showing several inches of long smooth thigh below the hem and, without undue vanity, she knew it would drag male eyes downwards, even as her newly exposed cleavage would drag them up again. With any luck, they'd go cross-eyed trying to look both places at once.

She swapped her false name badge over and took the cheap Makarov 9mm and a roll of duct tape out of her bag. She lifted one remarkable leg up onto the wooden bench and ran the duct tape around the top of her thigh, twice, to hold the nine in position, just out of sight. The pistol grip pointed downwards and she knew from hours in front of the mirror that she could yank the gun loose in a second.

She'd bought both pistols from a crooked military surplus dealer down near Miramar. Thad insisted on coming with her for the Beretta, had made a big thing about checking the gun over like he knew what he was doing, sighting along the barrel with one eye closed.

Layla had gone back later for the Makarov. She didn't have enough money for the two, but she'd been dressed to thrill and she and the dealer had come to an arrangement that hadn't cost Layla anything at all. Only pride, and she'd been way overdrawn on that account for years.

Now, Layla checked in the cracked mirror that the gun didn't show beneath her skirt. Her face was even more bland in its pallor and, just for once, she wished she'd been born pretty. Not beautiful, just pretty enough to have been cherished.

The way she'd cherished Bobby. The way he'd cherished her.

She left the locker room and collected a fresh tray from the kitchen. The chefs were under pressure, the activity frantic, but when she walked in on those long dancer's legs there was a moment of silence that was almost reverent.

"You changed your clothes," one of the chefs said, mesmerised.

She smiled at him, saw the fog lift a little as the disappointment of her face cut through the haze of lust created by her body.

"I spilled," she said, collecting a fresh tray. She felt every eye on her as she walked out, smiled when she heard the collective sigh as the door swung closed behind her.

It was a short-lived smile.

Back in the ballroom, it was all she could do not to go marching straight up to Venable, but she knew she had to play it cool. The four bodyguards were too experienced not to spot her sudden surge of guilt and anger. They'd pick her out of the crowd the way a shark cuts out a weakling seal pup. And she couldn't afford that. Not yet.

Instead, she forced herself to think bland thoughts as she circled the room towards him. Saw out of the corner of her eye Thad casually moving up on the other side. The relief flooded her, sending her limbs almost lax with it. For a second, she'd been afraid he wouldn't go through with it. That he'd realise what her real idea was, and back out at the last moment.

For the moment, though, Thad must think it was all going to plan. She stepped up to the Dyers, offered them something from her tray. The secretary still hadn't left his side, she saw. The girl must be desperate.

Layla took another step, sideways towards Venable, ducking around the cordon of bodyguards. Offered him something from her tray. And this time, as he leaned forwards, so did she, pressing her arms together to accentuate what nature had so generously given her.

She watched Venable's eyes go glassy, saw the way the eyes of the nearest two bodyguards bulged the same way. There was another just behind her, she knew, and she bent a little further from the waist, knowing she was giving him a prime view of her ass and the back of her newly-exposed thighs. She could almost feel that hot little gaze slavering up the backs of her knees.

Come on, Thad ...

He came pushing through the crowd nearest to Venable, moving too fast. If he'd been slower, he might have made it. As it was, he was the only guy for twenty feet in any direction who didn't have his eyes full of Layla's divine body. Venable's eyes snapped round at the last moment, jerky, panicking as he realised the rapidly approaching threat. He flailed, sending Layla's tray crashing to the ground, showering canapés.

The bodyguards were slower off the mark. Thad already had the gun out before two of them grabbed him. Not so much grabbed as piled in on top of him, driving him off his legs and down, using fists and feet to keep him there.

Thad was no easy meat, though. He kept in shape and had come up from the streets, where unfair fights were part of the game. Even on the floor, he lashed out, aiming for knees and shins, hitting more than he was missing. A third bodyguard joined in to keep him down, a leather sap appearing like magic in his hand.

There was that familiar crack of skulls. *Just like Bobby ...*

Layla winced, but she couldn't let that distract her now. Her mind strangely cool and calm, Layla stepped in, ignored. The fourth bodyguard had stayed at his post, but Layla was shielded from his view by his own principal, and everyone's attention was on the fight. Carefully, she reached under her skirt and yanked the Makarov free, unaware of the brief burn as the tape ripped from her thigh.

The safety was already off, the hammer back. The army surplus guy down in Miramar had thrown in a little instruction as well. Gave him more of a chance to stand up real close behind her as he demonstrated how to hold the unfamiliar gun, how to aim and fire.

She brought the nine up the way he'd shown her, both hands clasped round the pistol grip, starting to take up the pressure on the trigger, she bent her knees and crouched a little, so the recoil wouldn't send the barrel rising, just in case she had to take a second shot. But, this close, she knew she wouldn't need one, even if she got the chance.

One thing Layla hadn't been prepared for was the noise. The report was monstrously loud in the high-ceilinged ballroom. And though she thought she'd been prepared, she staggered back and to the side. And the pain. The pain was a gigantic fist around her heart, squeezing until she couldn't breathe.

She looked up, vision starting to shimmer, and saw Venable was still standing, shocked but apparently unharmed. How had she missed? The bodyguard had come out of his lethargy to throw himself on top of his employer, but there was still an open window. There was still time ...

Layla tried to lift the gun but her arms were leaden. Something hit her, hard, in the centre of her voluptuous chest, but she didn't see what it was, or who threw it. She frowned, took a step back and her legs folded, and suddenly she was staring up at the chandeliers on the ceiling and she had to hold on to the polished wooden dance floor beneath her hands to stay there. Her vision was starting to blacken at the edges, like burning paper, the sound blurring down.

The last thing she saw was the slim woman she'd taken for a secretary, leaning over her with a wisp of smoke rising from the muzzle of the 9mm she was holding.

Then the bright lights, and the glitter, all faded to black.

***

The woman Layla had mistaken for a secretary placed two fingers against the pulse point in the waitress's throat and felt nothing. She knew better than to touch the body more than she had to now, even to close the dead woman's eyes.

Cindy, the name tag read, under the trickle of the blood. She doubted that would match the woman's driver's licence.

She rose, sliding the SIG semiautomatic back into the concealed-carry rig on her belt. Two of Venable's meaty goons wrestled the woman's accomplice, bellowing, out of the room. She turned to her employer.

"I don't think you were the target, Mr Dyer, but I couldn't take the chance," she said calmly. She jerked her head towards the bodyguards. "If this lot had been halfway capable, I wouldn't have had to get involved. As it was ..."

Dyer nodded. He still had his arms wrapped round his wife, who was sobbing, and his eyes were sad and tired.

"Thank you," he said quietly.

The woman shrugged. "It's my job," she said.

"Who the hell are you?" It was Venable himself who spoke, elbowing his way out from the protective shield that his remaining bodyguards had belatedly thrown around him.

"This is Charlie Fox," Dyer answered for her, the faintest smile in his voice. "She's *my* personal protection. A little more subtle than your own choice. She's good, isn't she?"

Venable stared at him blankly, then at the dead woman, lying crumpled on the polished planks. At the unfired gun that had fallen from her hand.

"You saved my life," he murmured, his face pale.

Charlie stared back at him. "Yes," she said, sounding almost regretful. "Whether it was worth saving is quite another point. What had you done to her that she was prepared to kill you for it?"

Venable seemed not to hear. He couldn't take his eyes off Layla's body. Something about her was familiar, but he just couldn't remember her face.

"I don't know—nothing," he said, cleared his throat of its hoarseness and tried again. "She's a nobody. Just a waitress." He took another look, just to be sure. "Just a woman."

"Oh, I don't know," Dyer said, and his eyes were on Charlie Fox. "From where I'm standing she's a hell of a woman, wouldn't you say?"

Off Duty
intro

This was the fourth short story I wrote featuring Charlie Fox. In this, she and her former boss and now partner, Sean, have moved to New York City and are working for Parker Armstrong's prestigious close-protection agency. But Charlie is on enforced leave—a bodyguard without a body to guard—and feels somewhat adrift.

This story was written specially for the US paperback edition of book six in the series, SECOND SHOT. During the events of that book, Charlie was injured protecting her principal, Simone Kerse, and at the end of it Charlie is still rehabilitating from the double-gunshot wounds that almost killed her.

As part of her recuperation, she takes off on her new Buell Firebolt motorcycle, and heads for an out-of-season health spa in the Catskill Mountains. There she encounters guests and staff who turn out to be more—or sometimes less—than first meets the eye. Charlie handles them all with her usual downbeat inimitable style.

Incidentally, the damage sustained by the Buell during this story was referenced in the next book in the series—THIRD STRIKE. Only a small mention, but enough for fans to spot!

Instead of appearing as a bonus story at the end of SECOND SHOT, Off Duty was selected for inclusion in CRIMINAL TENDENCIES—GREAT CRIME STORIES FROM GREAT CRIME WRITERS, part of the proceeds of which went to breast cancer charities. The story also appeared in *Ellery Queen Mystery Magazine*, and was chosen for THE MAMMOTH BOOK OF BEST BRITISH CRIME 8, edited by Maxim Jakubowski.

Off Duty

The guy who'd just tried to kill me didn't look like much. From the fleeting glimpse I'd caught of him behind the wheel of his brand new soft-top Cadillac, he was short, with less hair than he'd like on his head and more than anyone could possibly want on his chest and forearms.

That was as much as I could tell before I was throwing myself sideways. The front wheel of the Buell skittered on the loose gravel shoulder of the road, sending a vicious shimmy up through the headstock into my arms. I nearly dropped the damn bike there and then, and that was what pissed me off the most.

The Buell was less than a month old at that point, a Firebolt still with the shiny feel to it, and I'd been hoping it would take longer to acquire its first battle scar. The first cut is always the one you remember.

Although I was wearing full leathers, officially I was still signed off sick from the Kerse job and undergoing the tortures of regular physiotherapy. Adding motorcycle accident injuries, however minor, was not going to look good to anyone, least of all me.

But the bike didn't tuck under and spit me into the weeds, as I half-expected. Instead it righted itself, almost stately, and allowed me to slither to a messy stop maybe seventy metres further on. I put my feet down and tipped up my visor, aware of my heart punching behind my ribs, the adrenaline shake in my hands, the burst of anger that follows on closely after having had the shit scared out of you.

I turned, to find the guy in the Cadillac had completed his half-arsed manoeuvre, pulling out of a side road and turning left across my path. He'd slowed, though, twisting round to stare back at me with his neck extended like a meerkat. Even at this distance I could see the petulant scowl. Hell, perhaps I'd made

38

him drop the cell phone he'd been yabbering into instead of paying attention to his driving ...

Just for a second our eyes met, and I considered making an issue out of it. The guy must have sensed that. He plunked back down in his seat and rammed the car into drive, gunning it away with enough gusto to chirrup the tires on the bone dry surface.

I rolled my shoulders, thought that was the last I'd ever see of him.

I was wrong.

***

Spending a few days away in the Catskill Mountains was a spur-of-the-moment decision, taken in a mood of self-pity.

Sean was in LA, heading up a high-profile protection detail for some East Coast actress who'd hit it big and was getting windy about her latest stalker. He'd just come back from the Middle East, tired, but focused, buzzing, loving every minute of it and doing his best not to rub it in.

After he'd left for California, the apartment seemed too quiet without him. Feeling the sudden urge to escape New York, and my enforced sabbatical, I'd looked at the maps and headed for the hills, ending up at a small resort and health spa, just north of the prettily-named Sundown in Ulster county. The last time I'd been in Ulster the local accent had been Northern Irish, and it had not ended well.

The hotel was set back in thick trees, the accommodation provided in a series of chalets overlooking a small lake. My physio had recommended the range of massage services they offered, and I'd booked a whole raft of treatments. By the time I brought the bike to a halt, nose-in outside my designated chalet, I was about ready for my daily pummelling.

It was with no more than mild annoyance, therefore, that I recognized the soft-top Cadillac two spaces down. For a moment my hand stilled, then I shrugged, hit the engine kill-switch, and went stiffly inside to change out of my leathers.

***

Fifteen minutes later, fresh from the shower, I was sitting alone in the waiting area of the spa, listening to the self-consciously soothing music. The resort was quiet, not yet in season. Another reason why I'd chosen it.

"Tanya will be with you directly," the woman on the desk told me, gracious in white, depositing a jug of iced water by my elbow before melting away again.

The only other person in the waiting area was a big blond guy who worked maintenance. He was making too much out of replacing a faulty door catch, but unless you have the practice it's hard to loiter unobtrusively. From habit, I watched his hands, his eyes, wondered idly what he was about.

The sound of raised voices from one of the treatment rooms produced a sudden, jarring note. From my current position I could see along the line of doors, watched one burst open and the masseuse, Tanya, come storming out. Her face was scarlet with anger and embarrassment. She whirled.

"You slimy little bastard!"

I wasn't overly surprised to see Cadillac man hurry out after her, shrugging into his robe. I'd been right about the extent of that body hair.

"Aw, come on, honey!" he protested. "I thought it was all, y'know, *part of the service.*"

The blond maintenance man dropped his tools and lunged for the corridor, meaty hands outstretched. The woman behind the reception desk jumped to her feet, rapped out, "Dwayne!" in a thunderous voice that made him falter in conditioned response.

I swung my legs off my lounger but didn't rise. The woman on the desk looked like she could handle it, and she did, sending Dwayne skulking off, placating Tanya, giving Cadillac man an excruciatingly polite dressing down that flayed the skin off him nevertheless. He left a tip that must have doubled the cost of the massage he'd so nearly had.

"Ms Fox?" Tanya said a few moments later, flustered but trying for calm. "I'm real sorry about that. Would you follow me, please?"

"Are you OK, or do you need a minute?" I asked, wary of letting someone dig in with ill-tempered fingers, however skilled.

"I'm good, thanks." She led me into the dimly lit treatment room, flashed a quick smile over her shoulder as she laid out fresh hot towels.

"Matey-boy tried it on, did he?"

She shook her head, rueful, slicked her hands with warmed oil. "Some guys hear the word *masseuse* but by the time it's gotten down to their brain, it's turned into *hooker*," she said, her

40

back to me while I slipped out of my robe and levered myself, face-down, flat onto the table. Easier than it had been, not as easy as it used to be.

"So, what's Dwayne's story?" I asked, feeling the first long glide of her palms up either side of my spine, the slight reactive tremor when I mentioned his name.

"He and I stepped out for awhile," she said, casual yet prim. "It wasn't working, so we broke it off."

I thought of his pretended busyness, his lingering gaze, his rage.

No, I thought. You *broke it off.*

***

Later that evening, unwilling to suit up again to ride into the nearest town, I ate in the hotel restaurant at a table laid for one. Other diners were scarce. Cadillac man was alone on the far side of the dining room, just visible round the edges of the silent grand piano. I could almost see the miasma of his aftershave.

He called the waitress "honey", too, stared blatantly down her cleavage when she brought his food. Anticipating the summer crowds, the management packed the tables in close, so she had to lean across to refill his coffee cup. I heard her surprised, hurt squeak as he took advantage, and waited to see if she'd 'accidentally' tip the contents of the pot into his lap, just to dampen his ardour. To my disappointment, she did not.

He chuckled as she scurried away, caught me watching and mistook my glance for admiration. He raised his cup in my direction with a meaningful little wiggle of his eyebrows. I stared him out for a moment, then looked away.

Just another oxygen thief.

***

As soon as I'd finished eating I took my own coffee through to the bar. The flatscreen TV above the mirrored back wall was tuned to one of the sports channels, showing highlights of the latest AMA Superbikes Championship. The only other occupant was the blond maintenance man, Dwayne, sitting hunched at the far end, pouring himself into his beer.

I took a stool where I had a good view, not just of the screen but the rest of the room as well, and shook my head when the barman asked what he could get me.

41

"I'll stick to coffee," I said, indicating my cup. The painkillers I was taking made my approach to alcohol still cautious.

In the mirror, I saw Cadillac man saunter in and take up station further along the bar. As he passed, he glanced at my back a couple of times as if sizing me up, with all the finesse of a hard-bitten hill farmer checking out a promising young ewe. I kept my attention firmly on the motorcycle racing.

After a minute or so of waiting for me to look over so he could launch into seductive dialogue, he signalled the barman. I ignored their muttered conversation until a snifter of brandy was put down in front of me with a solemn flourish.

I did look over then, received a smug salute from Cadillac man's own glass. I smiled—at the barman. "I'm sorry," I said to him. "But I'm teetotal at the moment."

"Yes, ma'am," the barman said with a twinkle, and whisked the offending glass away again.

"Hey, that's my kind of girl," Cadillac man called over, when the barman relayed the message. Surprise made me glance at him and he took that as invitation to slide three stools closer, so only one separated us. His hot little piggy eyes fingered their way over my body. "Beautiful *and* cheap to keep, huh?"

"Good coffee's thirty bucks a pound," I said, voice as neutral as I could manage.

His gaze cast about for another subject. "You not bored with this?" he asked, jerking his head at the TV. "I could get him to switch channels."

I allowed a tight smile that didn't reach my eyes. "Neil Hodgson's just lapped Daytona in under one-minute thirty-eight," I said. "How could I be bored?"

Out of the corner of my eye, I saw Dwayne's head lift and turn as the sound of Cadillac man's voice finally penetrated. It was like watching a slow-waking bear.

"So, honey, if I can't buy you a drink," Cadillac man said with his most sophisticated leer, "can I buy you breakfast?"

I flicked my eyes towards the barman in the universal distress signal. By the promptness of his arrival, he'd been expecting my call.

"Is this guy bothering you?" he asked, flexing his muscles.

"Yes," I said cheerfully. "He is."

"Sir, I'm afraid I'm gonna have to ask you to leave."

Cadillac man gaped between us for a moment, then flounced out, muttering what sounded like "frigid bitch" under his breath.

After very little delay, Dwayne staggered to his feet and went determinedly after him.

Without haste, I finished my coffee. The racing reached an ad break. I checked my watch, left a tip, and headed back out into the mild evening air towards my chalet. My left leg ached equally from the day's activity and the evening's rest.

I heard the raised voices before I saw them in the gathering gloom, caught the familiar echoing smack of bone on muscle.

Dwayne had run his quarry to ground in the space between the soft-top Cadillac and my Buell, and was venting his alcohol-fuelled anger in traditional style, with his fists. Judging by the state of him, Cadillac man was only lethal behind the wheel of a car.

On his knees, one eye already closing, he caught sight of me and yelled, "Help, for Chrissake!"

I unlocked the door to my chalet, crossed to the phone by the bed.

"Your maintenance man is beating seven bells out of one of your guests down here," I said sedately, when front desk answered. "You might want to send someone."

Outside again, Cadillac man was going down for the third time, nose streaming blood. I noted with alarm that he'd dropped seriously close to my sparkling new Buell.

I started forwards, just as Dwayne loosed a mighty roundhouse that glanced off Cadillac man's cheekbone and deflected into the Buell's left-hand mirror. The bike swayed perilously on its stand and I heard the musical note of splintered glass dropping.

"Hey!" I shouted.

Dwayne glanced up and instantly dismissed me as a threat, moved in for the kill.

OK. Now I'm pissed off.

Heedless of my bad leg, I reached them in three fast strides and stamped down onto the outside of Dwayne's right knee, hearing the cartilage and the anterior cruciate ligament pop as the joint dislocated. Regardless of how much muscle you're carrying, the knee is always vulnerable.

Dwayne crashed, bellowing, but was too drunk or too stupid to know it was all over. He swung for me. I reached under my jacket and took the SIG 9mm off my hip and pointed it at him, so the muzzle loomed large near the bridge of his nose.

"Don't," I murmured.

And that was how, a few moments later, we were found by Tanya, and the woman from reception, and the barman.

***

"You a cop?" Cadillac man asked, voice thick because of the stuffed nose.

"No," I said. "I work in close protection. I'm a bodyguard."

He absorbed that in puzzled silence. We were back in the bar until the police arrived. Out in the lobby I could hear Dwayne still shouting at the pain, and Tanya shouting at what she thought of his stupid jealous temper. He was having a thoroughly bad night.

"A bodyguard," Cadillac man mumbled blankly. "So why the fuck did you let him beat the crap out of me back there?"

"Because you deserved it," I said, rubbing my leg and wishing I'd gone for my Vicodin before I'd broken up the fight. "I thought it would be a valuable life lesson—thou shalt not be a total dickhead."

"Jesus, honey! And all the time, you had a gun? I can't believe you just let him—"

I sighed. "What do you do?"

"Do?"

"Yeah. For a living."

He shrugged gingerly, as much as the cracked ribs would let him. "I sell Cadillacs," he said. "The finest motorcar money can buy."

"Spare me," I said. "So, if you saw a guy broken down by the side of the road, you'd just stop and give him a car, would you?"

"Well," Cadillac man said, frowning, "I guess, if he was a pal—"

"What if he was a complete stranger who'd behaved like a prat from the moment you set eyes on him?" I queried. He didn't answer. I stood, flipped my jacket to make sure it covered the gun. "I don't expect you to work for free. Don't expect me to, either."

His glance was sickly cynical. "Some bodyguard, huh?"

"Yeah, well," I tossed back, thinking of the Buell with its smashed mirror and wondering who was in for seven years of bad luck. "I'm off duty."

Truth And Lies
intro

This is a brand new story, written especially for inclusion in the e-anthology (e-thology?) of Charlie Fox stories—FOX FIVE. As such, it's longer and more detailed than the others—I had no word-counts to restrict me, so I could let Charlie's character have free rein.

I have been deliberately non-specific about the precise location of this tale. It's nowhere and everywhere, both at the same time. There was so much trouble going on, and so many news teams reporting from civil war zones or other areas of conflict that I wanted to write something that was pertinent to them all. I hope I've succeeded.

In this story, Charlie is working as a full-fledged bodyguard for Parker Armstrong's prestigious New York City agency. She is part of a three-man team sent to escort a news reporter, Alison Cranmore, and her cameraman, Nils, out of a beleaguered country on the brink of civil war.

However, things start to go bad very fast and, as the regime begins to disintegrate, it is up to Charlie, with the help of a local fixer, to work out a plan that will get her principals safely across the border.

It comes at a price.

Truth And Lies

As long as they didn't strip-search me at the airport, I knew I'd be OK. Not that I was trying to bring in anything suspicious, never mind illegal. The government security forces were jumpy enough without giving them more of an excuse to imprison or expel yet another foreigner.

But I *was* attempting to enter the country as a harmless civilian, and I knew if I was forced to undress there was no way anyone could misinterpret my scars. Old knife and bullet wounds are hard to disguise, especially from people who are experts at inflicting them. To me they were a physical reminder of past mistakes—lessons painfully learned and not forgotten.

Three of us had set off from New York twenty-four hours earlier. A rush job—emergency evac. Some news team who'd got in deeper and stayed in longer than was good for them and suddenly needed out. Now. Probably a month after common sense should have told them to leave.

I'd seen it happen before to those exposed to long-term danger. A gradual dulling of the natural flight response until a fifty-fifty chance of living or dying on the job seemed like workable odds.

I had some sympathy with that. Before the evac team left, we'd been briefed by experts on the current political situation here. When they'd told us our chances of survival were not much better, we'd shrugged and carried on packing.

We travelled separately, via half a dozen different neutral countries. I'd dressed with authority rather than intimidation in mind, safely dowdy, and careful to avoid any kind of contact—eye or otherwise—that might have aroused attention. I'd also reverted to my British passport—the one without the Israeli stamps. But in the end I think the success of my infiltration was down to good old-fashioned chauvinism.

The soldiers who'd taken over the immigration process, with casually slung AKs and obligatory dark glasses, simply did not believe that a woman travelling alone posed any significant threat.

Maybe they were right.

They let me pass with a grubby fondle through my belongings that was cursory at best. Still, as I walked out of the building I was half-expecting the shouted order to stop, to drop to my knees. It was not only the blistering heat of late afternoon which caused the sweat to pool between my shoulder blades.

I ignored the garrulous taxi drivers who pushed and shoved for my notice by the kerb, knew they were weighing up my worth both as a fare and a potential hostage in equal measure. And I kept a firm grip on my bag, even though I was intending to dump it anyway. For now it was valuable camouflage.

A piercing whistle momentarily silenced the drivers. A man sailed through the crowd towards me, dressed in the local flowing robes. He might once have been handsome, until a large sharp blade—probably a machete—had bisected his face on a ragged diagonal from temple to jaw, destroying the line of his nose and his left eye in the process, and giving him a permanent lop-sided grimace.

The others fell away at the sight of his ruined features. He seemed almost to revel in their revulsion.

"I am Zaki—Zak, yes?" he announced, as if I might not recognise him from appearance alone. "We go please, yes?"

"We go," I agreed, and followed him to a dusty Toyota not so much parked as abandoned on the far side of the road. I climbed into the back seat—a pale-haired woman sitting up front beside a local man would have had us pulled over within minutes.

Zak cranked the engine and shot out into traffic without troubling his mirrors. A dented Mercedes, old enough to be a classic, fell into step behind us. The two men in the front seats were wearing dark glasses and identical moustaches. Security forces. Following foreigners was considered something of a national sport.

"Did my ... friends arrive yet?" I asked.

Zak shifted in his seat so he could let his good eye roam over me while he drove seemingly more from memory than observation. He shook his head, regretful.

"They did not make it."

48

All kinds of nasty scenarios flitted through my mind. "Didn't make it *how*, exactly?"

He shrugged, a gesture that involved both hands as well as shoulders. "They were arrested," he said simply. "It was not to be, yes?"

Shit. So I'm on my own.

"Will they be OK?"

Another shrug. "A few nights in jail. A few bruises, broken bones. Nothing serious. Then they are put on next flight home." The grin broadened. "My government, it does not like mercenaries, yes?"

"We're not mercenaries," I murmured automatically. "We're bodyguards."

Zak's roaming eye lifted to my face for the first time. "You fight and die for money, yes?" he said. "What is difference?"

***

The Hotel Royale had once boasted an elegant ambience, a blend of western decadence and eastern mystery. It was now a pockmarked survivor with faded paint and barred windows all along the ground floor. The management had placed a number of large concrete blocks outside, making it hard for anyone to take a run at the lobby with a truckful of explosives. A strategy born of experience.

Zak pulled up as close to the entrance as the concrete landscaping would allow. The government watchers in the dented Mercedes hung around long enough to see us get out, then U-turned in the road and headed back for the airport. It was reassuring to know they weren't taking their duties too seriously.

I had a handful of folded dollars ready to pay Zak for the trip—removed discreetly from the money belt around my waist in one of the brief periods when his focus had actually been on the road. He might be my contact here, a man to be trusted—but only to a point. It would not be wise to put undue temptation his way.

As it was, he waited expectantly while I shouldered my bag. I paused a beat, then said, "Could I have my *other* bag, please? I believe you put it in the trunk."

Zak beamed, as if he'd been testing me and could not be more delighted that I'd passed. He opened the Toyota's boot and lifted

49

out a small holdall I'd never seen before. He'd been given careful instructions about what was needed, and I hoped he'd been able to get everything on the list. After all, I could hardly check it right there in the open. Still, it felt reassuringly heavy.

I palmed him the cash and he slammed the boot lid. The sun was almost down and the city would soon be in curfew. A scruffy kid slithered over and tried to con me with a fake bellboy act, gesticulating angrily when I refused to cooperate.

Zak took a step towards him, raising his arms like a bogey man as his face caught the light. The kid ran. Zak laughed, but there was something hard and bitter behind it.

"I'll see you tomorrow morning—as soon as you can get through," I said. "We're counting on you."

Zak beamed. "Honour is mine, thank you, yes," he said, sketching a small bow.

He jumped into the Toyota and roared away, for all the world like a man who really did think himself honoured, instead of being involved in a crazy suicidal rescue scheme that was already two-thirds down on manpower.

***

If I'd had nerves about the security of the Hotel Royale, they were settled as soon as I entered the lobby area. The occupants of the shabby chic room were three-quarter female and clearly of a professional bent. But if the local hookers felt safe enough to ply their trade here, the chances are it would be OK for the rest of us. For one night, at least.

I signed in under a false name and slipped the manager a hundred when he asked for my passport.

"Thank you, *madame*," he said with a flash of teeth as the note disappeared into his sleeve. "That seems to be in order."

He offered me a room on the ground floor, which I bullied him to change to the third. High enough to make anyone breaking in work for it, but not so high I'd die before jumping if there was a fire. I took the stairs, pausing on each landing to listen for footsteps behind me. There were none.

Safe in my room, I checked the locks and turned on the radio to a raucous local station before finally unzipping the holdall Zak had given me. Inside, as per his instructions, was an assortment of useful items including old clothing, a thin paper map of the city, compass, field medical kit, duct tape, survival knife with a

20cm blade, and an old Sterling Sub-Machine Gun with a spare magazine and two boxes of 9mm rounds. All essentials I dare not risk trying to carry through the airport. Never mind the gun— just having the map and the compass was likely to get me condemned as a spy.

I stripped the Sterling and reassembled it. It had a folding stock that made it short enough to deploy inside a vehicle, but gave the shooter some stability for more distant targets. A long time ago I'd trained on just such a weapon, back when the SMG was standard issue to all members of the Women's Royal Army Corps. When I started my Special Forces training we'd moved on to more sophisticated armament, but sometimes simplicity was best.

This old faithful had probably come from India, not in the first flush of youth, but plenty reliable and accurate for the job in hand. Plus it was sturdy enough to clout someone over the head with if I ran out of ammo. All points in its favour.

I loaded thirty rounds into each magazine rather than topping them off, slotted one into the receiver, and nestled the gun back into the top of the holdall where I could reach it easily if I left the bag partially unzipped. Then I changed into a selection of the shapeless clothes Zak had provided. Somewhat disturbingly, the smell of their last owner still lingered.

Two flights up, the fifth floor had largely been taken over by those hardy or desperate or unbalanced enough among the press contingent to still be in-country. I passed a couple of obvious ex-squaddie contractors who were supposed to be guarding the corridor, but who let me through without a second glance. Black marks all round.

When I banged on the door to the room number as per the briefing, there were signs of rapid movement inside. Shadows came and went behind the Judas glass. Eventually, a man's voice called out curtly, "Who is it?"

I sighed and slid my passport, face down, beneath the door. It was yanked out of my fingers before it was halfway under. For my own safety, I'd brought nothing to identify me as working for Parker Armstrong's New York City close-protection agency. If a Brit ID wasn't enough to convince them, it would just be me and Zak heading for the border tomorrow.

Eventually, the door opened a crack and a narrow section of a woman's face stared out above the chain. She was small and blonde and totally wired. I recognised the slightly freaked-out eyes of someone who is only keeping it together because they don't quite believe what's happening is real.

"Alison Cranmore?" I said, not adding "I presume" because she didn't look like she'd appreciate the Livingstone joke. "I'm Charlie Fox."

The eyes flickered in something that might have been dismay. She closed the door without a word, opening it again a second later, the chain removed. I stepped past her and waited while she fumbled with the chain and lock. I reached into the holdall and picked out another item that had been on Zak's procurement list—a simple wooden doorstop. I slid the narrow end under the door and kicked it into place with the toe of my boot. When it comes to flimsy hotel locks, you can never be too careful.

When I turned, I found Alison had moved back to sit on the bed as if her legs had given out on her, and was staring at me again. She was pretty but not to the point of frivolity, with good bone structure that came across well on camera. Since she'd been in-country, she'd acquired a leaned-down slimness, as if long exposure to heat and stress had stripped her of any excess weight.

The male voice I'd heard belonged to the only other person in the room, a gaunt man sprawled in a chair over by the curtained window. His hair was pale almost to white, and he had the high cheekbones and startling blue eyes that made me think instinctively of Scandinavia.

"*You're* Charlie?" Alison said at last, her voice blankly incredulous.

I looked from her to the man. He was eyeing me with flat amusement, as if his luck had been bad for so long he expected nothing else, and the only recourse left to him was to laugh in the face of it.

"You were expecting some hulking great grunt like that pair outside," I said, jerking my head towards the corridor.

"Too right!" Alison shot back. On the news reports I'd seen her deliver, her voice had a carefully cultivated classlessness, a neutrality designed to convey the information without you noticing the person behind it. Tension made it ragged. "Where are the others? We were told there would be more of you—three or four at least."

I smiled. "Sadly, what you see is what you get."

The blond man spread his hands and shrugged, reminding me of Zak. He'd obviously been in-country a long time. "We are going to die, for sure," he announced, his accent Swedish.

"Not for sure," I said. I reached into the bag and pulled out the SMG, hefted it. "Do you honestly think—if I looked like the gorillas out there—I would have managed to walk in here carrying this?"

***

We talked for a couple of hours. At least, Alison and I talked, while the blond guy—who turned out to be a freelance cameraman called Nils from Stockholm—drank cheap vodka and smoked cigarettes down to the knuckle.

At the end of it, I knew more than I wanted about the injustices going on inside the country, and less than I needed about the situation we were in. I was already aware that the president was a poster-boy for corrupt dictators the world over. The current unrest was being generated by his former right-hand man, who had somehow managed to survive being purged to mount the first viable opposition in years. Beyond that, I didn't need to know the details.

"So," I said. "What's stopping you going out the same way I came in—via the airport on the first commercial flight to just about anywhere?"

Nils harrumphed into his shot glass—no easy feat. "This is what they are waiting for," he said.

I glanced at Alison. "You think the government would try to prevent you leaving?"

It was Nils who answered. "No way," he said. "It is their dream that we go—get us out of their head."

I was pretty sure he meant 'hair', but I didn't correct him. Mainly because his English was a hell of a lot better than my grasp of Swedish, which was limited to mild obscenities and ordering beer.

"So," I repeated, "what's stopping you?"

"They'll let *us* go, but not the story," Alison said.

"You've been here for six months, sending out stories all the time," I said. "What's special about this one?"

That's when they began to act cagey. And shortly thereafter, I began to lose my patience.

Eventually, I returned to my room on the third floor, having told Alison and Nils to be ready to move as soon as curfew lifted in the morning. As I left, I suggested quietly to Alison that she try and separate Nils from his bottle of vodka before he hit the bottom—mentally and physically. Some people get maudlin when they drink. Clearly, Nils was one of them.

I tried not to let the cloak and dagger attitude irritate me. It's not unusual for clients to try to keep you in the dark. I suppose they made the same assumption as Zak—that they've bought your services and so can anyone else, if the price is right.

The reality is that the close-protection business is all about reputation, and Parker Armstrong's outfit had a name for utter reliability. With the rest of my team blown, the responsibility for maintaining that reputation rested squarely on my shoulders.

No pressure, then.

***

I woke in the middle of the night to find I'd rolled out of bed on a reflex and grabbed for the SMG which I'd left close to hand on the side table. I lay there on the floor, hard up against the side of the mattress with my heart hammering against my breastbone and my ears straining in the dark.

For a moment I wondered if I'd merely been in the grip of some weirdly realistic nightmare. Then the noise that had woken me came again. Incoming fire—close proximity.

Keeping low, I crabbed over to the window, slithered up the wall alongside it and peered out. Tracer rounds were arcing through the night from the south, aimed not for the city itself, but further east. I didn't need GPS to work out they were targeting the airport.

Ah well, there goes that escape plan.

There had been plenty of collateral damage before the gunners got their eye in. Isolated fires were dotted all over the city, their flames licking up into the night sky until the underside of the clouds themselves seemed to be burning.

Through the single-glazed window I could hear the distinctive rattle of AK fire in the streets below. It was this development, I knew, that had penetrated my subconscious. The AK was the weapon of choice for all sides in this conflict, so it was hard to know who was shooting at what.

I considered our options. The hotel itself did not seem to be a direct target. Moving in the dark would be ludicrous. Staying put was the only logical choice.

I wrapped myself in several layers of spare clothing and crawled to the far side of the bed, away from the window and possible shrapnel, with the holdall close to hand and the SMG cradled in my arms. If the worst happened and the building collapsed around me, the bed would not be squashed completely flat, creating a survival pocket alongside it. And if we received a direct hit, well, there wasn't much I could do.

Either way, I didn't intend to lose sleep over it.

***

On the grounds that you should never pass up the opportunity to eat, I was down in the lobby early the following morning in hopes of breakfast, only to find Alison and Nils had beaten me to it.

Alison gave me a wan smile as I sat down at their table.

"I never could sleep through a bombardment," she said. And as if to highlight her point of view, another distant explosion rumbled in.

Nils looked the worse for wear, too, but that could simply have been down to fallout from the night before's vodka.

"You might want to change before we leave," I told him. He was wearing digital-desert pattern trousers and a khaki shirt.

"What for?"

I shrugged. Zak must be rubbing off on me, too. "You look like a soldier," I said. "We're going to have enough trouble getting out of here without both sides mistaking you for an enemy combatant."

Nils grunted. He took a sip of coffee the colour and consistency of road tar, and said with a certain arrogance, "This is why we have you."

"Actually," I said mildly, "this is why *she* has me. You're just along for the ride."

Alison blinked. "But—?"

"It was *your* news agency who contracted us—Nils is freelance," I told her, flicked my eyes across both of them and added with as much diplomacy as I could manage, "I'll do my best to keep everyone safe, but if it comes down to it, I am bound to protect Alison first."

"And I get to go fuck myself into a cocked hat," Nils said morosely.

The intricacies of that manoeuvre were lost on me, but I got the gist. "That is your prerogative," I agreed. "But it doesn't mean I'm going to let you do the same to the rest of us." I let that settle, then put effort and quiet force into my voice. "Now—go and change."

The Swede sat for a moment, anger swirling behind his features, then he got up without a word and strode away towards the lobby. AK fire in a neighbouring street seemed to echo in time with his footsteps.

I'd noticed that the lobby area had been crowding up—it seemed we were not the only ones proposing to make a rapid exit in light of the collapsing situation. The manager didn't look unduly upset by the exodus. I gathered that there would soon be a new influx of war zone junkies to replace those leaving. Not just news teams, but private military contractors, too. Some of them were legit, but some of them were just gun freaks who wanted a chance to take out a live moving target, without spending the rest of their life behind bars for the privilege.

Probably best to be gone before any of them arrived.

Alison leaned across and touched my arm. "I *need* Nils," she said, low and urgent. When I raised an eyebrow, she flushed. "Not like that. I need him for this story. Without him, I have nothing. It's just *my* word, you know?"

I stared at her. "You mean you don't have proof?"

"Oh, we have proof," she said. "On digital video—*Nils's* video. And without it, they'll say I've gone completely off my rocker."

"Couldn't you have beamed it out by satellite or something, if it's so important?"

"Nils won't let go of it. He says that once it's out there, anybody could steal it."

"Better that than never getting the damn thing out at all."

She gave an unhappy shrug, the reporter in her understanding Nils's reluctance to let go of his baby for anyone to exploit.

I would have pushed her for more, but the Swede's return made her clam up completely. His manner was one of sulky confidence, as if he knew exactly what Alison might have told me during his absence. Still, at least he *had* changed, into a flowered shirt and blue lightweight hiking trousers with the lower half of the legs zipped off to turn them into comically long shorts. He'd gone from looking like a weekend warrior to a bad tourist.

"So, when do we go?" he demanded.

That was a question I'd been hoping nobody was going to ask. Zak was late. Not just 'delayed'—even by the generally relaxed timekeeping standards of this place—but seriously, worryingly, late. Time edged round. Other breakfasters came and went. I began to think I might have to resort to Plan B, which was basically to steal an abandoned vehicle and make a run for it by ourselves.

About half an hour later, I spotted the two moustachioed watchers from the dented Merc, who slid into the lobby and were loitering conspicuously behind the drooping fronds of a potted palm. I swear hotels only include potted palms in their decor for exactly this purpose. I silently christened them Tweedle-Dumb and Tweedle-Dumber.

I tried not to read too much into their arrival. Maybe they figured it was safer here than out on the streets when they were so clearly aligned with the current regime. And maybe Zak's alarm clock had failed to go off and he'd simply overslept.

Yeah, right.

***

Just when I'd begun to seriously consider luring the Tweedle brothers outside and nicking their Merc, Zak finally turned up, looking freshly showered. He was full of shrugs and bows and apologies as he led us out to his old Toyota, which also now glistened wetly in the morning heat.

"*Please* tell me you didn't stop to wash your car," I said.

He gave another of his voluminous shrugs. "Water cannon, yes?"

I gathered from the huge cracks in the windscreen and the sopping interior that he wasn't joking. The front seats had taken the brunt. This made Nils even more grumpy when I pointed out that, strictly for propriety's sake, Alison and I should ride in the back.

We loaded our gear. I'd transferred anything I needed from my original luggage to the holdall Zak had provided, and abandoned my old bag in my room for the cleaning staff to make use of or sell, as they wished. I'd left the bag carefully spread open on my bed—people were having a bad enough time here without adding an unnecessary bomb scare into the mix.

As we climbed into the Toyota, the Tweedles emerged and trotted towards their own car with much surreptitious glancing in our direction. People had been leaving since curfew lifted and the pair hadn't taken much notice, which meant they had been specifically waiting for us.

Not good.

I leaned forwards and tapped Zak on the shoulder. "Do you have any friends you can rely on who might help us?" I asked.

He pursed his lips, torn between being paid for his own helpfulness and being forced to split whatever money I was prepared to spend. "Maybe yes, maybe," he said at last.

"Call them," I said. "Tell them to steal or borrow a car and be ready to move." With reluctance, Zak dragged out an ancient mobile phone the size of a brick, and prodded in a number. As he waited for the connection, I tapped his shoulder again. "Oh, the car—make sure they take it from someone they don't like."

***

I don't know if the antiquity of Zak's phone had anything to do with it, but he was unable to get through to his friends. "Network is down," he announced casually over his shoulder as we careered out into traffic. "We need to make side-show to go see them, yes?"

I glanced out of the rear screen. Beads of water still rolled down the outside of the glass, and every time Zak cornered both front seats squelched. The Merc had slotted in behind us as if on a long tow. The Tweedle brother in the passenger seat was talking on his own phone, arms waving wildly as he did so. Put handcuffs on half the guys in this part of the world and they'd be struck instantly mute.

"Our watchers are back and they appear to be spreading the word." I stabbed a thumb over my shoulder towards our tail. "I thought you said the network was down."

Zak looked pained. "*Civilian* network is down," he explained, twisting in his seat without regard for obstacles in the road like burning buses and strewn rubble from the occasional half-collapsed building.

Alison spun back from staring out of the rear window. We'd both covered our face and hair with local scarves, so all I could

58

see of her was a pair of accusing eyes. "You *knew* you were being followed?" she demanded.

"Everyone is followed *to* the hotel," I said. "Looks like they really don't want to see you leave." I unzipped the holdall, which sat alongside me on the rear seat, and brought out the SMG, keeping it below the level of the glass. "Do you know how to load a magazine?"

She shook her head.

"Don't worry," I said grimly, "you'll soon learn."

***

The city was a mix of wide open squares and narrow twisting streets. It was as if the head of planning had grand designs, but the rest of the committee conspired against him during his lunch hour, surreptitiously crowding houses and offices and shops into every available space.

Zak tore through the open areas as if trying to avoid a missile lock. Some of the squares were still awash, but at least it was only water.

Water cannon ...

"Why didn't they just shoot you?" I asked suddenly.

"Thank you, please, yes?" Zak queried over his shoulder. I'd noticed that if he didn't understand the question, he tended to just throw words at you, hoping to land on the right answer by a process of elimination.

"There's been artillery fire all over the city during the night. If it was government forces—and I can't see the rebels bothering with water cannon—why didn't they just shoot at you?"

"Too many news peoples," Zak said, his grin becoming wider and slightly more grotesque. "Both sides wanting support of international community, yes?"

"Water cannon looks bad enough on camera," Nils said from the front seat, where he was bracing himself during the wild ride with both hands and a knee wedged hard against the dashboard. "But killing civilians looks worse, for sure." And the bitterness was back in his voice again.

Zak swerved round a corner and a shabby café came into view, one window boarded up with corrugated iron sheeting and bullet pockmarks in the walls. Outside was a motley collection of cars and scooters. They weren't so much parked as huddled together like flotsam in the corner of a dirty harbour.

"Ah, luck is with us," cried Zak, taking both hands off the wheel in his delight. "My friend—he is here."

He ran the Toyota into the melee until the bumper docked with the car in front, and jumped out before I could stop him. I cursed under my breath. Going after him meant leaving the gun behind—carrying it openly would be inviting trouble. I went after him with a wad of money folded tight in my hand, leaving the SMG on the back seat for now and my door open. I had already tucked the survival knife through my belt, hidden beneath the folds of baggy clothing, and I made sure my scarf was pulled tight around my face.

The dented Merc pulled up on the other side of the street. This area was not a government stronghold, and the Tweedles looked as out of place here as they did uneasy.

They were so close I had to keep my voice low as I explained to Zak what was needed. If the Tweedles had wound down their windows, they could have joined in without needing to shout. These guys must have called in sick the day the Beginners' Guide to Discreet Surveillance class was run.

Zak disappeared the cash with a magician's skill and hurried into the café, sandals flapping. I gave the street a slow once-over, then climbed back into the Toyota, still leaving my door open.

"Where's he gone?" Alison demanded.

"We need some help to get rid of our tail before we run for the border," I said, eyes sliding towards the Tweedles. "As it is, if those two follow any closer we'll be able to slap them with a paternity suit."

Nils frowned, nodded to the gun by my leg. "So—why not shoot them?"

There were any number of tactical reasons why that would be a Very Bad Plan but before I could explain any of them, Alison rounded on him. "Is that how we get our story out now—kill whoever gets in our way?" she asked. "We're supposed to report the problems, not become a part of them, remember?"

Nils gave another shrug that would have done Zak proud, and slumped back into his seat. The sudden silence between us grated. Alison muttered, "Come on, come on," under her breath. "What's taking him so long?"

I reckoned she'd been here long enough to realise that every business transaction started with drawn-out cups of tea or evil coffee. But even I didn't like the time Zak had been inside. If nothing else, the distant AK fire that had formed a constant backdrop seemed to be growing in pitch and volume. And the deserted street was not quite so deserted any more. There were faces, movement, in once-deserted doorways and windows around us. I kept a wary eye on the slow convergence.

The Tweedle brothers were becoming increasingly agitated, too, to the point where I entertained a vain hope they might jump ship without waiting for further discouragement. They clearly weren't happy with their current location, though—a fact which was not lost on Alison.

She ducked in her seat to get a better look at the buildings surrounding us, as if getting her bearings for the first time since the journey had begun. "This Zak—whose side is he on?" she asked abruptly.

"His own, I think," I said. "If you think he might sell us out, I agree that's crossed my mind, but this is a strictly cash-on-delivery kind of job. His promised fee is waiting for him at the border, so it's in his best interests to get us there."

Not to mention what I'll do to him if he tries anything ...

She nodded, and then I had to open my big mouth to add, "If it helps, I don't think he's a closet admirer of *El Presidente.*"

She didn't flinch. Flinching would imply involuntary movement. Instead, she went utterly still, like a fat rabbit who's suddenly realised that hawk-shaped shadow directly overhead is not a novelty cloud formation.

"We need to get out of here," she said, a fine serration of panic sawing through her voice. "It's not safe—"

"Get a grip," I snapped, surprised and not a little annoyed by the cracks in her cool. "Of course it's not *safe*. We're in a country that's had months of unrest and is heading downhill rapidly into full-blown civil war. Not exactly Leamington Spa on a wet Bank Holiday Monday."

"You don't understand," she said. She broke her immobility, twisting as if trying to cover all angles at once. "We can't trust him! We need to go."

I confess I'd been reluctantly edging towards a similar conclusion, but maybe with slightly less hysteria. I ducked my head to check the Toyota's ignition. It was empty.

Shit.

"OK," I said, "Let's—"

Before I got any further, a trio of skinny figures slithered out of a narrow alley next to the café and approached the car from the driver's side, peering in. They were mid-teens, but I didn't make the mistake of thinking of them as children. Nevertheless, although I put my hand on the SMG I kept it hidden—for now.

"English? American?" they demanded. "Manchester United? Red Sox?"

"No, Swedish," Nils called back. And then, perhaps realising that replying in English might not have been too smart, added quickly, "*Jag är Svensk. Svensk!*"

"*Français*," Alison declared, not to be outdone.

The pair ducked to look directly at me. "Irish," I said, putting all the threat of East Belfast into the single word.

They paused, not quite sure what to make of our replies. I flicked my gaze briefly to the café, the open doorway now thronged with faces watching the show. Nothing like the possibility of a lynching to brighten a dull morning.

I felt my heart rate step up, adrenaline pumping. I knew that when things went bad here, they tended to reach flashpoint very quickly. Zak might be setting us up, or he might be lying inside the building with his throat cut. Alternatively, he could be sipping his mud coffee and navigating the formal dance of small talk on his way to a deal.

Hope for the best, but plan for the worst.

I glanced around me, forcing my focus outwards to assess the whole scene. The Merc was only metres away with the engine running. It was a heavy vehicle—heavy enough to use as a battering ram if I needed to force our way through. If it came to it, I would have to take out the Tweedles and to hell with Alison's sensibilities. Still, the prospect of getting my principals transferred from one vehicle to the other, in the face of hostile and no doubt readily armed opposition, was not a choice to be made lightly.

"Maybe we should ask those watching us to watch *over* us?" Nils suggested out of the corner of his mouth. He'd twisted in his seat and followed my gaze—if not my intent—to the pair in the Merc.

"Not exactly what I had in mind," I murmured. "Just be ready to move."

Then, just as I tightened my fingers around the pistol grip of the Sterling, Zak pushed his way through, talking loudly, waving his arms as if to shoo away crows. The youths scattered and Zak climbed back into the car.

"All OK," he said, smiling. "We go, yes?"

He rammed the gear lever in reverse and the Toyota leapt back from the pile of vehicles, coming within a gnat's whisker of whacking another dent into the side of the Mercedes as it did so.

Tweedle-Dumb, behind the wheel, rapidly shifted the big car backwards away from a collision. Maybe any damage was deducted out of his pay. Looking at the state of the Merc he hadn't received his full packet in quite a while.

Meanwhile, a nondescript car turned into the street behind us and approached so fast I thought the driver was going for full ramming speed. I was just about to call a warning when Zak shoved the Toyota's transmission into first and stamped on the accelerator. We shot off with the second car so close up behind us I couldn't see enough of the front grille to identify the make. The Merc wheelspun in pursuit.

The Tweedles could not have been happy about having this buffer between us. The two rear cars weaved from side to side in the narrow street in an attempt to pass or avoid being passed. All it needed was sets of running boards and men in pinstripe suits and I'd be in the middle of a classic Chicago gangster movie.

Looking out of the back window, all I could see of the chase car's occupants was their eyes. There were four people inside— that they were all men was a fairly safe bet—with their faces covered. If their gesticulating arms were anything to go by, they were all talking at once. Even the driver.

"Hold very tight please, thank you, yes," Zak yelled over his shoulder, then spun the wheel to launch us into an alleyway with barely half a metre spare on either side. The chase car followed, slicing off its door mirrors as it ricocheted through the entrance.

The alley was lined with houses, narrow doorways that spilled straight out into the roadway. I prayed nobody stepped out of their front door as we thundered past.

I turned to look back, just in time to see the nose of the chase car dip as the driver slammed on the brakes. The front wheels locked, smoke and dust billowing up, until the car finally came to a halt. All four doors opened. All four occupants leapt out. They scarpered into the nearest buildings, which swallowed them up as if they'd never been, leaving a stalled roadblock firmly in the path of the Mercedes.

We burst out of the far end of the alley and fishtailed away, leaving the Merc boxed in behind us.

Zak turned and grinned at me hugely over his shoulder. "My friends, they follow plan, yes?" he said.

"Absolutely," I agreed.

Nils had twisted to watch the foiled pursuit. For the first time I thought I caught a glimpse of bone-dry humour. "*You* planned this?"

I shrugged. "Only works if you've got a chase car following close behind," I said. "But if Princess Di's security had done the same instead of trying to outrun the paparazzi that night in Paris, who knows how things might have turned out?"

Zak kept his foot wedged down on the throttle and made a series of random turns. With every passing minute, the Tweedles' chances of reacquiring us diminished until they were somewhere between slim and none.

I wondered if they'd have that taken out of their pay, too.

*****

We drove for nearly three hours through the hottest part of the day. The Toyota's air conditioning system consisted of opening the windows. At speed, the inrush of dust and grit blowing across the raised desert highway acted like the roughest facial you ever had. After the first ten minutes my eyes were full of gravel, but it was preferable to dying of heat exhaustion.

Alison had calmed down after her panic outside the café. In a manner that always struck me as terribly English, she attempted to over-compensate for doubting Zak's allegiances earlier by being extra nice to him now, giving his every pronouncement more attention than it warranted, smiling and nodding.

Zak, as if to demonstrate his debonair side, had the radio tuned to a local station and was singing along. By that, I mean he was singing at the same time *as* the music, rather than in time *with* it. His accompanying hand slaps on the steering wheel were equally erratic.

Nils coped with the racket by feigning sleep. I could tell by the way his chest rose and fell he was faking it.

64

The road was heavy with traffic, foot as well as vehicle. There were the ubiquitous boys on donkeys, overladen pickup trucks with vociferous goats in the back, mixed in with new BMWs and SUVs. Hardly anyone was heading towards the city. The flood of refugees had started—all making for the border just like us.

"We need to get off highway, yes?" Zak suggested over the roar of wind noise as we slowed for yet another broken-down donkey.

I hadn't missed the fact that when we *weren't* moving, we were attracting the wrong kind of attention from our fellow travellers. Their country's conflict might be mainly internal, but that didn't mean they'd pass up the chance to stone a group of foreigners, just for someone else to blame.

"You wouldn't by any chance know an alternative route, would you?"

Zak turned to look at me, his distorted features pulled almost into a leer. "Maybe yes, maybe," he said.

***

Zak's alternative route involved the kind of terrain I'd only previously encountered on army tank courses. It was brutal, but the old Toyota scrambled gamely on, encouraged by Zak's random wheel-slapping and tuneless yodels. Nils feigned coma by this time. I was tempted to join him.

Eventually, just when I thought my eyes would never line up with their sockets ever again, we bumped off the rutted track and rejoined something that nearly resembled a metalled road.

"All OK now, yes?" Zak said, beaming at us as he put his foot down.

It was clear that he was not the only one who knew about this detour, but at least the traffic was light and the slow-moving stuff kept to the shoulder to let us by. We were moving through sparse desert scrub, flanked by huge outcrops of rock blasted smooth by the elements. Settlements huddled close to the roadside as if fearful of what lay beyond it, out in the wilderness. The few people we saw stared at the passing vehicles like floats in a parade. They were mainly women, kids, and the elderly— over here that seemed to encompass anyone over the age of thirty-five.

Where are the men?

"How far to the border?" Alison asked.

"Not far," Zak said with a vague gesture to the road ahead that could have indicated anything from an hour to a week. "All OK now."

The road had begun to twist around the rock formations, creating natural chokepoints and elevated strongholds that made my defensive antennae twitch like crazy. And maybe it was because this was one of the rare occasions when Zak actually had his eye on his driving so I couldn't see his face, but something in his voice worried me. A tightness, a faint harmonic that had been absent during the rest of our journey.

He's nervous, I realised. *Why now?*

I sat forwards in my seat. "Any likely problems up ahead I should know about?"

"No, no, all OK, thank you, yes."

There it was again—more of it this time.

Fear.

"Zak, stop the car."

"No, we must go," he insisted, sweat in his voice now. "All OK."

"What is it?" Alison demanded. "What's wrong?"

That's what I'm trying to find out.

Desperate measures were called for.

"Stop the car or I'll pee here," I improvised loudly. "Your choice, but it's going to stink."

Zak flung me a single horrified glance over his shoulder and stood on the brakes.

We were in the middle of a corner at the time and the Toyota didn't take kindly to the manoeuvre, skating on the loose gravel that coated the road until we eventually came to an untidy halt.

Still, in other ways the timing couldn't have been better. Up front, about three hundred metres in the distance, was a narrow bridge across a dried-up riverbed. The entrance to the bridge was currently blocked by a line of rusted oil drums. A dusty Land Cruiser with vaguely military markings sat nearby. Guarding the drums was a group of four guys in sloppy fatigues. The only thing impressive about these troops was their obvious familiarity with the weapons they carried.

"You didn't mention we'd have to pass through any checkpoints on this road," I said.

Zak gave a subdued shrug. "They come and they go," he said, striving for the philosophical air of someone describing the seasons. "All the time."

I moved my face closer to his ear, shifting the SMG across and into my hands at the same time. "Are you sure about that?"

"Of course he is sure," Nils said impatiently, reaching for his passport and papers from the outside pocket of his rucksack. "We stop, we give them money, and they let us pass. Like the man said—it happens all the time."

"On a side road in the middle of nowhere?" I said, not taking my eyes off Zak. "With no backup nearby?"

Zak didn't answer but I saw his Adam's apple dip rapidly in his skinny throat. Meanwhile, one of the slower vehicles we'd passed—a battered pickup, its exhaust smoking like a wet bonfire—overhauled us and lumbered towards the roadblock. The soldiers tensed for a moment, clutching their weapons, then rolled the drums aside and waved the pickup on.

"Well, they do seem to be letting people through," Alison said.

"Either that," I said, "or they're waiting for someone in particular."

She frowned. "We can't go back, so ... what do we do now?"

My turn to shrug. However tempting it was to push on regardless, sometimes going back was by far the most sensible—and safest—option. But, still ...

"We go forwards," I said.

Zak stretched an arm to put the Toyota into gear. As he did so, I slid the SMG across my lap and jammed the muzzle hard into the back of Zak's seat. The elderly Toyota had only a passing nod to lumbar support, and I knew from the way he arched that Zak had not only felt it, he knew exactly what it was. He tensed in automated response, and then relaxed.

"Is all OK, no problems," he said and before I could react he'd stuck his head out of his open window, yelling, "Unarmed! We are unarmed." And he launched into more of the same in several different local dialects.

What the hell ...?

I gave him a vicious prod with the gun through the thin seat back. "Zak, shut up."

"Is OK," he said again, a patent untruth as the soldiers readied their weapons in front of us.

What happened next is known as tachy-psyche effect. The way time slows in moments of duress as if squashed and stretched by the extreme pressure.

Tick.

Suddenly, between one second and the next, I had all the time in the world to assess the situation. Apparently random images flashed through my consciousness in a continuous stream that flowed to form a single bright cohesive strand.

All the soldiers at the checkpoint were wearing army uniforms that didn't quite fit, as if borrowed from another owner—with or without consent. Their vehicle could have been mocked up or simply stolen. They should have been carrying standard-issue AKs, but only two were armed with the classic assault rifle. One of the others had what looked like an old Mac-10, and the fourth cradled a 9mm SMG.

Just like the one in my hands—the one Zak had supplied. The one he seemed so relaxed about when I jammed it against his spine ...

Tick.

Although I'd put thousands of rounds through similar weapons in my time, I'd had no chance to test-fire this particular SMG, and there are plenty of ways to subtly sabotage a gun that would not be immediately obvious—even during the strip-down inspection I'd given it the night before.

A few fractions of a mil shaved off the firing pin and all I'd get when I squeezed the trigger would be the dull clack of the mechanism trying to strike the primer cap of the first round, which would be just out of reach. No primer cap detonation, no ignition of the main charge, no projectile leaving the end of the barrel.

It was a good job the SMG *was* sturdy enough to use as an emergency club, because if my suspicions were correct, that was all it was good for.

Tick.

I let go of the gun and ripped the survival knife out of concealment, firm in the knowledge that there's not much you can do to interfere with a knife that isn't obvious, especially if you've spent time checking the blade is sharp.

This blade was plenty sharp enough to pierce the thin vinyl back of the Toyota's seat, slice through the flimsy internal padding, and out again through the front. I only stopped when I felt the point's resistance as it entered skin and flesh.

This time, Zak jerked forwards with a hoarse cry. I snaked my left arm around the headrest and clamped my forearm hard across his throat, gripping the other side of the headrest to keep him pinned there.

Alison, sitting alongside me, had an unobstructed view. "Charlie!" she shouted, aghast. "What the hell are you *doing?*"

"Shut up," I said calmly. "Zak—drive."

***

Zak did nothing. He simply sat, with the tip of the knife he'd given me now embedded in his back.

"I cannot," he said at last. "I am very sorry." The clown personae he adopted to fit his bizarre distorted appearance dropped away. His voice was different again, less ingratiating, more dignified. He sounded resigned, too, as if the fates had taken things out of his hands and he was OK with that.

Two of the soldiers started to approach us, yelling for us to not move, to get out of the car, to put our hands up, to lie on the floor. I resisted the urge to shout, "Make up your minds!"

I slid the knife out of Zak and his seat, shifted my grip and laid the blade across his right cheek, close to his one remaining eye. His eyelid twitched as he flicked his gaze down to it, and I knew he had not missed the fact the tip was still smeared with his own blood.

"Drive, or I will blind you," I said tightly.

"I cannot," Zak said again. "Please—I am much sorry."

The soldiers were only a few metres from us now, crabbing forwards. One carried an AK, pulled up hard into his shoulder, the other the SMG. They were younger than I'd first thought, probably only in their late teens, and they looked scared and excited in equal measure.

Firearms and bravado—never a good combination.

Surprisingly perhaps, it was Nils who took action. He lifted his booted foot over the centre console and stamped down on the Toyota's accelerator. Zak's feet had been covering the brake and clutch, but the shock of Nils's move and the instinctive fear of a man in sandals for having his toes mashed made him jerk them out of the way. The Toyota lurched forwards, engine revving into a loose-fanbelt squeal. Nils grabbed for the wheel.

The soldiers opened fire in reflex at the car's sudden move. Nils and Zak fought for control and neither of them won. The Toyota veered wildly towards the driver's side, striking the soldier with the SMG. He disappeared so fast under the front wheel he didn't have time to make a sound, the suspension bouncing sickeningly as the car rode up and over him. Then the front corner hit the rock face, and Nils's short-lived break for freedom came to an abrupt halt.

The other soldier raked the passenger side with fire. I heard the Swede cry out as I grabbed Alison by the collar of her shirt and punched open my door to bail out.

I found myself staring straight down into the wide-eyed corpse of the soldier we'd just hit. The front tyre had rolled across his chest, forcing his insides out through every available orifice. Which was not, I judged, a pretty way to die.

On the bright side, the SMG he'd been holding was both accessible and intact. I snatched it up as I got out, ignoring the greasy stickiness on the strap, and forced the pair of us round the back of the Toyota.

"Keep your bloody head down," I growled to Alison, knowing that civilians—especially reporters—have a habit of wanting to gawk, thus turning themselves into very inviting targets.

The soldier who'd shot Nils had seen me get out and was expecting my head to pop up above the roof line, and that's where he was aiming. I took advantage of his distraction to lean out from behind the far rear tyre and put a three-round burst into his pelvis. He dropped, screaming.

The remaining pair of soldiers had initially hung back, only starting their run for us when the Toyota hit the rocks.

Laying down an accurate field of fire while sprinting towards a hostile target takes training and practice. They had neither. Still, there was always the chance of a lucky shot. I stayed low, braced on my elbows, and stitched across them as they ran, then rolled away.

The echo of blood and gunfire lifted slowly, leaving only a stark, static silence. I was aware of a low moaning from inside the car, the rasp of my own breath, and the hiss of steam from the Toyota's ruptured radiator. My eyes raked the landscape, looking for movement, threat. There was nothing. It all seemed to have happened in the space of a heartbeat.

You go into another zone in a firefight, one where normal morality is suspended, normal feelings of fear or revulsion are put aside. Sometimes it was hard to tell when everyday reality recommenced. Some soldiers never returned.

I swallowed a throatful of bile, starting to come back. My hands, gripping the SMG, were not quite steady. When I staggered to my feet, using the back end of the Toyota as a makeshift crutch, I found my legs were not quite steady either.

Four on one, and we survived—mostly. How the hell did that happen?

Alison took standing up as her cue to move, too. She scrambled up and dived back into the car, as if that might provide cover.

"Charlie, Nils is hurt!"

The soldier that had shot Nils was no longer screaming, I noted. He was no longer making any sound. I stepped over his body and yanked open the passenger door. Nils all but fell out into my arms. He'd taken a couple of AK rounds at close range in the arm and shoulder and had already managed to bleed enough to give the Toyota's front seat upholstery a colour change.

There was no arterial spray, which was a good thing. If we could patch him up long enough to get him across the border, and if he didn't go into shock first, Parker's people would take care of him from there.

The shoulder wound was a fairly straightforward hit. The 7.62mm round had smashed his collarbone and gone straight through the flimsy seat back to bury itself around where Alison and I had been crouching, before I'd pulled her out of the car.

Nils hadn't been so lucky with the second round. That looked to have entered his forearm at a shallow angle, ploughed a furrow into his flesh like a diving submarine, and exited, messily, through the back of his elbow. I was no orthopaedic surgeon, but one look was enough to tell me his lower arm was completely screwed.

I retrieved the rudimentary first-aid kit and roll of duct tape from my holdall on the rear seat. Alison ripped open a couple of field dressings and I taped them in place. There wasn't much I could do with the arm except tape it back together and hope for the best. Duct tape is tough enough and waterproof enough to contain bleeding in an emergency. I wouldn't go anywhere without it.

71

Nils had blenched beneath his tan—any paler and we'd be able to see right through him. His skin had that waxy tint and he was panting around the pain, swearing in several different languages when he had the breath to do so. Shock was already setting in.

Alison used her scarf to fashion a sling, keeping his injured arm tied close to his body for support. I went and checked the Land Cruiser, found the keys were not in it. That meant going through the pockets of the dead men for the keys. Not a task I relished.

It did tell me part of the reason I'd been able to kill them, though. They were all young, without the toughened hands of professional soldiers. Only one had army-style boots on. I did not allow myself to dwell on it. I'd done what I had to.

I went back to the car. Alison had managed to get Nils out and was trying to persuade him to lie down to ease his depleted circulation, something he refused to do.

"Get him into the Land Cruiser," I told her. "We're leaving."

Alison looked at the bodies as if seeing them for the first time. "What about—?"

"Now, Alison."

I leaned into our wrecked car across Nils's empty seat and looked at Zak. He hadn't moved since the soldiers had opened fire on us, and I expected to find him dead, but his eye opened and swivelled slowly in my direction. His body was beyond still, it was immobile. I glanced down, saw the blood on the side of his clothing and realised he'd taken a stray round in the ribs that had probably lodged somewhere near his spine. He was paralysed.

"I am sorry," Zak said again, little more than a whisper.

"So am I," I said gravely. "Was it for money?"

Zak's face twitched into something that was more grimace than smile. "No," he said. "It was for my country. For honour, yes?" His gaze followed Alison and Nils as they stumbled across towards the other vehicle. "They will ... ruin us."

***

I didn't expect to see Alison Cranmore again except on the news—and there I couldn't miss her. The dramatic—not to mention dramatised—story of how she and her intrepid cameraman had escaped from a war zone, pursued by all sides, was syndicated to every channel who would give it air time.

Alison looked good on camera, with a black-and-white *keffiyeh* slung casually around her neck, steady of eye and serious of voice. I was glad she didn't try to rope me into her personal media circus, and to begin with she didn't.

Then about six weeks after the extraction, I got word she was asking for a meet. I had a London stopover on the way back from a job in Saudi, and—more out of curiosity than anything else—agreed to meet her in Soho House on the corner of Greek Street.

The once-seedy area was now filled with TV production companies and trendy wine bars where the movers and shakers of the arts world could not only be seen but heard as well.

The more things change ...

It was summer in London and the city was wilting in the unaccustomed heat. It was a relief to climb the stairs to Soho House's upper-floor bar where the open windows allowed cross-flow ventilation.

I was early as a matter of course, but Alison was already there, having an intense discussion with a man I judged from his clothes and manner to be a TV producer of some kind. I sat at the bar nursing a tonic water until they were done. He gathered up his iPad and strode away with the air of a man who has far more important places to go and people to see.

"Sorry about that," Alison said, coming over. "Come and join me."

She looked fit and well, and far more relaxed than when I'd last seen her. She was dressed to blend with her surroundings, fashionable and expensive, her hair styled and nails shaped and polished. I'd just got off a long-haul flight and what felt like an equally long-haul taxi ride, and it showed.

We skated round the pleasantries while we ordered food and the waitress departed.

"I was hoping you might agree to an interview," Alison said then. "About your part in our escape."

A little late for that, isn't it?

"I can't," I said, trying to make a show of regret. "There's no way I can blend into the background well enough to do my job if you put me centre stage. I'm sorry."

She nodded, as if she'd half-expected that response, but it was something that had to be tried. "Well, at least let me buy you lunch—as a thank you."

I picked up my glass. "So, how's Nils?"

"Recovering well, as far as I know," she said, smiling now. "It's amazing what they can do with prosthetics these days. He's even talking about getting a camera built into his new arm."

"A pity Zak wasn't so lucky," I said.

The smile faded. "Excuse me?"

"Zak," I repeated. "There was nobody to medevac him off to a private Swiss clinic, so he had to rely on the local butchers. Infection got him in the end—took him about a fortnight to die."

"Oh ... that's—" she searched for the right word, "—sad," she came up with at last. "But he did lead us into a trap."

I looked at her. "So he deserved what he got, is that it?"

She flushed, but I didn't miss her sideways glance to check who might be listening in. She needn't have bothered—I was purposely keeping my voice down. For now.

"No, but you know what I mean. We could have been killed," she said, gaining confidence. "Nils lost an arm, for heaven's sake. You can't expect me to weep for someone who would do that."

"He did what he believed was right," I said. "It's the most any of us can do. The most any of us *should* do."

She stiffened. "What's that supposed to mean?"

"I thought you told Nils, outside that café, that you were there to report the news, not become a part of it."

Alison lifted an uncomfortable shoulder. "I *still* believe that," she said in a low voice.

I shook my head. "So, how did you end up as the next TV Dangerwoman, then?"

She grimaced. "Not my first choice, I admit, but I had to give them *something* to justify the expense of being out there."

I put my glass down, wiped a trickle of condensation from the side of it. "And what happened to your earth-shattering original story?"

Her face turned wry. "They squashed it."

I raised an eyebrow. "Who—your network?"

"Yes ... well, not really." She started to shake her head, then stopped. "Pressure from above. They caved."

"Does that mean I'm never going to find out what that whole damn thing was all about?"

She hesitated, shifting awkwardly on the squashy sofa. The open window was to her left, the breeze stirring against her artfully casual hair. A motorbike with a raucous exhaust roared past in the street below. She looked a million miles away from the terrified and bloodied figure I'd pulled from that desert ambush.

"Well, I did sign a confidentiality agreement and—"

I leaned forwards, lowered my voice. "Aren't you people always banging on about the public's right to know? Don't you think at least that *I* have a right to know?"

Her shoulders came down. "Yes," she said at last. "Yes, you do." She took a deep swig of her drink, something in a tall glass with a lot of fruit salad—probably Pimm's—and set it down carefully on the low table in front of her. "We managed to get hold of some video from about a year ago—government archives," she said. "Amazing how often these tin-pot regimes record stuff like this for their own amusement. It showed the massacre of a group of dissidents. A big group of them. They were just herded into the desert and machine-gunned, for sport." Her face contorted at the memory. "The kind of thing you could only watch once, and that was once too many."

"Massacres happen all the time," I said calmly. "What was special about this one?"

She glanced at me in reproof. "The people behind the guns," she said. "The president himself was one of those pulling the trigger and laughing while he did so. We tracked down and interviewed some of the survivors, got their stories to intercut with the original footage. It was compelling and horrifying both at the same time."

There was a wistful note in her voice, though. Stories that were both compelling and horrifying were the ones that tended to win Pulitzers. Maybe that was her biggest regret.

I shrugged. "Sadly, that happens all the time, too."

She sighed, as if she'd been hoping that part of the tale might have been enough to satisfy me. The waitress arrived then with our salads, deposited them with a flourish and bustled away again. I let Alison pick at her food for a few moments, then nudged her to continue.

"What was special, Alison?"

She put down her fork. "One of the other people involved was the ex deputy president," she said flatly.

75

That took a moment to penetrate. "Hang on—isn't he the one who denounced the president and broke away to lead the opposition—?"

"The one who's just routed the old regime and been sworn in as new leader?" she said, a cynical note in her voice now. "The one the west is courting? That's him."

This was the man Zak had supported, the one he'd spoken of when he'd claimed to act in honour. *For my country.* He had wanted to kill the story, and the storytellers, to prevent the public disgrace of a disgraceful man. He'd given his life for that loyalty.

"They will ruin us," he'd said of Alison and Nils. Maybe it was better of have a strong dictator than a nation in chaos. Events in Iraq and Libya had proven that. Was it also worth the price in civil liberties? Somebody thought so—somebody high enough up to make it happen.

I glanced at her. "So, what was it all for—personal glory?"

Her face twitched. "It's never clear-cut, Charlie," she said. "It wasn't my first choice to make myself into the story, but I *had* to do something to justify the time and expense. I couldn't put the original story out, and I couldn't take it elsewhere—"

"Why not?" I interrupted. "Why couldn't you take it to another station, another network?"

"Because I have a contract that wouldn't let me do that," she said with the exaggerated patience of someone talking to a child. "And if I'd broken it, I might have been blacklisted, never got another job."

"Bollocks," I said shortly. "It might have delayed your next promotion, but it would have made your name as a journalist of principle."

She eyed me cynically. "I could have gone to jail."

"Same answer applies—possibly with a longer delay."

Alison let her breath out in an annoyed spurt, still looking past me, I noticed, to see who was paying attention to our quiet disagreement. "Charlie, that's simply not how things happen in the real world—"

"No, it damn well isn't," I shot back, low but harsh enough for her eyes to jump back to mine. "In the *real* world, Alison, I killed four men—little more than boys—to protect you and your bloody story. If you were never going to have the balls to use it, you could have left via the airport weeks before it all went bad and

76

saved me the trouble." I let that settle for a moment, then added. "And Zak would still be alive, too."

"But he betrayed us."

"So you told the world," I agreed dryly, and the pink stain rose again above her collar. "But in the *real world* you're so fond of, Zak was the one who behaved with honour. Misguided perhaps, but honour of a kind nevertheless." I got to my feet, looked down at her for a long moment. "You were the one who betrayed, not just yourself, but everyone in that godforsaken country."

She flinched. "That's a low blow, Charlie."

"Is it?" I said. "Whatever happened to that old newspaper saying—'publish and be damned'? What happened to having the courage of your convictions?"

"There were consequences—not just for me!"

"There are always consequences, Alison," I said tiredly. "Sometimes the truth hurts like hell, but—trust me—it's nothing compared to the pain of a lie."

Across The Broken Line
intro

Thuis is a brand new Charlie Fox short story, never before published. I always wanted to write something with a very broken-up timeline, but my first attempts ended in frustration. I originally conceived this tale to be the final story in the FOX FIVE Charlie Fox e-thology, but put it to one side and wrote something else instead.

As is always the way, though, the basic idea wouldn't leave me alone. Fortunately, I was able to write the bones of it and then put it aside for several months to ferment gently in the back of my mind. The time jumps, backwards and forwards from three weeks ago to right now, still proved a challenge, but also a great framework.

Here, Charlie is tasked to protect a principal on the run-up to the holiday season in New York City. Not everyone is going to get exactly what they wish for as a Christmas gift. Some, though, might just get what they deserve …

Across The Broken Line

Fifteen minutes ago ...

Shoving a loaded gun in somebody's face is never going to make you friends but it certainly works for influencing people. The uniformed guy on the business end of my SIG Sauer P229 looked both unfriendly *and* influenced, that was for sure.

He froze halfway through bringing his own weapon clear of the holster on his hip. From what I could see of the hammer and the top of the slide it looked like a big Colt. A useful piece. I was glad he didn't get chance to finish the draw.

I couldn't blame the guy for trying, though. I'd just crashed a reinforced Lincoln Navigator through the security barrier he was supposed to be manning. That kind of thing tends to have that kind of effect.

Behind us was a huge warehouse, looming. Even by American standards it was enormous—practically big enough to have its own motto and design of flag. It stood in rather sterile landscaped grounds, made bleaker by the unmarked covering of snow. The place was apparently deserted apart from the security post—and the slightly dented Navigator I'd just skid-parked by the main entrance.

"Where are they?" I demanded.

The security guard didn't answer, nor did he take his eyes off the gun in my hands, watching for his opportunity. Now I got a good look at him I saw he was at least six-four and probably two hundred and thirty pounds, most of it muscle. He also had the narrowed calm of previous armed contact—an ex-military man.

Just my luck.

"My name is Charlie Fox," I said, speaking clear and loud. "I'm the bodyguard."

79

Something of that went in. I saw a flicker of understanding. I took a calculated risk, brought the SIG's front sight up off target and uncurled my finger from the trigger. His shoulders dropped slightly in relief. Mine probably did the same.

"Mrs Duvall left strict instructions," he said then, brusque with residual tension. "No interruptions. Not for anything."

"Well, you might say Mrs Duvall was under duress."

He nodded, still wary. "Mr D—her husband—he went in 'bout a quarter hour before she arrived," he said, as if that confirmed it.

Shit.

So much for risking my neck on the snow-slicked roads trying to get here ahead of them. New York in the winter can be a bitch.

"Call the cops," I said, starting for the entrance to the building.

The guy moved as if to block me. "Hey, you can't go in there!"

"If I don't, one of them will be coming out in a body bag," I said. "Your choice."

He hesitated as if I might be overstating it, saw from my face that I was not.

"You don't understand," he said, waving an arm towards the warehouse. "This whole place is fully automated—state of the art. The motorised stock-retrieval system moves pretty damned fast. No way can you go in there unless they shut it down. You'll get yourself killed."

"Well, that's *my* choice." I threw the security guard a last look over my shoulder. Tall and powerful, with a neck that cried out for a bolt through it, his hand resting on the butt of the Colt in reflex. "Be sure to tell them you tried to stop me."

***

A week ago ...

"Ah, Charlie, come on in. This is Olivia Duvall," Parker said. "Ms Duvall has just engaged our services. You'll be looking after her."

An elegant, dark-haired woman rose from one of the client chairs in Parker Armstrong's office, turning as I shut the door and came forwards. She was wearing designer sunglasses, but I saw from the angle of her head that she gave me the usual once-over. There was a momentary hesitation while she compared her mental expectation of a female bodyguard with the reality. I'm not built like a member of the Bulgarian ladies' Olympic weightlifting team, so I rarely match up. I was used to that.

She probably wasn't quite what I expected either.

I held out my hand and we shook. Olivia Duvall came roughly up to my nose, which was saying something because I wasn't exactly supermodel-tall myself. She was carefully put together and neat as a miniature doll. Classy suit over a high-neck blouse—style that had been hard won rather than inbred. She had a firm grip, seemed vaguely disappointed when I didn't grind her bones into dust in return.

"If I *looked* like a bodyguard," I said mildly, reading her thoughts, "I wouldn't be much use to you." A standard reply. One I'd found myself compelled to use many times before.

She paused, then gave me a somewhat tremulous smile. "Ah … no, of course not." But she looked in my boss's direction while she said it.

"Charlie's one of my best operatives," Parker said. "She'll take real good care of you."

Olivia did not necessarily look reassured but she sank back into her chair. I sat opposite, unbuttoning my jacket so the gun behind my right hip didn't pull it out of line.

Parker looked to the woman opposite as if for permission to expand. She lifted her shoulder a fraction.

"Ms Duvall is having a little trouble with her husband—"

"A *little*? Try a *lot*! The bastard tried to kill me." Olivia stopped, took a shaky breath and let her gaze drop to the hands clasped tightly in her lap. "I still can't believe Joe would do that to me—to *us*. Not after all these years."

"What happened?"

"Ms Duvall is seeking to dissolve her marriage," Parker said, his voice dry and cool, offering no judgements. "She believes her husband may have a more … permanent solution in mind."

Olivia's head came up sharply, as if hoping to catch an expression of disbelief. Almost defiant, she reached up and removed the sunglasses. Worn indoors I'd thought them to be an affectation. They were not.

Beneath the tinted lenses, the whites of her eyes were streaked with red.

"He tried to smother me with a pillow two nights ago," she said, her voice flat. "I woke up with it over my face. I couldn't breathe, I just went crazy, managed to get my head turned so I could get some air." She gave us both a defiant glare, as if we'd doubt she was capable.

I looked at her hands. They were small and narrow, nails painted a delicate coral pink. Not the kind of hands you could imagine successfully fighting off a larger, stronger attacker.

Parker glanced at me, still nothing in his voice. "Ms Duvall's two children were asleep in the house at the time," he said.

I raised my eyebrows. "Has your husband ever behaved violently towards your children?"

She hesitated. "No," she said quietly. "At least ... not yet."

And there it was—out, stark and edgy.

Voiced.

Every mother's nightmare. The reason she had sought out the kind of protection offered by someone like Parker. By someone like me.

"Did he offer any excuse—try to explain?" Parker asked.

Olivia shot him an old-fashioned look, as if only a man could ask such a question, and directed her answer to me. "I–I must have passed out for a second. When I came to, got my breath and shoved the pillow off of me, the bastard was standing in the bathroom doorway, pretending like nothing had happened and asking what all the noise was about," she said, her voice neutral almost to the point of detachment.

I glanced at Parker. "I get the impression this wasn't an isolated incident."

There was another fractional pause. "As I was leaving the office, about six weeks ago, someone tried to run me down," she admitted. "I didn't get a look at the driver—it was dark—but it was the same make and model as Joe's truck. And when I got home he was in his workshop, said he hadn't left the house all afternoon."

There was something in her face. "But?"

"The hood of his truck was still warm."

"Had he any previous history of violence?"

She didn't shake her head right away, as if loyalty were overcoming truth. "Joe was in the military for a while," she admitted. "He was discharged. Doesn't like to talk about it much, but—with the kind of training they get—well, I always wondered ..."

... if it turned him into a killer.

"And what has he done since then?"

A flicker of annoyance crossed her features. At the question or the coming answer, I wasn't sure.

"For work, you mean? He doesn't *do* anything. After he shipped home he worked the mill for a while, like his daddy before him—'til they laid him off. Could hardly seem to get a job after that and when he did he couldn't seem to keep it." She was trying not to condemn—just not too hard. "Eventually, it was just easier all round for me to go out and find work, and that's what I did."

I checked out the designer suit, the matching accessories, the flash of jewellery at ears and wrists and fingers. The work Olivia Duvall had found clearly did not involve scrubbing floors. It seemed to surprise her that my face was blank.

"Ms Duvall has enjoyed no small measure of success," Parker said, and I heard the dry understatement.

She sighed, shifted in her seat. "I started up an online home-electronics company right out of my kitchen," she said with the matter-of-fact tone of someone who's recited this story many times. "I studied the market and simply ... supplied that demand—straight from the manufacturer. No stock, no overheads."

"Ms Duvall is being modest," Parker said blandly. "She now controls one of the largest warehouse and distribution networks in the United States. I believe her turnover last year was well into eight figures."

"So, I assume—should you divorce—that Mr Duvall's current lifestyle would be somewhat adversely affected?" I said, matching my tone to Parker's.

Her mouth twitched again. "End of the line for the gravy train, you mean? Oh yeah." She paused again, uncomfortable. "His name isn't Duvall, by the way, it's Dabrowski—Josef Dabrowski."

I nodded without asking awkward questions, watched her face relax a little in response.

"You could go to the cops—get a restraining order."

She shook her head. "I have a high profile," she said, like that fact embarrassed her rather than being the peak for which she'd strived. "It would be all over the tabloids before the ink was dry on the paperwork."

Parker cleared his throat, "There are other steps—"

"Getting a gun, you mean?" Olivia interrupted. "I already did that. But the boys are at an age where they're fascinated by anything that goes bang. I have to keep the damn thing locked up so tight I'd never get to it before Joe—"

She broke off, drew in a long shaky breath. "I'm scared," she said, something in her voice that might have been reluctance to admit such a personal failing. "For me and for my kids. It's not just the money thing with Joe. He's always been so jealous ... possessive. Even if he gives me a divorce, I know I'll be looking over my shoulder for the rest of my life. Unless ..."

Her voice drifted away into a heavy silence, eyes still on her own whitened knuckles, and Parker's eyes flicked to mine. I caught acquiescence in their cool grey depths.

"We may be able to help you with that," I said, and watched her head come up as if jerked on a wire. I rose, made sure she got a glimpse of the SIG on my hip. Not locked away tight to keep it out of the hands of children, but ready, instant. "We may be able to find a more ... *permanent* solution of our own."

She allowed the hope to creep into her face, her cheeks flushing with a kind of guilty relief. "I just want to feel safe," she said at last. Evasive, but as close to tacit approval as we were likely to get.

I looked her straight in the eye, unblinking. "Don't worry," I said. "When I sign on to protect a principal, I'll die before I let any harm come to them."

***

Ten minutes ago ...

"Olivia!"

My voice bounced off the stacks of electronics stretching up to the vast roof above like skyscrapers in an enclosed city.

I jogged along one of the main north-south aisles, past what appeared to be crated-up washing machines and refrigerators. Everything was swathed in enough plastic and polystyrene packaging to pollute a small ocean. Or a large one come to that.

No doubt in an effort to save on running costs the lighting inside the warehouse was dim, but there were no staff to complain. The whole place was empty like an abandoned ship. I expected the floor to start listing at any moment as the vessel began her final dive for the seabed.

A faint squeaking noise behind me had me turning fast, the SIG in my hands, only to find a mechanical monster bearing down on me, two giant blades aiming for my stomach.

I leapt clear, flattening against the nearest racking. The unmanned electric forklift glided past oblivious, its electric motor almost silent. Only the sound of the rubber tyres on the painted concrete floor had warned me of its approach. As I watched, heart bumping against my ribs, the forklift stopped precisely level with a stack of steam ovens and began to telescope upwards to fulfil its pre-programmed instructions. I eyed the twin blades as they rose.

"Christ," I muttered under my breath. "Who designed this place—Freddy Krueger?"

The security guard's warning came back to me in a rush. Clearly he had not been exaggerating the dangers.

The buzz of my cellphone in my inside jacket pocket nearly had me jumping out of my skin. I fumbled for it, left-handed, saw Parker's name on the display and almost dismissed the call. Almost.

Instead, I flipped the phone open, said tightly, "Not a good time."

"I realise that," my boss said dryly. "But this changes everything ..."

***

Three weeks ago ...

"I think my wife is maybe trying to get rid of me."

Josef Dabrowski had once been a handsome man, but time had not been kind to him. He was well over six feet, broad shouldered and narrow hipped but with a belly just starting to overhang his belt. His fair hair was thinning backwards and his blue eyes were bagged beneath and crowded with laughter lines at the sides. He wore an old T-shirt and denims faded from too many rounds with the washing machine rather than designer stressing.

At a casual glance I would have taken him for an out-of-work actor who'd just been to a casting call for construction workers. The too-clean hands gave him away.

Dabrowski certainly did not look at home in the living room of this mock Tudor mansion in a leafy suburb of New York unless he was there to quote for renovations.

He perched on the edge of a buttoned leather sofa, one of a matching pair that framed the ornate fireplace. There was a thick earthenware mug of coffee on the delicate table in front of his clasped hands. It seemed as out of place as he did in the elegant surroundings.

Opposite sat Parker Armstrong, slender by comparison and younger looking despite the prematurely grey hair. He was apparently relaxed, one arm draped along the low back of the sofa. A convincing illusion.

I stood to one side where I could see out of the front window along the driveway, just in case of visitors. Dabrowski had said he wasn't expecting anyone. We didn't like to take that for granted.

"Why not go to the cops?" It was Parker's standard opening question, and how people answered—or evaded—usually told him plenty.

"Go to the cops with what?" Dabrowski asked now, his voice bitter. "Sides, my Olive is already prepping me as the bad guy."

"How?"

Alongside him, vibrating with a kind of righteous anger, was Bill Rendelson. I would have described him as Parker's right-hand man, except I knew Rendelson would take great offence at the remark. He'd lost his right arm to the shoulder in a parcel-bomb attack on the principal he'd been protecting some years previously. He made up for the loss by ruling the office with an iron fist, and seemed to nurture a deep resentment for those of us still active in the field.

Dabrowski shifted restlessly, making the leather squeak beneath him. It was left to Rendelson to jump in, which he did with barely concealed impatience even towards his boss.

"Acting in public like she's real nervous of Joe, when he's never laid a hand on her," he growled. His eyes drifted over me. "However much she had it coming."

Dabrowski murmured a protest, automatic rather than heartfelt. "Hey, come on, Bill. *Someone* tried to run her down in my truck—it just wasn't me behind the wheel."

"You only got her word for that, Joe." Rendelson's tone was quiet but final. "No witnesses and it all happened where there just so happened to be no security cameras. Convenient, huh?"

Dabrowski opened his mouth then shut it again, whatever he was about to say interrupted by a fair-haired boy, possibly just into his teens, who catapulted into the living room doorway.

"Hey, Dad, tell Adam it's my turn! He won't—"

"Not now, Tanner," Dabrowski said, more heavy than sharp. "I got people here. Later, OK?"

Tanner looked downcast. "Adam *always* gets what he wants," he complained. "It's *so* not fair."

As if in victory, a burst of loud distorted music thundered down the stairs from the upper floor.

"Excuse me," Dabrowski muttered, rising. He stepped around Tanner, stood in the open doorway and yelled upwards, "Adam, turn that noise down! And play nice with your brother."

There was brief silence before the music returned, this time with a booming rap overlay:

"Ad-Ad-Adam. T-t-t-urn that noise d-d-down. Noise down. And play nice. Playnice, playniceplaynice—"

"ADAM!" Dabrowski roared, army in his voice now. "Turn it down right now or every last scrap of that gear goes on eBay in the morning. You hear me?"

The music cut off in mid note. Dabrowski waited a moment longer, then nodded and headed back for his seat.

"Wouldn't happen if'n I had my own stuff," Tanner muttered as his father passed.

"Wait see what Santa Claus brings you," Dabrowski replied. It sounded like an automatic response to an oft-made request.

His younger son rolled his eyes behind his father's back, then saw me watching and gave a sly grin. I kept my expression stony. I've never been exactly maternal but sneaky kids are the worst kind. Undeterred, he disappeared and shortly after came the pound of teenage feet up the stairs.

Dabrowski shrugged helplessly to Parker. "Boys, huh?"

"How old are they?"

"Tanner just turned thirteen," Dabrowski said. "Adam was sixteen last fall. I guess he's starting to find his younger brother a drag."

From what I'd just seen of Dabrowski junior, I couldn't blame the older brother for that.

"If your wife wants out," I said mildly, getting us back on track, "then surely a divorce would be easier?"

Rendelson gave a snort that might have been twisted laughter. With him it was difficult to tell. "Not when you're on the rich list," he said.

He gave an abrupt twitch of his right shoulder, the kind that might once have resulted in the dismissive flick of a hand. I tracked the direction, saw a framed picture on the wall just behind a grand piano that had the look of furniture rather than instrument.

I stepped closer, recognised it as a front cover of *Forbes*—the money mag. I unhooked the picture and carried it across to Parker.

The cover photo was of a woman standing with one fist on her hip, the other holding the hand of the boy who'd just ratted out his older brother. Adam stood a little way back from his mother and Tanner, both kids scrubbed up and shiny. The perfect family.

The headline read:

'OLIVIA DUVALL—SELF-MADE MILLIONAIRE SUPER-MOM'

"Ah," I murmured as I handed it to my boss. "You're married to *that* Olivia Duvall."

Dabrowski hesitated a moment, then nodded, as if caution on the subject had become a habit hard to break. "She done good," he said, his voice a mix of shame and pride.

"So, she doesn't use the name Dabrowski?"

"Not any more—something to do with 'brand image' or something." He shook his head. "She did explain it to me one time but ..." He glanced at the pair of us briefly, a shy smile on his face. "I didn't take it in much. She calls herself Olivia now. Don't like it when I tell folks it ain't so."

I looked for malice, saw only a hurt bewilderment. He looked for all the world like a man who was still in love with his wife, but she had reinvented herself. The woman he'd married didn't exist any more.

"I'm guessing there was no pre-nup agreement," I said dryly. "So a divorce would cost Ms Duvall big bucks."

Dabrowski's face took on a stubborn cast. "She worked hard for what she's got. I only want what's fair and no more."

I heard his unspoken *"but"* and queried it.

"She knows I'd never let go of my boys," he said simply. "I raised 'em single-handed, near as dammit. Ever since I got laid off and my Olive set up on her own. Internet stuff." He spread hands so big he could have scooped up a litter of puppies in them, and jerked his head in the direction of upstairs. "Truth be told, the boys probably understand it better than I do."

"They're fine boys," Parker said, his eyes still on the picture.

Dabrowski ducked his head in acknowledgement. "We didn't always have money," he said. "Might be that way again—this economy, who knows? I've tried to keep their feet on the ground. They still do their chores, earn their allowance. I want to see 'em raised right."

"You could come to some arrangement over joint custody," Parker suggested.

"My Olive's an all-or-nothing kinda girl—always was," Dabrowski said. "I guess that's why she's done what she's done."

For a moment I thought he was referring to her business empire. It was left to Bill Rendelson to expand.

"She rigged his truck to explode."

I didn't respond to that immediately. It seemed a little outrageous, put baldly like that. And where would a middle-class suburban mother-of-two get the components for ...?

"Ah," I realised, almost to myself, "she just happens to run an electronics company."

Bill Rendelson flicked me a brief look of surprise as if he hadn't expected me to put it together.

"It was kind of obvious to be a serious attempt," Dabrowski said quickly, like that excused the whole thing. When Parker raised an eyebrow, he shrugged. "I seen a lot of IEDs back when I was in the military."

"She really wants the boys that badly?" Parker asked.

"She's built her whole image on being some kind of super-mom," Rendelson said, twisting the words with contempt, "but she barely sees the kids from one day to the next. She just hates to lose."

"So you think getting rid of Joe might be a cheaper option for her," I said.

Rendelson began to bristle. "If it's the money you're so damn worried about, *I'll* pay the agency's going rate myself—"

"I'll pay what I can," Dabrowski said stoutly. "I ain't asking for charity."

Parker paused, considering. Bill Rendelson leaned in, as if about to plead and loath to have to do it in front of me, muttered, "Joe and I served together. I don't often ask for personal favours, boss ..."

Parker got to his feet, buttoning his jacket, and it might have been my imagination but his gaze lingered over the two kids in the photograph. "Let's worry about the money later," he said. "Mr Dabrowski, we offer a very special service in cases like this. Not just close protection in the traditional sense, but a more ... proactive approach."

I saw the man's frown at the sideways terminology and simplified it. "What he means is, we draw out the threat and neutralise it."

Dabrowski rose also, suddenly uneasy. He was half a head taller than Parker, and towered over both me and Rendelson.

"I just need to know I'm gonna be around for my boys," he said again.

"I think we can arrange that."

"Yeah? How?"

I smiled. Was it really only three weeks ago? It seemed so easy then.

"By offering to help your wife."

***

Five minutes ago ...

"Olivia!" I called again. "We need to get out of here before we all get killed."

"Isn't that what you want?" her voice yelled back. The echoes made it harder to define direction. But at least she was talking to me.

I skirted the forklift as it began to retract, balancing a pallet-load of HD flatscreen TVs. I watched it whirr away quietly into the gloom.

"Things have changed," I said. I crabbed forwards with great care, keeping close to the stacks. "Whatever's happening here, it's not what you think."

"Oh really?" There was a harsh bark of laughter. "What made you betray me, Charlie? Did he promise you a fat bonus if I didn't make it to the final decree? Well, I got news for you, honey.

Anything happens to me, every cent goes to the boys." Her voice caught audibly. "If the bastard hasn't killed them already."

My ears finally got a fix. I dived through one of the cross-streets—there was no other way to describe the gaps between the racking. One up and two across.

And there she was, staring around her with fear-filled eyes. She was clutching the little revolver she'd bought for her own protection after claiming her husband tried to kill her. I moved into view with the SIG up and levelled.

"Put it down, Olivia," I said, loud enough for there to be no mistake, soft enough not to startle her into a negligent discharge.

She spun with a gasp, even so, staring at me. If I expected to find her dishevelled I was disappointed. She still looked like she'd stepped out of the pages of a fashion mag.

"Not while that bastard's out there," she said. She gestured to the SIG. "What—are you really going to shoot me?"

"No," said another voice, deep and bitter. Joe Dabrowski came rushing out of the shadows with his own gun raised and pointed straight at his wife. "But I will."

And then, out of nowhere, the darkness came whistling in on us and Dabrowski's hand jerked.

He fired.

***

An hour ago ...

"The bomb was a blind," Parker said.

I felt the Navigator twitch slightly as I reacted to the news. I almost dropped my cellphone—which served me right for not taking his call on hands-free while I was driving. It had begun to snow again and the roads were lethal, even with four-wheel drive.

"Charlie—you still there?"

"Yeah, I'm still here," I said. "What do you mean, it was a blind?"

"It was too complex for an amateur to have put together. Olivia Duvall may run an electronics company, but that doesn't mean she has the knowledge on how to build an improvised device, so I had Bill check it out. We've been waiting for his tame IED expert to rotate home from Afghanistan and he's gotten an expert opinion—she couldn't have done it."

"Come on, Parker, any school kid with an internet connection can find out how to build an improvised device in about twenty minutes."

"True," he allowed, "but you've been alongside her twenty-four/seven for the past week—when does she have the time?"

"It's like anything—you want it badly enough, you *make* the time." But even as I said it, I realised that Olivia Duvall ran to the kind of schedule that would make presidents and prime ministers wilt.

"So, what are we saying?" I demanded. "That she had help?"

"Or that Dabrowski put the thing together himself," Parker said flatly. I could almost hear Bill Rendelson simmering in the background. "He did admit to having extensive experience during his time with the military."

"But if Joe built the bomb he claimed his wife used to try to kill him does that mean—?" I began.

"That we've been taken for a ride?" Parker finished for me. "I hope not." His voice was grim. "Where are you?"

"On my way to meet Olivia at the house."

"What's your ETA?"

I took the phone away from my ear just long enough to use both hands on the Navigator's wheel. I swung the big vehicle through a gap in the dirty banks of ploughed snow and into the tree-lined driveway. "I'm there now," I said. The house came visible through the sparse foliage. I glanced across, saw the front door standing slightly ajar. "I'll call you back."

For once I didn't bother taking the Navigator round to the side of the building to the tradesman's entrance. I left it sprawled untidily on the cleared stone setts of the driveway and ran to the doorway, sliding the SIG from its holster as I went.

Taking a deep breath, I nudged the heavy oak door open with the toe of my boot and slipped inside fast. Nobody fired at me while I was silhouetted in the opening. A good sign.

I went from room to room, moving quickly, quietly. The place had been festooned with Christmas decorations since my visit with Parker and Bill Rendelson, and the living room smelled of pine from the eight-foot tree near the grand piano. The time of seasonal ill-will was rampantly upon us.

But I found nothing out of place—except the people. There was nobody at home.

It was a Saturday, late morning. Joe Dabrowski should have been there with the boys. Olivia had said she wouldn't be working for once. They had planned a family brunch, but when I stuck my head into the kitchen everything was squared away. There were no signs of food preparation.

I looked into Joe's workshop, which was empty and unlit. Tanner's room was its usual muddle, scattered with dirty clothes that Olivia refused to allow the cleaning service to pick up for him.

The room of the older boy, Adam, was neater, just cluttered with his music paraphernalia, the latest piece of which he'd bought second-hand from eBay. Joe had told me that the kid had bitched about the fact that Olivia sold all the latest gear through her company, but wouldn't give him more than staff discount. They were trying to teach him the value of things. It was taking a while to sink in.

I went back downstairs and stuck my head into Olivia's study. Her handbag and briefcase were both sitting on the desktop. If the open front door had sounded the first note of alarm, that sent it up a notch. Olivia never went anywhere without her cellphone, laptop and diary. To find them apparently abandoned was worrying.

I scanned the desktop, saw the message light blinking on the answering machine. Suddenly wary, I used the butt of the SIG to tap the replay button.

"Hey Olivia." Joe's voice came raspy and barely recognisable out of the tinny speaker. "I've got the boys. Unless you want to be burying them, you'll ditch the bodyguard and meet me at that mausoleum you call your empire. And you better hurry."

"Shit," I muttered under my breath. I punched the redial button on my cellphone. While it rang out, I paused the message, set it to replay. "Hey Parker," I said. "I think you—and Bill—need to hear this ..."

***

Now ...

The motorised forklift caught Joe Dabrowski little more a glancing blow. Even so, I heard the bones of his shoulder give way like an old dry branch as it flung him out and to the side. If he hadn't heard that betraying squeak at the last moment, started to turn, it would have mowed him flat.

As it was, at least the shock of it deflected his aim enough to go wide. The discharge was still brutal in the echoing cavern, then the gun was falling from his grasp.

I darted forwards and kicked the weapon out of his reach. It was an old Beretta, a standard military sidearm, something that was no doubt familiar to him.

I scooped on hand under his good arm and dragged him back against the stacks just in case another forklift bore down on us. He slumped there, breathing hard. The shock was taking care of the pain—for now. He was grey with it.

I turned back, to find Olivia Duvall was covering both of us with the little revolver.

Give me strength.

"Olivia," I said sharply. "Put that down before you hurt yourself—or I have to do it for you."

"Damn right she'll hurt you," Dabrowski told his wife through gritted teeth. "And she'll keep hurting you until you tell us what you've done with my boys."

"What *I've* done?" Olivia demanded. "It's *you* who's threatening to bury them, you bastard!"

I said calmly, "Olivia, we can sort this out, but now here and not at gunpoint." And to prove it I slid the SIG away, ignoring Dabrowski's groan. I held out my hand towards her, palm out.

She wavered for a moment, then I saw the determined glint come into her eyes.

"Not until—"

"Look out!" I yelled, and rushed her.

There was no incoming forklift this time, but the possibility was real enough to make her look. As she did so I rammed my elbow into the fleshy vee just below her ribcage. It knocked the stuffing out of her just as effectively.

By the time she'd recovered enough to curse me, I'd spun the cylinder of the little revolver and dropped the live rounds out into my pocket.

And then another forklift *did* come whooshing out of the murky darkness. We stepped back quickly.

"Now you've temporarily finished trying to kill each other," I muttered, "can we please get out of here before we all qualify for the Darwin Awards by removing ourselves from the gene pool in the most inventive way possible?"

After the dimness of the warehouse interior, it seemed unnaturally bright outside, sunlight gleaming from the pristine snow around the exterior. I blinked a few times and saw Parker waiting with the security guard, standing by another of the company Lincoln Navigators.

The two boys, Adam and Tanner, slouched between them. They looked like they'd rather be anywhere else.

Their parents both stopped dead. Dabrowski tried to wipe his forehead, suddenly realising his arm didn't work properly. He stared at it like he couldn't for the life of him work out when that happened.

His eyes, when they turned to me, were bewildered. "But—?"

"Let me guess, Joe," I said gently. "You got a message, apparently from your wife, telling you she had the boys and unless you wanted to arrange their funerals, you'd meet her here."

Dabrowski's brow furrowed. "How the hell—?"

"Olivia got the same message," I said. "From you."

Olivia's attention finally tore away from her sons and towards me. "What?"

"You were set up—both of you," I said. "I had a phone call from Parker inside to confirm it. He analysed the messages. Your voices were sampled and digitally manipulated. They could have made it sound like you were saying anything."

"But ..." Olivia stumbled into silence. "How ...?"

"The 'how' is the easy part," I said. "It's the 'who' you're not going to like."

They had moved instinctively closer to each other, I noticed. Which was possibly a good sign.

"That can't—" The look Olivia threw me was fast and vicious. "You've crossed the line, Charlie."

"Trust me," I said. "That line was already broken."

And despite the fact it was Olivia who'd had the drive and intelligence to start a major business from the ground up, it was Joe who put it together first.

"Adam has one of those electronic synthesisers," he said slowly. "He was always recording our voices—even made it sound like I could sing."

95

"No, no," Olivia said, shaking her head as if that would make it all go away. "But ... someone tried to smother me ..." She put a hand to her throat. "No, not Adam! That's ridiculous! I'm his mother—"

"No offence," I said, "but if someone the size and weight of your husband wanted to suffocate you, you'd be dead."

"And the bomb?" Joe asked, sounding hollow.

"Olivia hasn't the time or the expertise to put have put it together," I said, "but the average teenager, spending hours on the internet, and with access to your workshop at the house, could have something of that level of sophistication constructed in a couple of hours. Particularly," I added, "if their father just so happened to have spent time dismantling IEDs after Desert Storm, and told them a few war stories."

For a moment they both stood there, then Olivia said in little more than a whisper. "Adam was learning to drive your truck, Joe—ever since he got his learner's permit."

They both turned, in unison, and looked at their children again. Only this time their gaze was very different.

Adam gave his younger brother a vicious jab in the arm. "I *told* you," he complained.

Tanner's cheeks were burning. "Adam, shut *up!*"

I began to change my mind about which of them had been the ringleader in this enterprise.

The security guard calmly pulled them apart before they could come to further blows. I handed Parker the weaponry I'd collected from husband and wife.

"Good work, Charlie," he said.

"Same to you, boss," I said. "If Bill hadn't analysed those tapes so fast, we'd be scraping bodies out of there right now." I thought of my own near-miss with the forklift. "Probably mine included."

Olivia Duvall was looking almost as shocked as her husband. He put his good arm around his wife and for what I imagined was the first time in months, she didn't pull away from such a public embrace.

"Why?" she murmured then. She cleared her throat, gave her sons a piercing stare. "Why the hell would either of you want us dead ...? I mean, *why*, for God's sake?"

Their answer was sullen silence. I glanced back at their parents. They'd been prepared to fight over custody of their ungrateful children in the divorce. Maybe now the fight would be to see who didn't have to put up with them.

I shrugged. "You gave the reason yourself, Olivia. 'If anything happens to me,' you said, 'every cent goes to the boys.' Maybe they just wanted Christmas to come early this year."

ABSENCE OF LIGHT
a Charlie Fox novella

'In the absence of light, darkness must prevail.'
—Buddhist adage

A major earthquake sees ex-Special Forces soldier-turned-bodyguard Charlotte 'Charlie' Fox on a transport plane headed for the scene of devastation.

The way things are coming apart at home with Sean Meyer, she welcomes the chance to get away.

Tasked as security advisor to the specialist team at the centre of relief efforts, Charlie knows it won't be easy. The team members are willing to put themselves in constant danger as a matter of course. But what kind of other risks are they prepared to take?

As Charlie soon discovers, it's not just the ground beneath her feet that cannot be relied on. Her predecessor died conveniently while investigating rumours that the team were on the take, Charlie's been instructed to quietly uncover whether his death was as accidental as the official verdict suggests. If it was an accident, why are they so obviously lying to her?

Charlie must move with care through a shifting landscape to find the answers before there are more than just earthquake victims buried in the rubble. And when disaster strikes she will learn not only whom she can trust, but whether she can she survive the darkness that comes with a total absence of light.

One

The last time I died they didn't get a chance to put me in the ground for it. Mind you, back then my apparent demise proved neither long nor durable. A brief but interminable period of nothingness between one stumbling heartbeat and a thousand-volt jumpstart.

It seemed the gods were determined to make up for that lapse by being unreasonably prompt this time.

The weird thing was that I remained fully conscious through it all, from the first violent buckling of the earth under my feet to this silent tomb.

Because it is silent now, and it shouldn't be.

The aftershock hit with very few of the warning signs I'd come to recognise. No initial trembling, no gradual increase in tremors as the seismic waves magnified from their distant, buried hypocentre. This one must have had its genesis almost directly beneath us, and not far down. The abrupt assault of released energy was more shocking than bullet or blade.

As I went down I didn't have time to offer more than a brief scream. One moment I was on the surface and the next the ground caved in around where I was standing. I smacked myself about quite a bit on the way to hell before I came to rest, lying trapped in utter darkness while the graunching shudders of the planet died away and I wondered if I'd be next to follow.

"Well, *shit*," I said aloud. My voice sounded muffled and very close.

The first small bubble of panic began to form under my ribcage. It brought with it a swell of nausea that prickled the hair on my scalp and sent a ripple of hot and cold rushing across the surface of my skin. I fought it all back, folded it up until I couldn't fold it any tighter, and packed it into a very small box hidden at the centre of me.

99

Lately that box had been getting overfull.

I ran through a quick mental checklist. Clearly I could still breathe although the solid weight pressing into my chest restricted how deeply. My left arm was wedged tight to my side. In fact, when I experimented I think it might have been pinned there by something that had pierced both forearm and abdomen and spiked the two together. I could feel an annoying trickle of blood under my shirt.

I could move my right arm and hand a little. Illogically, I wished I had a weapon in it, even though it would have done me no good. It wasn't that kind of fight.

My legs were numb. Best not to worry about what that might mean.

The normal rules of gravity did not seem to apply down there. With no real idea of my orientation I sucked up a ball of saliva and let it dribble from my lips. It ran diagonally outwards across my right cheek and ended, annoyingly, in my ear. Well, that answered the which-way-is-up question at least.

Carefully, I screwed my head round maybe half an inch or so to the left, scraping my forehead. My eyes strained for the faintest glimpse of daylight.

Nothing.

I might as well have been sealed into a sarcophagus.

I shut my eyes and diverted all sensory perception to my ears. I tried to tune out the ominous crunch of who knows how many tons of settling masonry and rubble above me and searched instead for anything that might conceivably have a human source.

It was then I caught the sound of sobbing.

"Hey!" I croaked, throat raw with dust. "Can you hear me?"

The sudden outward breath caused a flurry of grit to drop onto my tongue. I coughed and spat for a minute or so then worked my chin until I could nip the edge of my scarf with my teeth. I tugged the thin cotton up over my mouth as a filter before I tried again.

"Yes, yes, I'm here. Please!" came a distant voice. "Please, I'm bleeding. Help me!"

You and me both.

"Just keep calm," I called back. "They'll get us out."

The answer was laughter—harsh bordering on hysterical. I let them laugh-cry themselves back to speech without trying to

100

hurry them through it. I wasn't exactly going anywhere. Christ, my left arm might have gone dead but the wound in my side felt as if it was starting to *boil*.

"They won't come for us," the voice managed eventually. "The *last* thing they'll do is get us out of here. Can't afford to. We know too much, you and I. We could tell too many stories. Stories they want to stay buried with us."

I didn't respond right away. Mainly because there was too much truth in the words to allow for an instant denial.

And also because the people who might be still up there, on the outside, were the very ones who had most to gain from the unfortunate accidental death of the pair of us.

"It's not just a job to them." I tried to push conviction into my tone and heard only a raw desperation. "It's a vocation. It's who they are. They will not abandon us."

They can't.

"Of course they will—in a heartbeat," my tomb partner insisted. "You think they have a choice?"

My suddenly arid mouth was a good excuse not to answer. In reality I was straining my ears, stretching out my senses as if they could be persuaded to catch the faintest sounds somewhere up there on the surface.

Sounds of a rescue team searching for us, digging for us, doing their best to keep us alive for long enough to bring us out to safety.

I heard nothing but silence.

And I saw nothing but the particular darkness that comes with a total absence of light.

Two

It was only a few days earlier that I got my first taste of what life was like in a major earthquake zone. People behaved differently, I found, as if to survive having their world quite literally turned upside down brought about a radical change in attitude.

The first sign was a certain ambivalence to the concept of danger. Perhaps that explained why the ex-Israeli Air Force pilot who nosedived us towards the half-destroyed runway laughed like a loon all the way down.

At the last moment he pulled back sharply to float the Lockheed C-130 Hercules into an approximate landing attitude and dumped the old heavy transport onto the ground from about six feet up, hard enough to make the airframe shudder. The pallets of netted-down cargo levitated briefly in the hold. I made sure to keep my feet well clear when they thumped down again.

The plane performed a couple of giant bounces that wouldn't have been out of place in a rodeo. Then the pilot yanked on the brakes as if hoping we'd all shoot forward to join him in the cockpit so we could congratulate him on his aviation prowess.

By the time we'd taxied off the flight-line my stomach was more or less back where nature intended. When I boarded the Hercules outside New York early that morning I hadn't expected comfort and amenities, which was fortunate. Our in-flight refreshment was a matter of helping yourself from the coffee urns strapped into the tail section.

Eventually we lurched to a stop and the four huge turboprops spooled down. After so many hours in the air, even wearing ear defenders, the relief was immense.

"There you go, guys," the pilot said, jumping down from the elevated cockpit and threading his way aft past the cargo as we unbuckled and stretched. "Perfect demonstration of the Khe Sanh Approach."

"Very impressive, Ari," I agreed. "Except we weren't trying to avoid groundfire on the way in."

He grinned. "Works just as good for short runways."

"At least he remembered to stop instead of just opening the ramp at the back and kicking us all out," said the guy next to me. "Had that happen a time or two."

He was a redheaded Scot called Wilson who came from one of the dodgier areas of Glasgow. An ex-Para now working for Strathclyde Police and currently on some kind of cultural exchange with the NYPD. He'd explained how a group of US officers had volunteered to help with the relief efforts and, for want of anything better, he'd stuck his hand up too.

Wilson had been fascinated by the idea of my work in close protection, envious of the pay and what he perceived as the glamour of travelling the world by private jet in the company of rock stars.

"Yeah," I told him, indicating the interior of the Herc. "Tell me about it."

He had a fund of war stories from his present and previous careers that had helped alleviate the boredom of a long flight with no creature comforts.

Even back in the military I'd never got used to the loo on a Hercules. It involved perching on a caravan-style construction built into high step at one side of the fuselage with a flimsy curtain pulled around you and very little to hold onto. Good job nobody had been attempting to use it during that final approach.

Transport aircraft pilots, in my experience, were different from jet jockeys in that they were mostly normal. Just my luck to end up with a lunatic who'd insisted on showing us how things were done during the Vietnam War. I was pretty sure Ari wasn't old enough to have seen action in that particular theatre, even if the venerable old aid-agency Herc he was flying might well have done.

We grabbed our kit bags and jogged down the lowered ramp which had already begun to swarm with ground crew off-loading supplies. I skipped sideways to avoid a forklift truck being driven with more gusto than expertise and stuck close to Wilson as we exited. At least he was a big enough target for them to avoid.

As I stepped down onto the concrete the warmth of the time and place finally hit me. I shrugged out of the jacket I'd worn for most of the flight. Like I said, a stripped-out transport plane doesn't even rival cattle-class on the most downmarket of budget airlines.

We headed towards what was left of the main terminal building. The control tower was still standing but the far end of the terminal itself had collapsed. It was my first glimpse of the damage a major earthquake leaves behind, this careless swatting of man's best construction efforts.

When I looked back I saw the reason for Ari the pilot's heroics with our landing. About two thirds of the way along, the runway had a diagonal line chopped across it as neatly as if someone had used a giant rotary saw. The concrete had split apart and heaved. One side of the small crevasse now stood a good two feet higher than the other.

"*That's* not going to be a cheap fix," I murmured.

Wilson slid me a quick smile. "Aye, an eight-point-six will do that to a city," he said. He hefted his bag onto his shoulder. "I assume you already know the roads between here and just about anywhere are out, by the way?" He nodded in the direction of a gleaming Eurocopter sporting the full-dress livery of the national police force. "That's my lift, by the looks of it, but I could probably get the local LEOs to drop you somewhere if you need it. Where you headed?"

The local Law Enforcement Officers he mentioned were standing around the helo all wearing combat-style uniforms along with equally uniform aviator sunglasses and moustaches. They had the look of men who would only be too delighted to drop me somewhere, providing it was a long way down.

"I'm fine, I think," I said. "I'm supposed to have a lift waiting but—"

"Coo-ee!"

The banshee cry was enough to make just about everyone in the vicinity turn and stare. A small bow-legged guy was ambling towards us. He had his hands in the pockets of his dusty combat pants and his booted feet scuffled the ground like he couldn't be bothered to lift them.

Above the combats he wore a multi-pocketed waistcoat of the kind favoured by fishermen and photographers, with no shirt underneath. Perhaps this was to show off the complexity of scars across his torso. From the tight irregularity of his skin I guessed he'd been badly burned at a time when the level of cosmetic surgery available had been a lot more rudimentary. So either he was proud of this visual history of his suffering or he simply didn't care.

I'd time to study his approach because he was completely focused on the guy standing next to me. I took in the newcomer's apparently relaxed face, deeply lined and tanned. It was completely at odds with the wariness I saw in his eyes.

"Charlie Fox, right?" he said to Wilson, sticking a hand out. "G'day, mate." His initial cry was suddenly explained by the strong if not slightly exaggerated Australian accent.

Wilson studied him for a beat, frowning, as if he'd seen the discrepancy between the face and eyes too and was working out what it might mean.

"Not me, pal," he said then, and jerked his head in my direction. "I think your lift has arrived." He took in the little Aussie's obvious consternation and gave me a slap on the shoulder. "See you round, Charlie. Our paths are bound to cross somewhere. And don't forget to mention me to your boss, next time he's recruiting, eh?"

"OK. Will do," I agreed, surprised he'd meant it serious enough to ask twice. "And good luck."

As Wilson strode away the Aussie said incredulously, "You're Charlie bloody Fox?"

"I've been called worse."

"But we asked for a security advisor, and you're ..."

"Cheap, available, and here," I said cheerfully. "You're with Rescue & Recovery International, I take it?"

"R&R." His mouth corrected automatically while his brain was still playing catch-up. "Folks just call us R&R."

"And what do I call *you* that I can repeat in public?"

He shook his head although if he was hoping to shake some sense into it. I doubted it had much effect.

"Riley," he said then, and shook his head again.

I shifted my kit bag from one shoulder to the other. "Look, I've just had a very long, very uncomfortable trip with a pilot in desperate need of a nice white coat with sleeves that knot at the back," I said with tired calm. "I know damn well that your outfit's lead doctor is a woman and you've other female staff, so it's not like you've never seen anyone with lumps down the front of their shirt before. What's your problem with me?"

He finally gave me the same big friendly grin he'd broken out for Wilson, but this time with a sheepish tint to it.

"Jeez, sweetheart, it's nothing personal," he said, reaching for my bag. I swapped it to my furthest hand and kept a firm grip on the straps. "It's just that we've been having trouble with the locals. Supply chain's all to shit and natives have been getting a mite antsy. I was hoping for someone the size of your mate back there so I could hide behind 'em, y'know? I mean, you're practically as small as I am. Didn't eat your Wheaties as a kid, eh?"

"I know," I said, "but if it makes you feel better I move quick and I've got a very bad temper."

For a second he rocked back on his heels and regarded me, head on one side. "I'll bet," he said at last. "Y'know, Charlie, I get the feeling I'm gonna like you after all. C'mon then, the old bus is over by what's left of the hangar there, and light's a'wasting."

Three

Riley's "old bus" turned out to be a Bell 212—the civilian version of the twin-engined UH-1 Huey that's been a staple of battlefields the world over since the late sixties.

Not that this helicopter looked quite that old—or particularly civilian. It had been painted some kind of matt-finish sludge khaki colour with 'R&R' stencilled not quite straight on the tail.

The passenger compartment, which could hold up to fourteen seats, had been stripped down to the minimum to leave room for cargo. It was currently half filled with a cling-wrapped pallet of what looked to be medical supplies. I wedged my kitbag alongside it and clipped a safety line through the straps just to be sure.

I climbed into the co-pilot's seat, dragged on a set of headphones held together with duct tape, and fastened my belts. As I did so I noticed the butt of an old Ruger .357 Magnum sitting upside down in a canvas pocket slung alongside the pilot's seat.

"You expecting elephants?" I asked as Riley hauled himself in.

He grinned at me. "Wouldn't be the first time."

He let out a galumph of breath and rubbed both hands vigorously over his stubbled face. It reminded me of a long-distance truck driver who's already been on the road all night and still has too far to go.

Oh great. I survive being killed at the hands of a mad Israeli only to die at the hands of an equally mad Aussie.

"Been flying these things long?" I asked over the whine of the Pratt & Whitneys going through start-up.

"Got my licence about three months ago." Riley threw me a laconic smile as he juggled the controls and the Bell made an initial half-hearted attempt to get off the ground. "Well, to be

107

fair, I should say I got it *back* three months ago. Here we go then!"

And with that he rammed the aircraft upward like an express elevator. We yawed drunkenly sideways as we rose, our downdraft flattening the wide grass runoff that bordered the service road. That was probably one of the reasons it was there.

Riley caught me gripping the bottom of my seat in reflex and didn't so much laugh as guffaw. The action that brought on a fit of coughing that made the Bell twitch in response to his hands.

"Relax, Charlie," he said when he could speak again. "It's like riding a bike. You don't really forget how to do it."

"Easy for you to say," I shot back. "Last time I was up in one of these damn things, we crashed."

"Hey, me too!" he said. "How about that?"

I was beginning to get the creeping sensation I was being taken for a ride in more ways than one but I didn't call him on it. I'd been through worse hazing, that was for sure. Better to let him have his fun and get it over with early.

Instead I adjusted the boom mic from my headset and asked, "So when did you R&R guys get in?"

"We set down inside about eight hours of the initial quake. Been working round the clock since then, more or less. She's a monster."

From the way he was slouched in his seat I realised he'd long ago adapted his wiry frame to the most comfortable position so he could keep to the schedule. Either that or all the scar tissue was twisting his body out of shape.

I looked out through the canopy and the Plexiglas panel by my feet, trying to ignore the jerkiness of the ride. Below me were swathes of destruction, buildings knocked flat as if a petulant child had gone rampaging across a beach full of sandcastles wearing bovver boots. From up there the whole scene lacked a sense of reality.

Most scary to me were the gaping holes that had opened up in the roads, fields and where the houses used to stand. I shivered. Having a building fall around your ears was one thing. Having the earth open up underneath your feet to sending you plummeting into the bowels was quite another.

The ground had contracted as well as split. I saw a wooden fence that had once been straight and was now an absurdly wiggled line, and a section of railway track that was distorted as a painting by Salvador Dalí.

"How bad are the casualties?"

Riley shrugged. "Over three hundred confirmed dead so far. We haven't really started digging out the bodies yet—still concentrating on finding survivors, y'know?" he said in a flat voice. "But if they don't get their supply lines sorted soon, that figure's going to rocket. There's already trouble about aid distribution, been some looting, stuff like that. Can get a bit hairy out there."

One of Wilson's tasks, so he'd told me on the flight, was likely to be ironing out those distribution kinks and maintaining order. I'd lay bets the big Scot would be good at it, even if he was going to have his work cut out.

"In that case I'm surprised you came in-country without a security advisor in place," I said as casually as I could manage.

Riley flicked me a quick look and gave another shrug. The action caused us to sideslip wildly to the left. "Never know how bad it's gonna be 'til you get here," he said, overcorrecting. "Besides, we lost our regular guy last time out."

"'Lost'?" I echoed. "'Lost' as in 'misplaced'? What happened?"

Before he could reply the cockpit radio squawked. Riley cut the intercom connection between us to answer it.

"Yeah doc, go ahead," I heard him say, only just audible to me over the roar of engine and rotor. "Not far. I'm giving Charlie the ten-dollar tour." There was a pause while the person on the other end clearly asked who the hell he was talking about. "Our new security expert," he said then, flashing his yellowed teeth. "Yeah, that's right. I tell you, I feel safer already."

I turned my head deliberately to stare out across the ruined cityscape. Columns of smoke still rose from the sporadic fires that had yet to be dampened. I could see groups of people scattered about the debris. Most wore fluorescent jackets or bibs. I knew it was a co-ordinated effort but their movements seemed small and futile against the sheer scale of the disaster.

There was a click in my ears and Riley's voice was back.

"Gotta make a small diversion," he said.

"As long as the meter's not still running."

He laughed again. I waited in alarm for one of his lungs to make an actual appearance but he managed to choke it back down. "No worries," he said. "This one's on doctor's orders. Wants me to pick something up for her on the way in."

He swooped the Bell into a sudden stomach dropping right-hand turn that tipped my side of the cockpit over by almost ninety degrees. It was like being back in the Hercules all over again.

I made another grab for my seat and realised, as the Aussie's wheezy laughter echoed in my ears, that he had just very neatly sidestepped answering my last question. The one about what had happened to my predecessor.

Perhaps, if I survived this flight, I'd get to ask him again.

Four

When you said you were going to 'pick something up' on the way, I thought you were talking about a pint of milk," I said.

"Jeez, don't put that idea in the doc's head for Christ's sake or she'll have us running all over this bloody city looking for unsweetened organic soy or some shit like that."

Riley put the Bell into a clumsy hover above a cracked roadway that curved dangerously close to the edge of a steep drop-off. He held it there for a moment or so while he checked around him and then didn't so much land as dump it onto the skids. We hit hard enough to loosen a few fillings—and the teeth that contained them.

If this was all part of his act to scare the newbie, I decided, it was getting very old very fast.

Still, better that than the alternative explanation—that he really *was* a dreadful pilot.

The Aussie climbed out and staggered for a few strides until his joints began functioning normally, leaving the Bell's engines on tick-over and the rotors turning lazily overhead. He was small enough that he didn't bother to duck.

I hopped out to join him without waiting for an invitation that clearly wasn't about to be issued. I assumed he left the helo in Park with the handbrake applied.

By the time I caught up, Riley was standing a foot or so back from the precipice next to another man. The newcomer was maybe a few years younger, his hair dark but flecked with grey. He wore coveralls with a rappelling harness and fluorescent bib over the top, and carried heavy gloves. There was a large coil of climbing rope at his feet.

Even without the high-and-tight buzzcut and the unbending stance, I would have pegged him as ex-military. There's an air about former US Marines they never seem to lose.

Both men were peering downwards. I moved alongside and did the same.

It immediately became clear why the narrow road appeared to run so close to the edge. Before the quake, it had been a dual carriageway positioned what should have been a safe distance back.

Now the entire left-hand lane and shoulder—plus a good chunk of safety fencing—were about sixty feet below us, balanced precariously on the slope. It must have been at least another hundred feet to the valley floor below.

A truck and two cars had been on the breakaway section when it fell. They lay jumbled on the makeshift ledge. Fluoro-jacketed rescue workers swarmed around them. I saw four people on stretchers and three zipped body bags.

"The doc wants him out of there yesterday," the former Marine was saying in a soft American drawl. "Day before that would be even better."

"Why not strap him in and drag him up the cliff wall," Riley suggested, frowning. "Bumpy ride but safer than me going down there that's for bloody sure."

The former Marine gave him the kind of stare that must have had raw recruits shivering in their boots.

"We drag the kid up the cliff face and he loses the use of his legs."

Riley took a step closer to the edge, leaned out cautiously. As he did so, the former Marine seemed to notice me for the first time. His eyes narrowed. I gave him a nod of greeting he didn't return.

Riley stepped back between us. "Shit, boss. I got a half-load of cargo in the back of the old girl. She must weigh in at about eight thousand pounds. The downdraft alone could send the whole bloody lot heading for the bottom of the hill like a giant rock toboggan."

The former Marine raised an implacable eyebrow in a *So?* gesture.

Riley scowled. "And it's bloody close. I'll practically be weed whacking with the main rotor to get far enough in."

"Nothing you haven't done before," the former Marine said, and added, "By accident or design."

"What about winching him up?" I asked, nodding to the Bell.

"Ah." Riley looked embarrassed. "Local cops 'requisitioned' my winch yesterday. Bastards. I'm still trying to steal it back." He passed me a sour look and muttered, "Wouldn't have happened if we'd had decent security."

"Hey," I said, "yesterday I didn't even know I was coming."

The former Marine swung toward us in exasperation. He pointed a finger at me but his eyes were on Riley. "Excuse me," he said, "but who is she, exactly?"

"Stephens' replacement." Riley said with deliberation. He gave a leer. "Smaller muscles but bigger ti—"

"Yeah, I guess I can see that for myself," the former Marine cut in dryly. He held out his hand and we clasped briefly. He had a steel grip. "Joe Marcus."

"Charlie Fox."

He gave me a fractional nod then dismissed me from his mind and turned back to Riley. "You gonna to get your ass back in that heap of junk, fly down there and pick up our casualty, or do I just kick you over the edge right now, save us all a heap of trouble?"

"Might cut out the middle man," Riley grumbled.

He took a final look over the precipice and spat for good measure, as if timing how long it would take the gob of saliva to reach the bottom.

"Ah, shit mate, why not?" he said at last. "Gotta die of something, right?" He started ambling toward the Bell, calling cheerfully over his shoulder, "Just in case the worst happens, I leave all my debts divided equally between my ex-wives."

I glanced across at Joe Marcus but clearly he had heard all this before. I turned and jogged for the helo. By the time Riley reached the cockpit I was already climbing in alongside him. He favoured me with a brief stare.

"You fed up with us already Charlie? Aiming to go home in a body bag yourself?"

I strapped in. "A Bell Twin Two-Twelve has a forty-eight foot rotor diameter," I said. "That ledge can't be more than twenty-five feet out from the cliff wall. If you're going to keep this thing out of the scrub you're going to need someone to spot for you."

For a moment he sat with his hands slack in his lap, then he shook his head and reached for the controls.

"Jeez," he said. "Stephens would have shit his pants."

"Yeah well, think of it as an added bonus," I said. "And that's on top of having bigger tits."

Five

When it mattered, Riley flew like an angel. I'd kind of hoped that might be the case.

If I'd been wrong we would both have been dead.

But he juggled the manual throttle, the cyclic and the collective, and the anti-torque pedals with a sure and delicate touch. He carefully sidled us, a few inches at a time, toward the wreckage on the fallen section of roadway while I hung out of my open cockpit door and guided him in.

Below us, the rescue team crouched away from the spinning rotors and sheltered the casualties with their own bodies. The protection they offered was more psychological than actual. If we'd touched the exposed cliff face with the rotor tips the resulting explosive disintegration would have probably wiped out everybody down there. As it was, the vicious downdraft beat them flat and grit-blasted them while it was about it.

As we crept closer I watched the longer fronds of stringy vegetation clinging to the rock wall until they became whipped into frenzy by the displaced air. The Bell rocked and plunged like a small boat caught in a cross-current, dipping the main rotors perilously close to the cliff with every jagged roll.

"Is this as good as it gets?" I demanded.

"You think you can do better, sweetheart, you're welcome to give it a shot," Riley managed from between clenched teeth. "I'm losing half my bloody lift over the outboard side. Now then, hang about."

His hands shifted. The Bell gave a lurch and then steadied with the pilot's side of the helo maybe a foot lower. Instead of the aircraft having to cope with a long drop on one side and a very short one on the other, the space underneath us was more equalised. He feathered the controls just enough to hold station and grinned at me. It wasn't exactly glass-like, but it was a big improvement.

"Hey, would you look at that? Piece o' cake."

I hauled myself back into the door aperture and watched the rotors. The angle opened up room for us to edge another vital couple of feet closer.

"OK, that's close enough!" I ordered. The skid on my side was directly overhanging the mangled guard rail that had dropped, as one lump, with the rest of the section of road.

I straightened back into my seat, wedging the door ajar with my knee, and glanced at Riley. "Can you keep it steady right there?"

"'Course, mate." The Aussie even managed to sound a little bored. "There's not a fart of wind. Long as it stays that way, no worries."

"Good," I said. "Because if I can get down there in one piece, chances are we can get the casualty back the same way."

I pulled off my headset without waiting for his comments, shoved open the door again and got out.

I tried not to think about the hundred feet of nothing beneath me as I clambered onto the skid and used the guard rail as a stepping stone before jumping down onto the cracked concrete. And all the while I made sure to keep my head low.

A slim dark-haired woman half rose to meet me. Her face was perfectly calm, as if total strangers walked out of mid-air helicopters in front of her every day of the week.

"Doc?" I guessed, shouting to be heard. She nodded. "This is close as we get. Where's your patient?"

She beckoned. Four people hurried forward carrying a stretcher between them. The boy strapped onto the stretcher was wearing a surgical collar to stabilise his neck. He looked no more than seventeen. His eyes were closed and there was a mess of blood tangling his hair. Another rescue worker jogged alongside the stretcher carrying a drip that was plugged into his arm, and pumping the resus bag covering his nose and mouth.

"'Ow do you propose we do this?" the doctor asked. She had a heavy accent I couldn't place with all the background noise.

"Bloody carefully," I said. "We'll slide him up and in across the cargo bay. I'll go first. Be ready."

She nodded again without argument. I turned back to the hovering Bell. From the ground, getting back into it seemed a hell of a lot more difficult than getting out had done. The vicious downdraft buffeted me and I couldn't help the horrible feeling that the rotors were skimming my hair the same way as that vegetation.

I took a deep breath and leapt for the guard rail and the skid at the same time. I'd been aiming for the rear door but as I landed the helicopter gave a sudden outward lurch. My foot slipped off the railing. I hurled myself forward, grabbing messily for the cockpit door handle instead, wrenching it open. I tumbled back inside with my heart hammering against my ribs so loud it must have drowned out the noise of the engines.

Riley sat slumped and impassive in the pilot's seat. Relief made me grin stupidly at him. "Miss me?"

Without waiting for an answer I squeezed between the front seats, staggered into the rear and tugged the cliff-side door open. It slid back alongside the fuselage.

As soon as I'd done so the dark-haired doctor climbed up coolly onto the guard rail and put her hand out without waiting to be invited. I hastily clasped it and yanked her inside. In contrast with my own graceless efforts she landed with the ease of a dancer. Bitch.

The front two stretcher-bearers lifted one end high enough to reach the cargo deck and everybody pushed. The doc and I took hold and between us, with amazingly little further drama, we hauled the stretcher on board. I slammed the door shut again.

Riley didn't need any further signal, moving away instantly.

The doctor nodded to me just once, then reached for a headset and gave Riley instructions about which medical centre to head for. As she spoke she checked the boy's airway and worked the resus bag to keep him breathing. I hung the saline pouch feeding his drip line high enough not to become a drain instead and strapped down the stretcher.

When I was done I threaded my way to my front seat again and stuck my own headset back on. Riley flicked me a glance that was suddenly serious.

"Nice going, Charlie," he said. "Thought I'd lost you for a moment there."

"Yeah," I agreed. "You'll have to try a damn sight harder next time."

Just for a second he looked startled but then he grinned at me. "No way would old Stevo have given that a go."

"Thanks," I said. I re-fastened my belts, although after the last ten minutes it seemed an oddly redundant gesture. "You never did tell me what happened to him."

"He got careless," Riley said. "And then he got unlucky."

Six

The doctor's name was Alexandria Bertrand and the accent I hadn't been able to discern amid all the other distractions turned out to be French. She was a highly regarded trauma specialist who'd jacked in her career at one of the best hospitals in Paris and done five years with *Médecins Sans Frontières* before joining R&R. So I surmised she'd seen the very worst people could do to each other anywhere TripAdvisor warned you not to go.

She was also a qualified forensic pathologist and as soon as the rescue efforts started to scale down she would begin the heartbreaking and laborious task of identifying the dead. Maybe she had more affinity with them than the living. She certainly didn't impress me with her bedside manner. But, having a top class surgeon for a father I was only too familiar with that haughty clinical demeanour.

I found out most of her background from staff at the medical centre where we transported the injured boy from the roadway collapse. The centre was located in an area of the city least affected by the quake, although the sheer numbers of incoming casualties meant most of the injured were going through military-style triage and then being treated in a makeshift field hospital. Requisitioned tents and marquees stretched out across the parking areas.

Dr Bertrand saw her patient into the care of the surgical team and handed him over with a concise recitation of his injuries and the treatment he'd received so far. There was too much blood on his forehead for her to write the traditional 'M' there to indicate she'd given him a hefty dose of morphine and she made a pain of herself insisting they make proper note of it.

119

"I 'ave risked too much to bring this boy 'ere," she told them in that icily exotic voice, "only for you to overdose 'im on the operating table."

"I *have* risked ..."

So, not only a complete lack of bedside manner, but no concept of being a team player either.

She and my father would have got on like a house on fire.

As they hurriedly wheeled the boy away to pre-op she peeled off her latex gloves and dropped them into the nearest waste bin. There was a symbolic finality to the act, a washing of hands.

Then she turned to me. I expected some form of greeting but instead she gave me a swift cool appraisal and asked, "Where is Riley? I must get back to my work."

I jerked my head toward the landing area nearby where we'd just set down. "Offloading medical supplies."

"Then tell 'im to 'urry," she responded, and swept out past me.

"Yes ma'am," I said under my breath. "And it's a pleasure to be working with you, too ..."

It wasn't until we were in the air again twenty minutes later that she deigned to offer me her full attention. We were travelling in the rear of the helicopter on flip-down seats facing each other, so it was harder for her to avoid it.

Riley was left to his own devices in the cockpit. He seemed put out that he could no longer play the inept rookie with me, and as a result he flew a smooth straight course, forsaking drama as well as conversation. Maybe it was simply the dampening effect Dr Bertrand had on him.

Without its cargo the interior of the Bell seemed vast. The empty space beat with reflected flight noise like a giant drum.

"So, Charlie," she said via the headsets we both wore, curling my name into something more than it was, "why are you 'ere?"

I had my official story down pat. "To advise your team on personal safety, minimise risk, protect you if necessary, help out where I can."

"That is not what I meant." She frowned. "But your actions out there today," she went on, her fingers making a small gesture to indicate the helicopter and all that had gone into the rescue, "were they safe—or advisable?"

"I think that falls under both protecting you *and* helping out."

"But you did not seem to give much regard to your own safety. 'Ow can we be sure you will give regard to ours?"

120

"I said *minimise* risk. I know I can't eliminate it entirely, so my job is to put myself between you and whatever hazards I can, but still allow you the freedom to do your work," I said. I paused. "I understand you lost a team member recently. I'm sorry. Please be assured I will do everything I can not to let that happen again."

"Thank you." She favoured me with a vaguely regal nod. "I confess that I did not like Kyle Stephens, but in most ways 'e was a professional and I could at least admire that."

"Why didn't you like him?"

She gave me a slow blink, almost in surprise that I had the temerity to ask.

"'E did not think much of women," she said at last.

"Can I ask ... what happened to him?"

She stiffened. "Why do you ask?"

"I try to learn from past mistakes in order to avoid repeating them. Other people's as well as my own."

"It was ... 'e did not ..." She gave a growl of frustration and tried again: "Natural disasters are often followed by great lawlessness ... people who wish to take advantage of the situation for their own gain. This can make such places very dangerous, as Monsieur Stephens found out to 'is cost."

"Dangerous how?" I persisted.

She flashed me a quick look of irritation. "We were in an area of Colombia where the rule of law is somewhat ... tenuous," she said at last. "The local guerrilla fighters were determined to come in and take what they wanted—including our equipment and supplies. We needed time to make a successful evacuation." She shrugged. "Perhaps 'e should 'ave advised us to move out sooner. 'E paid the price for that oversight."

All of which was precisely no help whatsoever towards finding out what actually caused the death of my predecessor.

And no help either towards planning how best to avoid following in his footsteps.

Seven

The dead lay in rows in a temporary mortuary established at an army base about ten klicks from the capital.

In the weird way of earthquakes, while some areas were totally destroyed this whole place had escaped totally unscathed. Everyone fervently hoped it would stay that way. Even so, whenever an aftershock hit there was a fractional pause before they carried on. Outside, there was the constant rumble of engines from the line of commandeered refrigeration trucks being used for storage.

Dr Bertrand briefly explained the cataloguing system used for each victim as they were brought in. Every piece of clothing and personal items had to be removed, photographed and bagged.

She seemed to take it for granted that I wouldn't freak out in close proximity to so many corpses. Particularly ones who had not exactly died peacefully in their sleep. Her only concern was whether I could be trusted to operate a camera with enough skill to be useful.

"This is not in my brief," I pointed out. "Wouldn't I be more—?"

"Tomorrow—maybe," she interrupted, thrusting a Canon digital SLR and a clipboard into my hands. "But the teams are already scattered across the city. For now you are more use 'ere."

I shrugged. "Where do I start?"

And so I began. The quake had been no respecter of age, race or social status—an equal-opportunity killer. That first day I listed and photographed toys found clutched in the hands of children, lavish rings from well-manicured fingers, and the rags of the homeless.

I was handed all these possessions to arrange and record as they were stripped from the bodies. In some cases blood and other debris had to be cleaned from them first.

"We try to make an initial identification from family or friends recognising the property found with the victim," I was told by the girl I was working with. She introduced herself too fast for me to catch her name and there never seemed to be opportunity to ask a second time.

The level of concentration I felt compelled to maintain in order to give these people the respect they deserved made it an engrossing but dismal task.

There were four DVI teams—Disaster Victim Identification— from different countries working alongside each other. Apart from the murmuring of the pathologists dictating their observations and the occasional rapid rattle of a bone saw, the only sounds were the muted pop of camera flashes and the flutter of Canon motorwinds.

No chatter, no jokes, no music.

The Japanese team, so experienced in dealing with situations like this, held a sombre minute's silence before starting on each new victim. An overwhelming sense of sadness pervaded the place. By the time I'd been there a couple of hours I was mentally and emotionally flattened.

"Charlie." Dr Bertrand's voice, loud and unexpected, made me jump. "I need you over 'ere."

I turned, saw the young guy who'd been photographing for her stumbling away with his shoulders hunched.

"'E is too tired to work efficiently," Dr Bertrand said, following my gaze. "I 'ave sent 'im to get some rest, and so I must make do with you."

I bit back my instinctive sarcastic comment and said instead, "What do you need?"

She laid a hand on the naked thigh of the overweight middle-aged male cadaver on her table, like a butcher contemplating which cut to take from a side of pig.

"This man 'as an artificial 'ip," she began.

"Which will have a unique serial number tied to the patient who received it."

She gave me a small sideways glance but stopped short of actual praise.

"I will, of course, need to expose that area of the implant for you to document," she warned.

"Of course," I repeated blandly.

I had seen the dead up close before. In fact I had been the cause of death more times than was probably good for my eternal soul. And once I watched my father carry out an emergency procedure to clamp a man's severed brachial artery by the side of a road, armed with no more than a Swiss Army knife and the rusty toolkit from a Ford pickup truck.

But I had never witnessed such a swift and brutal partial dismemberment as Alexandria Bertrand performed. Her incisions were precise and practical, without a wasted stroke or hesitation. The image of her as a butcher returned as she peeled back the dead man's skin and flesh with no more drama than if she'd been boning a joint of meat for Sunday lunch. Then she stepped back with an impatient flick of her fingers.

"There. Be sure it is entirely visible and in sharp focus."

I snapped away and checked the results on the view screen at the back of the camera, zooming in as far as it would allow. But when I offered to show the good doctor she waved me away. It brought to mind generals who give orders and expect them to be carried out without question, but who would never lower themselves far enough to actually check.

We worked on into the evening. By then I had confirmed my first impression of Dr Bertrand. She was tireless, ruthless and humourless. But bloody hell she was good at her job.

Exactly the same qualities were much admired in contract killers.

"Hey, Al!" called a voice from the doorway.

My head jerked up and I realised Dr Bertrand and I were the only two people left in the mortuary amid a sea of empty stainless steel tables.

The former Marine, Joe Marcus weaved his way between them. He had exchanged his coveralls for lightweight trousers and a cotton shirt but everything about him carried the authority of rank.

"Clear up and give the new kid a break," he said. "Chow time."

Dr Bertrand let out her breath and frowned as if considering whether or not to comply. The fact he'd called her "Al" didn't seem to cause a flicker. Marcus reached us and stood silently across the other side of our work station. She had just finished with the burned body of an old woman and I had carefully put all her documented charred belongings back into a labelled archive

124

box and shelved it in the ante room next door while she completed her notes.

From that point of view Marcus's timing was excellent. It didn't stop Dr Bertrand having a short stare-out competition with him, though. I reckoned they were fairly evenly matched, but in the end the former Marine beat her on points.

"You're only as good as the most exhausted member of your unit," he said.

I would have argued about that, but realised it would not do me any favours.

"OK," Dr Bertrand said at last. She peeled off her gloves and dropped them into a flip-top bin, in the same way she'd done earlier at the medical centre after we'd delivered the boy from the roadside. I followed suit. Marcus nodded at her capitulation.

At the doorway she stopped and looked back almost longingly.

"Dead is dead. Another few hours isn't gonna make any difference to them," Marcus said quietly. "But it will to you."

She switched off the light without replying and we stepped outside into the humid wash of evening.

While Dr Bertrand locked up Joe Marcus shifted his eyes to me.

"You were lucky out there today," he said. "Nice reflexes."

For a moment I went blank on his meaning then realised he was talking about that slip as I'd jumped for the helicopter. The rescue on the cliffside seemed to have taken place days ago.

"Yeah well," I said with a smile, "I told Riley he'd have to try harder than that if he wanted to get rid of me."

His eyes narrowed and I didn't miss the quick look that Dr Bertrand flicked in his direction. And in that instant I had sudden flash-recall of launching myself for the Bell, of the helo jinking away from me at exactly the wrong moment.

Or had it been exactly the *right* moment?

Not enough to appear deliberate—just a correction for an unexpected gust of wind buffeting the aircraft. But coming after Riley had stated there was "not a fart" of a breeze, even allowing for the difficult angle, it sent a shiver of delayed reaction along every nerve.

And when I met Joe Marcus's gaze I saw that he either knew anyway or he'd already worked it out. He stared back at me steadily.

I'd thought Dr Bertrand was a cold one, but I realised that he was infinitely colder.

"Let us eat," she said abruptly. "There is still much work to do."

She strode away along a narrow path bordered by whitewashed stones. Marcus indicated I should go before him with a sweep of his arm. Good manners precluded my refusal, but I found I didn't like him walking behind me.

I'd come here looking for a potential killer.

Instead I'd found three.

Eight

Only a few hours before I boarded that Hercules I'd never heard of an outfit called Rescue & Recovery International. Nor had I ever crossed paths with a former US Army Ranger called Kyle Stephens. The fact that he was dead was of little interest to me.

I had other things on my mind.

Foremost of these worries was the state of my relationship with Sean Meyer. Sean had been my training instructor during my short and bitterly inglorious military career. The toughest of a tough bunch, he was the one who had goaded me towards excellence. And just when I thought he was the coldest bastard I'd ever encountered, he confounded me by offering a glimpse of his human side that provoked an incendiary desire.

Our affair while we were still in uniform was short-lived, illicit, and ultimately doomed not only to failure but to personal and professional ruin for both of us.

I never would have dreamed back then that Sean and I would reconnect, or would end up living together in New York working for Parker Armstrong's prestigious close-protection agency. We'd certainly had our share of high points, but there had been some equally stunning blows as well.

The previous winter I nearly lost him for good. For more than three months I pilgrimaged daily to his bedside while he lay in a coma and on some subconscious level made up his mind between holding on and letting go.

And during all that time I loved him and hated him in equal measure.

In the end my prayers were answered but with a sick twist neither of us could have prepared for. We came back to each other changed from who we were—and not for the better. Just when I finally became more like Sean—more like the old Sean *wanted* me to be—he became less like himself.

Everyone from the neurosurgeon who dug the fragments of skull out of his brain, to the coma specialists and psychologists, had warned us he might be different afterwards. *If* he lived.

The one thing I clung to was that if he made it back then the bond between us was strong enough to cope with whatever might follow. In the event, I found myself devastated by his sudden unexpected enmity towards me. For someone in a profession that stands or falls by its anticipation of every obstacle, I admit *that* one took me completely by surprise.

We still shared the Upper East Side apartment Parker had arranged for us as part of our relocation deal, but I moved my things into the second bedroom. At first this was a temporary measure while Sean acclimatised to the fact we were a couple. His last waking memory of me was as someone he despised.

As is always the way with temporary measures, the move soon became permanent. But it also seemed to ease the tension between us. He took some tentative steps toward me and I thought, finally, we might be making progress.

And then it all changed again.

The day that eight-point-six earthquake hit I sat watching the news coverage and teetering on the cusp of melancholy. And that's when Parker Armstrong rang me.

"Charlie!" he greeted. There was surprise in his voice, as if he hadn't expected to catch me at home when he knew that's where I'd be. "How you doing?"

"I'm fine."

He let the lie pass, said instead, "I have a client coming in at three this afternoon. I'd like for you to be here, meet with them."

I poked my brain doggedly into work mode. "Is this a solo job or part of a full detail?"

Parker hesitated. "Not exactly either," he said. "Best if the client explains it to you herself."

"OK, so what's the threat?" The question lacked finesse, but hell—people didn't hire Armstrong-Meyer unless they needed protecting from something bad.

"Your guess is as good as mine," he said, not sounding at all fazed.

I felt my eyebrows rise. Parker was usually meticulous. He possessed a wariness born of long experience at the sharp end of close-protection work. He did not normally offer his services—or those of his operatives—on such an open-ended basis.

In spite of myself, I was intrigued. And almost anything was better than this frantic inactivity.

"OK," I said. "I'll be there."

I made sure I reached the midtown offices of the Armstrong-Meyer agency a good half an hour before the appointed time. Excessive perhaps, but Parker always stressed that we were there to wait on our clients, not the other way around.

As it was, I was told to go right in as soon as I stepped out of the lift into the marble-tiled lobby. The Armstrong-Meyer nameplate was still displayed behind the reception desk. I wondered how long Parker could continue to keep Sean as a full partner when he no longer played an active role.

I knocked briefly and opened the door to Parker's office. His domain occupied a corner of the building. It had a fabulous view out over the Manhattan skyline but I didn't get chance to admire it.

Parker was not alone, I saw immediately. There was a woman with him who was sitting in one of the low client chairs that bracketed a coffee table in the centre of the room. She was in her forties and the best word to describe her was sleek.

She was dressed with a careless elegance only the long-term wealthy ever truly manage well. I couldn't pull it off with a gun to my head. What little jewellery she wore was antique and expensive without being gaudy. Her hair and nails were flawless. And she was a redhead—one of Parker's weaknesses.

My boss was standing behind his desk, leaning both fists onto the polished surface, his arms braced. His head came up sharply when I entered.

For a horrible moment I thought I'd walked in on a situation that was personal rather than professional. There was definitely something going on even if I couldn't put my finger on what. I heard the tension fizzing in the air and saw the flash of stubbornness in the woman's eyes. Eyes that widened when I walked in on them.

I froze with one hand on the door handle.

"I was told you were ready for me, sir," I said quickly, keeping it formal just in case. "But I can come back later if you're—"

"No, no, come on in," Parker said. He straightened and lifting a shoulder as if to ease the tension in his neck. "Mrs Hamilton," he went on, "this is the operative we've been discussing—Charlie Fox."

I shut the door and came forward. Mrs Hamilton rose to meet me, neatly pushing aside all appearance of irritation, and gave me the kind of smile that makes you believe it really *is* a pleasure. Nevertheless, I caught the way her eyes slid questioningly to his and the bland look he passed her in reply.

I pretended not to notice, taking a seat opposite and crossing my legs. I was glad I'd taken the time to put on a decent black suit for the occasion. What made me less happy was the fact I'd chosen to wear an open-necked shirt with it.

The old scar around the base of my throat had faded to a thin line that didn't tan well. I was still touchy about it even though it was only noticeable if you knew to look—and for some reason Mrs Hamilton seemed to know. I returned her gaze evenly. She flushed slightly and glanced away.

Parker, who'd missed nothing of this, gave her a brief reassuring smile.

"Thanks for coming in at such short notice, Charlie, but we have something of a time-sensitive situation."

"No problem," I said. "What's the brief?"

He nodded to Mrs Hamilton. "If you'd care to fill Charlie in on some of the background?"

Again there was more in the tone than the words but the redhead simply gave a reluctant nod.

"I guess I ought to tell you right away that I am finding it hard to maintain a level of emotional detachment from all this," she said.

Most clients who came to us suffered the same problem, but to have her admit it up front was refreshing.

She took a deep breath. "My husband died in the Tōhoku earthquake in Japan," she said. "He was over there on business, decided to take an extra day or two at the end of his trip to see the sights, and as a result he became one of nearly twenty-five thousand dead, injured or missing."

I did a quick mental calculation and worked out the Tōhoku earthquake was several years previously. Not long enough to sate her grief, clearly, but enough to dull the pain just a little.

"I'm very sorry for your loss," I murmured.

She nodded her acknowledgement, went on. "He was in the hotel restaurant when the building simply ... came down around him, trapped him in the rubble. Afterward, well—" she turned diffident, "—they said he might have survived if help had gotten to him sooner."

I said nothing. Slow deaths are harder to bear, I knew, than if he'd been killed instantly.

Instead, it was Parker who said, "Mrs Hamilton is now a major donor supporting an outfit called Rescue & Recovery International."

I felt my lips try to quirk inappropriately upwards and controlled them only with effort. Parker's face showed no inner amusement. Had he never watched the puppet *Thunderbirds* series as a kid? The Tracy family living on their private island and running International Rescue on the side?

"Yes," Mrs Hamilton said, reading me with uncanny accuracy. "I guess that makes me Lady Penelope, doesn't it?"

I let go and grinned at her. "And not forgetting her trusty butler-turned-chauffeur."

"Of course!" Her eyes flew to my boss. "His name was Parker."

Parker's face remained impassive. I suppose one of us had to behave like a grownup.

"And you have concerns with this Rescue & Recovery?" I asked. I couldn't bring myself to include the "International" part.

"Yes," she agreed, her eyes on my boss.

Parker said, "Rescue & Recovery—they're known as R&R—was formed as an emergency response team shortly after that Japanese quake in two-thousand-ten. Their mission statement is to provide rapid emergency assistance on the ground, anywhere in the world, twenty-four/seven, three-sixty-five days a year."

I nodded. All very interesting but so far I didn't see where I came in. I silently indicated this to Parker with a face that asked, *So?*

"They go into areas which, by their very nature, are experiencing upheaval and a degree of civil unrest. It is a requirement of their insurance to have a security advisor on board. Until three weeks ago that was a guy called Kyle Stephens."

He lifted a manila folder from his desk and held it out to me. I flipped it open and saw a head and shoulders shot of a thickset man with a bull neck and a nose that had seen some action. He was uniformed in the mug shot. I recognised the red lightning streak cap badge of the US Army Rangers.

131

"Is there a problem with Stephens?" I asked, skimming his impressive résumé. "He looks like an ideal man for the job."

"He's dead."

I blinked. "How?"

"That rather seems to be the question," Mrs Hamilton said. She sighed. "Three weeks ago they were in South America. Mudslides in Colombia. Four hundred dead—many of them children. Two schools were destroyed. It was a nightmare, not just the continuing heavy rains but increased guerrilla activity in the area causing havoc as well. It was dangerous in many ways but that's all part of the job."

I heard an edge to her voice and wondered who she was trying to convince. I said nothing but Parker gave her an encouraging nod. Her answering smile was grateful but there was still something slightly strained between them. I wondered again what they'd been arguing about before my arrival.

"At first it all seemed normal—as normal as their work ever gets. They took the rescue operation as far as they could and moved on to recovering the bodies." She shook her head. "All those children. It was heartbreaking."

"I read the reports," Parker said gently. "It was a tragedy."

"And the next thing I know I get a call on the sat-phone from the team leader, Joe Marcus. Anyhow, Joe tells me Kyle has 'met with an accident'."

"Did he say what kind of an accident?"

"No, but it wasn't *what* he said, it was the *way* he said it. It's hard to explain. Joe can be a tough man to read but there was just too much anger."

"That wouldn't be unusual," Parker pointed out. "Losing somebody you feel responsible for can make you … rage."

He didn't look at me as he spoke. I didn't look at him either.

"But it was as though he was angry *with* Kyle, not because of something that happened *to* him," Mrs Hamilton said. "It was as though Joe was taking it personally somehow."

"Same rule applies," I said. "If someone dies because they made a mistake—especially a one-off stupid mistake—that would do it, too."

"Funny." She eyed us both. "When I pressed Joe about it later, that's exactly what he said."

"But?" I put in, because in situations like these there's always a "but".

Mrs Hamilton paused. She uncrossed and re-crossed her elegant legs. Eventually she said, "Do you trust your instincts, Miss Fox—when it comes to people, I mean?"

"Mostly," I said, because there were times when my instincts had let me down big time. And other times when I'd refused to listen to my internal warning system. Usually to my cost.

She heard all that in my one-word answer, smiled and said, "Well then, if you 'mostly' trust your instincts, do you then follow up on them, or do you let it slide?"

It was a good point. I couldn't come back with anything except agreement. I shrugged.

"All right," I said. "What does your instinct tell you about Kyle Stephens?"

She hesitated again, because now we were drifting from facts into feelings. She glanced at Parker again for support.

"That I might have gotten him killed."

"It was brought to Mrs Hamilton's attention that there had been a number of *incidents* that coincide with the arrival on scene of R&R's people," Parker said.

"What kind of 'incidents'?" I asked, echoing his emphasis. "You mean threats against them?"

Parker shook his head. "Thefts," he said bluntly.

Mrs Hamilton's body shifted in protest. "In the confusion following the kind of natural disasters they deal with, it's easy for things to be ... lost, but this is more than that," she said, her voice hollow. "It's deliberate, organised theft, and I won't have any part in it."

"What proof do you have that anyone who works for R&R is involved?" I asked.

"An anonymous tip, delivered via a third party I knew slightly," she said. "A warning to ... disassociate myself before it becomes a scandal."

"Which you're reluctant to do," I surmised.

"Wouldn't you be?" she demanded. "Whatever *else* they may be up to, my team does amazing work, locating and rescuing the injured and then recovering, identifying and reconciling the dead. Rebuilding shattered infrastructure. My people bring hope and help and closure to thousands—"

My team, I thought. *My people ...*

"I realise that and I do entirely appreciate your dilemma," Parker said soothingly, cutting her off before she could get into her stride.

"No, you don't," she shot back. "You don't appreciate just how *guilty* I feel."

That brought both of us up short. I flicked my eyes to Parker's.

"Mrs Hamilton," he said carefully, "what exactly do you have to feel guilty about?"

But she wouldn't look at either of us. "Kyle was there for security. Not only to keep the team safe but to help maintain law and order. So I asked him to ... look into what I'd heard," she said, speaking low. "And now he's dead."

"And you feel his death was a little too convenient?"

"Isn't it?" Anger pulsed through her voice. "Either it's a coincidence and he was just plain unlucky, or he was silenced. Silenced because of something *I* asked him to do," she said. "I can't take the not knowing. It's destroying my faith in R&R and the work they do. How can I be proud of something that might be so tainted? To steal from the dead, the dying or the injured. It's a desecration."

"Which is why I propose sending in Charlie," Parker said. "To put your mind at rest."

She made a brief gesture of frustration with her hands, and I realised this was probably the point where I'd come in.

"I'm sorry, Miss Fox—Charlie," she said. "I mean no offence, but Kyle Stephens was a decorated veteran of two Gulf Wars and Afghanistan, and yet still he ended up dead. And now Mr Armstrong wants to send in a young woman who can hardly have the same kind of experience or—"

"One of Charlie's many strengths is the fact people woefully underestimate her abilities," Parker said. "Trust me, she is more than capable of handling herself. If she wasn't, do you honestly believe I'd propose sending her?"

Mrs Hamilton's eyes skated over me. They lingered again on the scar at my throat and I couldn't quite decide if the sight of it reassured her or not. She bit her lower lip.

"It's very short notice," she said, as if that final point might dissuade me.

I was wearing the TAG Heuer wristwatch Sean had given me as a 'welcome to New York' gift shortly after we arrived. I checked it and did some fast mental calculations. Not for the first time since some bastard ran my Buell Firebolt off the road I cursed the fact I had yet to replace the bike. It would have halved my travel time.

"I keep a go-bag ready packed at home," I said. "I can be ready to leave in less than an hour."

Mrs Hamilton was silent for maybe half a minute. We let the silence run.

Eventually she sighed and got to her feet. "All right," she said, checking her own watch. "An hour? That's good, because the next transport plane out is due to leave the Air Cargo centre at JFK a little over three hours from now."

I smiled. "Should give me plenty of time then."

***

Parker ran me out to the airport himself, despite my protests. I appreciated the ride, but if he played personal chauffeur for me too often I was going to start getting knowing leers from the other guys and comments about how the boss was trying to get into my pants.

The problem was they wouldn't have been far wrong.

Not that Parker would ever be quite so crass, but he'd shown beyond any doubt that it would only take the slightest encouragement from me to turn our relationship into something much more personal.

He wanted me, maybe even loved me. And part of me recognised that it would have been such an easy step to take.

It would also have been totally wrong for both of us.

"Any hunches, doubts, suspicions, you call me, a-sap," he ordered as he dropped me off outside a hanger belonging to the freight company that was co-ordinating the latest earthquake relief supplies. "And Charlie—watch your six."

"I will," I said, answering both questions. I grabbed my bag from the footwell and climbed out, then paused while the howl of a jet powering through take-off made speech temporarily impossible. Then I said, "And if you hear anything from Sean …?"

His face hardened. "I've got people working on it. *When* we find him—not *if*—I'll call you," he promised. "Just as fast."

Nine

The morning after my arrival I met the final two regular members of what Mrs Hamilton had described as "the core team" that made up R&R. A thin waiflike girl and a leggy blonde bitch.

As I arrived at the mess hall where non-stop breakfast was being served, Joe Marcus was just leaving. We did the usual dance in the doorway before he stepped back and beckoned me through with a slightly impatient jerk of his head.

"You'll be working with Hope this morning. Girl over by the far wall—looks like she hasn't eaten for a month and won't eat for another," he said by way of description. "That's Hope Tyler. Don't let the appearance fool you. She's the best I've seen in a long time. But you'll get to judge that for yourself later."

I followed his eyeline and saw a girl whose youth was exaggerated by her thinness. She was all bones and sharp angles. In view of Marcus's description I eyed the way she was tucking into the typical carb-laden stodge being provided by the army camp's catering corps and concluded she had a lightning metabolism, hollow legs, or a tapeworm.

The leggy blonde bitch sat alongside her.

The bitch's name was Lemon. She was a four-year-old yellow Labrador retriever possessed of an extremely sensitive nose and the most expressive eyebrows I'd ever seen on a dog.

I loaded up my own tray with food before I went over to introduce myself. I'd eaten in hundreds of such places during my time in uniform. The country, climate and cap badges might be different but the smell remained exactly the same.

As I approached the dog sidled in and leaned heavily against my thigh. Normal rules about keeping animals and food separated did not apply in the military. If you had a dog in your

136

unit capable of sniffing out Improvised Explosive Devices, you kept it close at all times.

"Hello, and what do you want, hmm?" I murmured. "Yeah, like I couldn't guess."

The yellow Lab beat her frantic tail against my knees while she trampled on my feet. It was my most enthusiastic reception so far.

When that didn't get the dog the attention she wanted, she gave a couple of restrained barks and bounced stiff-legged off the floor a few times. I reckoned she was just trying to take a sneaky look at what was on my tray.

"Lemon, leave her alone!" Hope said, lifting her eyes from her plate for the first time. "Cor, sorry about that. If she's not wearing her harness she thinks she don't have to listen to a word I say. Lemon!"

Her accent was British, from an indeterminate mixture of regions with maybe a hint of south London at the base of it. I threaded my way towards her between the tables with the dog lurking round my heels.

"Better than the other way around I suppose. And it's no problem—I like dogs." I looked down at Lemon who had the most amazing green eyes. She put her head on one side appealingly as she tried to persuade me that she was in danger of imminent starvation unless I slipped her half my food. "Not a chance," I told her. "This bacon may need carbon dating but it's all mine."

Hope laughed. "Oh, she's got your number all right, Lem," she told the dog, rubbing the gold-tipped ears.

"Too right," I agreed. "Mind if I join you?"

"Make yourself at home," Hope said. "Always nice to come across a fellow Brit."

She had finished shovelling down her fry-up and now she straightened, wiping her mouth almost delicately before reaching for her mug. From the colour and smell, it was filled with the thick strong army tea I remembered so well and disliked so much. Like I said—some things never change.

"Joe Marcus pointed you out to me," I said once I'd unloaded my tray. I stuck out my hand. "I'm Charlie Fox. Apparently we're working together today."

Hope didn't respond right away. She just sat and stared at me with a strange look on her face as if I'd said something that didn't quite compute.

As if sensing the awkward moment developing, Lemon stuck her snout under the edge of Hope's elbow and turfed it upwards, splashing lukewarm tea all over the surface of the trestle table.

Hope protested with a cry of, "Oh, *Lemon!*" But she was laughing as she said it.

By the time we'd mopped up, and one of the squaddies had smilingly brought her a replacement mug of tea, the tension had passed. Lemon sank onto her haunches and continued to dust the floor with her tail, but more half-heartedly now. Her soulful eyes switched back and forth between the two of us like a spectator at a tennis match.

"I don't believe it," Hope said then. "When Riley said he was off to pick up the new bloke at the airport yesterday I thought, well, that you'd *be* a bloke."

She rested her elbows on the trestle table and held the mug up close to her lips. The fingernails on her skinny fingers were bitten down so far past the quick it made me wince.

"Yeah," I said. "I get that a lot."

"So you've taken over from Kyle Stephens full time then, eh?"

I shook my head. "Just until they can sort out someone permanent," I said.

She looked disappointed. "Oh, would'a been nice to have another girl to hang out with," she said. "Dr B—Dr Bertrand—well, she doesn't hang out much."

"I can imagine," I said. "We met yesterday. The frostbite hasn't started to heal yet."

Hope hid a giggle behind her mug, watching me with one bright eye over the top. "She's all right once you get to know her," she said, and seemed to surprise herself with that statement.

"How long have you been with R&R?"

"About three months," Hope said. "Only got the job 'cos I pestered 'em non-stop until they'd give us a trial." She put a hand on top of the dog's head and smoothed her fur. "Soon showed 'em though, Lem, didn't we? Soon showed 'em, girl." She looked up, a fierce pride bringing colour to her pale cheeks. "She's the best search and rescue dog ever."

Her vehemence made me wary.

"Well, apparently I'm partnering you this morning, so I'll get the chance to see her in action," I said. "I'm looking forward to it."

Lemon edged her muzzle onto the tabletop. Her eyes really were beautiful, a fact which she was only too well aware of. She fixed them on my plate and let out a gusty sigh.

"Had one of the local cops out with us yesterday," Hope said. "But they're spread so thin that if they get a call they naff off and we're all on our tod."

"Well I promise not to naff off and leave you."

"Great," she said and lowered her voice a little. "Gets a bit creepy out there sometimes. Puts the wind right up us, doesn't it, Lem?"

The dog's eyebrows rose in response. She gave another exaggerated sigh and licked her lips. I did my best to ignore her.

"Have you had any trouble?"

Hope lifted a bony shoulder. "Not as yet but it's coming. Soon as people's stocks run out and they gotta start scavenging, that's when things can get a bit hairy. And we tend to work on our own, y'see. No point in having a crowd of diggers standing around with their thumbs up their backsides until Lem's found something for 'em to dig up, is there girl?"

I assumed that last question was either rhetorical or aimed at the yellow Lab anyway. Hope didn't strike me as an ideal dog handler. Her movements were too quick and nervy. I would have thought she'd turn even the most placid animal into a twitching wreck inside the first week.

Lemon rolled her eyes in my direction causing her eyebrows to bob again. It was hard not to paint human emotions onto the gesture, as if she'd sensed my doubts.

"You worked with Kyle Stephens quite a bit then?" I asked casually.

Hope stilled. Lemon cocked her head on one side, her ears raised in query. Hope stroked her until she subsided, then mumbled, "Yeah, sometimes."

"Do you know what happened to him?" I asked. I dropped my voice to match her earlier conspiratorial level and pushed my luck. "I mean, I know he died but nobody seems to want to say how and if it's something I need to know about—so I can try to stop the same thing happening again—"

"It won't!" Hope blurted. She checked to see who might have overheard but the mess hall was busy, the level of background conversation and clatter high enough to conceal her outburst. "It won't," she repeated more quietly. "Joe told him not to but he did it anyway."

I had to lean in to hear her words. "Joe told him not to do what?"

She glanced at me quickly then, as if aware she'd already said too much. "Go into buildings that was unsafe," she said hurriedly. "That's what I heard. Joe's an engineer so he knows all about stuff like that, but Kyle didn't do what Joe told him and he got himself killed for it."

She got up, almost leapt to her feet. "I gotta go get sorted," she said. "I'll pick up our search grid and meet you out front in twenty minutes, yeah?"

And she scurried off without waiting for a reply. Lemon let her go. The dog had her head back glued to the tabletop near my plate.

My turn to sigh. I picked up the last piece of bacon and offered it to her. Lemon snatched it out of my fingers and devoured it in one swift burnt crunch before lolloping off after Hope.

I sat for a moment after they'd gone, trying to figure out how Joe Marcus had frightened the girl so badly and why.

Had she seen what happened to Kyle Stephens, I wondered, or had they simply threatened her with the same fate?

Ten

R iley flew us in low over the city. Hope, Lemon and I, along with a dig team made up of Thai, Japanese, Brit and US members, and another shrink-wrapped pallet of emergency supplies bound for who-knows-where. We squeezed around it inside the cargo bay, which didn't make for easy conversation. Neither did it make for comfort.

Some time during the night Riley had managed to beg, steal, or borrow a replacement winch for the Bell and refitted it. It may even have been the same one he'd accused the local police of filching for their own aircraft but I didn't ask and he wasn't saying.

It was bright enough that I could slip on a pair of sunglasses and stare without being obvious about it. If I thought I'd imagined him trying deliberately to dislodge me when I'd leapt for the helicopter the previous day, that period of observation confirmed my fears. His flying was flawless but his expression betrayed a conflicted man. At least it would seem he hadn't been *happy* about trying to kill me.

Well, that was always comforting to know.

But the question remained—why? Was it his own idea or was Joe Marcus pulling everyone's strings behind the scenes?

Riley was as relaxed about aviation inflight rules as he was about everything else, so we flew with the side door slid back, which at least created a swirling influx of cooler air inside the fuselage.

We made one stop along the way, to drop the dig team at their start-point location. They left with cheery goodbyes to Hope and pats to Lemon. I received the occasional nod—the new recruit who has yet to prove themselves in combat.

Lemon seemed perfectly happy to be up in a helicopter, if not actually blasé about it. She lay panting beneath Hope's canvas seat, wearing a harness with a fluorescent vest built in and bootees on all four feet. The bootees were clearly styled after human hiking boots. Bright colours, hi-tech shape, rugged soles, held in place with Velcro straps. It was rather unsettling to see a dog wearing them, doubly so when she lay down between us and stretched out her front legs.

Once we were under way Hope had recovered something of her balance. As if she was only really at ease when she was working.

Well, I can relate to that.

Now, she noticed my bemused glance at the dog's feet. "You never know what's going to be out there on the ground," she shouted over the rotor noise as though forgetting that we were both wearing headsets. "If Lem cuts her feet she could be out of action for weeks. She was a bit embarrassed about wearing 'em at first, but she's used to 'em now, aren't you, girl?"

She ran her hand over the dog's head. I could have sworn Lemon rolled her eyes again.

"Coming up on your search grid, ladies," Riley warned from the pilot's seat. "Please keep your arms and legs inside the car at all times and remain seated until the aircraft has come to a complete stop at the gate and the captain has switched off the Fasten Seatbelts sign."

Now it was Hope's turn to roll her eyes. "One of these days, Riley," she said, "you're going to do that routine and it will actually get the laugh you think it deserves."

He chuckled and managed not to cough. "Well I'm going to bloody well keep doing it until it does," he said. "Grab your gear."

Even though I'd checked through my pack before we left, I gave it another quick onceover, aware Hope was doing the same. We both carried food, water, a basic First Aid kit, GPS locator and two-way radios with a hands-free earpiece. Hope also had extra food and water for Lemon and two large cans of aerosol paint. I didn't ask what she planned on gang-tagging while she was out.

In my pack I also had four spare magazines for the SIG Sauer P229 in the small of my back beneath my shirt. Overkill maybe, but if the US Marines' motto is *Semper Fi*, meaning Always Faithful, then I preferred the Coast Guard's version—*Semper Paratus*, Always Ready. I made sure Hope didn't get a sight of the gun. No point in making her more uneasy.

Her final piece of equipment was a bedraggled-looking chew toy clipped to her belt. Every now and again I noticed Lemon giving the toy a longing glance and guessed that play time was her reward for making a successful find.

Hope had expected me to carry the extra gear and she was put out when I refused. I guessed from her slightly affronted surprise that my predecessor had done so without argument.

That told me a lot about Kyle Stephens, Gulf Wars veteran or no.

So I gave her the usual speech. She didn't like it much, but they never do.

"I'm not here to be your pack mule—you carry your own kit," I told her. "If I have to, I'll carry you *and* whatever of your stuff I can't leave behind, but let's just pray it doesn't come to that."

"What about Lem?"

I shook my head. "I can't protect both of you. Your job is to look after your dog and my job is to look after you," I said. "If anything happens, I'll get between you and the threat. If I tell you to get down, get down. Don't ask why, just do it. There won't be time to start a debate and I will not be kidding. But unless we're actually under fire don't drop flat—just crouch as low as you can and be ready to move. If Lemon's out of sight and you tell her to stay put, will she do it?"

She seemed almost offended. "'Course. I trained her myself since she was a puppy."

"Well that's what you should do then. And if I tell you to run, you run like hell and find a place to hide until I shout for you. That's when you'll know it's safe."

"I don't care about me," Hope said, "but sometimes, if people are desperate to find someone, well, they think if they get hold of Lemon they can, I dunno, jump the queue, bypass the system. So—," her eyes skated over me, dubious now, even a little scared, "—how will I know they're not forcing you to shout out?"

I met her eyes. "They won't force me."

"But supposing ..."

"I didn't say they wouldn't try," I agreed, "only that they won't succeed. I will not lure you into a trap, Hope. You can trust me on that."

She did not look convinced.

After Riley dropped us off at our designated point he was airborne again without hanging around. Anyone would think he

143

expected incoming fire. I was reminded of the mad Israeli C-130 pilot, Ari.

Maybe they were all a little touched.

Maybe they had to be.

As Riley lifted off, with the Bell's rotor wash like a physical force pressing down on us and blasting dust into our faces, I heard his voice in my ear.

"Comms check, ladies."

"Five by five," Hope said.

I went for the slightly more conventional: "Loud and clear."

"Roger that. Be careful out there. And good hunting."

Eleven

Seek on!"

Hope's instruction to Lemon was always the same, and every time the dog responded in the same way, bounding forwards with the kind of enthusiasm only Labrador retrievers really have nailed. She soon settled into an apparently meandering search pattern, leading with her nose.

I stayed a little way back and let the pair get on with it unhindered. The teamwork between the two of them, the sense of total trust, was fascinating to watch.

Every now and again Lemon would pause to stare back at her handler as if making sure of her approval. Hope never missed these glances and was always ready to urge her on. That they needed each other was obvious, as was the fact that neither of them wanted it any other way.

We were on what might once have been a fancy shopping street lined by old-fashioned buildings that had not stood up well to a quake of such magnitude. Many of the buildings had not stood at all. Of the ones that *were* still upright, it looked as though when the first tremors hit most of the revamped façades had simply sloughed away from the brickwork behind. Each had come crashing down like a concrete portcullis, crushing whatever happened to be below at the time.

I looked at the devastation and wondered how anybody, caught in such a location, could possibly have survived.

And if by some miracle they had, how the hell we were going to get them out without serious construction equipment and lifting gear, or possibly use of a Sikorsky S-64 SkyCrane.

In many ways the violently disturbed landscape reminded me of the Balkans immediately after the civil war. Constant bombardment reduced many of the once-beautiful cities to ruins such as this. Only the blast damage and the individual bullet holes and craters were missing.

That feeling of familiar unease put me on edge. It was totally against everything I'd ever learned, to be standing out in the open rather than using the jagged structures for cover and concealment. It felt even more wrong to allow my principal, Hope, to skyline herself on top of a mound of rubble as well.

Keeping her position always in the back of my mind, I scanned the wasteland as if expecting to catch the sight-flare of an enemy sniper. Everywhere I looked I saw the same indications of panic and sadness that always came with sudden attack regardless whether its origin was natural or man-made:

A single shoe, abandoned jewellery, a broken toy or a spilled shopping bag containing some kind pastry treats now gone bad and swarming with insects.

Lemon picked her way delicately over all this in her hi-tech bootees and squeezed between the twisted metal of cars that had once been parked nose-in toward the kerb. They were now squashed to the height of their wheels by the fallen masonry. She started at one end of the parade of boutique stores, disappearing in and out of tiny gaps without a qualm. Whenever she emerged she'd shake herself vigorously from nose to tail as if to get the dust out of her fur and look to Hope.

"Good girl, Lem. Good girl. No problem," Hope would tell her. "Seek on. That's my girl. Seek on."

And Lemon would trot off hunting for the next hidey hole to slip through.

The only other sound was Hope shaking the rattle cans of paint. Every time the dog left one of the buildings without indicating, Hope sprayed a prominent red square onto it, with the number 441 inside it. I was curious, but not so curious I wanted to disturb them long enough to ask about it.

Then, halfway down the west side of the street, Lemon came out of a building and immediately sat down, her expression anxious. Hope's hand shaking the paint can faltered. If it hadn't been for that, I might have thought the dog was simply tired. Hope looked hard at the building for a moment and then wordlessly replaced the red can in her bag and picked out the yellow instead.

She sprayed the same square with the same 441 inside, put the can away and took the chew toy off her belt.

146

Lemon leapt to her feet and lunged for the toy. Hope whisked it out of her way and launched it in a looping overhand throw. Lemon scrabbled for grip and galloped in pursuit, scudding up spurts of grit and small stones.

I moved up alongside Hope. She glanced at me and read the question I didn't need to ask.

"Body in there," she said briefly, jerking her head back towards the building. "When we've cleared somewhere it gets marked in red. Yellow means there's someone inside needs to be brought out. That way, when they're done the recovery team can overspray the yellow with red and there's no confusion."

Her voice was flat. It struck me again how young she looked to be working amid all this death, how she and the dog needed each other for emotional support as much as anything else.

I looked at the building again. There was no signage left on the front of it to show what kind of a store might have been in business there. Through gaps in the fallen masonry I surmised that the adjoining one, which we'd just cleared, had once sold clothing. I could see dismembered manikins still wearing the remnants of high-fashion labels with price tags to match. Now they were strewn like rags amid a glittering sea of broken glass.

Lemon reappeared with the chew toy in her mouth, head held high so it didn't snag on the debris at her feet. She looked inordinately proud of herself for this act of retrieval, delivering her spittle-covered gift into Hope's hands and grinning over it with her tongue lolling sideways. Hope dug out water and a treat from her pack. Lemon snatched the treat down in one gulp. I was reminded of my disappearing bacon.

"She's very polite," I said as Hope made a big fuss of her. "Most dogs I've come across make you work for it or just toss the thing at your feet."

"I taught her she always has to hand it over," Hope said, nodding to the glass that crunched beneath us. "Don't want her eating none of that."

I looked down and this time saw not only glass but something else sparkling amid the shards. Clear stones with far too regular a shape, ones that had been cut to show off their brightness and brilliance. And having seen one, I suddenly saw others. The significance of the colours slowly dawned on me. Not simply green, blue and red glass, but emeralds, sapphires and rubies.

Well, that answered the question of what kind of store it had been I supposed. It also supplied one of the reasons R&R needed a security presence. The prospect of bumping into looters out here was a very real one.

I nodded to the yellow spray, the corners beginning to dribble where the paint had gone on too thick. "What's with the four-four-one?"

"International phone code for the UK, which is forty-four, plus Lem and I are Team One." Again that hint of pride. "Joe says it's the easiest way to let the other teams know who marked it, so they can keep track. The Japanese crew tags with eighty-one, the New Zealanders sixty-four. That's pretty standard, I think. It was Joe came up with the colour scheme though."

"It's a good system," I agreed. The former Marine, it seemed, had a practical mind-set when it came to dealing with death.

But then, I'd already worked that one out.

"He's the best at what he does," Hope said as if reading my thoughts. Her face turned a little wistful. "That's why I wanted to work with him."

"How long have you been doing this kind of stuff?"

"Long enough." It had been a casual question but she stiffened as if I'd implied she had no experience on which to base her claim.

"I wasn't casting aspersions," I said mildly. "You have to admit, though, you don't look old enough to drive."

"I'm twenty," she said quickly. "That's old enough, isn't it?" She busied herself with packing away the dog's water bowl and clipping the chew toy back onto her belt. Lemon watched her with that slightly anxious expression back on her face.

Me and my mouth.

"Look, I'm sorry—" I began.

"'S OK. I 'spose I just get that a lot," she mumbled. "Hey, we really need to get back to work. Come on, Lem, you ready? Seek on then, girl. Seek on!"

Lemon bounced away again, sniffed a circle in front of the next storefront and limbo'd through another impossible gap.

As we moved off I glanced down but Hope was tidy and methodical. There was nothing left behind except the glittering shards of broken glass with the brighter sparks of diamonds among them.

But maybe—just maybe—I couldn't see quite as many as there were before. I would have asked her about that, but with perfect timing, Lemon chose that moment to reappear.

She shoved her head through and then wriggled her tight-packed body out of the narrow gap. She stood alert and quivering, her gaze totally focused on Hope, and let out half a dozen rapid barks.

Hope went rigid. Despite the heat of the day, all the hairs came up along my forearms.

"A live find," she mumbled for my benefit, although I hardly needed to be told. "Means she's made a live find."

I glanced over, saw the pallor of her thin features, the tension in her body.

"What colour do we spray for that?" I asked but she shook her head.

"We don't," she said, reaching for her radio. "We wait."

Twelve

The dig team turned up half an hour later, by which time we'd already checked the remaining stores on that side of the street.

Lemon had shown little interest until she stopped abruptly and sat down again when she neared the end of the row. I was the one who ventured close enough to discover a family of three dead inside their flattened car. The child in the back was still strapped into his booster seat.

Hope made sure she threw Lemon's chew toy in the opposite direction as if she didn't want the dog to see what it was she'd found. Maybe that was simply my take on things and it was Hope herself who didn't want to see.

All in all, it did not feel like a good time to ask about the gems lying in the street.

The dig team was a mix of nationalities led by a redheaded figure I instantly recognised, despite his borrowed local police coveralls.

"Well, well, Charlie," Wilson said. "We meet again."

I shook the Glaswegian copper's hand. "Couldn't stay away, huh?"

He grinned at me, but when his eyes shifted across to Hope I saw his eyebrows lift a notch.

It was hard not to see what he saw—an impossibly young-looking girl and a Labrador who wasn't helping matters by acting like a brainless family pet on a run in the park.

"How are you liking the work with R&R then?" he asked.

"Early days yet."

"Well, let me know if you get fed up, eh?"

"Hang on. I thought you were after a job with Parker?"

He grinned. "Just keeping my options open. I hear it's quite a cushy number."

I thought of the near miss jumping for the Bell and gave him a wry smile. "It has its moments."

"Right then, we better get started," he said. "Want to show us the spot?"

Hope led him there with Lemon ambling beside her, the chew toy still clutched in her mouth and those remarkable green eyes unblinking. By the time they reached the place where Lemon had indicated, he was frowning.

"You're quite sure, eh?"

Hope flushed and put a defensive hand on the dog's head. "'Course," she said.

He glanced at me as if hoping to glean some information about how seriously to take this. "Joe Marcus tells me she's the best he's seen in a long time," I said without inflection.

Wilson considered this and then nodded. "Good enough."

"Isn't he coming—Joe, I mean?" Hope demanded.

"Not for this one," Wilson said. "Don't worry yourself though. I like my own skin too much to risk losing it needlessly. I've had a bit of experience myself, so we'll be careful, eh?"

Once the dig team got started it seemed clear to me that they knew what they were doing. They scanned with a portable gas leak detector before the two-stroke masonry saw came out. The fourteen-inch circular blade soon created a gap large enough for a man to crawl through.

The smallest of the diggers—a Japanese guy—was selected to go in. He wore a miner's hard hat with an LED lamp, as well as a safety harness with rope attached. They paid out the rope as he ventured further inside just as if he'd been caving. In a way I suppose he was.

Hope waited off to one side with Lemon. The girl's tension had communicated itself to the dog and the chew toy was failing to distract either of them. Lemon was snuffling around in the dirt and picking up small pebbles in her soft mouth which she solemnly offered to Hope. Hope took each one, ignoring the coating of slobber and put it absently into her pocket as if she didn't want to offend the dog by throwing away the gift. Her eyes were glued to the dig team as she wiped her hand down the side of her trousers.

Eventually the rope went slack and they began slowly to reel it in. The Japanese guy emerged with a mixture of concrete and brick dust smeared into the sweat on his face.

"I found a couple near the front wall of the main structure about ten yards back thataway. Man and a woman," he called across in a strong California accent. He looked at Hope. "I'd guess they've been dead a while. I'm sorry."

Wilson's gaze passed over me with a faint trace of scepticism before it landed on Hope. "Sorry, pal," he said. "Luck of the game, I guess."

"But ... that can't be right." She stumbled over the words. "Lem told me ... there's no *way* she's wrong ..."

Wilson shrugged. "Well, we tried, eh?"

Hope's colour rose and fell fast as a traffic light. She moved nearer, put out a staying hand to the Japanese guy who'd just crawled from under the rubble. "You *have* to go again," she pleaded. "Lemon don't get it wrong. Once she's had a sniff of something she can follow it anywhere. You have to ... please."

The Japanese guy hesitated and looked to his team leader, alarmed not so much by her vehemence as the possibility she was about to burst into tears.

"Hey, now," Wilson said. He went to put a placatory hand on Hope's arm but she jerked away from him. The habitual goofy smile on Lemon's face disintegrated into a snarling growl as she jumped stiff-legged between them.

Before I could intervene, Wilson jerked back instantly. He'd clearly encountered enough guard dogs in his time, both police and military, to be leery of them. Hope spun away with a wordless click of her fingers. Lemon followed as if attached to her leg by a very short chain, staring up at her handler and letting out a series of small high-pitched squeaks.

I came up alongside Wilson and watched her rigid stance with concern.

"Now what the feck was *that* all about, eh?" he asked softly.

I had my suspicions but I wasn't going to voice them. That would have raised too many questions, least of all about how I'd come by my knowledge. I shook my head.

"Supposing she *is* right? Do you want that on your conscience?" I waited a beat. "Do me a favour will you? You're here now. Just get your guy to take one more look."

The Japanese guy who'd discovered the woman's body was hovering, helmet in hand and the straps loosened on his harness. His eyes flicked between us, wary of the atmosphere. "I don't mind going again, dude. Better to be sure, huh?"

Wilson looked from one of us to the other and sighed. "How tight is it for space in there?"

The Japanese guy shrugged. "Once you get past the cars it opens out a little onto what used to be the sidewalk," he said. "We might need some help finding a way into the store itself, if we need to go that far."

Wilson nodded. "I better come with you then, pal," he said. "Give you a hand."

The Japanese guy pulled his harness tight again quickly, as if worried either of them might change his mind.

We watched in silence as the two men adjusted their hard hats and knee pads. Wilson folded several body bags into his coveralls, knowing he'd need a couple and, I supposed, hoping he wouldn't need more.

Then they crawled carefully back through the gap they'd created. Even Hope edged closer again while Lemon plonked herself down in the dust and twisted round to nip at an itch on her back. Flies buzzed around our heads, their drone mixing with the distant chop of rescue, police and military helicopters.

Two of the dig team held the men's safety lines, letting them out steadily through their gloved fingers as the pair worked their way deeper inside. It struck me then that they weren't actually safety lines at all—they were recovery lines, should the worst happen.

And just as that cheery thought formed in my head, the ground began to tremble under our feet.

153

Thirteen

Somebody shouted, "Aftershock!" and there was a concerted rush away from what was left of the nearest buildings while we could still stand.

The tremble became a shudder that grew in violence until it was like being back in the Hercules dropping through holes in the sky. I'd never experienced the feel of severe turbulence while still at ground level before. I half dropped to my knees before I was thrown the rest of the way. Around me the others flattened themselves too, an instinctive reaction.

I lifted my head briefly to check on Hope's position. She was well out in the open, crouched on knees and elbows as the training dictated. She had one hand wrapped round the back of her neck and the other latched through the dog's collar. Lemon lay on her belly alongside, crowding in with her ears flat, trying to lick Hope's face. I wasn't sure if she was offering comfort by doing this, or taking it.

The rumbling through the ground was like the biggest heaviest subway train passing directly beneath us. It must have had a load of carriages, too, because it went on and on for more than twenty seconds before it finally began to die away.

I had to remind myself there *was* no subway and no train.

Staggering to my feet, I struggled to get my balance now the earth was still.

"Everybody OK?" I called. I got a series of cautious nods and waves by way of reply. I moved quickly over to where the safety lines snaked out from between the cars. To do so I had to hop across a crack in the road that I was damn sure hadn't been there a few minutes previously. Wisps of dust or steam rose gently from it like an outward breath.

"Wilson!" I shouted, ashamed that I didn't know the other guy's name. I listened a moment. Nothing. I turned to nearest member of the dig team. "Let's get them out of there. Do they have their radios?"

A handset was shoved at me. It was the same as mine, just tuned to a different frequency. I pressed the transmit button.

"Wilson, this is Fox. You guys OK in there?"

I half-expected an eerie silence but instead the Scot's laconic tones came back to me right away.

"Aye, but I'd appreciate you not stamping around out there in the big boots, pal," he said, coughing. "That last one brought down a mite of debris, but we're clear and Ken thinks we may have a way through, so looks like it's done us a favour, eh? We'll bag up the two dead and hook up our lines so you can pull them out—give us more room to work with. Three birds, one stone, eh?" He began coughing again.

"Have that," I said. "Standing by."

We waited until there was a jerk on his recovery line and then dig team began the slow and solemn process of hauling the first corpse out of the rubble.

Wilson and the Japanese guy, Ken, appeared briefly at gap between the cars to help push the body bag the last few feet. Their clothing and faces were caked in dust. I unclipped Wilson's line and passed it back to him.

They repeated the process with the second body, which was larger and took more effort. We were all sweating in the heat by the time we were done. Wilson took off his helmet briefly to wipe his face.

"All right, we'll go take another look for this live one. Standard radio checks every five minutes," he said to one of his team. He put a hand on the body bag we'd just pulled clear. "Let's hope we don't need another of these, eh?" And with that he disappeared back into the void.

Between us we carried the bodies of the dead couple clear and laid them down gently. Two labels were written in clear characters, assigning each of them a Unique Reference Number that would stay with them until they were finally identified and reconciled.

The rest of the dig team had been working to retrieve the family in the crushed car. There were already another couple of body bags laid out on the open ground and we put our burden alongside it, also with URN labels attached.

From the size of one of the bags, I judged that was the child from the back seat. A member of the dig team crossed himself, lips moving in some silent prayer.

I turned away, just in time to see a new group approaching, picking their way along the half-blocked road. Something about the way they moved had me reaching a hand for the SIG at my back, but then I stilled. The coveralls they wore were the same as the police officers I'd seen waiting to pick up Wilson at the airport. Even the moustaches and the aviator sunglasses looked the same, too. They were all armed. Old-fashioned leather holsters with a press-stud flap, making it impossible to gauge what lay inside.

Again I checked on Hope's location, made sure she was well back, and then waited for them to reach us, calling a casual hello before they got too close.

They stopped, as I'd hoped they would, before they were among us. One man pushed forward, giving a desultory wave.

"The aftershock came just after we landed," he said, indicating some unseen helo off behind his group, hidden by the tumbled buildings. "We're just checking everyone here is OK, yes?"

He was middle-aged and slim apart from a protruding belly, but he was coping well with the heat and didn't look out of breath having to pick his way over rough terrain.

"We're fine," I said, noting the way his eyes slid to the body bags and the team members crouched by the gap between the cars with the two recovery lines stretching inside. "I didn't know anyone else was working this sector."

He regarded me for a moment, his eyes impossible to read behind the aviators. "I'm Peck," he said at last, motioning to the police insignia on the breast pocket of his coveralls. "Divisional commander."

His official ID was on a lanyard around his neck, with the plastic badge tucked out of the way into the pocket. I wore my own the same way and now I lifted it clear between two fingers.

"Charlie Fox, R&R," I said, adding pleasantly, holding it level for him to read. "And now you've seen mine I'm sure you won't object to showing me yours?"

Clearly he *did* object but there wasn't much he could do to refuse. He freed his ID and would have flashed it briefly but I managed to snag it for a closer look. I matched the picture to the man in front of me and surreptitiously checked the laminated edges for tampering.

"Thanks. Sorry about that," I said with a shrug as I handed it back. *Only following orders, guv.* "But I'm under strict instructions from Joe Marcus to verify everyone."

Marcus hadn't mentioned anything of the sort, but the name had resonance for Peck, I could tell, even though he tried to hide his reaction behind a noncommittal grunt.

"Of course," he added quickly. "It would be my advice to you also." He stepped around me and headed for the body bags. Now I'd confirmed he was there in an official capacity I didn't see how I could reasonably object. I settled for being annoying rather than outright obstructive and ambled alongside him instead. That seemed to work.

"Where did you find these people?" he asked.

I let one of Wilson's team fill him in as the final body from the car was laid with the others.

When Peck spoke again his words might have been casual but his tone allowed little room for discussion. He pointed to the line of zipped bags and said, "I'd like to take a look."

Fourteen

Commander Peck pulled down the zip on the first bag, revealing the woman from the car. She'd been in the passenger seat and closest to the falling masonry. Peck zipped the bag up again quickly and moved to the next. I glanced at the faces of Wilson's people and saw from their horrified reactions that this was a long way from normal procedure.

To everyone's relief, I think, Peck passed over the child's figure and unzipped the second bag. The man who'd been driving had survived a little longer and at least had a face Peck could frown over.

I heard movement behind me. Hope was scrambling towards us.

"Hey, what's he doing?" she demanded. "Leave them alone."

Peck barely glanced at her. "It is my duty to make immediate identifications if that is possible," he said. "This is my area and I have received many missing persons' reports. Some of these persons may well be known to me."

He took longer looking at the male corpse Wilson and Ken had dragged out, although I would hazard a guess that the man's own mother would not have recognised his face. Peck was thorough, patting all the pockets, but he found no ID, closed the bag again and bent over the woman.

"You shouldn't be doing that!" Hope protested, more loudly now. Her eyes shot to mine. "Charlie, can't you make him stop?"

"Commander," I snapped, "I'm sure you'll get your chance to make formal IDs once the bodies have been transported to the official mortuary."

But he'd already opened the body bag and was dipping his hands into the woman's pockets without taking any notice. When he straightened, he had a wallet in his hands which he flipped open.

"Hmm. This one I think I do know of. I will check with headquarters," he announced. "You will be informed." And he shut the wallet again before slipping it into the side pocket of his coveralls.

Hope moved forward and got in his face. Her eyes were barely on a level with the base of Peck's nose, but she suddenly seemed bigger. Maybe that had something to do with the fact that Lemon was standing beside her, growling deep in her chest. A line of fur had risen from the back of her neck and tapered away down her spine.

Peck was watching the dog very carefully. Lemon pulled back her lips and treated him to a display of every one of her impressive teeth. Without taking his eyes off her, his right hand slid up and meaningfully unsnapped the stud securing his holster.

By the time he'd done so the SIG was out in my hand and lined up on the bridge of his nose.

"Hey," I said quietly. "She—and the dog—are under my protection. Think carefully before you act."

Peck shifted his eyes from the end of the SIG's barrel to my face and beyond it. He showed his teeth in a similar way to Lemon and said then, "I would strongly advise you to do the same, my friend."

Behind me I heard the unmistakable metallic click of the hammer being thumbed back on a service pistol.

"Oh, I always think before I act," I said. "And either way it goes, the outcome for you does not look promising, does it?"

He absorbed that in glowering silence before signalling curtly to the man behind me. I heard the hammer released, the rasp of leather, and only then allowed my arm to drop.

Hope was staring at the pair of us, wild-eyed. Wilson's own dig team looked as though they were praying for another aftershock—one big enough to open up a massive sink-hole and swallow the lot of us.

The radio clipped to the shoulder of Peck's coveralls began to squawk then. He reached for it, adjusted one of the knobs and tilted it towards his mouth, pointedly turning his back on me. I used the opportunity to glance behind me and met the stony faces of his men. It was difficult to tell which of them had drawn on me. They all looked eager for the task.

Peck finished his transmission and rapped out orders. He turned back and gave us a nod. "I am needed elsewhere," he said.

I'm sure I wasn't the only one who resisted the urge to say, "Good."

His men had already begun to move off but before could do so himself, Hope stepped forwards. Unaccountably, I saw she was offering him a shy smile.

"I'm sorry—about before," she said in a slightly breathy voice. "I didn't mean to be rude. And Lemon's just a bit over-protective of me, aren't you, girl?" She looked down to the dog who was staring back up at her adoringly. "She's just a big softy really." Hope seemed to give a little twitch that might have been a shrug.

Lemon skipped over to Peck and butted him in the knees in a clumsy display of affection. Reluctantly, he leaned down to pat her flank and, seemingly encouraged by this, she bounced up and got her booteed feet nearly to his shoulders. He staggered back under the unexpected weight with a sharp curse.

Hope gave a rather ineffectual cry of, "Lemon!" and dashed to grab the dog's collar, but struggled to drag her off him. Then she started frantically brushing the dirt and dust bootprints left by the dog's feet from his clothing. She wasn't too careful where she put her hands and after a moment he paddled her away, face flushing. And all the time, Lemon leapt around them, barking.

"Please!" Peck said stiffly. "Please, it is no matter. I am dressed for the work."

It was neatly done. The noise, the dancing dog, the profuse apologies and exaggerated waving of hands that acted as a complete distraction. So I was probably the only one who noticed Hope's nimble fingers slip into the police commander's coverall pocket. When they came out again the dead woman's wallet was pinched between them. But by the time the girl had pulled Lemon a few stride away and calmed her, her hands were empty and her face was without guile.

Into the quiet that followed came a burst of radio static. Not from Peck's police network this time, but from one of the handsets issued to the dig team. And then, loud and clear, I heard Wilson's voice over the air:

"Hey! We got someone here. We got someone. And he's still alive!"

160

Fifteen

I sat in a hospital corridor waiting to talk to a man who might or might not regain consciousness. Been there, done that. Didn't like it much the last time.

It was only mid-afternoon but already it had been a very long day that was barely halfway over.

The whole atmosphere had changed out there with the realisation of a live find. A sudden energy and purpose swept over everyone as they put their strategies into operation. There was nothing worse, I was told, than finding someone alive but bringing them out dead.

I could think of a few things that were infinitely worse, but I kept them to myself.

Commander Peck and his men slipped away before they could be volunteered to help dig. And as soon as they were out of sight Hope used the increased level of activity to cover her return of the wallet to the dead woman's body bag. Just for a second I debated on tackling her about that deft sleight of hand, but decided against. Her ability was curious, but until I knew if it was significant to the death of Kyle Stephens it was better to pretend I'd hadn't seen a thing.

That was the trouble with uncovering secrets—you couldn't pick and choose.

Getting the injured man out of the ground was a painstaking task that called for many different kinds of expertise. Keeping him alive until he could be freed, and not bringing down the rest of the building on top of him in the process were the two main difficulties. Wilson radioed in for reinforcements and it did not surprise me that the two figures next on scene were Joe Marcus and Dr Bertrand, arriving in the khaki-coloured Bell with Riley at the flight controls. He set down with a casual elegance onto the uneven piles of bricks at the end of the street.

Dr Bertrand swept past us and immediately started interrogating the dig team about the condition of the casualty. But Joe Marcus took a moment to have a word with Hope. She seemed bursting to tell him something, but he put a hand on her arm to stay her. Even from a distance I could see his lips form a single word: "Later."

As he turned away and caught me watching the pair of them, his gaze issued a flat challenge:

You may think you've just seen something but you haven't, and if you're wise you won't push this further.

What makes you think I'm wise?

But the most interesting thing about the encounter, to my mind, was the fact that when Joe Marcus touched her, Hope didn't flinch at all.

Lemon was sent in twice more, under Hope's direction, to pinpoint the position of the trapped man more accurately. I heard her barking in there as if to say, "It's so obvious. What's the matter with you people?"

I helped load the three bodies into the Bell. They had each been tagged with a Unique Reference Number, with the same URNs added to the bags of personal items collected from close nearby.

It was not the first time I'd handled body bags but I can't say I've ever enjoyed the experience, and it's not something you want to get used to. The bodies inside graunched and folded in places they were not supposed to fold when fully intact.

"I'll drop them off at the morgue after we've got this other guy to hospital," Riley said. But he glanced back frowning at the lumps of masonry that were being cleared away from the man's position. "Or maybe I'll only have to make the one stop, you reckon?"

But against all the odds, they brought the buried man out alive. He was bleeding from a vicious head-wound, crazed, dehydrated, barely conscious and with the bones of his left forearm visible for the world to see, but he appeared to have escaped the worst of what might have been.

Dr Bertrand pumped him full of painkillers via a rapidly inserted cannula into the back of his right hand, stabilised his left arm, put a neck collar on him and set up a bag of fluids. She moved with brisk efficiency and inside a couple of minutes he was on a stretcher being carried towards the Bell.

162

"Charlie, go with 'im and get 'is identity," Dr Bertrand ordered. "Oh, and see if the woman found nearby was known to 'im, also."

Maybe it was the lack of "please" or "thank you" that made me dig my heels in enough to argue. "My place is here, with Hope," I said. "I promised I wouldn't go anywhere without her."

The doctor had been already turning away and she stopped as if amazed to be questioned. It was Joe Marcus who stepped in.

"Hope's done enough for the day. She'll be heading back with us so there's nothing for you here," he said quietly, a host of meanings concealed beneath his measured tone. "But that guy will have family waiting for him. Going with him—maybe finding out his story—will put someone else's mind at rest."

Not much I could say to that, really, which was how I came to be sitting on an uncomfortable plastic chair in a hospital corridor at midnight, waiting.

He was in surgery for a fractured skull, I was told. They would let me know as soon as he was in recovery.

By chance I saw one of the same nurses who'd taken charge of the boy from the roadside the day before. I stopped her briefly as she hurried past and asked about him.

"I'm so sorry. He ... didn't make it," she said. "We did everything we could but in the end we lost him." She frowned at me, weariness in her face, her voice and her body. "I called Dr Bertrand last night. Didn't she pass on the news?"

"No." I shook my head. The nurse seemed disturbed enough for me to add a harmless fiction: "I'm sure she meant to—when she had a moment."

The nurse nodded and dashed away.

I settled back in my chair. It seemed only yesterday that I had waited, on and off, for nearly four months in chairs like these. Waited for Sean Meyer to come back to me.

And he almost had.

163

Sixteen

Even though the Sean Meyer I got back was not the same man who left me behind in that split second between the finger pulling the trigger and the bullet leaving the gun, I still thought there might be a chance for us.

Right up until Mexico City.

Not that Sean went to Mexico City, and perhaps that omission was at the heart of the matter. His first time out in the field since his recovery had not ended well and he was vacillating about his whole future in the close-protection industry.

Parker refused to accept his resignation and instead persuaded him to take care of glad-handing clients at the office in New York while Parker himself went back to the sharp end of the game as needed.

For this reason, when a high profile assignment came up south of the border Sean stayed to co-ordinate things at home and I flew out there as part of a team that included Parker.

The Mexico City job had been hazardous but successful—one of those rare occasions when everything just goes right. It hadn't been without incident but, even when we came under fire, the plans, backup plans and contingencies we'd put in place all unfurled like a dream and the clients were left seriously singing our praises.

In the army they drummed into us that no battle plan ever survives first contact with the enemy. I suppose there has to be an exception that proves every rule.

We landed at La Guardia on the return journey and Parker drove us into the city. He was still on a post-combat high. I'd never seen my normally calm and contained boss so buzzed up but his enthusiasm was infectious.

It hadn't abated by the time he pulled up at the kerb outside my apartment building. Living closest to the office I was the last of the team to be dropped off, so it was just the two of us.

We sat there for a while in one of the company Navigators with the engine running quietly, still going over the details, trying to work out how something good could be made even better. Eventually—with reluctance, I admit—I climbed out to retrieve my bag from the back. When I slammed the Navigator's rear door and turned, I found Parker waiting for me on the kerb.

"Thanks again, Charlie," he said, a smile crinkling the corners of his eyes.

"What for?"

"For being a superstar," he said. "Money can't buy the kind of great publicity we'll score from this job."

He was grinning like a kid. On impulse, I stepped forward and gave him a hug.

Mistake.

Before I knew it he'd lifted and swung me round off my feet.

"Parker! You idiot, put me down."

He did so, still grinning, but I saw the moment his expression shifted, saw those cool grey eyes flick down to my mouth and felt his arms tighten around me.

"Parker—" I said again. A warning this time, but it was already too late.

His head dipped. His kiss was a taste, a delicate nip that became a headlong plunge. His hands came up to frame my face, thumbs smoothing the line of my jaw, the hollow under my cheekbone, fingers at the base of my skull.

At that moment it would have been so easy to let myself fall into him, weightless. All the pent-up frustration, the feeling of utter rejection, the longing, suddenly came flooding out of me as I began to tumble. Just for a second I kissed him back almost on a reflex. Then reality jolted in.

I brought my hands up to grasp his wrists but he had already broken the kiss. He wrapped his hands protectively around mine and touched our foreheads together, still holding me close.

"I know, I know, I'm sorry. I promised myself I wouldn't do this," he muttered. "But ..."

His voice trailed away. I swallowed and found it took effort to speak.

"I'm sorry too," I said. "I should learn to keep my distance."

He gave a soft laugh. "Well, every now and again I'm glad you don't," he said. "If only it could be 'now'. *And* 'again' ..."

I made a noise of protest in my throat and shifted my hands. He released me at once.

"I'll see you in the office tomorrow morning," he said, stepping back and striving for normal. He cleared his throat. "Debrief is at oh-nine-thirty."

"Yessir," I said, smiling. "Nine-thirty? You going soft on us, boss?"

He grinned as he turned away, making a 'don't go there' gesture with his hand, and threw back over his shoulder, "Get some rest, Charlie. You've earned it."

I was still smiling as picked up my bag and slung the strap over my shoulder, watching the Navigator move out into traffic. I glanced up at the apartment block. I knew which windows belonged to the apartment Sean and I shared but there was no sign of life behind the glass.

I rode the lift up to our floor with the feel of Parker's mouth still on mine like an imprint. I scrubbed my hands across my face not caring if I smeared my makeup. I never wore much anyway and a very long, very hot shower was first order of business.

As I unlocked our front door and moved along the hallway I called out, but there was no reply. The place was silent and empty. I felt my shoulders droop and wondered if it was with disappointment or relief.

At the edge of the living area I let the bag strap slide off my shoulder, unzipped it and dug inside for my gun case. I'd cleaned and stripped the SIG for transport in secure hold baggage, and I would clean it again before I reassembled it in the morning. But right now the shower beckoned.

I shoved the weapon and my boxes of spare ammunition into the gun safe mounted in the floor of the main bedroom, taking a quick glance round while I was in there. Sean kept the place so orderly it bordered on impersonal. I wondered if it was an indication of his state of mind.

I abandoned my travel bag and headed straight for the bathroom, stripping off as I went and leaving my travel-stained clothing where it fell. Then I stood under needles of water dialled lethally hot with my eyes closed and my hands braced against the tiles.

I don't know how long I'd been in there but the glass walls of the shower cubicle were steamed opaque when Sean Meyer's voice cut through the drumming downpour.

"Trying to wash away the guilt along with the smell of him are you, Charlie?"

I twisted blindly in the direction of the sound, gasping into the humid air, but the combination of wet hair and water in my eyes meant I could hear but not see him. All I knew was he was somewhere close.

It seemed a long time since Sean had wanted to see me naked to the point where he'd deliberately invaded my space like this. We still shared the apartment but very much separately. We hadn't shared a bedroom—never mind a bed—for months. It never occurred to me to lock the bathroom door because he hadn't shown the least inclination to walk in on me.

After the shock of his arrival, it took longer for the words themselves to penetrate.

"Trying to wash away the guilt along with the smell of him ..."
What the—?

Furious, I swiped a hand across the glass at head-height and glared out. Sean was leaning in the doorway still dressed for the office. As a nod to being off duty he'd discarded his tie and the jacket of his dark grey suit, and rolled back his shirtsleeves. With his arms folded across his chest the action showed off the muscle bulk he'd worked so hard to regain after the coma.

He couldn't have made me feel more trapped if he'd set his mind to it.

I prayed that was not the case.

"I didn't realise you were here," I said, struggling to keep my voice neutral, as if nothing unusual or unsettling was taking place. There was no way I wanted to start an argument from this kind of disadvantaged position. "I'll be out shortly. Can you give me a few minutes?"

Instead he levered away from the doorframe and stalked forwards, letting his arms drop. I resisted the urge to cover my body from his gaze. Even with all its wounds and scars, it was nothing he hadn't seen before.

But not like this.

Even so, I didn't expect him to yank open the cubicle door heedless of the pounding spray. The steam roiled out, sucking a billowing waft of cold air in over my skin which goose bumped instantly.

"Sean!" I protested, low and shaky. "Get out!"

But he just stood there, subjecting me to a long scrutiny while his hair and clothing absorbed the sodden heat.

I felt my chin lift, my shoulders square. I met his gaze with defiance despite the colour flaring in my cheeks.

"What I asked," he repeated with deadly precision, "was—"

"I know what you damn well asked," I threw back, not bothering to waste my breath on questions when it was only too obvious what he'd been asking. "But if you think I'm going to discuss that kind of wild accusation in here like this—"

"What better time?" he demanded. "And where better place?"

And before I knew it he'd swung the door wide and stepped fully dressed into the shower with me.

The water beat his hair flat to his skull and ran from his brows, pushing his eyes into shadow behind the flow. The shirt turned transparent in a moment, the dry-clean-only suit trousers ruined.

The shower cubicle was a generous size. We'd shared it in the past but back then we'd been more than happy to occupy the same footprint, the same heartbeat. Now, when I was trying to keep him from touching me, it seemed impossibly small.

Sean bunched me back into the tiled wall, grabbed both wrists and wrenched my hands above my head, holding them there bracketed in his left. He was right-handed, but the gunshot wound to his left temple had affected his right side and he was still building back the strength of his grip. The fact he'd deliberately chosen to use the hand currently stronger, going against natural dominance, sent alarm bells clanging inside my head.

"I wasn't 'here' when you arrived, but I was close by all right," he said then in a savage whisper. "Close enough to see your fond farewell to Parker. The man *you* work for. The man *I'm* in partnership with. The man I'm supposed to trust."

I jerked my hands but he tightened his grip, stretching my arms a little more taut overhead until my muscles began to quiver. He leaned in, right hand fisted into the wall alongside me for balance. And all the time the water lashed down on the pair of us like a tropical typhoon.

"So how long's it been going on between the two of you, Charlie? Were you using him as a substitute for me all those months when I wasn't around to … satisfy you? Just how long did you wait before you and he—"

"Enough!" I snapped, my voice vibrating with anger. "Think the worst of me if you want, Sean. Why not? You always did before. But leave Parker out of this!"

"How can I?" he demanded, "when I saw the way you went to him out there, and I saw the way he kissed you. Got it bad, hasn't he?" He leaned in closer still, so the water splashed from his face down onto mine. I told myself that was the reason I shut my eyes. "So I think I have a right to know—does he touch you like this?"

I began, "You have no rights—"

Sean's free slicked up my ribcage to cup my breast, tormenting with fingers that knew how to cause both intimate pleasure and pain. Too long denied, I responded in spite of myself. Heat blossomed low in my belly, flushing the surface of my skin.

Sean sensed it and gave a mirthless laugh.

"Or this?"

He claimed my mouth in punishment while his hands balanced me teetering between restraint and caress.

I gasped onto his tongue and he swallowed the little mewl as if stealing my voice and my soul. From the first, Sean had seemed to know all my body's secrets. Hell, he had created most of them. I tore my mouth free.

"I've never slept with Parker!" I cried wildly. "Yes, I know how he feels about me. But he knows I can't give him what he truly wants and he would never force me to try."

I don't know what finally got to him. Maybe it was the word "force" that did it. That and the fact that Parker—his friend, even his mentor—would not stoop so low.

Sean's head lifted. I felt the shift in his balance, braced my right arm and jerked down hard with my left, rotating my fist against the joint between his forefinger and thumb—the weakest part of his grip. Pulled in opposite directions, his hand sprang open.

I let my knees sag until I was almost squatting in the shower tray, then drove my heels downwards and surged up again. I kept my arms bent close to my chest and used the power from my legs instead. Both clenched fists landed in the fleshy vee beneath Sean's ribs, angled sharply upwards, with enough force even in the confined space to paralyse his diaphragm.

He fell back, chest heaving as he tried to claw air into his lungs. Without bothering to shut off the water I looped my arm through his from the front and kept him going. Before he knew it I'd marched him backwards out of the shower cubicle, stumbling through the bathroom and into the hallway.

The punch was an improvised close-quarter technique that came from the necessity of fighting in an enclosed space. The arm lock was standard for neutralising and removing troublemakers from a crowd. I wondered if Sean would find it ironic that he was the one who'd taught it to me.

In the living area I manoeuvred him around my open travel bag and sent him sprawling over the arm of the sofa. He landed heavy on the cushions, still shuddering for breath and now shivering in his drenched clothes.

The suit was past repair in any case, so I wasn't careful how I stripped him of his trousers and everything beneath. Why should I be the only one naked?

He didn't help but I didn't need him to. About half the shirt buttons remained attached. The rest were scattered to the four corners.

At least his Breitling wristwatch was waterproof to greater depths than we'd just plumbed. I was unfastening the strap by the time he had the breath to speak.

"Charlie," he rasped. "What the hell are you doing?"

He tried to bat my hands away but he was still in enough respiratory distress to make it a poor attempt. I twisted his wrist into another lock, one I could maintain using only two fingers and my thumb. With my free hand I reached for him, let him feel my nails curve against the most sensitive area of his skin.

He froze. I could almost see the beads of sweat pop out among the water on his forehead.

"What am *I* doing?" I echoed tightly. "What do you bloody well think? I'm doing the same to you as you were going to do to me."

I watched his eyes as I said it and watched the flare in them, the way his pupils dilated. It might be lust rather than love, but I told myself at this stage I'd settle for what I could get.

I tightened my grip, relentless. He might have forgotten the last four years we had together but I had not. Every place I'd ever touched him, every time I'd sent him up in flames for me, I could recall in clear and utter detail.

And now I used that knowledge coldly, ruthlessly, to drive any jealous thoughts of Parker, disdain for me or disgust with himself, right out of his head. By the time I released the lock on his wrist he could do nothing but hold onto me.

But in the morning, he was gone.

Seventeen

All I could think about was getting out of there."

The man in the hospital bed had his eyes fixed on mine but I knew he didn't see me. His voice was raspy from the screaming and the acid-etch of concrete dust in his throat.

"How much can you remember?" I asked, but he let his head drop and I realised I should have reworded the question. *How much are you willing to remember?*

"I mean, it would help if we could start with who you are?" I said, trying to give out an encouraging vibe, "You weren't carrying any identification when you were found."

He frowned for a moment and then said, "My name is Santiago Rojas. I came here from São Paulo in Brazil, I think ten years ago. This much I know. I remember my past, my family back home, my work there, but here?" He gave me a hesitant smile and gestured toward his head. "I am struggling to recall anything about the last few years, never mind last week, or yesterday."

"Don't try to force it. It will come back to you in its own time," I said but I looked at the dressings around the surgical repairs to his skull and could not prevent the voice in the back of my mind from adding, *if it's going to come back at all ...*

He nodded and used his unbroken arm to push himself uneasily straighter against the thin hospital pillow. There was only one to cushion him against the angled metal bedframe, but the way the casualties had been coming in steadily from all over the city, he was lucky even to have a bed.

"Can you perhaps tell me," Rojas asked, "was I found at my place of work? I know I have a store in the tourist district—I sell jewellery and deal in precious stones."

His voice carried a hint of something, as if he was trying to remind himself as much as inform me. And suddenly it was

172

fiercely important to me that he *did* remember. For those close to him, if not for himself.

Don't project, I told myself. *It's not the same.*

Something about Rojas told me he would have been a good salesman of jewellery. Standard-issue hospital gowns are a great social leveller but he had well-looked after skin and expressive eyes. The fingernails that weren't torn were well manicured and polished smooth.

And more than that, he was aware of what he did with his hands, even the one in the cast. Each little gesture was imbibed with forethought and meaning, maybe even that certain sensuality that women seem to require when buying precious gems. I'd watched enough of them do so to have formed a theory. It was as if they needed to feel precious themselves, to feel worthy. Rojas's manner, his eyes and his hands, would have given that to them.

I explained what had happened to the street of boutique stores where he had his business, about the stone façades and the devastation. I didn't set out to give him nightmares by describing exactly *how* he'd been buried after the collapse of the storefronts, but when he pressed me I wasn't going to lie to him.

Rojas looked down at his hands as if amazed to find them still attached to his body.

"Holy Mother of God," he said, genuine awe in his voice. "I asked the wrong question. It should not have been 'where' did you find me, but 'how'?"

"For that you have to thank a very talented search and rescue dog called Lemon," I said. "And Hope, who is Lemon's very persistent handler. She's the one who made them keep looking for you."

"Hope," he repeated softly. "What a beautiful name for a woman with such dedication."

For a moment I thought he'd got the wrong person. It seemed a strange description of the skinny girl with the quick fingers and the dog who was, it seemed, trained for far more than just searching.

"She's a constant source of wonder," I agreed.

"It is *my* hope," he said with a smile, "that I am able to meet with her? To express my thanks."

"I'm sure she'll appreciate that, although it was a team effort." And I told him about Wilson and California Ken, who

173

were both volunteers from police forces on different sides of the world. I told him about Joe Marcus keeping him safe, about Dr Bertrand keeping him alive, and Riley airlifting him to hospital to ensure he had the best chance of remaining so. But that meeting any of them in person might be tricky. "There is still a lot to do out there—still a lot of missing people to be found."

He looked momentarily shocked. "I would not expect her to interrupt her work, of course," he said quickly. "Perhaps there is some small way I can repay her ...?"

He let his voice trail off suggestively. I gave him a bland stare. "Hope works for an organisation called Rescue & Recovery International," I said. "They are supported by grants and donations. I'm sure they'd welcome any amount you'd care to give them, however modest."

In fact, I'd no idea what R&R's policy was on people who wanted to pay them for their efforts, but I hardly thought they'd be turning money away.

Not if the rumours were correct ...

I thought of Mrs Hamilton's concerns about R&R, and remembered again the way Hope's nimble fingers had dipped into the police commander's pocket so smoothly he never felt a thing. But I also remembered the way she'd put the wallet back among the dead woman's possessions, all without knowing I'd clocked what she was doing.

How did that square with the rumours?

"Do you know if I was alone?" Rojas asked now, a little diffident. He gestured to his head. "I do not even know if I have staff who work for me, or if they were working yesterday."

It was two days ago now, but I didn't think I ought to tell him that. One of many things I didn't ought to tell him, no doubt.

I hesitated. "If there was anyone else alive in the store with you when the earthquake hit," I said, "then it seems they didn't survive. They sent in the dog again after you were brought out and she didn't indicate anyone else. I'm sorry."

"But if they were dead, perhaps, and hidden from—"

"Lemon can tell the difference," I said. "Trust me. I've watched her work. She found you even though there was a couple who were buried very close by who did not survive."

He frowned. "A couple ...?" he repeated slowly. "A couple. Yes! I remember a couple. They came in to buy an engagement ring. A beautiful three-carat marquise-cut ruby. It had, I think, pave set diamonds in a rose and white gold setting. She was so happy—"

He cut off abruptly and blinked at me. "How is it that I can remember some things so clearly and not others?"

Rojas shifted his position again, lips thinned against the pain. They had realigned and plastered the compound fractures of his arm so that only the tips of his fingers protruded from the cast, yellow with iodine. He was still getting used to the weight of it and he moved awkward and slow.

"You've suffered a serious head injury," I said. "It's bound to have affected you more than you realise."

"You mentioned the couple who were found nearby. Did she ...?" He looked on the verge of weeping. "Was the lady wearing a ring as I describe? If so, I may be able to help you identify her."

I had a brief recall of the way the body bag behaved when we had loaded it into the Bell. I had no idea what state the woman's face might have been in.

"It's possible you may not be able to visually identify her," I warned.

"Ah. Then I could at least identify the ring perhaps?" he said. "If I can help, I want to do so."

"I'll ask," I said.

He met my gaze with very dark liquid eyes and smiled. "Thank you," he said. "It feels important that I do this. I *need* to know."

A harried nurse appeared in the doorway and told me my time was up.

"If you have more questions, you will have to come back tomorrow," she said, "when he has rested."

I rose, pushed my chair to the side of the room.

"Is there anyone you would like me to contact for you, Mr Rojas?" I asked, looking back as I reached the doorway. "Your wife or family?"

"I am not married," he said automatically and then gave a quick smile. "At least, I do not believe so." His expression became stricken. "Do you think it is possible that I might have forgotten a wife? Children even?"

I thought of Sean, of what he'd remembered—and what he'd forgotten.

"Yes," I said gently. "I'm afraid that *is* possible."

175

Eighteen

I calculated the time difference and called Parker Armstrong back in New York.

It was late afternoon there. The weather before I left had been edging into a late autumn, the leaves falling in copper swathes to coat the grassy expanse of Central Park. The weather swung between being not quite cold enough for winter coats, but too chilled for summer wear. The streets and subway trains were filled with people who sweated or shivered accordingly.

Here it was hot with a humid overtone that made the day seem sullen. I stood by an open window while I made my call, but all that seemed to do was blow hot air into my face.

"Charlie!" Parker greeted me, as if hearing from me was the highlight of his day. I sincerely hoped that was not the case. "How's it going?"

"Fine." I paused. "Any word?"

"From Sean? No, I'm sorry," he said, at once more subdued. "Is that why you ...?"

"No," I said. "I need you to check something out for me. Or I should say some*one*."

"OK. Shoot."

"There's a young girl here as part of the R&R team. A Brit—Hope Tyler—she's a dog handler. Search, rescue and recovery."

"Rescue *and* recovery?" Parker queried. "Unusual. In my experience they typically have specialised teams for search and rescue and then bring in the cadaver dogs when they're pretty sure there's nobody left to rescue."

I shrugged. "Well, Lemon seems to do just about everything bar tap dance and make the tea. And come to think of it I wouldn't put either of those things past her."

"Lemon?"

"Hope's dog. A rather beautiful yellow Labrador retriever."

"I have a great deal of respect for working dogs of any kind," Parker said with the fervour of an ex-military man himself. "But you think this Hope—and Lemon—may be involved in what happened to Stephens?"

"Possibly not," I said. "But like I said, she's young—and she's scared of something. She went very cagey as soon as I brought up Stephens' name."

"When you say 'young', how young?"

"Twenty apparently, but she seems a very young twenty," I said. "I don't ever remember being that young."

At Hope's age I'd been in and out of the army, lived through humiliation and disgrace and was halfway out the other side. I'd been beaten down to my knees and refused to be beaten further.

"So you don't have her tagged as a potential suspect?"

"I wouldn't rule out anything at this stage, but if she *is* caught up in this I'd say she was labour rather than management."

"Oh?"

There was a wealth of quick understanding in the single-word question. Another of the reasons I enjoyed working with Parker so much.

"The rumours Mrs Hamilton heard related to thefts," I said. "And whatever else Hope may be, from what I saw of her today she's also a very talented fingersmith."

"A what?"

"A pickpocket. She liberated a wallet from the local police commander in front of all his men and none of them saw a thing, although she had the dog deliberately running interference, which helped. They're quite a team—in more ways than the expected."

"If she's stealing from the cops, that kinda confirms the rumours, don't you think?"

"Hmm," I said, still undecided. "The wallet she liberated wasn't the good commander's to start with, and she took it in order to put it back where it belonged. Not the behaviour of your average thief."

"Sounds intriguing. I'll have Bill do some deep background and I'll get back to you soon as I can."

"There's one more thing about her," I said and hesitated. "It's only an impression and I could be wrong but—"

"I trust your instincts, Charlie," Parker said. "So should you."

177

"Thank you," I said. I took in a long warm lungful of air, let it curl out again. "She shows signs of having been through some kind of sexual assault. Could be in her distant past for all I know, but it still resonates. As soon as a male stranger gets too close she locks up and Lemon goes crazy."

Parker, to his credit, didn't ask if I was sure, but his tone was grave. "OK Charlie, leave it with me. I'll see that Bill makes it a priority to find out what we can about this girl."

"I suspect she might have been through the system," I said. "After all, she didn't acquire those sleight-of-hand skills overnight. Not without a few false starts that probably got her nicked for it once or twice. She said she had to work hard to persuade Joe Marcus to take her on. Wonder what kind of a job interview *that* was."

"Good call. Anyone catch your eye apart from Hope?"

I gave a short laugh. "She's about the only one of them who *isn't* capable of murder, to my mind, although the way Lemon reacted earlier when she thought the girl was under threat makes me wonder if Hope needs to be capable herself. I wouldn't put anything past the others, though. I suspect they've already had one pretty good go at getting shut of me."

I heard Parker's indrawn breath, his muttered, "Let's hear it, Charlie."

So I told him all about the rescue on the fallen section of roadway, the precise jink of the Bell at exactly the right moment to throw me off balance, and how close I'd been to falling. And the reactions of Dr Bertrand and Joe Marcus afterwards.

"I guess if I said I wanted you on the next flight out it wouldn't do me any good, would it?" Parker asked. "Your job is to protect them from threat, not become a human target."

"But that's exactly what I agreed to," I pointed out. "And in fact it was what *you* promised Mrs Hamilton I was more than capable of doing. Don't make liars of both of us, Parker."

The long moment's silence at the other end of the phone line was not solely due to the signal bouncing off a telecommunications satellite. Eventually Parker said with clear reluctance in his voice, "All right, Charlie. These days I find I like the thought of sending you into danger less and less."

"Sean never had a problem with that—before," I said equably. "I suspect he'd have even less of a problem with it now."

That brought another intake of breath and somewhere in there I could have sworn I heard an underlying wince.

"Well now, maybe that's something you need to get your head around," he said then. "For better or worse—I am not Sean."

Nineteen

When I walked out of the hospital it was to find Joe Marcus waiting for me.

He was leaning against the front wing of a dirty white Toyota Land Cruiser, drinking from an insulated aluminium mug. As I neared I recognised the smell of strong coffee.

"Jump in," he said. "I'll give you a ride back to base."

"I didn't think the roads were clear enough to get through."

"Well, that was yesterday," he said. He peeled the top off his mug and threw away the dregs. "You all set?"

I shrugged and opened the passenger door while he got behind the wheel and cranked the engine.

"So, what did you get from him?" he asked as he swung the vehicle round in a wide circle and headed out.

"From the survivor? His name is Santiago Rojas—the owner of the jewellery store where we found him. He reckons he was probably there alone when the quake hit. His memory's a little shaky, which is not surprising considering the crack on the head he took."

Marcus nodded briefly but there was something vaguely disapproving about him. I tried to work out if it was a general demeanour or if it was something I'd done—or might do. Well, if he was giving me the cold shoulder because he had a guilty conscience that was his problem.

The first half mile was slow. We were still moving through the city. Buildings had fallen sprawling across the roadway and had yet to be cleared. In places the road was only passable because the Toyota had four-wheel drive, all-terrain tyres and Joe Marcus had clearly driven off road before.

"Rojas thought he might know the couple we found nearby— that they might be customers. He said if that was the case the

180

woman would be wearing a ruby engagement ring, and he asked if he could take a look at her, just to be sure."

"At the body?" Marcus shook his head. "Not happening," he said. "We learned a long time ago that visual identifications are a waste of time."

"Even by close relatives?"

"You got any siblings, Charlie?"

"No."

He gave a snort. "Figures," he said. "I got a brother I haven't seen for twenty years. I could walk right by him on the street and never know. For all I know he could have a shaved head, be covered in tattoos and every hole in his body pierced."

I didn't point out that apart from the silver in his hair and the lines cut deep around his eyes, Joe Marcus probably hadn't changed a bit in the last two decades. His brother, I decided, would know him anywhere.

"We tried visual IDs in the past," Marcus went on. "People are either so desperate for their loved ones to be found, dead or alive, that they'll claim anyone even vaguely similar, or they're in complete denial. Too many false positive and negatives."

"OK, that sounds logical, but can we at least check the woman's possessions for the ring he mentioned?"

"I'm sure that's one of the avenues Dr Bertrand will explore," he said and there was a finality to his words.

OK, that's me told.

I turned and stared out of the passenger window. Dusk was starting to fall hard, creating gloomy shadows from the ruined buildings. The streets were devoid of human life but we passed a pack of assorted dogs, half of which wore collars. They looked up hopefully and picked up their pace as we passed, like hitchhikers at the prospect of a ride, then fell away when we didn't stop. The animals would be as lost and confused as everyone else.

"You coping OK?" Marcus asked suddenly.

I turned back. "With what?"

"Your first day out there. Digging out the dead."

"And the living," I put in. I paused. "Tell me, did you ask Kyle Stephens the same question?"

His face gave a tic that might have signified irritation. "Meaning?"

"Meaning that do you think someone like Parker Armstrong would have sent me out here if he didn't know I could cope with whatever came up?"

"Everyone has their limits," Marcus said. "And yes, I did ask Kyle Stephens the same question."

Something in his voice alerted me. "But you didn't like his answer."

He glanced at me sharply then, no expression on his face. He had cool grey eyes very much like Parker's—a little darker maybe, a little closer to stone.

"Not much," he said. "It's a fine line we tread here between empathy and self-preservation. Some people have difficulty maintaining that balance."

And Stephens, I guessed, had been all about himself.

"You have to care, but not to the point of burn-out. I get that."

"You should do in your line of work," Marcus said. He flicked me another assessing look, only taking his eyes off the road for a second. "You lost a principal not so long ago."

That rocked me. "It happens. I'd be foolish to think it was never going to."

"Since then your boss, Sean Meyer, has not been back into the field," Marcus said, his neutral tone sending my heart rate rocketing, "but you have. And that makes me wonder which side of the line *you* tread."

"I care but I put it behind me and do my job—and technically he wasn't our principal," I said. "How do you know about that anyway?"

Marcus's voice hardened. "You think *I'd* let anyone just walk into *my* team without checking them out first?"

"No. I just didn't think you'd had the time."

"I made the time." He gave a dry smile. "And from what I hear, you'll go out on a limb for what you feel is right. That a fair assessment?"

"Pretty fair," I agreed.

"And who gets to choose what's right—you? What makes you qualified to take that decision?"

The intensity in him ensured I didn't come straight back with a glib reply. Eventually I said quietly, "Why not? You'd rather I abdicated responsibility to someone further up the line? So I could say, 'I was only following orders'?"

"But you're not much of one for following orders either, are you?"

"Depends on the orders—and who's giving them."

His fingers tightened on the rim of the Land Cruiser's steering wheel. "When I give an order I don't do it just to hear myself speak."

I recalled his order to Riley, back there above the fallen section of roadway, to put himself and his aircraft in serious jeopardy to effect a rescue that had turned out to be in vain anyway.

"Did Stephens follow orders?" I asked.

"Sometimes," Marcus returned. "When it mattered."

Hope had told me Stephens died because he didn't do what Joe Marcus told him. But given the number of conflicting stories I thought a fishing trip was worthwhile.

So I said, "Is that what he was doing when he died—following your orders?"

We'd cleared the city boundary now and were into an area that had escaped relatively undamaged. Marcus put his foot down and the Land Cruiser picked up speed.

"Kyle Stephens was a damned fool. He'd come through two Gulf Wars without a scratch and he thought he was indestructible," he said. "But are you asking me do I blame myself? Am I responsible for what happened? Then yes I am."

Twenty

It was dark by the time we got back to the army base. The gate sentry made a perfunctory check of our IDs and waved us through. Joe Marcus swung the Land Cruiser to a halt outside the mess hall and cut the engine. In the glare from the floodlighting the insects swirled as components of a larger mass.

"Grab some food, Charlie and get some rest," Marcus said. "It's been a long day and tomorrow won't be any shorter."

"I know," I said. "'The only easy day was yesterday', right?"

"You're thinking of the SEALs," he said, climbing out.

"Before we call it a day, I'd like to check on the items found with the woman—the one Rojas mentioned."

He turned back, flicking his head against the airborne bugs. Maybe that was why he looked annoyed to have his plans interrupted.

"I think Alex has her on tomorrow's list," he said. "What's the hurry?"

"There won't be time for me to wait around for the results in the morning, and I'd like to see her things—just in case the ring is there."

Or if it's been miraculously disappeared ...

"Now?"

"Yes, now," I said, standing my ground. "If I'm going to call in on Rojas again on one of the hospital runs tomorrow, he'll want to know."

Marcus eyed me with a dispassionate gaze. "Chances are, by tomorrow, there won't be any more hospital runs," he said. "They'll all be coming here to the morgue."

"Even more reason not to leave it any longer than I have to then," I said. "You have a better idea?"

184

"Yeah," he said, exasperated. "Eating is a better idea than getting emotional over a piece of jewellery that still won't give us the woman's name."

"The credit card authorisation Rojas used will give us her name," I argued. "Five minutes is all I ask. In fact, all you need to do is unlock the door for me."

After another moment's grumpy silence Marcus let his breath out and reached into his pocket. He came out with a small bunch of keys which he threw across to me. I wasn't foolish enough to try to catch them, so I just stuck a foot out to stop them skidding off the path into the grass. You never knew what might be lurking there.

"Knock yourself out," Marcus said as I bent to retrieve the bunch. "Bring 'em back when you're done."

"Where will you be?"

He gave a now familiar snort as he turned away. "Eating," he said over his shoulder. "Where d'you think?"

I watched him walk away. Eating sounded like a very good idea, particularly as the smell of cooking drifted from the mess hall windows. If he hadn't been so stubborn I probably would have held off until morning but the more he'd tried to talk me out of the idea, the more important it seemed to find out the information tonight, dammit.

I headed in the opposite direction, trying to ignore the disaffected growling of my stomach.

Is that really what R&R did—robbed the dead of their belongings while they lay in cold storage nearby?

I thought again of those loose gems lying amid the broken glass outside the jewellery store. I wouldn't swear in court to the fact that their numbers had diminished in the time I'd been there, but it had certainly looked that way. The trouble was, it wasn't only R&R personnel who'd been on site. Any one of a host of other people, from the members of the dig team to the local police, could have pocketed a few stones in the time they were there. Perhaps it didn't feel like stealing if they were lying on full view in the street?

The lock to the hall being used as a makeshift mortuary had a piece of yellow insulating tape stuck underneath it. The same colour tape had been wrapped around the head of the key. An easily recognisable system that worked irrespective of language barriers. I felt the hand of Joe Marcus in there somewhere.

185

The key turned noiselessly in the lock. I opened the door and slipped inside, closing it again quietly behind me. Too much noise would have seemed disrespectful to the dead.

I paused just inside. Now I was there, alone and unsupervised, should I take the opportunity to have a nosy round? I smiled in the dark, mocking my own intent.

Yeah, Fox, and just what are you expecting to find? A treasure map with a convenient X marking the spot? A document marked 'Our Secret Plan'?

There was enough light coming in from outside that I didn't switch on the overhead lights. The personal possessions and clothing of the victims had been placed in archive boxes, all marked with a URN, and stored in an ante room off the main hall. The army had dragged in racking that, by the faint pervasive odour of gun oil still lingered around it, had once been used in their armoury.

I pushed open the dividing door and walked in. The windows were smaller in this room, and the height of the shelving made it darker still. I wasted time groping for a light switch I couldn't find. Eventually I gave up, standing for a moment in utter stillness, listening.

It was then I caught the thump of a full box dropping onto the hard tiled floor, and the scuffling sound of rapid footsteps.

Twenty-one

I took a fix on the direction of the sound and started running. It was no surprise that the noise had come from the row housing the boxed possessions of the latest victims to be found. By the time I reached the end of the racking and catapulted around it, I'd just time to see a darkened figure disappearing at the far end. Automatically, I gave chase.

In the centre of the row was a mess of spilled boxes and their contents. I had to half step, half jump over the obstacle it created. Whatever they'd been looking for, our intruder had not been tidy about it. So, the object itself was more important than hiding the search. Or was this simple robbery?

As I pounded to the end of the row some sixth sense kicked in. I skidded to a halt just as a large fire extinguisher came swinging around the end of the racking. It hit the upright of the shelving unit a fraction of second before it would have connected with me, sending a reverberating clang through the whole length of it.

The intruder had put everything into his attack, relying on the weight and momentum of his chosen weapon to do the job for him. Missing had not been in the game plan. Neither was an opponent who didn't cower back after the first volley.

I'd learned a long time ago that even the most overwhelming odds can be successfully countered by speed and aggression. Now I used both, darting sideways and leaping to attack.

Even in the dark I managed to ram an elbow into the side of his neck just below his ear. He grunted in pain and stumbled forward. As he went down on his knees I spun, grabbed the back of his collar to locate him and kicked him in the ribs, my other arm outstretched for balance, giving it my all.

In the muted darkness I heard his breath explode out, heard the dull crack as a couple of ribs let go on his left-hand side. Still, he managed to fling his arm back, catching me low in the stomach with a clenched hammer-fist. It was only the pain from his busted ribs that took all the force out of the blow but it hurt enough to warn me to be careful of this man. He'd had training and he didn't give up easily.

I caught his flailing arm, hooked it up and back, starting to twist it into a lock. He countered by lurching sideways, despite the ribs, pivoted and kicked for my legs. I stamped on his ankle and booted him in the ribs again, eliciting an outraged squawk.

But just when I thought I might be winning fate threw a spanner in the works in the form of the fire extinguisher he'd used originally. By rolling him I'd inadvertently put it back within his reach. With a roar of pain and effort he grasped the metal cylinder, hoisted it overhead and hurled it straight at me like a medicine ball throw.

His aim was spoiled by his sudden inability to use his stomach muscles to their full potential. Even so, the cylinder weighed close to thirty-five pounds. It hit me low—across the chest rather than in the head as he'd no doubt intended—but hard enough to send me tumbling backwards.

I tucked and rolled, got my forearms up and mostly avoiding the damn thing landing directly on top of me. The extinguisher landed just below my sternum and toppled, skimming the side of my head as it went, rebounding off into the darkness.

Nevertheless, it knocked the wind out of me sufficiently to allow the intruder time to scramble to his feet and make a bolt for it. I heard him clatter away, gasping, while I took a vital couple of seconds to drag air into my spasmed diaphragm before I could follow.

Wary now of counterattack and with my head still ringing, I ran back through into the mortuary area taking great care at the doorway. I was slaloming between the empty stainless steel tables when I caught a peripheral glimpse of a figure sliding out of cover behind me. I crouched, had already started to turn when a voice cracked out:

"Hold it!"

And without needing to be told I knew the owner of that voice was either the best actor I'd ever come across, or he was holding a gun. There are not many people who can inject that kind of authority into their tone without firepower to back it up.

I froze, letting my hands come up and away from my sides to shoulder height. It was only then, as the red mist of combat dissipated like smoke, that I recognised the voice.

I let my hands drop back to my sides and turned around fully. "What the *hell* do you think you're doing, Marcus?"

He was indeed holding a gun, I saw, a big .45 calibre Colt 1911. It took him a moment to bring the muzzle up off target. He straightened out of a stance, relaxed his shoulders.

"I heard noise," he snapped. "What happened?"

"We *had* an intruder," I said, barely keeping hold of my temper. "But he'll be long gone by now."

"What was he after?"

I jerked my head back towards the ante room. "Come and see for yourself."

Marcus let the Colt drop alongside his leg, his finger outside the trigger guard, and followed me through. We split at the doorway—me heading left, him right. He found the switch for the overhead lights without difficulty. They rows of fluorescent tubes threw long shadows over the stacked boxes. Their significance as all that remained of the dead was suddenly very apparent to me.

I glanced along each row as I passed—saw Marcus doing the same thing at the far end—but everything was undisturbed until we came to the one housing the newest arrivals. I reached the mess of spilled boxes first and squatted on my haunches to survey the worst of it.

"This your doing?" Marcus asked.

I looked up sharply to find him approaching. He was carrying the errant fire extinguisher in one hand.

"Not exactly," I said, getting to my feet. "Although he threw it at me, if that's what you mean?"

Marcus put the cylinder down. It landed with a solid metallic thump on the hard floor. He moved forwards, eyes on me intently. I almost stepped back in response to the anger I saw there, had to force myself not to flinch when he reached for me.

"Let's see that." It was an order, not a request.

His fingers were cool against my cheek as he nudged my face to the side, angling it to the light. He wiped his thumb across the corner of my eyebrow and I felt the rasp of dried blood I hadn't realised was there.

"We should get that looked at," he said.

I shook myself out of his grasp. "Later. It's nothing," I said, ignoring the radiating headache. "It was a glancing blow. If he'd caught me full on I'd still be unconscious."

I'd once had my life saved by just such a fire extinguisher. I reckoned this made us even.

"Would you recognise him if you saw him again?"

"Probably," I said. "Depends if he bruises easily, but I broke at least two of his ribs, lower left. That's going to put a crimp in his day for a while."

Marcus's eyes narrowed as if trying to work out how much flippancy to ignore. Then he released me and nodded. "Good job."

"No, not really," I said grumpily. "If I'd done a good job I'd have him zip-tied face down on the floor right now and we'd know exactly what he was after."

Twenty-two

W hy go to the trouble of breaking in 'ere to steal from the dead," Dr Bertrand demanded, "When we all know that items of value lie unguarded in the streets? It makes no sense."

She finished applying adhesive Steri-Strips to close the small cut to my eyebrow and stepped back with a nod of satisfaction at her own handiwork.

My smile of thanks went unacknowledged, so I asked, "Do we know which boxes were disturbed?"

Joe Marcus hesitated for a moment then said, "They targeted the people found close by where we pulled Santiago Rojas out of the jewellery store. The family in the car, the couple found outside the store, a man on the sidewalk, plus two more in an art gallery on the opposite side of the street."

"What was taken?"

He sighed. "That we don't know. It's all handwritten notes made by the recovery teams. Only as the victims are processed is everything photographed, formally catalogued and transferred to the computer system. There isn't time to do it in the field."

"Then they should make time!" Dr Bertrand said firmly. "As it is, we 'ave lost sources of valuable information. Without them, some of the identifications may be in doubt."

She was clearly taking this as a personal affront. I knew from the dossier Mrs Hamilton had provided on the R&R staff that the doctor prided herself on her track record when it came to reconciling the dead.

"Alex, it's close to a hundred degrees out there," Marcus said, his voice reasonable. "The longer it takes for the bodies to be gotten back here and into cold storage, the harder time you're gonna to have with 'em."

She gave a very Gallic shrug, stripped off her gloves and strode away across the deserted mortuary to replace the First Aid kit.

I hopped down from the steel post-mortem examination table where I'd been perched, and hoped it was a good few years before I found myself on one again.

As Dr Bertrand made her somewhat flouncy exit, Riley appeared with a stack of three archive boxes piled so tall in his arms he had to walk sideways to see where he was going. The muscles in his stringy biceps stood out starkly with the effort.

"That's everything gathered up," he said, dumping the boxes onto the table I'd just vacated. "He'd even ripped the inventory sheets off the outside of the boxes. Thorough bugger, wasn't he?"

"Not as thorough as he would have liked to be," I said. "Let's hope he left us *something* behind."

"Wallets and purses are gone," Riley said cheerfully. Most you've got is some jewellery and personal items."

"Is there a ruby engagement ring?" I asked. "It should have belonged to the woman from outside the jewellery store."

"Half a mo," Riley said, unstacking the boxes and removing the lid of the bottom one. He rummaged around inside, moving bags of clothing and shoes until he came to a bunch of smaller clear plastic zip-lock bags. I saw earrings in one, a thin gold watch, and finally a ring.

"How's that?" Riley handed it across. I looked through the plastic at the central stone. It was a beautiful deep clear red cut into a pointed oval and surrounded by smaller diamonds.

"I'm not an expert, but I'd guess that's a marquise-cut ruby," I said. "So if his memory was working right for that bit, we know this woman had just been into Rojas's store. If they paid by credit card there'll be an electronic trail with an ID at the end of it. Maybe we can trace her that way."

Joe Marcus had been looking through the box of items taken from the male victim found nearby. The bagged jacket and shirt, I noticed, were covered in darkly dried blood that gave them a similar tone to the ruby.

"No wallet for him, either," he said. He held another bag up for me to see. "Would you classify this as a fancy watch?"

I recognised the matte-black face and rubber strap. "I'll say. That's a Hublot, and they don't come cheap—ten grand at least."

Marcus frowned, unimpressed, and dropped the watch back into the box. "I'll take your word on that," he said. "Looks like we have a pair of tourists with more money than sense. Maybe somebody got wind of that and wanted what they had."

"So why take their IDs and leave the valuables behind?"

Riley laughed. "Because they weren't expecting to run into bloody Wonder Woman," he said. "You really reckon you bust the guy's ribs?"

"I heard them go." I kept my eyes on Marcus's face, wondering if he was going to mention the woman's wallet first, or whether I was going to have to bring it up. The latter, it seemed. "This wasn't the first attempt at taking the woman's ID, was it?" I murmured. "The police commander—Peck—he tried it, too. If it wasn't for it … falling out of his pocket when Lemon jumped up at him, it would have been in the hands of the police by now."

Marcus regarded me with a bland expression, refusing to rise to the bait.

"I'll contact him tomorrow and see if he remembers who she is. Meanwhile, Alex," he called across to where Dr Bertrand was jotting down notes for the morning's lists, "you better move these people up the priority lists. The woman especially."

"She was first on my list for tomorrow morning in any case," she agreed.

Marcus nodded, began to turn away when I stopped him with a question that should not have thrown him, given the circumstances.

"Does this kind of thing often—robberies from the dead?"

I saw the quick glance the three of them exchanged. It was Marcus who shook his head. "From our own morgue? Unheard of. And the curfews organised by the local police cut down on looting. Most people who break curfew are looking for missing family or pets."

"So there haven't been any recent cases?" I persisted.

"No." Another exchange of brief looks, more uneasy this time. "What are you getting at, Charlie?" Marcus asked, his tone a little harsh.

"Just trying to work out if there's a precedent," I said mildly, recognising that now was the time to back off a little. "If it's unusual then that makes it more significant, don't you think?"

He rolled his shoulders but they remained stiff. "Yeah, well, maybe I'll discuss that with Commander Peck tomorrow." He stepped back, gestured for all of us to head for the door. "Now let's get some rest, people. One way or another, we're gonna need it."

It was only as he pulled the door to the mortuary shut behind us and twisted the key in the lock that I voiced my final point.

"One thing you worth bearing in mind for tomorrow," I said. He paused, raised an eyebrow. "When you ask Commander Peck about this mystery woman, you might want to check if any of his ribs are broken ..."

Twenty-three

I spent the following morning combing another shopping district with Hope and Lemon. We discovered and marked the location of a further four bodies. There were no more live finds.

The general feeling among the dig teams was that we'd now moved on to the recovery stage of the operation. They were matter-of-fact but subdued about it. Didn't stop them running whenever they thought there might be a possibility, though. A triumph of hope over experience.

I was expecting to put in another long day so it was a surprise when I heard rotors sweep low overhead and recognised the R&R Bell circling as Riley picked his landing spot.

He put the helo down in the middle of a car park, one side of which had disappeared into a crater, and came jogging across. In the short time I'd known the laidback Aussie, I'd never seen him look in such a hurry.

"Hey Riley," Hope called. "Where's the fire?"

"G'day, ladies," he called back with a grin. "How's it going?"

"Depends on your point of view, I think," I said. I nodded to the line of body bags. "If you're heading back to base we've four passengers for you."

"Better make that seven," Riley said. "Joe Marcus wants you back at the morgue right away. And Hope—and her ladyship of course."

"What for?"

He shrugged. "I'm just the oily rag, sweetheart, not the engine driver."

Hope appeared by my shoulder with Lemon at her side. "So, what's the rush?" she asked. "Lem's on a roll."

He shrugged. "All I know is, the boss said it was urgent. And when he speaks I don't argue."

The on-site dig team—mostly from New Zealand where they'd gained their experience during the 2011 Christchurch quake—helped us load the body bags into the Bell. Hope and I climbed aboard without speaking and Lemon jumped in, turned around twice and plonked herself down at Hope's feet. She seemed unfazed by her proximity to so much dead meat.

It didn't take long to get back to the army base. Nowhere takes long when you can take a crow-flies route and don't ever meet traffic. But all the way there I tried to work out the reason for this abrupt summons.

Do they know why I'm really here? And if so, how did they find out? Or did they guess?

Perhaps my question about the frequency of thefts from the dead had struck too close to home. But with no sign of obvious forced entry to the morgue or the ante room, it was looking decidedly like either a pro at work or an inside job.

I half expected to find Joe Marcus waiting on the landing pad with my kitbag at his feet and an instruction not to bother getting out because I was on my way straight back to the airport.

But the only people waiting for us when we set down were the army stretcher teams—Riley must have radioed ahead. Between us we quickly offloaded our cargo.

It was Hope who looked about her, puzzled, and said, "Are you going to go find Joe? I want to know what's worth dragging us off site in the middle of the day. He wants his bumps feeling for that."

I agreed, even if I wasn't going to volunteer to be the one to do it. I asked one of the stretcher bearers if they'd seen Joe Marcus and was told he was in the morgue with Dr Bertrand.

Hope pulled a face and said she'd take Lemon to the mess hall and see what they could scrounge between them.

"You'll come and find me when you're done with Joe?" she asked.

I assured her I would.

I found Marcus in the mortuary as predicted, together with Dr Bertrand and, to my surprise, the police commander, Peck. The two men were standing back from one of the post-mortem exam tables, watching Dr Bertrand peeling open the chest of a lean male cadaver. His face was a mess, crushed and misshapen, the features offset as if wearing a horror mask that had badly slipped.

It was damage I recognised.

"Ah, Charlie," Marcus said when he caught sight of me, adding dryly, "You already met Commander Peck, I understand."

"Yes sir," I said, holding my hand out as I approached. Automatic good manners had Peck reaching to shake it. I gave it a few hearty pumps with a friendly smile on my face, watching him for signs of discomfort. He showed only bemusement at my enthusiastic greeting.

Damn. That's that theory out the window.

Marcus gestured to the body on the slab. "This is the guy who—"

"Was found outside the jewellery store with the woman," I finished for him. "Yes, I know."

He raised an eyebrow.

It was Peck who demanded, "You *know* this man?"

"Not his identity, no. But I got a good look at him yesterday ... when you were searching the bodies after they were brought out," I said. "It's not a state of face you forget in a hurry."

Dr Bertrand glanced at the body with a frown, as if unable to work out what made it memorable. I guessed she'd seen a lot worse in her time.

"That is immaterial," she said. She indicated the gaping chest cavity with a gore-spattered glove. "What I found 'ere is of greater concern at present. See for yourself."

The invitation was issued in an off-hand manner with just an underlying hint of smug. She clearly expected me not to spot whatever it was she was indicating. Then I would be compelled to ask and she would have the opportunity to sledgehammer home her superior knowledge.

I moved closer, leaned over the body, remembering to breathe shallowly through my mouth. It didn't stop the taste of death from settling on my tongue but it was better than the alternative.

Looking down, I saw the rib cage had already been cracked open and the breastplate of sternum and ribs removed in one piece. The heart and other organs still nestled in place but I noticed a blackened torn mass at the bottom edge of the left lung. I peered closer, then glanced up and met Dr Bertrand's quickly hidden look of surprise.

"Would you mind, doctor?" I asked politely, indicating the lower triangular flap of skin that she had folded back to hide the whole of the abdomen. With disapproval in every line, she lifted it for me to inspect. I saw what I was looking for almost at once, nodded and stepped back.

"He was shot," I said, drawing blank stares from the three of them. Not for my verdict but the fact I'd been able to reach it.

Twenty-four

Y"ou can see the front entry wound—here," I said, keeping my voice cool and level, pointing to the dead man's chest. "I'd say the round clipped the bottom edge of his lung. Without taking a look at his back I wouldn't like to guess on it being a through-and-through but it wasn't a large calibre if I'm any judge—maybe a thirty-eight or a nine mil. The wound was possibly not bad enough to be immediately fatal, but without immediate medical attention I doubt he would have lasted long."

And he didn't last long because—looking at his face—the earthquake got him before he had a chance to bleed out or suffocate to death.

For a second nobody moved and then Dr Bertrand gave me a stiff little nod, as if it grieved her to have to do it.

Commander Peck cleared his throat. "We are looking at homicide here and I shall be launching a full investigation."

"Maybe, maybe not," Joe Marcus said. "If the quake hadn't hit, he might have survived."

"With a bullet through his lung?" Peck scoffed.

"Why not?" I asked. "I managed just that a year or so ago. I have the scars to prove it."

Peck gave me a strange look as if he was pretty sure I was joking but he couldn't be sure. "Either way, you don't shoot a man in the chest without intending to kill him, regardless of what actually finishes him off."

I couldn't refute the logic of that. "Do we know who he is yet?"

Marcus lifted one shoulder. "Maybe," he said. "The woman he was found with is a French tourist, Gabrielle Dubois. According to immigration she entered the country last weekend, travelling with a man called Enzo Lefévre, her fiancé."

"That was quick," I said.

Marcus ducked his head in Peck's direction. "The commander remembered her name from looking at her ID," he said without inflection. "From there it was easy enough to check out her passport record."

I nodded, turning over this new information. If Peck had originally taken the woman's wallet to conceal her identity, why give it up voluntarily now? After all, it would have been entirely believable for him to say he didn't take a good enough look at the ID to recall the details.

"You seemed to think she'd been reported missing. Was that why you were looking for her?" I asked him.

He lifted a casual shoulder. "I thought I recognised her but I was mistaken." His face was expressionless, giving nothing away. Probably best never to get into a poker game with the police commander.

"So ... why drag us off the streets for this?" I asked Marcus, getting the perplexity into my voice without having to work too hard. "Couldn't it have waited until we got back later anyway?"

His face ticked in irritation. "Because there's a threat here you need to be aware of, Charlie," he said. "Somebody shot this guy right before the earthquake hit. We don't know why, and we haven't yet recovered a body clutching a gun. Plus there were no survivors other than the store owner on that street, so it looks like our gunman got away."

"He could well be the man you say broke in here last night," Peck said. "Although I have inspected all the points of entry and can only assume this man was highly professional, or that he had access."

It was an echo of my own earlier thoughts, and although he left that one dangling nobody wanted to make a grab for it.

"So, why steal their identification?" I asked instead. "What does that achieve?"

"Perhaps the robber was known to them." Peck made a vague flapping motion with his hand. "Perhaps he fears that if we were able to identify these people we might also make some connection to him?"

Marcus's stare lasted a second or two longer than it needed to, and spoke volumes as to what he thought of that idea.

"Or perhaps," I echoed the commander with a straight face, "Mr Rojas might be able to fill in some blanks."

200

Peck straightened to show the mild jibe had not passed unnoticed. "I will be questioning Rojas in due course. I trust that you will leave this in my hands." He gave a stilted bow of his head to Dr Bertrand and Joe Marcus but ignored me completely as he headed for the main door out of the mortuary.

"You know, Charlie," Marcus said as we watched the commander disappear. "I get the feeling he really doesn't like you."

"Oh-dear-what-a-pity-never-mind," I said cheerfully. "So, when do we go and see Mr Rojas?"

Just for a second Marcus's severe face cracked into a smile. "Any time you're ready."

"I'll just go and let Hope know what's happening," I said. "I'll meet you by the helo in five."

But Hope was not in the mess hall as I expected. I jogged across the parade square to the NCOs' quarters we'd been assigned, aware that if I went more than half a minute past the five I'd promised Marcus, he was likely to take off without me.

That was the reason I forgot my manners and just shoved open the door to Hope's room already calling her name.

And my voice died in my throat.

Hope was sitting cross-legged on her bed. Her head jerked up when I burst in and her mouth formed a soundless oh. Spread on a shirt in front of her was a pile of stones. Some of them were pebbles, of the type that I'd seen Lemon delivering to her so solemnly when we were out in the field.

But the others were far too small to have been picked up by a dog's mouth, however delicate. They glittered against the fabric, cut and graded and polished—the precious stones I'd seen scattered outside Santiago Rojas's jewellery store.

Hope tensed, her eyes darted wildly. They even flicked to where Lemon lay stretched out on a blanket with her favourite chew toy next to her. The yellow Lab had lurched from her side onto her belly when I made my entrance, letting out a couple of loud sneezes as she was woken from sleep. She lifted her head, recognised me and flopped back down again with a loud grumbling sigh.

Hope's flight reflex folded in on itself and collapsed, taking her composure with it. For a moment I thought she might cry.

I stood there frozen with one hand still on the doorknob until I heard footsteps and voices approaching. I stepped inside quickly and closed the door.

"What's going on, Hope?" I asked, keeping my voice calm and quiet. I'd seen how Lemon leapt to her handler's defence when it was clear the girl was being threatened and I had no desire to be on the receiving end of those teeth.

Hope bounced off the bed, tangling her bare feet in the blankets and stumbling straight into my arms in her haste.

"Please," she said, staring up at me. "Please, Charlie, don't tell anyone!"

"Hope ..." My voice trailed away helplessly. I shook my head, said tiredly, "Just tell me what the hell is going on, will you?"

That seemed to get to her more than harsh words would have done. She wrenched herself away and slumped down on the edge of the bed with her head bowed. Lemon rolled partly onto her back and gazed up at her with two legs waving and her tongue hanging out. Hope rubbed the side of the dog's belly with one foot.

"You picked these up on the street, didn't you?" I went on when she didn't speak. Let Joe Marcus go without me if he damn well pleased. As far as I was concerned this took precedence. Still, I didn't have all night. "Hope?"

"Yes," she said, lifting her head and showing me more than a hint of defiance. "They're just lying there, for fuck's sake. Anybody could help themselves. You think they'll be any left by the time that jeweller gets clearance to go back?"

"That doesn't mean they're yours to take," I said neutrally.

"Why not?" she cried. "I've seen everyone take things, even the cops. Even the birds!" She let her head drop again so her next words emerged as a mumble: "S'not like I was gonna keep them."

I opened my mouth to make a "yeah, right" kind of comment, but then I remembered again the way she'd put the woman's wallet back after she'd lifted it from Commander Peck and I stopped myself from coming out with anything too cynical.

"Who knows about this?" I asked instead.

"Nobody!" she assured me. If she kept bobbing her head up and down like this she was going to put her neck out. "Nobody else knows about it, and nobody else is doing it. It's just me, all right?"

I took in her mulish expression and realised there was no point arguing with her. Not right now. I checked my watch. "Look, Hope, I'm going back to see the jewellery store owner—"

"Oh, please don't tell him! I'll put them all back, I swear!"

I let my breath out. "I wasn't going to tell him," I said. "I simply meant I haven't time to talk about this now, but we *are* going to talk about it—later, when I get back, yes?"

Another mumble, less distinct this time. I took it for a yes anyway.

"Good," I said. I reached for the door handle again, paused as a final thought struck me. "Did Kyle Stephens know you were helping yourself to bits and pieces?"

Hope didn't answer that one, but from the sudden flare of loathing and fear that crossed her face, I didn't need her to.

Twenty-five

I was, I realised as Joe Marcus and I headed back towards the hospital with Riley in the Bell, getting far too used to travelling everywhere by helicopter. Being grounded was going to seem very restrictive after all this.

What I needed was to get out on a fast bike on an open road and blow the cobwebs out of my head. I still hadn't replaced my Buell Firebolt after it was written-off by a bunch of kidnappers. Sean's own bike remained under a cover in the parking garage below our building. I thought longingly of the Honda FireBlade I'd left behind in the UK, sitting equally dormant in the back of my parents' garage. Maybe I'd get over there this year and take it out for a blast—if the tyres weren't flat-spotted with standing and the fuel left in the tank hadn't gone off.

Or maybe not.

Unable to side-track myself any longer, I dragged my mind back to Hope Tyler. I knew I was putting off examining what I'd seen and heard, and what it might mean. Hope was a confirmed thief, no two ways about it. She was too quick with her fingers to be anything else and it would seem that she'd trained Lemon to aid and abet. I wondered what the RSPCA or PETA would have to say about that.

Still, if Hope had been helping herself from other disaster sites, would that really be enough to cause the rumours Mrs Hamilton had heard all the way back in New York? Hope struck me as a collector of pretty things rather than a serious player, but that didn't mean she hadn't tried to offload some of her booty in search of yet more pretty things. Wouldn't take much carelessness there for her activities to come to light.

Kyle Stephens had known what was going on—that much was clear from her reaction. When had he found out, and what had he been intending to do about it? I got the impression from Mrs

Hamilton that what she really wanted was not confirmation or denial of the thefts, but for the problem to be simply made to go away. She had asked Stephens to take care of it for her.

Instead he'd got himself killed.

I was still tumbling those thoughts over and round when Riley set the Bell down on the pad outside the hospital and the engines spun down.

"I never trust a woman when she goes quiet," Joe Marcus said as we hopped down onto the baked concrete. "What's on your mind, Charlie?"

"Life, death, the universe and everything," I said, keeping my tone light. "Any clues?"

"Given some thought to all of it over the years."

"And?"

He shook his head. "Never did come to any conclusions worth a damn."

We found Santiago Rojas looking both better and worse.

Better because he was out of his hospital bed and sitting in a low chair by the window. Worse because the bruising had blossomed across his face, turning his skin every colour of pain. He shifted awkwardly when we entered, making as if to rise. Marcus waved him back into his seat.

I introduced them. Rojas clasped Marcus's hand warmly, his eyes becoming moist. "So, you are one of the people responsible for getting me out of there alive," he said, his voice husky. "For that, sir, I am forever in your debt."

"It's kinda the whole point of what we do," Joe Marcus said without any hint of embarrassment. I guessed he'd received a lot of similar thanks in his time.

"I would like to give you something," Rojas went on. "A small gift, from my store. Something of value—"

"That won't be necessary," Marcus said quickly, and I couldn't help wondering what he might have said if I hadn't been with him. "If you feel you'd like to make a contribution to one of the disaster relief funds, well that would be more than enough."

"Ah, of course," Rojas said quickly, not wanting to cause offence. His eyes went from one of us to the other expectantly.

"We wondered if you'd had any more recollections of what happened—just before the earthquake?" I said.

He frowned. "I do not understand why it is so important for you to know this," he said. "There must be so many dead and injured."

"You remember the couple I told you about? They were found just outside your store—the woman with the ruby engagement ring?"

"Ah, you found the ring. So it is her?" He nodded sadly. "I am so sorry they did not survive. She was so beautiful. And she seemed so happy."

"Her name was Gabrielle Dubois," Marcus said. "What can you tell us about the man who was with her?"

"Her fiancé?" Rojas gave a confined shrug, as much as his injuries would allow. "He was a man of ... sophistication. A man of the world, I think you would say. Older than she, but good looking, of course, to have snared such a beautiful lady."

"Mr Rojas, our doctor has just carried out an autopsy on this man—we believe his name is Enzo Lefévre. He was shot in the chest shortly before the earthquake struck," Marcus said gravely. "Would you happen to recall anything about that?"

His level tone and gaze would have been enough to make a nun confess, but Rojas just stared with his mouth slightly agape.

"Shot?" he repeated. "Holy Mother of God ..." His focus went into middle distance as if trying to latch onto a fragment of memory. Eventually he murmured, "So, *that* was it."

"That was what?" Marcus demanded.

Rojas pulled his attention back onto us with an effort. "I've been having ... strange dreams," he said hesitantly. "Of violence, of someone crying out, of a loud noise and fear and falling. I thought ... I thought it was all to do with the earthquake, with being buried, but now ..."

"Now?" Marcus prompted.

He was not the subtlest of interrogators but his technique seemed to work because a moment later Rojas said, more firmly, "Now I believe that, just before the earth opened up and swallowed me ... I believe I was robbed."

Twenty-six

I remember the couple coming into the store," Rojas said. "They said they had just become engaged—that he had asked her only that morning, and she had said yes. She was still blushing, so pretty."

"Just that morning?" I queried and he nodded.

I was sure Peck had said Gabrielle Dubois was listed as travelling with her fiancé on the flight details. Perhaps it was just easier that way. In the past I'd wondered how I should introduce Sean. He was too old to be called "boyfriend", too practical be described as "lover", but the all-encompassing "partner" sounded so soulless.

It was all a bit of a moot point now …

"How long were they in the store?" Joe Marcus asked.

"Oh, almost an hour. She tried on a great many beautiful rings before she settled on the marquise-cut ruby. It was an exquisite stone. And the size, it was perfect for her. She said it was a sign that she was meant to have it."

His eyes began to fill again. Marcus said, "Take your time, Mr Rojas."

I plucked a handful of tissues from the box on the bedside cabinet and passed them across. Rojas took them with a nod of thanks.

"The doctors tell me it is the … relief of my rescue still coming out," he explained and we didn't call him a liar.

"Do you remember anything about the robbery itself?" Marcus asked after a few moments. I raised an eyebrow at him. What part of *"take your time"* did this fit into?

But Rojas was nodding. "Yes … yes, I think so. I have a remote lock on the door. I would have had to press it to let the couple out. I think that was when the man pushed his way inside. He pushed them back inside, also. He wore black, and a mask. And he had a gun. He forced me to open my gem safe. He threatened the lady … what could I do?"

"I'm sure you did everything you could," Marcus murmured.

"He was expecting more stones. I was waiting for a shipment, but it was delayed. I tried to explain but he was very angry. Eventually he took what he could, including the cash in the register, and just when I thought he might finally leave, he saw the woman's ring—the ruby. And he wanted it."

"And Monsieur Lefévre didn't want to let go of it," Marcus guessed.

Rojas nodded helplessly, his English breaking up in his distress. "He shoot him in the chest and he go. And then the building start to shake and I … I don't remember much after that."

He sagged back into his chair as if the retelling of the tale had physically exhausted him. I sat quiet for a moment, lining his story up with the holes in our own timeline. It would all seem to fit except for the unknown intruder who'd broken in to steal the couple's identities—and from a secure building in the middle of an army base at that.

I still didn't see the point of it. Unless Peck had been right and there *was* some connection between the couple and the robber that he thought too obvious to risk exposing.

"Do you have any ideas who might have robbed you?" I asked. "Or if there might have been any connection between the couple who came in, and the robbery?"

"How could there be, when he shoot that man?" Rojas demanded.

I exchanged a look with Joe Marcus, saw no enlightenment in his face either. Perhaps I needed to get Parker Armstrong digging on the French pair to see what he could come up with.

We got to our feet. Marcus reached a hand to Rojas, who clasped it again briefly, and did the same with mine.

"Well, thank you for your time and your patience, Mr Rojas," Marcus said. "We hope—"

"What in the name of hell is going on here?" said an annoyed voice from the doorway. Commander Peck came striding into the room and stopped dead when he caught sight of the man in the chair, his head bruised and still swathed in dressings.

"Ah, Commander Peck, is it not?" Rojas said, and there was a rueful note to his smile. "My name is Santiago Rojas. I believe you want to speak with me."

"Mr Rojas," Peck returned, so stiffly it made his treatment of us seem positively effusive. Enmity rolled off him like cold air from an open fridge door.

"You must excuse us, Mr Marcus, Miss Fox," Rojas said then, a bitter smile curving his swollen lips. "I'm afraid the commander and I have some ... history together, is that not right?"

Peck said nothing.

Rojas laughed. "The good commander works long hours," Rojas went on, "and his wife is a lonely and attractive woman." He shrugged as far as he was able. "Our ... friendship was over some time ago, but I think I am not yet forgiven."

Peck forced some of the rigidity out of his shoulders and jaw. "Our personal ... differences will not prevent me from doing my job," he ground out. "You can be assured of that."

Twenty-seven

W"e're working in the dark," Marcus said when we were outside and heading for the Bell.

"You should be used to that in your job," I said, which raised the beginnings of a smile that never made it any further. "Why don't you check with your sources—see what they have to say?"

"My sources?"

"You found out all the gory details about me fast enough after I arrived," I pointed out mildly. "You must have a good source of intel somewhere along the line."

"Good, yes," he agreed. "Sporadic, also. And right now my 'source' as you call him, is on deployment and out of regular cellphone contact."

"Well, it's fortunate that *my* source is sitting by his phone in New York," I said. "I can ask my boss to do some digging on this if you want?"

"We talking about Sean Meyer?" he demanded. "Or Parker Armstrong?"

My hesitation was only fractional. "Parker."

He regarded me for a moment and I could see the pros and cons circulating behind those stony eyes before he said, "Do it."

I pulled my cellphone out of my pocket and hit the speed dial number for Parker's direct line. He picked up on the third ring— a slow response for him.

"Charlie, how's it going?"

"Fairly quiet," I said, which he knew meant the opposite. I watched Joe Marcus walk over to Riley, who was fussing with the tensioning of the winch he'd reinstalled. "You got anything for me?"

"We looked into the girl," he said cautiously. "No record, not even a parking ticket. Although as she doesn't have a driving

210

licence maybe that's not so hard to believe. No late payments, no final demands, no credit card. The kid's practically a ghost."

"Hmm," I said. "Can I ask you to take another run at that?"

I almost heard his ears prick up. "Ah. Developments?"

"On that front, yes and I'll fill you in when I can," I said. "But there have been other developments, too." And I told him briefly about the robbery of Santiago Rojas's store, the dead French couple, and the intruder at the mortuary who'd stolen their IDs—and whose ribs I'd busted.

"This sounds like the kind of thing the local LEOs should be handling," Parker said when I was done. "It's way outside your remit."

"You know the scope of my remit as well as I do, Parker," I countered. "Besides, there was no forced entry into the mortuary—"

"Which means we can't rule out an inside job," he finished for me wearily. "Yeah, OK. I'll do what I can."

"Besides which," I added, "I don't entirely trust the local head honcho. For a while I thought he might even be our intruder. I can rule him out personally, but that doesn't mean he didn't get one of his boys to indulge in a bit of Breaking and Entering on the side. I can't go around hugging all of them to find out."

I still had my eyes on Joe Marcus, apparently shooting the breeze with Riley, both of them casual and relaxed. But just as Parker's voice in my ear asked, "So, are they still … treating you OK?" both men seemed to glance over in my direction at the same time. The look they gave me was anything but warm and fuzzy.

"For the moment at least," I said carefully. "Which is lucky really, because if they decide I need to follow in my predecessor's footsteps, so to speak, I don't think I'd get much backup from the local cops."

"Are you trying to give me grey hair, Charlie?"

"Parker, your hair's been grey practically since you were in short trousers—I've seen the pictures."

"Yeah, and that means I don't want it to start falling out from stress," he returned. "Watch your step and I'll get back to you as soon as I can, OK?"

I ended the call and ambled towards Riley and Marcus. Riley was wiping his hands on an old rag while the former Marine had donned a pair of heavy gloves and was trying the winch line to make sure it ran out and retracted smoothly.

"Well?" Marcus wanted to know as soon as I reached them.

"He's checking," I said. "As soon as I know anything I'll pass it on."

He gave a grumpy kind of a sigh at that, as though he'd heard such promises many times before and knew they rarely came to fruition.

"OK, Riley," he called to the Bell pilot. "We're good to go."

"Hop in then, mate," Riley said with a grin. "Now I've got the winch hunky dory I can set you down any place you fancy."

Marcus glanced at me. "Well, Charlie? You up for finding out what happened to that gun?"

I shrugged. "What's so important about this one? There must be thousands of weapons loose in this city right now."

"Thousands? Maybe," he agreed, "but not many we know for certain have been used as a murder weapon."

"There are plenty with the potential to kill far more."

"Maybe," he repeated. "You have that same potential but I'm not chasing you."

I opened my mouth to voice another objection then closed it again. Joe Marcus was suddenly very insistent to go back to the scene of the crime and all of a sudden I could think of several reasons for that which had nothing to do with a missing gun. What better way to find out?

I climbed into the back of the Bell without comment. It meant I couldn't see their faces easily. At least I didn't have the former Marine sitting behind me. Marcus took the co-pilot's seat. It wasn't until we were in the air that I spoke into the boom mic attached to my headset.

"If he got away clear before the quake hit, there won't be any weapon to find."

Marcus looked back over his shoulder. "And if he didn't?"

"Then Hope and Lemon would have found his body."

Marcus tilted his head and his mouth twitched. "They're good, Charlie, but they're not infallible."

"In that case," I said carefully, "I don't suppose this additional search might have anything to do with a bag of missing diamonds, would it?"

This time Joe Marcus didn't turn his head so I couldn't see his expression. He and the Aussie didn't even glance at each other.

After a moment Marcus said, "If it's missing, that means it can be found."

"Possibly a lot of money's worth there." I tried to keep my voice casual, as if I were seriously considering this. "You thinking there might be a reward?"

"Possibly." He echoed me in both tone and caution.

I pursed my lips even though he couldn't see me, knowing it would affect my voice just the same. "Slim chance," I said. "Do you honestly think Rojas has had time to even report the robbery yet? The man's still in hospital. He hasn't been back to the store to do an inventory—even if he was allowed near the place, never mind inside."

"I'm sure they take that into account."

"Will they? Or will they simply declare this whole mess an Act of God or whatever the terminology is and void everyone's insurance?"

"For property damage, they might," Marcus returned, "but according to Rojas the robbery took place before the earthquake hit. In theory he'd still be covered."

"Yeah, because we all know how honest and fair-dealing insurance companies are," I said sarkily.

I caught his smile, a flash of surprisingly white teeth. "You always look on the downside, Charlie?"

"It's part of my job description." I paused, decided to edge this forward just a touch. "Rojas said he was waiting for a big shipment that was delayed," I added, aiming for a note of calculation. "You really think there's enough out there to get excited about?"

Marcus shrugged, not taking the bait. "Let's see if we can find the gun first and talk about anything else later."

Damn. Ah well, may as well be hanged for a sheep as a lamb
...

"Why don't you put your cards on the table, Joe," I said. "Are you thinking of handing those gems in for the reward—assuming there is one—or are you thinking instead of not handing them in at all?"

It took him a beat or two before he answered. "I can think of a whole heap of better uses for them than left lying around in the street."

213

It was within a hairsbreadth of an admission, but not quite all the way there yet. I knew I needed to push just that little bit further.

"So, how many ways are you thinking of splitting it?"

Again came the little tilt of his head. The one that told me nothing. "This was your idea, Charlie, not mine," he said. "What exactly did you have in mind?"

"Hey, I'm just the newbie," I said with as much unconcern as I could muster. "How do you usually work it?"

Marcus was silent for a moment, then said with icy disdain, "I wonder what the illustrious Mrs Hamilton would have to say about your suggestion. But I'll wager this was not quite what she had in mind when she went to Armstrong-Meyer for Stephens' replacement."

"If you kids can stop haggling long enough to grab your gear," Riley cut in from the pilot's seat, "we're coming up on your search location now." There was little to be gleaned from his voice to know if he was for or against the idea of keeping the missing gems.

"Set us down where you can," Joe Marcus said, turning all business once again. I cursed long and silently behind a bland expression. If he knew who had gone to Parker, and why, then I was probably blown from the start. No wonder Riley had tried to shake me off the skid of the Bell on the very first day.

The Aussie made another deceptively casual landing and was in the air again as soon as we'd jumped down into the rubble. He hovered through our standard radio checks, then moved off with a jaunty wave through the canopy.

I returned the salute and watched him surf the rooftops until the Bell disappeared from view. As the thrum of the rotors began to fade into the distance I started to turn back to Joe Marcus. And as I did so I heard the unmistakable harsh metallic click of the slide being racked back to chamber the first round into the breech of a semiautomatic.

Twenty-eight

I completed my turn very slowly and found Joe Marcus with that big Colt .45 in his hands again. The only thing that kept my heartrate from going stratospheric was the fact the gun wasn't pointing at me.

Marcus was wearing a loose shirt over khaki cargoes but I hadn't picked up any sense that he was armed. Which meant either he was really good, or I was slipping. And as before I knew that he didn't carry just for show—he was more than capable of using.

The SIG sat snug in the small of my back under my own shirt. I knew I could get to it quickly but not quickly enough.

"You expecting to repel boarders?" I asked with a calm I did not feel.

He stared at me for a moment with no humour in his face. I fought to keep my shoulders easy and my hands relaxed by my sides. Then he tucked the Colt away under his shirt again and moved past me.

"No point in carrying a weapon that isn't ready to shoot," he said. He paused, found me still frozen. "You coming or what?"

"'What', probably," I muttered and followed him.

We picked our way over the rubble until we turned into the street where Lemon had found Santiago Rojas. Another building had partially come down during the night. We were getting perhaps half a dozen aftershocks a day, some worse than others. Unless they threatened to throw me off my feet I tended to ignore them. How quickly we learn to be blasé.

"So, if we're searching for something specific why didn't you bring Hope along?"

Marcus stepped across an eighteen-inch gap in the road surface without apparent concern.

"It's not exactly Lemon's specialty," he said.

"Oh I don't know. Hope reckons once that dog's had a sniff of just about anything she can find it again."

"Yeah, well, they both do enough to earn their keep," Marcus said with a flick of irritation in his voice. "And maybe I don't want to expose the kid to danger unnecessarily."

"She's an adult, as she's only too ready to point out. She's capable of making her own choices." I thought of the gems I'd seen Hope inspecting in the privacy of her room and added silently, *however poor some of those choices might be.*

He hesitated and a dark flicker crossed his features. "In many ways she's still a child. And she's on my team—my responsibility."

That hesitation made me curious. Time to push it again, gun or no gun.

"So, do you take responsibility for her actions too?"

Joe Marcus stopped then, turned to look back at me with his head tilted in a manner I was coming to know well. For a moment I thought I might be getting somewhere.

"Might be easier if we split up," he said then. "Keep your radio on. If you find anything, call me."

"Likewise."

"Of course."

I watched him walk away, hopping nimbly over tumbled blockwork and daggers of broken glass still fettered to their twisted wooden frames.

"Yeah," I said quietly, "I bet you will ..."

I headed for the nearest cross-street, a wider main road that bisected the tourist district. From there I cut down the service road running behind Rojas's jewellery store. In the mouth of the narrow street I halted, trying to get a feel for my quarry's train of thought.

The main road would have been a faster escape route for our gem thief but it was also more exposed. If I'd been him I would have stuck to the alleyways until I was well clear, but if he had enough bottle he could have shed his mask and gloves, disguised his booty in a brightly coloured shopping bag and strolled away like any other tourist. A studied lack of urgency would have proved very effective camouflage.

And this was a man, after all, who had robbed a high-end jewellery store, alone in broad daylight. Surely he must have known that as soon as he was out of the door Rojas would be straight on the phone to the cops—whatever his relationship with Peck might have been.

Ah.

Unless, of course, the unlucky Frenchman was not the only person the robber had been intending to leave behind him dead.

Logic told me the man was long gone but that didn't stop me from reaching very quietly under the back of my shirt and easing the pistol grip of the SIG into my palm. It said something about what my life had become that I always felt better with a gun in my hand.

Maybe that was one of the many things that had driven Sean away.

I shook my head as if to dispel flies. Now was not the time. *When is?*

Besides, the unknown robber was not the only person who might have a reason for wanting me out of the way.

I approached the shadowed service road in the same way I would a live-firing Close Quarter Battle range, moving quiet and cautious. I put my feet down with great care, making sure each step was solid before I trusted my weight to it, just in case I had to launch for cover. I led with the gun in both hands, my right forefinger close but off the trigger. Aware of their precarious nature I avoided hugging the buildings too much, instead spending as much time with my eyes on possible hiding places as searching the ground.

Nobody leapt out at me and I found nothing.

I had almost reached the end and was already mentally tossing a coin for right or left when the radio came to life in my earpiece.

"Charlie, you read me?"

I settled the SIG into my right hand and reached for the transmit button with my left.

"I'm here, Joe. Go ahead."

His next transmission was indistinct. I halted, frowning, thumbed up the volume on my handset.

"Say again?"

"I asked if you were due east of our insertion point?" His voice came over louder this time but I got the impression he was speaking softly.

I took a few paces forward so I was just out of the service road and glanced up at the sun, shielding my eyes. After some quick ready reckoning of direction I hit transmit again, swinging round as I did so. After the relative gloom of the service road it was uncomfortably bright out there.

"Negative. More like southwest."

"In that case—"

He never got to finish whatever he'd been about to say. At that moment a high-pitched whine zinged past my ear. The brickwork within a couple of feet of where I'd been standing disintegrated with a sharp, vicious crack.

Twenty-nine

I twisted on the balls of my feet and threw myself sideways, back toward the relative safety of the service road entrance. Another round followed the first. If I hadn't moved instantly, that one would have been right on target.

Thank God for the uncertainties of the first cold shot.

I loosed a single round in the direction of the storefront and then scuttled backward deeper into cover, moving on my elbows and toes, keeping the SIG up and alert for a target. None showed itself.

"Charlie!" Joe Marcus made no attempt to speak quietly now. I flinched at his voice in my earpiece. "Report! What's your status?"

"I'm being shot at, what do you think?" I responded in a savage whisper. "Not you by any chance, is it?"

"No ma'am," Marcus said more mildly. "I'm not nearly pissed enough at you for that. Not yet."

"Well I've pissed *somebody* off enough, that's for sure. Where are you?"

Did I imagine his hesitation? "I'd guess southeast of your position. I saw movement I thought was you but I guess that must be our shooter. Looters, maybe?"

"If that was the case he would have fired and run. This guy's dug in for the long haul."

"Stay put. No heroics."

I rested my forehead momentarily on my clasped hands. Moment of truth time. Did I trust Joe Marcus or did I think he was the one who'd just taken a pot-shot at me?

Ah well, only one way to find out.

"Any chance you can get yourself in a position to lay down a bit of covering fire for an exfil? By now he'll have lined himself up with the end of the service road and I'm caught like a rat in a drainpipe."

"You reckon that's where he's located?"

"Why not? It's where I'd be."

"Give me a couple of minutes. Riley's on his way in for an evac."

"Well unless he's managed to fit a GE Minigun to the Bell since he dropped us off, he better keep his distance until we're clear of groundfire. The helo makes a much more satisfying target than I do."

"Don't you worry none about Riley. Won't be his first time playing with the big boys."

"Speaking of which, how many extra magazines did you bring for that Colt?"

"A couple. You?"

"The same," I lied. Always good to keep one in reserve. "Let's hope that will be enough."

"I was trained by guys who believe you can never have a gun too big or too much ammo."

"I was trying to travel light or I would have packed my RPG."

He laughed briefly and was gone.

I lay very still with more rocks and half bricks digging into my ribs, pelvis and shins than I was happy about. A few insects buzzed around me. I was aware of the smell of something vaguely rotten permeating the air. Large areas of the city had now been four days without power. We might have pulled out the bodies but if there was any food in the vicinity then it was definitely no longer fit to eat. A tiny shimmer of movement caught my eye and I noticed a couple of suspiciously large ants tracking across the terrain just in front of me.

"Oh great. All supposing I'm not shot to death, instead I get stripped to my bones by bloody ants," I grumbled. "Just what I need."

I cricked my head over to one side and raised it just far enough to have a minimal view over the tumbled pile of broken concrete in front of me. Almost immediately I saw the muzzle flash and heard the echoing snap of a handgun report from the glassless window of a storefront on the far side of the main street.

The range was probably less than thirty metres, which was the length of a standard pistol range. If the unknown gunman

220

put in any practice time at all, then hitting me was well within his capabilities. I ducked rapidly but the round landed close enough to blast concrete dust and grit into my face. The ants went about their business unconcerned.

I didn't return fire just for the sake of it. Let him think I needed to conserve my supply. I almost keyed the mic on my radio to report the gunman's position but decided against it. If he had any sense Marcus would contact me before he took any offensive action. It seemed like a long time since we'd spoken, even though it could only have been a minute.

Meanwhile there was no great imperative to move—providing those ants *didn't* turn out to be some man-eating species. And providing my lone gunman wasn't biding his time waiting for a bunch of his pals to show up. It wasn't unreasonable to suggest they might be looters, although in my experience they tended to cut and run when faced with discovery rather than make a stand.

I unwound the cotton scarf I wore round my neck as a dust filter and wiped my face to keep my eyes clear.

"Whatever you're going to do, Joe," I said under my breath, "do it soon."

There was always the possibility, of course, that Marcus was already doing exactly what he came here to do, which was pin me down in an exposed location and wait until I panicked or did something stupid from sheer boredom.

I could think of any number of reasons why he might have decided that another convenient 'accident' was called for. Aware my time here was short and we'd promised Mrs Hamilton answers, I knew I'd pushed harder than was prudent. I recalled again the way Joe Marcus had carefully questioned who was my contact back in New York—Sean or Parker. It was no secret that I worked for Armstrong-Meyer, but did the fact that I was reporting directly to Parker give anything away?

With his well-informed source Marcus probably knew it was Mrs Hamilton who'd come to Parker for Kyle Stephens's replacement, and it wasn't a stretch from there to assume I'd also been briefed to finish the investigation Stephens had started. Was that enough to make him concoct this makeshift plan to get rid of me?

Perhaps Hope had called him about my discovery of the gems she'd lifted from the street. Or maybe I'd overplayed my hand on the short flight over and he'd simply decided I was going to be too greedy for my own good.

On the other hand, I could be way off base and it wasn't Marcus out there at all. I took small comfort from the fact that most of the US Marines I'd encountered were proficient enough with a weapon to have slotted me at their first attempt.

Still, Marcus was no longer in the Corps. It wouldn't take long to discover if it took him a while to get his eye in.

I twisted round very carefully and checked the service road behind me. As far as I could tell it was empty. The nearest piece of available cover was probably the same distance away as the man lurking in the storefront up ahead. That meant an attack— if and when it happened—could come from either direction. A fit man could sprint the thirty metres separating us in a little over four seconds. If he started his run when I was looking the wrong way, even for a moment, that didn't leave much time to react.

I shifted my position so I could swing the SIG to cover both vectors with the least effort. I learned a long time ago that the more naturally the muzzle points at the target, the more likely you are to hit it, even with your eyes closed. And the lack of reaction from across the street proved at least that my hips were not wide enough to stick up beyond the concrete in front of me when I was on my side. So, there's always a silver lining.

The time oozed by with exaggerated slowness. I forced myself to concentrate on the noises around me, trying to pick up on anything out of place. It was difficult when everywhere was far from silent. Apart from the distant helos constantly overflying the city and the squabble of scavenger birds, the buildings themselves rasped and groaned as they continued to settle. Plastic packaging snapped in the breeze. The occasional tile slithered and skipped off the roof and smashed on the concrete below. Every time one did so I tried my best not to jerk in surprise.

Eventually, I caught the faintest scuff of movement along the main street to my left, too regular to be anything but human, moving with care. They were good, whoever they were, but not quite good enough to disguise all sound of their approach.

I held the SIG stretched out loosely in front of my body, elbow resting on the ground to take the weight of the gun. I kept checking both ways like a kid whose parents have drummed road safety into them.

With an effort, I regulated my breathing. Slow in, pause, slow out. Nice and easy.

So when the shallowest outline of a man appeared around the brickwork at the end of the service road, I was already lined up on him.

"Like I said before, Charlie—nice reflexes," Joe Marcus said.

Thirty

This time when Riley arrived to pick us up Joe Marcus climbed into the rear of the Bell with me. The Aussie pilot didn't comment on the fact we both had weapons drawn. I kept one eye on the landscape below as we lifted off, as if hoping I might catch a glimpse of a fleeing figure.

Needless to say, I did not.

"OK mateys," Riley said after a few minutes in the air, "Somebody want to tell me what the bloody hell that was all about?"

Marcus tucked the Colt away under his shirt and slouched in his fold-out seat.

"One of the things I've always liked about you, Riley, is the fact you know when to follow orders without asking dumb questions."

"Great. Thanks. Put it in a letter of commendation," Riley said with dismissive irritation in his voice. "Now answer the bloody question—dumb or not."

Marcus shrugged even though Riley couldn't see it. "May have been a looter."

"You think?" Riley's words could have been my own. "Most folk aren't making it this far in. Still plenty of stuff to be grabbed from the outlying food stores and electrical wholesalers. Keep 'em quiet for another day or so yet, I reckon."

"That was no random looter," I said and Marcus's stony gaze swept briefly over me.

"You think it might have been the jewellery store robber?" Riley asked. "Come back to grab the rest while he had the chance?"

"Maybe," I said, not taking my eyes off Joe Marcus. "Or maybe the answer's a little closer to home."

That got Marcus's attention. He came upright in his seat. "Be careful what you say now, Charlie."

"Or what?" I said. "I have a convenient accident of some kind, hmm? I mysteriously fall out of a helo or get taken down by some rampaging looter. What a shame there are no rebels handy."

Riley said nothing, all his focus suddenly taken up with the business of flying the Bell, but Marcus's eyes narrowed ominously.

"And why exactly would you think something like that might happen to you?" he asked in a soft lethal tone.

"Why not?" I threw back. "Isn't that what happened to Kyle Stephens?"

Marcus sat back in his seat again and crossed his arms as if afraid of what his hands might unconsciously betray.

"Why would we have wanted Stephens dead?"

"Because he got careless," I said, echoing Riley's own explanation on the day of my arrival. "And then he got unlucky."

"Oh?"

I sighed, rubbed a hand around the back of my neck. It came away gritty like the rest of me.

"Look, let's cut to the chase shall we?" I said tiredly. "I know about Hope."

That got a reaction—from both men. I felt the slight tremor through the airframe as Riley's hands twitched at the controls. Joe Marcus's reaction was a more straightforward flare of compressed anger.

"What do you want, Charlie?"

"A good question. The truth might be a good start."

Marcus gave a snort that broke up into a mirthless smile. "And what do you intend to *do* with this 'truth' once you've gotten it?"

I shrugged. "I'll burn that bridge when I come to it."

From his face he did not find my mangled metaphor amusing.

"Hope is part of this team," he said with deliberation. "We think of her as family and we look out for each other as family."

So what did that make Kyle Stephens?

"Your apparent loyalty is admirable. Shame it doesn't extend to everyone on your team."

"Not everyone needs protecting," Marcus said. "Surely you get that we would want to look out for her?"

"Even though she's been lying to you since she joined R&R?" I asked mildly. "This can't have been a first time for her—not the way she's got her moves down—"

Marcus launched out of his seat. In the space between heartbeats he had his hand fisted in my shirt, his forearm wedged across my throat and his face thrust close to mine.

"Don't say another word about that kid," he bit out, "or you will be getting out of this aircraft before the next stop."

In reply I jerked both hands up, grabbed his ear with one and his chin with the other and started to wrench his head round. Marcus wisely dropped his chokehold before the vertebrae in his neck gave way. As he lurched back his eyes were wary and, I like to think, just a little more respectful. He made an exploratory movement of his head and winced.

Well, good.

"Looks like you're right," I said. "Not everyone does need protecting."

"Like you said, I'm loyal to my team," he said tightly. "You attack one of us, you attack all of us."

"But that proviso didn't extend to Kyle Stephens, did it?"

As soon as I spoke I knew it was the wrong thing to say. Marcus lost his defensive posture and seemed to uncoil. He sat back, his whole body relaxing.

And in that moment I knew I'd been on the cusp of an important discovery, and somehow I'd blown it.

Thirty-one

I was photographing teeth when Parker Armstrong called from New York. It was early afternoon, after Riley had returned me and Joe Marcus to the army camp. Almost immediately Dr Bertrand commandeered me. Apparently my skills with a camera were not as bad as she'd feared.

Besides, I didn't think spending further time with Marcus—or seeking out Hope—was a good idea.

So I spent several hours working with a forensic odontologist from the UK, who was carefully sorting through a scattering of teeth and allocating them to individuals. He was currently gluing them onto strips of card that resembled a dental X-ray. From this, he told me, it might be possible to identify victims too badly damaged to otherwise put a name to.

"There's always DNA, but that's expensive and often there's nothing to match it to," he told me, inspecting another tooth. "Superglue and cardboard is the more cost-effective option."

I snapped each completed mouthful with the URN giving the team who'd found the victim, the area they were found in, and the unique number. Only when the body was finally identified and reconciled to their family would that number finally be put aside.

I was so absorbed in the work that the buzz of my cellphone made me start. I checked the incoming number and gave an apologetic smile to the Brit odontologist.

"This could be important. I better take it, if that's OK?"

He waved me away cheerfully enough, his glasses perched on the end of a long nose.

"I'll shout when this one's complete," he mumbled, distracted. "Now then, upper left second bicuspid ... Ah, there you are!"

I took the call, moving away into the far corner as I did so.

227

"Hi boss, what do you have for me?" I asked, careful not to use his name just in case.

"You first," Parker said. "How's it going out there?"

I suppressed a sigh and gave him a brief rundown of earlier events. He listened in loud silence. When I was done he expressed a desire, again, to recall me. Again I refused.

I stood with my back to the wall watching the other teams at work while I talked. The military had laid down a temporary floor that could be scrubbed clean every night but the faint tang of disinfectant overlaying old blood still lingered. It did little for my appetite.

"You have information for me?" I said at last, trying to distract him.

Parker's own sigh was clearly audible across the international phone line. He knew exactly what I was doing and was prepared to go along with it, if under protest.

"Enzo Lefévre and Gabrielle Dubois are aliases," he said flatly. "At the moment we're still trying to uncover their real names but Interpol lit up like a Christmas tree as soon as we started a search."

"What's their interest?"

"Jewel thieves. Lots of skill and finesse—no smash and grab for this pair. I'm told Lefévre means 'craftsman'. Maybe that's why he chose it. From what I could squeeze out of my Interpol liaison, they've pulled off some major heists along the French Riviera, Monaco, Madrid and that one at the Cannes Film Festival last year. This is the first time they've operated so far from Europe, though."

"So how does that square with what Santiago Rojas told us about the robbery and this supposed third man?" I said, frowning. "The one who shot Lefévre and got away. If this pair were jewel thieves, how likely is it that they just so happened to be in a jewellery store—on the very day it was supposed to have a big delivery—at the precise moment it was turned over by someone else who was totally unconnected?"

"Honest appraisal? About the same odds as getting struck twice by lightning," Parker said dryly. "It happens, but you'd have to be pretty damn unlucky."

I thought of the man in the hospital bed who'd told such a heartfelt story about the woman with the ruby engagement ring.

"I suppose they *could* have simply been taking a holiday and decided to buy a ring like normal people. Would it mean more to a pair of thieves if they paid for something rather than just stole it?"

Parker made a "maybe" noise in his throat. "Might explain why Lefévre tried to intervene and got himself shot for it."

"A sense of professional outrage you mean?" I suggested. "That somebody had the gall to attempt a half-arsed job in front of him?"

"Something like that, yeah—if that's what happened."

I considered that one for a moment. Across from me, the fingerprint expert, also from the UK, was hunched over her workstation. She had just made a match between a palm-print taken from the kitchen counter at the home of a missing person and one of our victims. There was no sense of triumph or satisfaction, though, only sorrow. It was her first time with a DVI team. I wondered if she'd stay the course or volunteer again.

"I think I need to go back and talk to Rojas again," I said to Parker. "It sounds like he may not have been entirely forthcoming."

"He may not," Parker agreed solemnly. "But from what you've said he did suffer a nasty head injury, which we should take into account. After all, we both know the kind of effects something like that can have."

"We do." I scraped a hand through my hair, unwilling to venture much further along that line of thought. Instead I asked, "Is there, um, any news on the girl?"

"I'm still waiting for the London end to get back to me," he said. "They hit a few obstructions. Washington bureaucrats could learn a lot from the British Civil Service, huh? I'll call you as soon as I have something."

"Thanks." *Let's just hope it's soon.* I paused. "I don't suppose there's been any word ...?"

I didn't have to elaborate. Parker knew exactly who I was talking about. He cleared his throat and I knew immediately it wasn't going to be good news.

"We tracked Sean to Germany. A couple of days ago he flew from Frankfurt to Kuwait City."

"Kuwait?" I repeated. "What the hell is he doing there?"

"We believe he may have crossed the border into Iraq," Parker said carefully, "heading for Basra."

I opened my mouth to ask again what the hell Sean was doing but then closed it again, aware of a leaden weight settling in my chest. I had a horrible feeling I knew exactly why Sean might be going alone into bandit country and I hoped to hell I was wrong.

Thirty-two

The night I got back from Mexico City—the night things came to a head between Sean and me—I made what I realised later was a grave error of judgement. It wasn't my first and I daresay it won't be my last either.

Not by goading Sean into respond to me physically. That had been a long time coming—in every sense. Even though he'd left the army with the mistaken belief I was instrumental in ruining his career as I'd ruined my own, he still wanted me. Throughout our brief but clandestine relationship back then, the constraints of behaving with rigid formality towards each other while we were on duty led to break-the-furniture and wake-the-neighbours kind of sex when we were finally let loose.

That night my only thought had been to let it loose again.

So I held him down on the sofa in the living room of the New York apartment and released all those months of pent-up emotion. It was almost impossible not to ravage what had once been mine to take freely. His initial freeze almost made me weep but then his lips relaxed under mine and he began to kiss me back in anger.

I counted on the fact that it's very hard for a man to be raped by a woman he honestly does not desire without some kind of chemical inducement. By the time the shower water had all-but evaporated from our naked skin Sean needed no artificial stimulation.

When I relaxed the lock on his wrist he dived both hands into my short wet hair, dragging my head back to bare my scarred throat like a goat for sacrifice. With a groan that sounded close to torture he feasted on the line of my jaw, my neck, my breasts.

And when his hands slid down over my shoulders to trace my spine and grasp my hips, I cupped his face in trembling fingers and kissed him with aching tenderness, feeling his body rise to mine in the old way, guided by instinct and muscle memory.

I forced myself not to rush even though the need was clawing through me. I knew I had to tip him over the edge of frustration until he could do nothing but give in to blind lust and take what had once been given freely too.

I couldn't contain a harsh cry as we came together. Sean's face was a whitened mask, his eyes closed.

I jammed a hand under his jaw and muttered, "Look at me, dammit. I need you to *know* it's me."

His eyes snapped open. "Christ. Jesus," he managed. "How could it be anyone else?"

When he bucked under me with a growl I almost grabbed for his throat again before I realised he wasn't trying to dislodge me, far from it. I felt the slide of muscle packed under slick skin as he powered to his feet, lifting me, taking me with him. We made it as far as the wall by the bedroom, knocking aside a small table.

My back hit the door frame and my limbs wrapped tight around him as he thrust upward with his face buried in my neck, his teeth on my skin and my name on his lips.

That alone was enough to undo me. I came apart in his arms. If the neighbours had been sleeping, I would surely have woken them.

Almost at once Sean tried to pull back. I tightened my grip.

"Charlie!" His voice was raw. "I can't hold on much longer, and I'm not using—"

"Had a coil fitted," I gasped against his ear. "Not taking chances after last time ..."

If I could have taken the words back I would have done. I knew he'd registered the importance of them by the way he stiffened, then my body spasmed afresh and he was barging into the bedroom itself, tumbling onto the bed with me wedged beneath him.

I landed hard on the mattress still clenched greedily around him.

Afterwards we lay together, separated only by the width of our thoughts. We sprawled on our backs while the sweat cooled on our bodies and the only sound was the slowing beat of our hearts as we came back to ourselves.

I didn't speak. I couldn't think of anything to say that wasn't trite.

Sean shifted, his short hair rasping against the pillow as he turned towards me. I tensed involuntarily. I couldn't help it. Those dark unfathomable eyes probed mine. I knew I needed to say something but nothing came.

"I take it back," Sean said then and I couldn't get a lock on his tone. "If you'd been fucking Parker all the time you were away you wouldn't have been so ..."

"Desperate?" I supplied.

He almost smiled. "I was going to say 'ardent' but I suppose boils down to the same thing."

I stared up at the high ceiling and felt my heart splintering into shards like a bullet through glass.

"I've never been unfaithful to you Sean."

"It was mine, wasn't it—the child you lost?" And when shock kept me mute he recounted with deadly accuracy, "You said you'd had a coil fitted, because you weren't taking any chances 'after last time'. Was it ... before we left the UK?"

I rolled away from him slowly onto my side and curled my knees up toward my chest, resisting the urge to cry. "Was getting myself pregnant the only reason I got to tag along with you to New York you mean?" I asked with brittle dignity. "No, it wasn't."

I heard the gush of his outward breath, felt the mattress sway as he propped himself up on one elbow. His hand smoothed across my hip and gently tugged me over onto my back again so he could see my face.

"I'm sorry, Charlie," he said then, his voice low. "I know how hard this is—for both of us. We're neither of us the people we remember."

I recognised the olive branch for what it was, but still couldn't prevent a hurt question. "Was I *ever* the kind of person who would have tried to trap you with an unwanted child?"

He rubbed his fingers across the scar at his temple and shook his head as much to clear it as in denial. "I just ... don't know," he said helplessly. "It doesn't seem to matter what I *know*, I still can't shake the feeling we're bad for each other—a disaster waiting to happen."

"Maybe we are," I agreed as images of earlier times and places cartwheeled through my mind. I stared into his eyes. "But

I've risked my life for you, and I'd do it again tomorrow without hesitation."

His hand dropped away from his face, a sudden intensity about him.

"Those two spent rounds you carry everywhere with you like a talisman," he said at last, frowning as if until the words were out there he hadn't known what he'd been about to say.

I nodded. "We were facing a gunman with a hostage," I said, matter-of-fact. "I was wearing body armour. You weren't. So, I ... put myself between the two of you."

Sean's gaze flicked over my body as though searching for the extra scars. "Supposing he'd gone for a head shot?" he asked quietly.

"He might have done, but he didn't," I said. "I didn't think he was good enough—and he wanted to be sure. Two in the chest will usually get the job done."

His mouth twisted. "Is that something else I taught you?"

"Yes."

I could have said more—there was so much more to be said—but I lapsed into silence, for all the good it did me. Sean always had been able to read me like an open book.

"What else is there, Charlie?" And when I would have rolled away again he caught my wrist, held it fast and demanded roughly, "Tell me."

So I told him. It was only when I got that phone call from Parker I realised what a mistake it was but at the time it was a relief to finally get it out in the open.

About how being prepared to die for him was only part of the story. About how I discovered while he was in his coma that I was also prepared to kill for him. Not in the midst of a fire fight where saving one life gave you no choice but to take another. But later, with icy calculation. To stalk a target like prey.

"You told me once you thought I had all the makings of a cold-blooded killer. Someone who didn't just have the ability to aim—someone who had what it took to pull the trigger for real," I said. "Turns out you were right."

Thirty-three

On my fourth morning with R&R I found myself slated to work a new sector alongside Hope and Lemon again.

Hope was clearly uncomfortable about this. She was very subdued in the mess hall when I saw her first thing. Her anxiety communicated itself to Lemon, who remained glued to her side throughout breakfast. The dog even refused to be tempted by the offer of bacon strips from the squaddies manning the grill. Unsure of my welcome I didn't sit at the same table, and as soon as Hope had shovelled down her usual healthy serving she scurried away without making eye contact.

I would have gone after her then but Joe Marcus stopped me with an ominous, "Charlie—a word."

I followed him outside, noting that he pointedly turned away from the direction Hope had taken. I watched the yellow Lab trotting along at her heels, the dog's face upturned to fix her with those unwavering green eyes. I schooled my expression into one of polite enquiry.

"What can I do for you, Joe?"

He stared at me for a moment in an attempt to flatten out any sign of flippancy, then said, "Hope's acting kinda upset this morning."

"I'm not surprised," I said. "She's—"

He chopped off my words with an abrupt slice of his hand. "I don't need to know why. I just need her focused on the job. You hearing me?"

I nodded. I was hearing him all right.

"Without Hope—and Lemon—doing their jobs to the best of their abilities, everybody else on this team is just spinning their wheels. *Your* job is to let her work without distractions, not to be the cause of them." He paused. "Lives depend on it, Charlie. Got that?"

"Loud and clear," I murmured.

He gave a final sharp shake of his head as if he couldn't believe my density and spun on his heel. I watched him stride away toward the morgue where Dr Bertrand stood waiting for him. They spoke briefly and she glanced in my direction before they went inside. I don't know what they said and gathered from her bleak expression that I didn't want to know either.

I went out of my way to be pleasantly chatty with Hope on the ride over the city but she remained hunched and withdrawn, only replying to Riley's teasing banter in monosyllables. By the time we reached our designated sector even the laidback Aussie was handing me reproachful glances.

Great. She can't keep her hands in her own pockets and suddenly it's my fault.

Riley dropped us off with the usual comms check, to which Hope responded with a morose, "OK." He lifted off again with a frown that was visible even from the ground.

"Look, are you going to lighten up, Hope?" I asked once we were alone. "Or are we all going to have a miserable day?"

She threw me a look of almost teenage disdain.

"What's the point?" she demanded. "You're going to get me sent home anyway, aren't you?"

Joe Marcus's warning at breakfast was still looming large in my mind—that he valued Hope and Lemon's contribution to the team above almost all others. How far would he go to protect the girl, and why? I remembered the way she didn't flinch that time he touched her arm and I couldn't prevent a shiver of distaste. I hoped I was way off base with my suspicion—he was old enough to be her father for heaven's sake. In terms of maturity, more like grandfather.

Is that what Kyle Stephens did—discovered Hope was the thief he was sent to root out? Is that why she reacted with such force to the mention of his name?

If Marcus attributed so much of R&R's success to Hope, it wasn't just the girl's interests he'd be looking out for. I could just imagine what the other three might do if accusations were made towards the girl.

And what might they have done once already ...

"Hope—"

But she whirled away with a gesture that clearly meant 'leave me alone' and stomped off across another section of cracked paving towards what had once been an apartment block.

I knew if we didn't get things straight between us now, it would fester for days—or as long as I'd got left. Without thinking, I jogged after her and tagged her arm.

Hope gave a squeal that was more temper than anything else. I heard the scrabble of booteed feet and turned just in time to see sixty-five pounds of canine muscle pounding toward me at a flat run. Lemon's normally goofy expression had been replaced by a snarling mask.

I yelled, "GET DOWN!" at the top of my voice. Lemon was normally obedient to voice commands and however quickly she came to Hope's defence I assumed she was not a fully trained attack dog.

Her pace slackened, head ducking in confusion, but she didn't veer off. When she was three long strides away I braced myself and swung my left arm out and across my body, saw her focus on this new and tempting target.

As she gathered and leapt, jaws opening, I snatched my arm back and twisted to the side. The dog flew past me, her vest skimming my sleeve close enough to rasp as she went. I grabbed the cotton scarf from round my neck and wrapped it quickly around my left wrist and hand.

"Call her off, Hope," I warned as Lemon skated on the loose gravel in the gutter of the road and came about for another run. "I don't want to hurt her."

Hope snorted. "Yeah, right. Think you can?"

"Unless that vest she's wearing is made of Kevlar, I know I can," I said. "Don't make me prove it."

Hope hesitated. As she did so Lemon leapt for me again, although less forcefully this time. Again I whipped my arm back just as her teeth clacked shut on empty air. She was looking more puzzled than aggressive now but if I wasn't careful she was going to forget all about wanting to protect her handler and try to bite me out of sheer frustration instead.

"Hope!" I snapped.

She finally seemed to realise the danger she was putting her dog into. Seeing her waver, I started to move my right arm back as if reaching beneath the tails of my shirt.

She let out Lemon's name on a yelp and the dog went to her instantly. Hope dropped to her knees and wrapped both arms around the Lab's neck, sobbing into her fur. Lemon looked up at me over Hope's shoulder, breathless and, unless I was imagining it, ever so slightly sheepish.

I didn't attempt to go near the pair of them until the girl had quietened. Instead, I just stood far enough back that I'd have warning if she suddenly decided to send Lemon in for another go. I unwound my scarf from my hand and arranged it around my neck again. It was the one I usually wore when I was out on the bike to stop the draught whistling down the collar of my leather jacket. In the past I had vaguely thought it might do double duty as a makeshift bandage or sling if need be, but fending off attacking dogs had not been on my list of alternative uses.

"I wouldn't have hurt her unless you forced me to," I said gently. "It wasn't Lemon's fault so why should I take it out on her? She loves you enough to protect you. That's something she should be rewarded for, not punished."

That brought on a fresh paroxysm of weeping. I suppressed a sigh and waited her out. Eventually Hope's sniffs subsided. Lemon sidled out from her grasp and shook herself vigorously. Hope remained slumped on her knees. She spoke without lifting her head, her voice so low I hardly heard her.

"What do you want, Charlie?"

"Highest on the list at the moment would be not to get bitten," I said, deliberately light. "Second would probably be a bacon sandwich."

She didn't lift her head and her voice remained a subdued mumble. "But what do you want not to tell."

I sighed. "I don't *want* anything, Hope. No, that's not true. What I want is for you to stop stealing stuff from the streets. I want you to get on with your job without trying to get Lemon into trouble. I want you both to do what you're best at. You know Joe Marcus values you two above everyone else on the team. Don't let him down. And don't let yourself down either."

Thirty-four

As if to prove Joe Marcus's faith in them, later that morning Hope and Lemon made another live find in one of the old apartment blocks.

Word spread fast. Within twenty minutes the area was swarming with personnel. I gathered that the government had been about to declare the rescue phase of the operation officially over. Finding someone still alive at this stage was considered big news.

So, not only did Dr Bertrand arrive with Joe Marcus, flown in by Riley in the Bell, but the Scots copper Wilson also turned up with his dig team. He greeted me with a serious nod on his way to survey the lopsided building.

I stayed out of the way and kept an unobtrusive eye on Hope who stood off to one side. Lemon sat next to her, the beloved chew toy clutched in her jaws. Her gold-tipped ears flapped like pennants at each new burst of activity, as if she knew she was the cause of it all.

It was not an easy extraction—I was beginning to realise they never were. Once Lemon had indicated for them, the dig team were able to locate the survivors—a young mother and her baby—relatively quickly.

Getting them out was another thing altogether.

The pair had been the living room of their second floor apartment when the earthquake hit. The old building, mainly timber with brick protrusions that were nowhere near up to modern codes, had folded like a house of straw. The two of them were found in the cellar, still surrounded by the remains of the sofa on which they'd been sitting.

To complicate matters, the woman had apparently broken her pelvis in the fall. By the time they'd cut a small exploratory hole through to her she was so incoherent she couldn't even tell them her name. She was convinced the hands of the rescuers reaching out to her were those of the devil himself trying to pull both her and the child down into hell.

The last thing she could be persuaded to do was hand over the baby which she cradled mute and still in her arms. Initially Wilson thought it might be either dead or a doll until he caught the faintest movement. When this was relayed back the sense of urgency kicked up another gear.

"We need to separate 'er from the child, even if that means shooting 'er with some kind of tranquiliser dart," Dr Bertrand declared brusquely. "If the child is not already near to dying, it soon will be."

I was all for it, but the suggestion did not meet with general approval. Meanwhile, Joe Marcus had assessed the state of the structure and was not encouraging.

"It we weaken one critical piece of support, the entire building could pancake on top of them," he said. "I'm amazed it's lasted this long with the aftershocks we've gotten over the last couple of days."

A plan was hastily devised to dig down outside the footprint of the building itself and go directly into the cellar by tunnelling through what remained of the foundations. It sounded like lunacy to me but everybody else nodded their heads gravely. Wilson volunteered to be first into the hole.

"I'll drag her out by force if I have to, eh?"

But by the time they'd scratched their way through concrete, hardcore, earth and stone—a job which could not be done either quickly or quietly—the woman was in the throes of a complete meltdown. When Wilson squeezed in alongside her she lashed out with fists and whatever loose objects she could find to throw.

"Crazy bitch," Wilson said, climbing stiffly out of the hole and touching his fingers to a sliced wound on his cheek. "At this rate the lassie's gonna bring the thing down on herself and the wee bairn."

"Would it help to have a female face with you?" I asked.

Joe Marcus shook his head immediately. "I'm not risking Alex getting herself injured. She needs all her fingers working just the way they are."

"Actually, I was thinking of using someone far more expendable," I said. "Me, in fact."

It was interesting to note there were far fewer objections to that idea than to suggestions the French surgeon should put herself in any danger. Always nice to know your own worth.

Wilson rooted through his pack for a plaster large enough to cover his cheek. I borrowed a harness and what looked like a cycling helmet with an LED light attached from one of the other dig team members and waited for a final decision. It didn't take long before Marcus headed over.

"OK, Charlie, you're good to go. We're running out of time so this is your last chance to back out." His tone offered no opportunity for second thoughts.

I shook my head. "No thanks," I said. "I'm all set."

Wilson grinned at me. "Ladies first then, eh?"

I clipped the polypropylene recovery line to my harness and jumped down into the hole, then switched on my head lamp and slid head first into the short tunnel through the foundations. I low-crawled on my belly, using my elbows and the toes of my boots for purchase and wishing there had been time to dig a bigger hole.

When I emerged into the tiny cavern that was the cellar, the first thing that hit me was the four-day stench, acrid enough to make me gag. The second thing was a piece of brick, which bounced off the side of my helmet, accompanied by an inarticulate scream from the trapped woman.

"Please, I'm here to help," I said loud enough to be heard above her wailing. "We just want to get you out of here."

In the beam of my light her wild eyes showed briefly from beneath a matted tangle of hair. She threw another rock but with less force, as if she'd exhausted what little energy she had left. Still clutched in her left hand was the dirty bundle of rags. I feared the worst, but as I emerged from the tunnel she squeezed the bundle tighter and it let out a feeble squawk of protest.

I kept talking, trying to reassure her, but I knew I was fighting a losing battle. And when Wilson began to shimmy out into the cellar behind me, she became almost hysterical. Given the circumstances I couldn't really blame her for that.

"What the feck do we do now?" Wilson muttered.

I rolled my eyes. If we'd been faced with a berserk man he would have had no qualms but this had him floored.

"Get ready to catch," I said, and launched myself across the gap.

I tried to go as gently on the woman as I could, which wasn't easy when she rained blows on my head and shoulders as soon as I was within range. But barely being able to move her hips put her at a disadvantage. I was able to get behind her far enough to put a solid lock onto her neck and press hard with my forearms at either side, restricting the blood flow to her brain. Already weakened, she was unconscious inside ten seconds. A startled Wilson managed to grab the baby as it slipped from her grasp. I fumbled in a pouch on my belt and secured her hands with a plastic zip-tie while I had the chance.

"You want to take the bairn out and drag the stretcher back in here?" he asked.

I eyed the filthy dripping baby he was offering toward me and hastily nodded to the mother. "What if she comes round while I'm gone?"

He grimaced. "Ah, good point. Back in a jiffy then, eh?" As he squeezed himself into the confined exit I heard a muffled, "Jesus, wee feller, you stink to high heaven."

I thought I'd got the better end of the deal, but no sooner had the Scot's feet disappeared into the tunnel than the earth around me began to shudder.

Thirty-five

As soon as the aftershock hit, the building above me started to groan like an old ship. I'd never suffered from claustrophobia but that sound brought me close to panic.

Most of the time the threats I face are small. Even in Mexico City, where we came under attack from an organised fighting force, I knew it was made up of small individual units. Men, who lived and breathed and bled and died like the rest of us. An earthquake is an implacable monster bigger than a mountain. At five storeys high, the building we were in represented a fraction of it.

And suddenly I felt very small and very puny by comparison.

I swung my head so the beam of my light shone towards the tunnel entrance. No sign of Wilson.

"Come on, come. Get your bloody arse into gear." The shuddering picked up a notch. I eyed what was left of the cellar ceiling with alarm and muttered, "Not you!"

Dust speckled through the beam of the light as it fell. Over in a dark corner a skewed beam creaked and shifted and then let go with a tremendous dry crack like a rifle shot. I threw myself face down over the woman's upper body as shrapnel splinters peppered my back.

I glanced across at the hole again, willing myself not to dive for it while I still could. Beneath me, the woman stirred and moaned. I lifted away from her.

The earth gave a violent heave and I heard the slithering tumble of stones and roof tiles and crashing timbers. It was hard to tell if they were directly above or outside. But if they'd fallen into the hole at the far end of the tunnel ...

The woman came round groggily. She struggled against the restraints but without any force—she was spent. Nevertheless, I daren't leave her.

This time, when I looked to the tunnel I saw the flickering of a light, the beam widening as it came nearer. A moment later Wilson's grimy face shoved through, breathing hard. The relief was like a solid mass lifted from my chest.

"Aw, you could at least have brought me back a double espresso," I drawled. "And a couple of those little caramel biscuits."

Wilson grinned wearily. "I can go back if you like?"

He slithered round and dragged the rolled-up caving stretcher into the cellar behind him. It was made of canvas reinforced by wooden slats like the battens in a sail. We unrolled it quickly and tucked it underneath the woman as carefully as we could. She still shrieked with pain at every movement. We secured her in place with the kind of wide buckled straps you'd expect to see on a straitjacket. There was already a rope attached to the foot end.

We lined the loaded stretcher up with tunnel and Wilson jerked twice on the rope. Almost immediately the slack was taken up and the stretcher began to inch forward into the void. The ground shivered and the woman screamed again, in fear this time. I couldn't say I blamed her for that.

"Do you want to go first—give her a shove?" I asked.

"Better you do it," Wilson said.

I caught something in his voice and turned so I could put him in the beam of my light. I saw way he was holding his left arm stiffly, and the blood on his sleeve.

"Glass," he said. "Bloody window dropped on me as I was handing the baby over. Lucky it didn't cut the wee feller's head off."

My eyes widened, but I simply nodded and scrambled into the tunnel. There'd be time for talk later—or not at all. I put both hands against the woman's shoulders and dug the toes of my boots in harder than was necessary. The stretcher shot out of the other end like a champagne cork and was hoisted out of the hole. As soon as I was clear I turned, grabbed Wilson's outstretched right hand and hauled him free before the pair of us were hurriedly dragged back to ground level.

I saw the reason for the haste when I turned back to look at the building we'd just been underneath. I swear the whole thing was swaying gently, as if one more good shake would see it all come crashing down.

244

Thirty-six

As soon as Riley had mother and child strapped down he lifted off in the Bell, pirouetting as he rose, and headed straight for the main hospital with Dr Bertrand stabilising her patients en route.

It wasn't until I'd stripped out of my borrowed harness and helmet that I realised Hope and Lemon had gone too. I searched for Joe Marcus but realised the R&R team had all climbed aboard and left me behind.

Like I said—always nice to know your own worth.

I found Wilson sitting in the load bay of his dig team's police transport helo having his lacerated arm seen to. In daylight the wound looked far nastier than it had done underground in the dark.

"Hospital," one of the medics decided. "I hope your shots are up to date."

"If not they soon will be, eh?"

He saw me and gave a sober nod. The medic gave me a pat on the shoulder as he left. With these guys that passed for high praise.

"If you're heading that way, can I hitch a ride?"

"Don't see why not. Marcus left you behind, did he?"

I shrugged, not trusting myself to speak. Wilson's voice turned quietly serious.

"You wanna watch yourself there."

I stilled. "Meaning?"

He raised a hand in mock surrender. "Hey, don't be giving me the daggered looks. Just something I overheard, that's all."

"Wilson ... Just spit it out, will you?"

"Well, when I brought out the wee bairn and the whole bloody place started shaking and that bloody window tried to guillotine me—" he lifted the shoulder of his injured arm, "—I heard

Marcus say to that French doctor about how maybe this would be an ideal time to cut their losses."

"Cut their losses?"

"They were talking about leaving the pair of you down there, Charlie. Why d'you think I came back in, even bleeding like a stuck pig, eh?"

"Don't you mean 'knight in shining armour'?" I corrected.

"Forget it." He grinned again although he was clearly fast exhausting his supply. "No big thing, eh?"

"Yes it is," I said. "And I won't forget."

Wilson's stocky police pilot opened the door to the cockpit and hoisted himself in. He pulled on his headset and looked over his shoulder, making a thumbs-up or thumbs-down gesture of enquiry.

Wilson gave him a thumbs-up and eased back from the edge of the load bay. I hopped in alongside him and strapped in. The police helo had no more creature comforts than R&R's, except the seats were more firmly bolted down and had a fixture which, I assumed, was where they could secure a prisoner's handcuffs for transit.

The flight to the hospital complex didn't take long. Oh for one of these to beat traffic back home in New York.

But New York was not really my home, I realised suddenly. It was where I happened to be living. If the situation between Sean and me could not be retrieved, how much longer could I stay there?

I cursed the impulse that had made me confess my sins to him. All our troubles, it seemed, stemmed from me either saying too much or not enough. The next time I saw him I swore I would say everything I had to—everything I should have said a long time ago—even if it was the last time I got the chance.

If I ever saw him again.

I pulled out my phone intending to call Parker for a progress report on that front, but the noise inside the Eurocopter's cabin made it impractical. Reluctantly, I slid the phone back into my pocket, noting Wilson's eyes on me as I did so. I wasn't sure if the look he gave me was sympathy or cynicism.

The police obviously had priority landing rights and were able to set down closer to the main entrance in the spot usually reserved for air ambulances. As soon as we were on the ground and the engines began to spin down I patted the pilot on the shoulder by way of thanks and jumped out, snagging the first person I saw in medical garb.

Fortunately, Dr Bertrand made enough of an impression on everyone she dealt with that the doctor I collared was able to point me in the right direction. I knew I must be close when I spotted Joe Marcus leaning against a wall giving him a view of the lobby area. He was sipping a large coffee and gave me a slight nod of greeting when I walked in.

"What happened to the old infantry motto of 'leave no man behind'?" I asked.

The look he gave me was a sour one. "You expected us to wait around for you when we had casualties to transport?"

That wasn't what I'd been referring to and I was pretty sure he knew it, but arguing the point would not have got me far. I glanced about the lobby although I already knew he was alone.

"Where's Hope?"

He took another sip of coffee and swallowed before answering. "With Riley in the Bell. They don't allow rescue dogs in here."

Any question about why they'd left me behind would have sounded like a complaining child, so I restricted myself to pointing out mildly, "I can't protect her if you whisk her away from me the moment I'm not looking."

"Then maybe you should have been looking."

"Yeah, well, that's a bit difficult from a hole in the ground."

He raised an eyebrow as if I'd just answered my own question. "You're either a bodyguard or you're one of the team, Charlie. Can't be both."

"So you didn't consider Kyle Stephens one of the team either?"

Again he treated me to his best Marine Corps hard stare. It was getting harder to feign indifference to it.

"No, I believe it was Stephens who made that decision."

Before I could query that statement, the lift doors opened across the other side of the lobby and a man in a wheelchair emerged, being pushed by one of the nursing staff.

I recognised the man right away even in his street clothes. Santiago Rojas was pale and clammy under the artificial strip lights, his jacket hanging awkwardly around the cast on his arm. Half his head was still wrapped in dressings and he looked as though the short ride down from his bed had already exhausted him. Balanced on his lap was a paper bag which I assumed

247

contained his old clothing. They'd had to cut most of it off him so there can't have been much worth keeping.

Marcus spotted Rojas too and he levered away from the wall, dropping his empty cup into a cylinder bin while he waited for the pair to reach us. I wondered briefly if anything was better than staying to answer my questions.

"Señor Rojas," he said. "You leaving already?"

Rojas managed the majority of a smile. "All I do is lie down for most of the day and there are many others who need a bed here more than I. If my house still stands I can rest there as easily."

"He is not fit to go home," the nurse said stoutly. "Please, if you are his friends, convince him to stay another few days at least. His head injury—"

"I am OK," Rojas said, reaching back to pat her hand with his uninjured one. "Please, do not worry."

The nurse's pager went off. She checked it and relinquished her hold on the wheelchair with reluctance.

"Do not worry," Rojas said again. "Go. I have called for a car. It will be here soon. And thank you."

She flashed him a smile and hurried back to the lift, her shoes squeaking on the tiled floor.

"If you're going to be at home alone you might want to consider hiring someone to look after you," I said.

He frowned. "I am sure I do not need a personal nurse."

"Not a nurse," I said. "I meant someone to ensure your safety—a bodyguard."

Thirty-seven

Santiago Rojas glanced quickly between the two of us.

"A bodyguard?" he repeated. "But why?"

"We believe the man who robbed you may return," Marcus said after a short pause. He gave the jeweller the shortened version of our trip back to the street of boutique stores and of the unknown sniper. "It could have been a random looter, but you may not want to take chances."

Rojas nodded carefully. "I–I cannot believe all this trouble over so small a prize. If my delivery had not been delayed ..." He gave a lopsided shrug.

Behind him the lift doors binged and opened again. This time it was Dr Bertrand who strode into the lobby. Joe Marcus excused himself at once and went to meet her. I noticed they moved out of earshot before they began speaking in low tones.

"Who is the lady?" Rojas asked.

"Dr Bertrand. She's the one who treated you at the scene."

"Ahh, then I must thank her also before I leave."

"I'm sure she'll appreciate that," I said, mentally crossing my fingers.

"Did you find out any more about the beautiful young lady with the ruby ring?" he asked then. "Dubois, I think you said her name was."

I shook my head. "It turns out Gabrielle Dubois was not her real name. She and her partner, Enzo Lefévre, were jewel thieves wanted by Interpol," I said. "Looks like there may have been more than one plan in the works to rob you."

"No! I cannot believe it. They seemed so ... ordinary. And so much in love. Do you know ... what was her real name?"

"That we don't know—yet. We have someone working on it."

Marcus and Dr Bertrand finished their conversation and came over. To my surprise she offered the injured man a smile that was at least polite if not exactly effusive.

"*Hola Señor Rojas. ¿Cómo se siente?*" she rattled off in Spanish.

Rojas looked momentarily stunned, then he stumbled into speech. "*M–mucho mejor, gracias. Gracias a su pericia. Sin usted ...*"

My own Spanish had improved working for Parker, to the point where I could work out she'd asked how he was feeling and he'd told her he was much better, thanks to her expertise, because without her ...

She paused as if to consider and then nodded her agreement with his evaluation.

A harried-looking woman in a white coat appeared from a doorway and hovered where she could catch Dr Bertrand's attention.

"If you will excuse me, I 'ave a patient to attend to." To Marcus she added a curt, "I will not be long. Wait 'ere." And then swept out without waiting for a response from either man

Rojas subsided into his wheelchair looking a little overwhelmed by the encounter.

"She is a force of nature, is she not?"

Marcus's mouth twitched up at one corner. "That she is."

"I would very much like, if it is possible, to say thank you also to Hope and the dog who found me. Is she here?"

"They're outside," Marcus said. "You'll see R&R's helo sitting out on the parking lot. She's there with the pilot who brought you in." His eyes flicked to me. "I'm sure Charlie will be happy to take you."

"Excellent," Rojas said. "But I do not want to be any trouble?"

I wondered what Dr Bertrand intended to discuss with Joe Marcus that was so urgent, and too private to have me around. I hid my irritation behind a smile and gripped the handles of the wheelchair. "No trouble."

But almost as soon as we got outside, my cellphone rang insistently in my pocket. I halted to fish it out and check in the incoming number. Parker.

"I'm very sorry," I said to Rojas. "It's my boss and I really need to speak with him. Are you OK for a few minutes?" The wheelchair was not one the occupant could propel themselves.

"Do not worry. I think I see the helicopter Mr Marcus talked of—the parking lot is just behind those tents over there, yes? And I am sure if I become lost then I can ask the way. Please, I think I can manage to go to meet my rescuers on my feet, if you would not mind returning this?" He tapped the arms of the wheelchair.

The phone continued to ring. "Of course," I said, already stabbing my thumb on the receive button. "Thank you. If you're sure?"

He smiled. "It is no trouble," he said and hoisted himself slowly out of his seat using his unplastered arm. I watched him walk away, hesitantly at first and then with increasing confidence when he didn't end up falling flat on his face, carrying his bag of rags. Perhaps he wanted them as a memento of his close call.

"Hi boss," I said into the phone. "What's up?"

"You with someone? Can you talk?"

"I was seeing off Santiago Rojas, the guy we pulled out of the rubble of the jewellery store a few days ago. He's just discharged himself from hospital to free up a bed."

"Nice guy," Parker said. "He checks out clean, you'll be glad to know. No criminal record, no shady deals. He worked for a diamond merchant in São Paulo for years before family pressure made him leave to set up his own store over there."

I steered the wheelchair with one hand, turning it in an awkward circle and pushing it back through the glass doors into the lobby area. Joe Marcus, despite Dr Bertrand's order, was nowhere to be seen.

"Family pressure?"

"Yeah, the family are all devout Catholics. They didn't approve of his lifestyle, shall we say."

"He does seem to be a bit of a flirt."

Parker laughed. "Yeah, but you're not quite his type, Charlie."

I frowned, thinking of Rojas's manner, those sensual hands, his admission of the affair with Commander Peck's wife, and his reaction to Dr Bertrand's icy beauty.

"I don't get you."

"Well, they didn't approve of the fact he was gay, of course," he said, losing the smile in his voice now. "You mean you couldn't tell?"

251

"Not a flicker. Quite the opposite in fact. Are you sure he's not bisexual?"

"Not according to the information we have. Otherwise he would have given in and married one of the procession of eligible young ladies his parents kept presenting him with, just to make them happy. By all accounts he was a dutiful son."

"I don't like this," I said. "Something's not right here. Look, Parker, can I call you back—?"

"There's just one other thing before you go," he said quickly.

"Can it wait?"

"No, I don't believe it can. It's about Hope, and you need to hear it."

Thirty-eight

Joe Marcus reappeared just as I finished my call with Parker, putting away his own cellphone.

"Looks like we got that woman and her baby just out in time," he said. "I've just gotten word the whole of that apartment building collapsed about ten minutes ago."

I thought of Wilson's warning that they'd wanted to leave me in the cellar during the last aftershock and didn't respond.

To be honest, I was still reeling from the information Parker had given me.

"Joe, we need to talk."

"Oh?"

"Yes. About Hope—"

Behind us, the lift doors pinged and slid back, and Dr Bertrand came out at her usual speed. Perhaps she had been a greyhound in a previous life.

"I 'ave done what I can for them," she announced. "I must get back to work. There is much still to do."

Marcus started to fall into step with her but I moved in front of the pair of them.

"No," I said. "Nobody's going anywhere until I get some answers."

The two exchanged a glance and I didn't miss the way Marcus edged sideways a little to widen the gap between them, making two targets harder to watch.

"Is this about the Frenchman?" Dr Bertrand asked.

"What Frenchman?"

I'd opened my mouth to ask the same question only to find Marcus had beaten me to it.

Dr Bertrand looked irritated by our lack of understanding. "The man in the wheelchair of course."

"Rojas? But he's South American—from Brazil."

253

She shook her head, utterly devoid of doubt. "But when I spoke to 'im in Spanish and 'e answered, 'e speaks Spanish with a French accent. Couldn't you 'ear it?"

Marcus saw the wheelchair where I'd left it just inside the doors.

"Where is he?"

Where you sent him. "On his way to see Hope and Lemon."

"You left her alone with him?"

"No, I didn't," I said. "Parker called and I never got that far. If she's at the Bell, Riley will be with them."

I saw by the way Marcus's jaw tightened that he was regretting directing Rojas to Hope as I much as I was for not ignoring that phone call from Parker and accompanying Rojas all the way.

We started to run, out of the lobby of the hospital and through the maze of temporary structures and tents toward the open area where there were half a dozen helicopters from various aid agencies and rescue organisations were parked up.

I stopped, let Marcus come past me. He'd been in the helo when it landed so he surely knew where they'd left it. But when he stopped too, staring about him, I realised we were in serious shit.

"Where are they?" Dr Bertrand demanded, catching us up without appearing significantly out of breath.

"Gone. Dammit!"

"Gone?" For the first time the doctor's voice cracked with stress. "'Ow can they 'ave gone? And where?"

"It's a helo, Alex. They could have gone just about anywhere." He pulled out his radio and tried hailing Riley. There was no response.

"Tell him you've got a pickup for him," I said. "Make it casual."

Marcus gave me a dubious look but did as ordered.

"Sorry mate, I'm a bit held up at the moment." Riley's voice over the background noise of the Bell's engines sounded as laidback as ever. Only his choice of words gave anything away. "I'll get back to you when I'm free."

"Soon as you can then," Marcus said and clicked off. "'Held up'? Oh yeah, they're being held up all right."

"By Señor Rojas? What does 'e want with them?"

I shook my head. "It's not Rojas." That got their attention, although Joe Marcus was halfway to the same conclusion anyway. "I think the man we've accepted as Santiago Rojas is actually the French jewel thief, Enzo Lefévre."

"But Commander Peck, 'e identified the body in the morgue as Lefévre." She sounded outraged at the inferred slight to her professional reputation, as if someone had deliberately set out to blot her near-perfect record.

"The guy had no face, so maybe Peck *assumed*," Marcus corrected her, "based on his proximity to the body of the woman, Dubois. Without other means of ID—like the personal items that were stolen—we had no reason to think otherwise."

"And now?"

"You said yourself that he speaks Spanish with a French accent—"

"Circumstantial," she dismissed. "'E could 'ave 'ad a French nanny as a child."

"Rojas came over from Brazil because his religious family were putting pressure on him over his homosexuality," I said. "Yet he told us he'd had an affair with Peck's wife."

Marcus nodded. "And Peck backed him up." His eyes met mine. "Now why would he do that, hmm?"

I hit redial on my phone without breaking his gaze. When the call was answered I said briefly, "Parker, how quickly can you send me over a picture of Santiago Rojas?"

There were no superfluous questions, just the sound of computer keys in the background. "OK, it's on its way to your cell. Need anything else?"

"No—thanks. I'll call you."

A few moments later my phone bleeped to signal an incoming picture message. The jpeg image unfurled down the screen with agonising slowness. When it had finished downloading I handed the phone to Marcus.

"Not the same guy," he said flatly.

Dr Bertrand said nothing, but her lips had tightened into a compressed line and her face was white.

"'Ow do we find them?"

"We call the police," I said.

Thirty-nine

Wilson asked no questions when I told him simply that someone had grabbed the R&R's helo and taken hostages. We caught up with him, newly stitched and with his left arm in a sling, already aboard the police Eurocopter on the pad near the hospital entrance, with the engines fired up.

As the three of us ducked under the main rotor and would have run toward it, Joe Marcus grabbed Dr Bertrand's arm.

"Alex, you should stay here."

"No!" she said. "She is as much my responsibility as yours, Joe."

He shrugged and let go without further argument. We reached the Eurocopter and scrambled into the rear.

The pilot finessed the Eurocopter into the air and asked, "Which way?" over his shoulder.

Wilson twisted toward us carefully from the co-pilot's seat. "Any ideas where they're headed?"

"If he's any sense then I'd guess the nearest border," Joe Marcus said.

"And if he's no sense, eh?"

"For the moment, let's just get up there and see what we can see."

The pilot shrugged and powered upwards. The Eurocopter was newer than the Bell and faster by probably forty-five knots, but unless we knew where to chase that advantage was negated.

I checked my watch. Riley could have been in the air and travelling flat out at a hundred and twenty knots for fifteen minutes now. The diameter of the search zone was increasing all the time.

"Do we know who's taken your people hostage?" Wilson asked. "And what do they want?"

Marcus explained briefly about Santiago Rojas, our theory that he was Enzo Lefévre, and about Riley's cryptic radio message.

"If this Lefévre is a pro that's good," he said. "Means he's less likely to do something stupid with them."

"We know he's killed once already," I said. That earned me a sharp glance from Dr Bertrand. "If he swapped identities, who do you think shot the real Santiago Rojas in the chest—this mysterious third man nobody can find?"

"Sounds like your pilot can take the pressure, though," Wilson said. "What's his call sign? I'll get my guy to give him a shout and pretend to be Air Traffic Control, something like that. Worth a try, eh?"

"But there isn't any ATC operating over the city, is there?" I asked.

"No." Marcus gave me a grim smile. "We'll just have to hope Lefévre doesn't know that."

Wilson spoke to the pilot. A minute or so later he handed back to us a folded aviation chart with a heading scribbled onto it, wincing as he bumped his injured arm.

"Damn, I think he was wise to us. That bearing makes no sense unless he wants to end up on top of a mountain."

"I've worked with Riley for a long time," Marcus said. "He would have given us something even if he had a gun to his head."

I peered at the chart. From the hospital which had been ringed in pencil, the heading the Aussie had given took them out of the city to the northeast, which wasn't a logical route to anywhere. I opened the chart out and scanned it. Almost at once I recognised one of the areas Hope and I had been given to search.

"What about a reciprocal?" I said. "Rojas's store is directly southwest of the heading he's given you."

"Could be," Wilson said. "Better to go somewhere than nowhere, eh?"

He showed the chart to the pilot who swung the Eurocopter onto a new heading and gunned it. If he'd had lights and sirens he would have been using those too.

"Why would 'e go back there?" Dr Bertrand asked. "'E must know we are after 'im."

"Because of the gems," I said. "If there was no third robber then he and the woman—Gabrielle Dubois—must have robbed

257

Rojas themselves, but we know he didn't have anything on him when he was found."

"So he's gone back to look," Marcus said. "But we searched and didn't find anything."

"Yeah, but we didn't have Hope and Lemon with us."

His expression hardened. "All this for a few stones."

"Lefévre mentioned a new delivery that was supposedly delayed," I pointed out. "But he was lying about everything up to that point. Why not about the delivery as well."

"So you reckon there's a fortune in precious gems out there for the taking, eh?" Wilson said. "Not surprising he decided to risk it."

I shook my head. "I think there's more to it than that—"

At that moment the pilot leaned over his shoulder. "Coming up on the location."

"Put us down short," Marcus said. He pulled the Colt out from under his shirt and racked a round into the chamber. "I don't want the bastard to know we're here."

Forty

Joe Marcus might have been ten years out of uniform, but before that he'd been twenty years in the USMC and he hadn't forgotten a trick.

The two of us picked our way across the deserted streets and the rubble, moving fast but careful, guns out in our hands. The SIG felt inadequate for the task. What I wouldn't have given for an M16 or an HK53 compact assault rifle for this kind of urban combat.

We'd had difficulty persuading Dr Bertrand and Wilson to stay with the helo. Both had wanted to come with us and Marcus had been blunt in his refusal.

"You'll slow us down."

From the way Dr Bertrand scowled at him, it was probably the first time she'd been told she wasn't fit to do something. Wilson looked pained but seemed to accept the truth of it.

"Shout if you need backup though. We can always land the bloody helicopter on 'em, eh?" His pilot did not look overly enthusiastic at this prospect.

We worked our way in to the opposite side of the street to the location of Santiago Rojas's jewellery store. The only signs of life were carrion birds and the occasional scurrying rat.

It was strange to be in the midst of a city and have no traffic noise. Even the immediate airspace was quiet. When the broken canopy of a petrol station flapped in the rising wind, it was sudden enough to make me whirl, bring the SIG up. The canopy rattled again harmlessly and we passed on, dust clouds eddying through the gaps and crevices.

The only place to gain a decent vantage point was the row of buildings facing the jewellery store, none of which were in a particularly good state.

259

Marcus studied the structural damage with a professional eye and eventually led us into the end unit through a rear service door. The store was another one that had sold designer clothing and the sight of the fallen manikins inside the gloomy interior gave it a surreal air. There was the relentless drip of a cracked water pipe somewhere, too, so the ground floor was an inch or so deep in water. I just hoped the power was definitely off as we paddled through it.

A cast iron spiral staircase gave access to the upper storey. The whole thing had become detached from the building around it and now leaned at a slightly drunken angle. It trembled beneath our feet as we climbed.

Upstairs there was a crack in the outer wall so bad I could see daylight through it. The interior had been home to more display racks and fitting rooms. The racks were tumbled to the floorboards and every mirror in the place was cracked or lying in splinters. Looked like somebody was in for a shit-load of bad luck.

Marcus and I tiptoed our way across the glass to the empty window frames and peered out. Below us we had a good view of the street. Off to our far right the Bell was settled on the same landing site Riley had used previously.

The Aussie pilot himself was sitting on the ground, ankles and wrists secured with duct tape. His bound hands were pressing a bloody rag to the side of his head. I guessed from that he hadn't given in gracefully to being hijacked.

The man we suspected was Enzo Lefévre stood a little distance away. In his uninjured hand he was holding the huge Ruger revolver I'd last seen next to Riley's seat in the Bell. Alongside him was Hope, her skinny frame hunched as if expecting a blow. Of Lemon there was no sign.

"Too far for a clear shot," Marcus murmured, regret in his tone.

"Especially in this wind."

"Call her back to you," Lefévre was saying to Hope. He extended the arm holding the Ruger and thumbed back the hammer with a click I could imagine even if I couldn't hear it. "Call her back or you won't ever see your dog again."

"Fuck. You," Hope said clearly and raising her voice she yelled, "Lemon, STAY!"

"God *dammit*, Hope," Marcus said under his breath. "For once in your life do as you're told, girl."

"If she doesn't start playing along we're going to have to do something fast," I murmured. "If Lefévre can't get what he wants from her, she's no use to him."

"She's still a valuable hostage."

"At the moment she's just a pain in the arse. He won't let her back into the helo with the dog—asking for trouble in a confined space—and you know she won't leave Lemon behind without a fight."

Marcus flicked worried eyes to me but said nothing.

Below us the thief still had the gun aimed at Hope, although the Ruger weighed the best part of three pounds and his arm was starting to waver.

"Why are you being so stubborn about this, hmm? All I want is for this remarkable dog I've heard so much about to locate a bag for me. A small bag I had with me when I was trapped by the earthquake. Then you can go free—you have my word."

"What about Riley?"

"I need Monsieur Riley to take me out of here. After that I will release him, also."

Riley laughed and ended up coughing fit to burst a lung. "He's lying, sweetheart. Soon as he gets what he wants we're as good as dead."

Even so, we could see the indecision on the girl's face.

"Do it," Marcus willed her through his teeth. "Give him what he wants. Buy us some time, create a distraction."

"The building's not safe," Hope said at last, tears in her voice. "The gap they made between the cars to drag you out is caved in. What if there's another aftershock and the rest of it comes down on Lem?"

"The decision is up to you, of course," Lefévre said with an almost courtly bow, "but you may not like the alternative."

"What's that?"

Lefévre shifted his aim downwards and to the side, away from Hope.

"That I shoot your friend here through his left leg."

Riley grinned widely at him.

"Not a good idea, mate. Not unless you've got a couple of hundred hours' rotary wing experience under your belt. 'Cos there's no way I can balance the controls for the tail rotor on the old bus without two good feet."

Lefévre thought for a moment, then gave as much of a shrug as his injured arm would allow and shifted his aim back to Hope.

"I am nothing if not flexible in my plans. Call the dog or I will shoot *you* through your left leg, *mademoiselle*. And I can assure you that it will be very painful."

"Another bad idea, mate," Riley said, although there was an edge to his voice that hadn't been there previously. "Look at her. She wouldn't weigh a hundred pounds if you filled her pockets with rocks. That hand cannon is a three-fifty-seven Magnum. You'll blow her bloody leg off and she'll be dead before the dog finishes scratching its arse."

Lefévre let out an annoyed huff of breath and let the big revolver drop to his side. Then he transferred it into his other hand, holding it delicately as if he didn't trust his injured arm to take the weight.

"Ah well, I had hoped we could be ... civilised about this," he said, and backhanded Hope across the face.

The force of the blow had the girl stumbling back. She lost her balance, falling heavily. Riley shouted and swore and struggled against his restraints. Beside me, Joe Marcus surged up. I grabbed his arm, dug fingers and thumb into the pressure points on the inside of his wrist and twisted hard.

"For God's sake stay down," I hissed. "That won't help any of us—least of all Hope."

I nearly recoiled at the way his eyes loathed me at that moment but he subsided without speaking. I relaxed my grip and he roughly shrugged my hand away.

Hope did not get up at once, just lay sprawled on the uneven ground as though stunned. She pushed herself up to a sitting position very slowly, head hanging. When she finally lifted it, there was blood staining her upper lip and her eyes were drenched.

"I assure you this gives me no pleasure," Lefévre told her, "but it causes me no anguish either. I will keep doing it until you give me what I want."

"Go ahead!" Hope threw at him, her voice breaking. "You can't do any worse than what's been done to me already."

"Jesus Christ mate, she's just a kid!" Riley yelped, still struggling without result. "Hope, do what he wants sweetheart. Please. Don't put yourself through this."

"Riley knows, doesn't he?" I said close to Marcus's ear. "He knows about Hope—that she's only sixteen."

"Of course he knows." Marcus couldn't tear his eyes away from the scene unfolding below, but there was pain in etched on his face, and the kind of promise in his eyes that sees men die very unpleasant deaths. "We all know. Did you think we wouldn't?"

I glanced back outside. Hope was still on the ground, gathering herself. Lefévre had made no further moves toward her.

"Including Kyle Stephens?"

I heard his teeth grit together. "Yes."

"Then what the fuck were you thinking, letting her stay?"

"Making a mistake." And for once the contempt in his voice was not solely directed at me.

I rose to a crouch and handed the SIG across. He took it automatically before he realised what I had in mind.

"What the—?"

"He'll only take it away from me," I said, dumping my spare magazines in his hand too. "And he might decide that a forty-cal round is more survivable than three-fifty-seven. Just do me a favour—when you get the chance to shoot him, don't miss."

Forty-one

I walked into the street from the far end, keeping my hands in plain view. The dust swirled around my legs as I went, like some tumbleweed-blown town in the Old West. In the back of my mind I almost heard the jingle of spurs on my heels.

Lefévre saw me coming a long way back. He yanked Hope to her feet and steadied her in front of him, checking Riley's position at his back so nobody had a clear shot behind either.

No flies on you, sunshine.

"That's close enough, if you please," he called when I was maybe fifty feet away. "What do you want?"

"To negotiate."

He smiled. "With what?"

"Word from Hope's boss."

"And where is Monsieur Marcus—lurking somewhere nearby no doubt?"

"We split up to search. He went northeast," I lied, gesturing vaguely. "Could be anywhere by now."

"Let's see the gun."

I shook my head. "I'm not carrying."

"You will not be insulted if I ask you to prove it?"

I lifted my shirt up, baring my midriff, and turned a slow circle so he could see I had nothing tucked into my belt.

"Ankle holster?"

I leaned down and pulled up the bottoms of my cargoes.

"Never liked 'em," I said. "They play hell with my back."

"Sleeves, too, if you please."

I unbuttoned my shirt cuffs and rolled up both sleeves with the exaggerated movements of a stage magician showing there were no rabbits or white doves hidden there. I even removed the cotton scarf from around my neck and twitched both sides toward him like a matador tempting a bull.

"OK—talk. What does Monsieur Marcus have to say?"

"The gist of it is, let his people go or be hunted to the ends of the earth."

He pursed his lips. "And in return for this?"

"We give you what you want."

I heard Hope gasp but didn't take my eyes off Lefévre. He grimaced.

"You cannot give me what I really want."

"You have my sympathies," I said blandly. "Just out of curiosity, what was Gabrielle Dubois's real name?"

He looked momentarily startled then shook his head. "Better for both of us if you never find out."

"Did you really buy that ruby for her, or simply take it after Rojas was dead?"

And did she find it appropriate to be given a blood-red stone?

That brought a twisted smile to his lips. "Once a thief, always a thief," he said. "But our engagement was real. This was supposed to be our last job."

"For her, it was."

The smile vanished and he gave Hope a shove in the back that made her stagger. "Now, if you would be so kind—call the dog in."

Hope's eyes were pleading. "Charlie—"

"Please, Hope. Do as Joe asks."

And whatever you're planning Joe, you better do it soon ...

Hope cast me a final despairing glance, circled her forefinger and thumb, stuck them between her lips and blew sharply, letting out a piercing whistle.

Almost at once there came the scrabble of booteed feet and the yellow Labrador retriever appeared over a mound of fallen bricks. She was wagging her tail and looking inordinately pleased with herself.

With another careful glance behind him, Lefévre leaned to the side and picked up a discarded paper bag. I realised it was the one he'd been carrying when he left the hospital. So he hadn't kept hold of his clothes for sentimental reasons, then. He'd kept them for scent.

That made me feel a little better, knowing that it wasn't a spur of the moment decision born of opportunity that had led him to hijack the Bell. He'd probably been planning this ever since he discovered the dog's tracking abilities.

Yeah, Fox, and who told him about that?

I pushed that insidious thought aside and tried not to look around me for any sign of Marcus's approach. Lefévre was too canny not to spot it.

Lemon trotted right up to her handler and sat down so close in front of her she could prop her muzzle on the girl's thighs. Hope cradled the dog's head with both hands and looked about to cry again.

"Good girl, Lem," she said, her voice cracking. "Who's my best girl then?"

I studied the thin frame and wondered how I'd ever believed she might be twenty. Hell, she didn't even look sixteen.

Lefévre had put the paper sack down near her and now he nudged it with a foot. He had swapped the Ruger back into his good hand, I saw, just in case Hope got any ideas.

"No more delays, *mademoiselle*. If the dog is of no use to me ..." He let his voice trail away with another expressive shrug.

Hope shot him a look of pure venom and dragged the bag of clothing closer. She thrust it under Lemon's nose. The dog obligingly shoved her face inside until only her ears overlapped the top edge and made loud snuffling noises while Hope murmured words of praise to her.

"That's it, Lem. Now find it!"

Lemon almost quivered with excitement as she began to circle, moving outward until she neared the crushed cars where Wilson and his team had cut their way through during the rescue. Was it really only a couple of days ago?

Lefévre's attention was on the dog. I risked a quick glance around me. No sign of Marcus. I tried to catch Riley's eye but he seemed as anguished as Hope.

Lemon nosed around the blocked gap for a moment or so, then apparently lost interest. She feathered away further up the street, head down and tail up.

"What is she doing?" Lefévre demanded. "Call her back."

"She's doing her job," I snapped. "Let her get on with it."

Hope gave me a look of grateful surprise and when Lemon paused to check back, she called encouragement in a stronger voice than before.

Lemon disappeared from view. With her eyes fixed on that spot Hope asked in a brittle voice, "How much do you know?"

"Some. Most of it, probably. Hope's your older sister isn't she? And because she's mentally handicapped and cared for by your parents, you knew she was never going to leave home, get a job, or apply for a driving licence, or a passport, so you did it for her."

"It was my fault," Hope said. "A stupid dare when we were kids. I was only eight—didn't know any better. She always was afraid of heights. Sometimes … sometimes I think it would have been better if she'd died. Instead, Mum and Dad were left with a constant reminder of what they'd lost. Of what I'd done. I guess I don't blame them for taking it out on me."

"So you ran away."

She nodded. "Stuck it for a couple of years, but in the end you can only take the back of someone's hand so often before you've had enough." She glanced at Lefévre with hatred. He either ignored it or didn't hear. "I lived rough, learned to get by."

"Picking pockets."

"Better than the alternative. I was lucky. Met someone who taught me. Got caught a few times, taken back home, but they couldn't make me stay."

"And then you found Lemon."

For the first time she smiled. "Saw someone chuck a box in the canal. Though it might be something I could sell so I fished it out. Turned out to be pups, the sick bastard. Lem was the only survivor."

The unwanted girl and the unwanted dog. Perfect companions. Hope's face suddenly crumpled and she scrubbed away tears, meeting my eyes for the first time with a fierce promise. "If anything happens to her because of this, Charlie, I swear I'll bloody kill you …"

Forty-two

A further ten minutes went past in windswept silence before Lefévre glanced again at Hope and said, "I begin to think the abilities of your dog have been somewhat overplayed."

"She's working it," Hope said, her whole body tense. "Give her time."

"Time is a luxury I do not have. Perhaps you need some encouragement to persuade her to work a little faster." Lefévre lifted the Ruger and swung it in my direction. "Your friend here, for instance, I do not need."

Hope looked at me briefly and I knew she already regretted telling me so much. She sneered. "Shoot her then. She's done nothing but poke her nose in since she got here."

For a moment I saw Lefévre's knuckles tighten around the grip of the big revolver. I braced myself automatically, waiting for the shot. If I was lucky I wouldn't know much about it.

And then, muffled by layers of stone and concrete and brick, came the distinct sound of a dog barking.

Lefévre smiled. "Saved by the dog." He lowered his arm. "Although I think it was perhaps a bluff on your part, *mademoiselle*."

I glanced at Hope's set face. *I wouldn't be so sure about that if I were you.*

Hope shrugged and ignored him, just took a few steps forward and yelled, "FETCH, Lem! Bring it, girl."

A few more agonising minutes dragged past until there was a flurry of movement from further along the row of storefronts and Lemon emerged from a tiny hole. Her golden fur was filthy with dirt and mortar dust, and there was a patch of what looked like oil staining her flank.

But clutched in that soft retriever's mouth was a grubby canvas satchel.

"Good *girl*, Lem!"

The dog brought the find straight to Hope, head high to avoid bumping it on the uneven ground, and relinquished it directly into her hands.

I heard Lefévre mutter, "My God," with wonder in his voice. "That's it. She actually found it."

And a voice behind us a voiced called out, "Did you ever have any doubts?"

We all of us turned almost as one unit. Across on the other side of the street, Commander Peck stood just far enough back to cover the group of us with a HK53 compact assault rifle. How ironic that I'd been wishing for one earlier.

Standing alongside him was the Scottish copper Wilson, and Joe Marcus. For a second I could not think of a good reason for Marcus to be there that didn't have bad connotations for all of us. Me especially.

"Thank you, Miss Tyler, for retrieving my gems."

Lefévre took a step forward but wisely did not try to bring the Ruger up to make himself more of a target.

"We had an agreement, commander, if you recall? A seventy-thirty split in my favour."

Peck gave a negligent shrug. "Circumstances have changed, my friend." He gestured around him. "More people are now involved on my behalf and, if you'll forgive me for pointing this out, fewer on yours."

I checked Marcus's face but could glean nothing from it. Did that "more people" Peck mentioned include him or not? Where was the Colt he usually carried? And my SIG?

"But, a deal is a deal, surely?" Lefévre's mouth was smiling but I was close enough to see his eyes were scared. "You brought us in—my late partner and myself—for this job because you were told you could trust us. Is it unreasonable to expect that you will keep your word?"

"Unreasonable? No. Unrealistic in the circumstances? Yes." Peck's face was stony. "It was supposed to be a simple robbery. You had no need to kill Señor Rojas. That was not part of the deal."

Lefévre took a quick step back, opening his mouth to protest, but it was too late.

Peck fired a short three-round burst from the HK. The 5.56mm NATO rounds exploded into Lefévre's upper torso, dropping him instantly. He let go of the Ruger which skittered away out of reach. I watched his chest deflate slowly as his last breath expelled and he was unable to draw another.

Riley swore again, low and vicious. Hope merely curled herself around Lemon's shivering body as the dog cowered from the gunfire.

"Thank you all for assisting me to capture a dangerous criminal, who sadly resisted arrest," Peck said calmly. "Mr Marcus, if you would be so kind as to retrieve the bag of ... evidence from Miss Tyler, I believe I will now be able to close this case."

With only the briefest pause, Marcus walked across the gap separating us and grasped the satchel Lemon had brought out. As he bent over her, Hope raised a tear-streaked face to his.

"It's all right, Hope. Everything will be all right."

He walked back to Peck without hurrying. Peck held out his free hand for the satchel but Marcus made no immediate moves to hand it over.

"We agreed on a dozen stones," he said, "for letting you handle this your way."

Peck said nothing for a moment, then nodded.

I watched in disbelief as Marcus undid the straps and pulled out a black velvet pouch. He reached in without taking his eyes from Peck and came out with a handful of what might have seemed like chips of glass except for the way they sparkled as they caught the light. He let a couple drip back through his fingers, counted what remained, then put the pouch back into the satchel and handed it over without a word.

"This just gets better and better, doesn't it, Joe?" I said, my voice oozing with contempt. "Now I know why you had to get rid of Kyle Stephens."

Riley swore again, more quietly this time, and Hope's breath hitched in her throat.

Marcus gave me a long stare that went right through me as if it found no resistance. "You don't know anything for sure."

"Oh, of course not," I agreed, edged with sarcasm. "That's why you wanted to leave me in that damn cellar and hope the building would silence me so *you* didn't have to."

He frowned but before he could speak Wilson broke in.

270

"What about me, eh?" Marcus and Peck both turned to look at him. Their expressions were not encouraging.

"You only received your cut if you obtained the gems first. You did not," Peck told him. "That was *our* agreement."

"Wait a bloody minute there, pal. If I hadn't brought *them* here—" he gestured to Marcus and me, "—and tipped *you* off, you would never have got a hold of the stones."

"*You* brought them here?" Peck queried mildly. "I thought my pilot did that. Just as my pilot made the radio call that summoned me as soon as you were in the air."

The shock on the big Scot's face tightened into outright fury as Peck turned away, dismissing him. He launched for the police commander's back, managed to get his good arm around the man's neck before Peck brought the butt of the rifle back, jamming it into Wilson's ribcage.

I heard the air gust out of his lungs along with a grunt of pain. He tumbled backward, gasping. The effect of the blow surprised me. Either Peck was stronger than he looked or ...

"Bastard!" Wilson got out between his teeth. "I put my career on the line for you. You owe me! You needn't think I'm going to keep quiet about this, pal."

Peck regarded him for a moment and then started to bring the HK up to his shoulder again.

I moved forward. Peck's aim shifted slightly.

"Enough," I said. "Killing a murderer is one thing. Killing a man because he's threatening to expose you is quite another."

And I knew when I spoke that Joe Marcus would not have missed the significance of the words, even if he did not react to them.

"What about killing a man who has tried to kill you?" Peck asked. "Who did you think was sniping at you from the end of this very street yesterday?"

I looked down at Wilson. He was clutching his side as though it would come apart without the support of his hands, and trying without success to move around the pain.

"All's fair in love and war, eh?" he said with a grimace that tried to be a smile. "Couldn't let you get to those gems first. Him—" he flicked his eyes in the direction of Joe Marcus, "—he'd already offered me a cut, but you? You would have handed 'em in, you daft bitch."

I leaned over him, several other things becoming clear now. "How are the ribs?" I asked. "I should have booted you harder when I had the chance."

"Hey!" Riley shouted, making all of us jump. He was still sitting trussed on the ground. "Hey, there's—"

"Shut up!" Peck snapped, swinging the HK in his direction.

But even as he spoke we realised what Riley had been trying to tell us as the ground began to tremble, then to shake.

"Aftershock!"

But this one was not like the others. It was as if the whole of the surrounding area was being hit by intense artillery bombardment. It jarred and shuddered violently from each impact, except there were no explosions, no heat and blast waves, no shells raining down on us. I tried to drop to my knees, to get my head covered, only to discover the ground under me had already gone.

I screamed. A pure visceral cry of terror as my body lurched, leaving my stomach behind, and then I was falling feet first into the void.

Epilogue

I watched the Lockheed C-130 plunge towards the fractured runway with a feeling of relief that, this time, I was not on board. It was bad enough watching the tyres deform from the impact as they hit, seeing the puff of smoke and only afterwards hearing the chirrup, delayed by the distance between us.

"Your ride," Commander Peck said unnecessarily.

"It is," I agreed.

"It has been a pleasure to have you visit my country, Miss Fox," he said, offering his hand. "Please do not come back."

"They couldn't pay me enough," I said cheerfully.

His mouth twitched, almost a smile, although his eyes were hidden behind the usual Aviators. "Then we are in accord."

I climbed stiffly down from the back of the police Eurocopter. A silent Wilson followed me out. I watched him struggle with the pair of crutches he was relying on, his foot and ankle encased in plaster.

"I hope this is the last time we meet," I told him, not offering to help. "But if you ever decide to shoot at me again, *pal*, make sure you don't miss. Because I won't."

"I was never trying to hurt you, just shake you up a bit. Thought I could put in for your spot, eh? Seemed like a cushy number."

Wilson, I'd learned, was a man who could resist anything except temptation, the lure of easy money, at which point his scruples tended to take a holiday. I wondered what kind of a soldier it had made him, and what kind of a copper he'd since turned into.

"Ribs still hurting, are they?"

"Like a bastard," he admitted, his voice rueful. "It was Peck put me up to—"

"Good," I interrupted, meaning the ribs. "I don't need to hear any more. And as long as you keep your mouth shut, nobody else does either, do they?"

I walked away from him, far enough to watch the Hercules taxi off the flight-line and slot into its designated space in a line of other heavy transport aircraft. The rear loading ramp was already lowering before the engines finished spooling down, forklifts and refuelling tankers converging.

As the crew emerged there were two figures among them who didn't fit the usual mould. Manners dictated that I go to meet them. Surprise kept me static.

"Charlie," Parker Armstrong greeted me without inflection as he drew closer. Those cool grey eyes skated over the cuts and grazes on my face, the way I held myself, and I knew he was assessing the damage—both what he could see and what he could not. "Glad you're OK."

"Sir," I murmured, keeping it formal because alongside him was R&R's sponsor—in effect my employer on this job—Mrs Hamilton. She looked as cool and elegant as ever, the rigours of a long-haul flight in steerage notwithstanding.

"It's a miracle they got you out alive. It must have been terrifying," she said, ignoring my proffered hand in favour of a light hug and a kiss to both cheeks. "My God, I never expected … How long were you buried?"

"Only about six hours," I said, playing it down. It had felt like six weeks. "They had to stabilise the area before they could get to us."

I did not add that the initial surveys and gathering of equipment had taken Marcus and his team over four hours, during which time neither myself nor Wilson, trapped nearby, had known if they were coming for us or not. It had been a sobering experience.

Wilson had wept and wailed and raged himself into silence—something he was not proud of now and another stick I could beat him with if I so chose. Providing he kept to his side of the bargain, I'd keep to mine.

The infinitely slow tick of those first four hours had given me time to think about where I had been with my life and where I intended to go. About right and wrong. Trust and betrayal. And justice, whatever I deemed that to be.

"Ah, looks like we have company," Mrs Hamilton said, smiling over my shoulder.

I turned and saw the khaki-coloured Bell making a fast showy landing near the hangar where Riley picked me up on my arrival, less than a week ago.

As soon as the skids were on the tarmac the doors opened. Joe Marcus helped Dr Bertrand climb down as Hope and Lemon jumped out of the rear load bay. Riley stayed in the pilot's seat as if to be ready for a quick exit. He gave me a nod and a salute when he saw me watching, but for once he did not smile.

"The gang's all here," I murmured. Parker glanced at me sharply, but he made no comment.

The R&R team greeted Mrs Hamilton with respectful enthusiasm. Even Lemon was on her most appealing best behaviour. Hope could hardly bring herself to look at me.

"I expect you are all wondering about the reason for this impromptu inspection of the forces," Mrs Hamilton said, flicking her eyes to Parker. "I—"

"I think I can probably answer that," I said. "Mrs Hamilton did not simply employ me as a replacement security advisor for Kyle Stephens." I let my gaze wander across them. "She also employed me to find out how and why he died."

Mrs Hamilton took a breath as if to contradict me. I waited, but she said nothing, frowning.

"I'm very sorry," I told her, "but I'm afraid your trust was severely misplaced."

She flinched and I heard Hope take in an audible breath that hitched in the back of her throat.

"Misplaced how?" Parker asked.

"Kyle Stephens, for all his record in the Rangers, was not a man to be trusted," I said. "He stole from the dead and sold off what he couldn't trade or barter."

"So his death?" Mrs Hamilton queried. "It wasn't …?"

"Deliberate?" I shrugged. "You'd asked him to look into the rumours, so he must have known he was on borrowed time. Maybe that led to him being … reckless, who knows?"

She nodded, the slight drop of her shoulders the only giveaway to her relief. "And that's it?" she asked. "Nothing more?"

My gaze skimmed the R&R team once again, lingering on Hope. She paled, mutely pleading.

"No," I said. "There's nothing more."

"*Thank* you," Mrs Hamilton said. "For putting my mind at rest. I mean, I *knew*, but even so ..."

"You're welcome."

A man in uniform with a lot of gold braid across the breast and epaulettes arrived to claim Mrs Hamilton in some official capacity.

Parker touched my arm. "We've located Sean," he murmured, his face grave. "It's not the news we were hoping for."

"Let's hear it, Parker."

"Not now. I'll brief you on the plane. Wheels up in two hours, OK?" And with that he joined his client, giving me a brief nod that was not altogether satisfied.

As soon as they'd gone more than a few yards Hope flung herself at me and squeezed me tighter than bruising and stitches were happy to allow. Lemon skipped around the pair of us, squeaking like a puppy.

"Thank you, Charlie," Joe Marcus said quietly over the top of Hope's head. "We won't forget this."

"Neither will I," I said.

Hope released me, only to have Lemon leap up and slosh a sloppy wet tongue across my face. I wiped my face on my scarf as the pair of them dashed for the Bell. I saw her standing on tiptoe by the pilot's door, talking to Riley. After a moment or so he broke out a big grin.

Marcus put his hand out and I shook it without hesitation. Dr Bertrand kissed me on both cheeks then held my upper arms and stared into my face. "What kind of macho nonsense is this?" she demanded. "That you do not want to let anyone see 'ow badly you are 'urting?"

Parker's words about Sean came back to me. *"It's not the news we were hoping for..."*

"Because I'm not done yet," I said, still watching the girl and the dog. I turned back to face them. "I know you killed Kyle Stephens. By accident or design. Please tell me it wasn't over a few stolen gems."

"I know Hope told you she was the one who started this but that's not entirely true," Marcus said. "There's always a heap of valuable items just lying around after an event like this, like those jewels from Rojas's store."

276

"And if you didn't pick them up, somebody else would, is that it?"

"We donate them to a good cause."

"R&R, you mean?" I said, thinking of those dozen stones I'd seen change hands.

"No." Marcus's face ticked. "They don't line our own pockets. Those stones from Peck went straight to the local relief fund."

"Ah … but Stephens was not so altruistic and he wanted his cut," I surmised. "Was that the price of his silence?"

Marcus nodded. "But it wasn't why he had to die."

"'E found out about 'Ope—'er real identity. The bastard was blackmailing 'er into 'aving sex with 'im." Dr Bertrand said in a cool and deadly voice. The only clue to her inner rage was that her accent seemed more pronounced than usual. "It was rape, plain and simple. If 'e 'ad not taken the easy way out, I would 'ave killed 'im myself."

"Alex wanted to surgically castrate him without an anaesthetic," Marcus said. "I offered him a chance for redemption. He took it."

I thought of Hope, of the way she cringed when anyone other than Marcus touched her. He'd been more generous than I would have been, I decided, given similar circumstances. "I guess we're all of us looking for redemption one way or another."

"That we are," Marcus said.

And I realised that I hadn't given Sean a chance to redeem himself. Instead, I'd thrown it down like a challenge, not realising that's how he'd perceive it, or the lengths he might go to in order to see it through.

Whatever he did next—whatever he'd already done—was on my head. I shivered in the clarity.

Sometimes it takes the darkness before we can see the light.

From the Author's Notebook

For some time now I've been kicking around the idea of setting a book around the activities of a rescue and recovery team working as first responders after some kind of major natural disaster. It would be a fully international group, each with his or her very personal reasons for wanting to do this kind of work. I'd put together some character sketches and that was as far as I'd got.

Then in the summer of 2013 two things happened. The first was that I decided to write a novella featuring Charlie Fox and I needed a suitable situation for her to be plunged into that somehow felt different to the longer books in the series. I'd left Charlie and Sean's relationship in a precarious state at the end of the previous instalment, DIE EASY: Charlie Fox book ten. I already had an idea of where the next book was going, but I wanted to bridge the gap between the two, and a novella seemed an ideal way to do it.

The second happening was hearing about an illustrated lecture being given by a friend, Home Office Pathologist Bill Lawler, at a local venue. The lecture documented Bill's experiences with the Disaster Victim Identification (DVI) team which went out to New Zealand after the earthquake in Christchurch in 2011, to help recover, identify and reconcile the victims of that disaster. Hearing and seeing the fascinating details from such an expert clinched it, and ABSENCE OF LIGHT really began to take shape.

Obviously, Rescue & Recovery International do not exist, and in fact their brief is greater in scope than that of the standard DVI teams, but it's the job of an author to take reality and ask, "What if ...?" at every available opportunity. So, that's what I've done here.

And while Charlie leaves the R&R team behind at the end of this book, I have a feeling that one day I might just return to find out how they're getting on.

Acknowledgements

First and foremost, I'd like to thank Home Office Pathologist Bill Lawler, who headed the Disaster Victim Identification (DVI) team that travelled to New Zealand in 2011 to help identify and reconcile the victims of the earthquake in Christchurch. I have borrowed greatly from Bill's experiences and introduced my own take on the work carried out by the DVI team in the construction of the fictitious Rescue & Recovery International.

Information about what was and was not possible with a helicopter came from retired rotary and fixed-wing pilot, Andrew Neal, who also took me to RNAS Yeovilton where I had my opportunity to closely examine the interior of a C-130 Hercules.

Australian mystery thriller author LA Larkin was able to make some great suggestions for suitable Aussie-isms for my pilot, Riley, while Brit author Andrew Peters corrected my Spanish. Thank you both.

I'm very grateful to fellow author, Dr Caroline Moir, for her detailed criticism and suggestions at the early stages, as well as to Rhian Davies for help and encouragement toward the end of the writing process.

Fellow author and Ninjitsu expert, KD Kinchen was able to provide me with some choice moves, and thanks to Tim Winfield for being an early test reader. As always, the wonderful cover was designed by Jane Hudson at NuDesign.

Zoë Sharp opted out of mainstream education at the age of twelve and wrote her first novel at fifteen. She became a freelance photojournalist in 1988 and wrote the first of her highly acclaimed Charlie Fox crime thrillers after receiving death-threat letters in the course of her work. She has been nominated (sometimes more than once) for Edgar, Anthony, Barry, Benjamin Franklin, and Macavity Awards in the United States, as well as the CWA Short Story Dagger. The Charlie Fox series was optioned for TV by Twentieth Century Fox. Zoë blogs regularly on her own website, www.ZoeSharp.com, on the group blog, www.MurderIsEverywhere.blogspot.co.uk, as well as wittering on Twitter (@AuthorZoeSharp) and fooling about on www.Facebook.com.

KILLER INSTINCT
Charlie Fox book one
by Zoë Sharp
with Foreword by Lee Child

The first in Zoë Sharp's highly acclaimed Charlotte 'Charlie' Fox crime thriller series, complete with previously deleted scenes.

'Susie Hollins may have been no great shakes as a karaoke singer, but I didn't think that was enough reason for anyone to want to kill her.'

Charlie Fox makes a living teaching self-defence to women in a quiet northern English city. It makes best use of the deadly skills she picked up after being kicked out of army Special Forces training for reasons she prefers not to go into. So, when Susie Hollins is found dead hours after she foolishly takes on Charlie at the New Adelphi Club, Charlie knows it's only a matter of time before the police come calling. What they *don't* tell her is that Hollins is the latest victim of a homicidal rapist stalking the local area.

Charlie finds herself drawn closer to the crime when the New Adelphi's enigmatic owner, Marc Quinn, offers her a job working security at the club. Viewed as an outsider by the existing all-male team, her suspicion that there's a link between the club and a serial killer doesn't exactly endear her to anyone. Charlie has always taught her students that it's better to run than to stand and fight, But, when the killer starts taking a very personal interest, it's clear he isn't going to give her that option ...

"Charlie looks like a made-for-TV model, with her red hair and motorcycle leathers, but Sharp means business. The bloody bar fights are bloody brilliant, and Charlie's skills are both formidable and for real." Marilyn Stasio, **New York Times**

"Sharp deserves a genre all her own—if you are just discovering Zoë Sharp then you are in for a real treat." Jon Jordan, **Crimespree Magazine**

"Charlotte (Charlie) Fox is one of the most vivid and engaging heroines ever to swagger onto the pages of a book. Where Charlie goes, thrills follow." **Tess Gerritsen**

DIE EASY
Charlie Fox book ten
by Zoë Sharp

The tenth in Zoë Sharp's highly acclaimed Charlotte 'Charlie' Fox crime thriller series.

'In the sweating heat of Louisiana, former Special Forces soldier turned bodyguard, Charlie Fox, faces her toughest challenge yet.'

Professionally, Charlie's at the top of her game, but her personal life is in ruins. Her lover, bodyguard Sean Meyer, has woken from a gunshot-induced coma with his memory in tatters.

Working with Sean again was never going to be easy, but a celebrity fundraising event in post-Katrina New Orleans should have been the ideal opportunity for them both to take things nice and slow. Until, that is, they find themselves thrust into the middle of a war zone.

When an ambitious robbery explodes into a deadly hostage situation, the motive may be far more complex than simple greed. Somebody has a major score to settle and Sean is part of the reason.

Only trouble is, he doesn't remember why.

And when Charlie finds herself facing a nightmare from her own past, she realises she can't rely on Sean to watch her back.

This time, she's got to fight it out on her own ...

"Zoë Sharp is one of the sharpest, coolest, and most intriguing writers I know. She delivers dramatic, action-packed novels with characters we really care about. And once again, in DIE EASY, Zoë Sharp is at the top of her game." **Harlan Coben**

THE BLOOD WHISPERER
by Zoë Sharp

They took everything she had, but not everything she was

The uncanny abilities of London crime-scene specialist Kelly Jacks to coax evidence from the most unpromising of crime scenes once earned her the nickname of the Blood Whisperer.

Then six years ago all that changed. Kelly woke next to the butchered body of a man with the knife in her hands and no memory of what happened.

She trusted the evidence would prove her innocent. It didn't.

Now released after serving her sentence for involuntary manslaughter, Kelly must try to piece her life back together. Shunned by former colleagues and friends, the only work she can get is with the crime-scene cleaning firm run by her old mentor.

But old habits die hard.

Dealing with the apparent suicide of Matthew Lytton's wife at the couple's country home should have been a routine cleaning job. But Kelly's instincts tell her things are not what they appear—even if the police seem satisfied. She wants to trust Matthew but is he out to find the truth or silence the one person who can expose a more deadly game?

Plunged into the nightmare of being branded a killer once again, Kelly is soon on the run from police, Russian thugs and a local gangster. Betrayed at every turn, she is fast running out of options.

But Kelly acquired a whole new set of skills on the inside. Now street-smart and wary, can she use everything she's learned to evade capture and stay alive long enough to clear her name?

"Cracking action, shocking twists, thrills and brains, one hell of a ride." **Emlyn Rees**

"The Blood Whisperer is a cracking, compulsive read ... I loved every word of this brilliant, mind-twisting thriller." **Elizabeth Haynes**

CPSIA information can be obtained at www.ICGtesting.com
Printed in the USA
LVOW11s1702151213

365395LV00021B/2578/P